Fire Wizard

by

Pam Binder

The Dragon Curse

Cover Art by *Lisa Dawn MacDonald*

The Wild Rose Press, Inc.
PO Box 708
Adams Basin, NY 14410-0708
Visit us at www.thewildrosepress.com

Publishing History
First Edition, 2025
Trade Paperback Print ISBN 978-1-5092-6394-3
Digital ISBN 978-1-5092-6395-0

The Dragon Curse
Published in the United States of America

Dedication

To Robin Washam,
My dear, kind and generous friend.
You were an inspiration to all those who knew you.
You gave your love and devotion to those in need
and brought light into this world.
You will be missed.

Starve the fire and burn the wind.
Steal the earth and boil the seas.
Ashes, ashes, they all fall down.

~A poem thought to have been inspired
by the Bubonic Plague

Prologue

In Rowan's line of work, if you turned over a rock, what crawled out had fangs, claws or a bloodthirsty temper. Bad guys came in all forms, and it was his job not to neutralize them.

A bullet burned through the night air along a secluded Seattle waterfront dock and sped toward its target. Rowan, a Fire Wizard for hire, moved out of its path, feeling only the heat of its trail before it embedded in an abandoned car, setting off an alarm as ear-piercing as a Banshee's wail. He reached the gunman before he could squeeze off another round.

Rowan shoved the dirtbag against the warehouse wall and held him off the ground. Human, by the smell, the man he held had a loose-jointed, scarecrow appearance.

"Who are you?" the man choked, trying to pry Rowan's hands from his throat.

"Armageddon. But this is your lucky day. You're coming with me to the precinct."

"Aren't you going to read me my Miranda?"

"Don't know her. And anyway, I'm not a cop." He let the comment settle. "As an off-the-books undercover detective for the Seattle Police Department, I have my own set of rules. Rule number one. Stop bad guys by any means necessary."

Two heavily armed men eased out from behind a

dumpster. One moved to box Rowan in on the left and the other on his right. They looked like men itching for a fight.

Rowan swore under his breath. Detective Lyons was on his case about holding down the body count. Unless these men grew brains and surrendered, this wouldn't be one of those times.

He let them get close and shoved his dark glasses up the ridge of his nose. No sense spooking the humans unnecessarily.

He nodded toward the man he held against the wall. "Tell your friends to put down their weapons."

A tall lean man with a tuft of white hair pushed the barrel of his assault rifle against Rowan's back. "You know who I think we got here, boys? It's that guy who declared himself a one-man clean-up gang along the waterfront. Well, you met your match this time, buddy boy. It's three against one."

Rowan had seen the man's type all too often. More bravado than common sense. "Scary. You're like the bad-ass Three Musketeers."

Rifle-Guy grunted.

Human with no sense of humor. Tragic. The third man, with dead-looking eyes that reminded Rowan of a female vampire he'd dated once, edged forward into the light of a flickering streetlamp. He slipped a blade with a serrated edge out of its sheath on his belt. It was the kind of weapon that could have made the jagged Pentagram on the latest victim's chest and caused Detective Lyons to suspect that the killings were the work of a rogue half-blood or vampire, which was the reason Rowan was called in on the case. But these three weren't paranormal bottom feeders, they were human bottom feeders with a taste for the occult.

Deadeyes raised his blade and pointed toward Rowan's neck. "Nice ink. Unusual. Get them in prison? Let my friend down, and I'll make your death... memorable."

"Generous offer," Rowan said evenly. "For the record, my tattoos weren't inked. They were earned and burned."

Rowan eyed Deadeyes. It was his guess these humans had sold their souls when they'd started their five-state killing spree, leaving grieving families in their path of destruction and the part that made them human at the gravesites of their victims. But according to the law, they deserved a trial. More importantly, and the reason these men were still breathing, the families of the victims deserved justice and closure.

Rowan deepened his voice. "Counter offer. Tell me where you've stashed your victim, if there's anyone else working with you, and how you pick your victims, and I'll consider letting you live."

When Deadeyes followed Rifle-Guy's gaze, it confirmed Rowan's suspicion. They were hiding their next victim behind the dumpster. Hopefully, the victim was still alive.

Deadeyes had the good sense to back down, but Rifle-Guy wasn't as bright. He kept his weapon trained on Rowan. "You've got a lot of questions for a guy who is about to die. You're ballsy. Heard that about you. And since you asked so nice, and you won't live to tell anyone, I'll answer your questions. We like them young and pretty, and a new drug on the street makes them easy to handle." His gaze flicked on the other side of Rowan. "Kill him. Say your prayers, big man."

"You, first."

Rowan summoned the fire power from his core. It heated to the speed of a raging firestorm and raised his body temperature. Heat shimmered over the alley like the desert at high noon. Time slowed as Deadeyes drew back to plunge the knife into Rowan's chest, and Rifle-Guy cocked his weapon.

Rowan moved faster than a mortal could blink. In less time than it took to strike a match, Rowan let the man he held drop to the ground, pulled his knife out of his boot, slit Deadeyes' throat, and shot Rifle-Guy with his own weapon. His goal had been to deliver them to the precinct alive. That changed when Rifle-Guy made the mistake of describing their victims.

Flanked by two dead bodies and a man lying in a whimpering pool of fear and piss, Rowan sped behind the dumpster, praying the victim was still alive. She lay curled in a fetal position, unconscious. He let out a breath. Alive, but barely.

He dialed 911 and gave his location, then gathered the young woman in his arms, brushing a forgetfulness spell over her forehead as he moved her beneath the flickering lamplight. With luck, she'd chalk up her fuzzy memory to late-night partying. He set her on the ground, pillowing her head with his jacket, then turned to the remaining villain, who looked more like a scarecrow than a human being.

"Your victim is unconscious. What did you give her?"

"If I tell you, you have to promise me a deal."

"How about you tell me everything you know, and I promise not to barbeque your ass."

The man glanced toward his dead comrades and

swallowed as his teeth chattered. "It's called Magic Carpet Ride, and we heard it can really mess up even guys like you. We didn't want her screaming until we got her out of the city."

A raven cawed, as though intentionally breaking into Rowan's interrogation. The bird was perched on the top railing of the fire escape. Rowan swore under his breath. The surviving Musketeer wouldn't be a problem. No one would take him seriously if he claimed he witnessed a man burst into flames and move in a blur of speed that would make a comic book superhero jealous. They'd surmise the man was drunk or on drugs, especially after Detective Lyons' interrogation. That human had a way of twisting a person's words so that even a grocery list would sound like a conspiracy theory. Scarecrow-Guy would be sedated and in a padded cell before morning.

The raven was a different matter.

Was the raven spying for the female Water Wizards? He'd heard rumblings that they, and their allies, were launching a rebellion against the Grey Council, the governing arm of the Wizards. It was pointless, of course, and easily stamped out. But the domino effect might pit Wizards against Wizards, with the female Water Wizards taking the brunt.

Rowan gritted his teeth. Morgan, the woman he had loved and lost, was a Water Wizard. He fought the black wave of heartache that always threatened him when he thought of her. She'd died years ago, but the pain and guilt were as raw as though it had happened yesterday. It was especially rough this time of year, right before Bealtaine, the annual Wizards' Fertility Festival where they'd first met.

Focus. You've got a job to do.

If the raven was a shapeshifter, and Rowan was betting it was, it wouldn't care about what happened to humans, so Rowan's secret identity was safe for another day. The Grey Council and their human counterparts, the Talons, didn't approve of him doing freelance crime-fighting gigs. But as long as he kept a low profile and the body count reasonable, they left him alone.

If the raven was a spy sent by the magical community of female Wizards, Rowan had a new set of headaches.

Chapter One

Restless waves attacked the shoreline as though they meant to drag Bealtaine Island, in the Canadian San Juan Islands, farther out to sea. The roar of the ocean's despair was swallowed by an icy breeze. As though searching for a target, the winds wove through the hastily constructed smoke-gray, ash and charcoal colored tents erected for the Wizard's Fertility Festival. The wind paused, then sped up the hillside toward the only permanent structure on the island: the replica of an eighteenth-century German castle, where it blew against the building's walls as though it meant to tear it down stone by stone.

Then, as though fulfilling its intention all along, it awoke Morgan from her sleep in one of the castle's ground floor chambers.

"I hear you," Morgan said as she threw off the covers, eased away from the current lover she had taken to her bed and rushed to the window.

She pressed her hand against the leaded glass panes as she observed the path of the wind and sent a telepathic message of thanks to the Air Wizard who had sent the storm. He was letting her know that the Air Wizards remained secret allies of her and her sister Water Wizards. But she and her sister Wizards didn't need gestures. They needed action.

A knock on Morgan's bedroom door thundered over the roar of the waves and the howl of the wind. A healer, with power over water, Morgan was next in line to hold the position of priestess, a position she did not want. She did more than most already and even now had planned a small rebellion of sorts. But she knew the one who knocked demanded more.

Morgan touched her lover's forehead, assuring he would continue in a restful sleep, and retrieved her silk robe from the bed as Caitlin, leader of the female Wizards and head priestess, entered Morgan's chamber.

"I will not be part of your rebellion." Morgan slipped on the robe, cinching it tight, knowing the question Caitlin would ask.

Over the years, Morgan had given all she had, and lost her heart in the process, to help save the few Wizards she could without drawing undue attention. To rescue the numbers Caitlin asked of her would expose them all and risk further deaths.

Morgan sank in front of her dressing table, crowded with lotions and bottles of lavender and rose water, while her friend stared out the open window. A floatplane, flying from the direction of Seattle, battled the storm as it circled over the harbor. Even from this distance she could sense that its occupants included a Troll and an Earth Wizard, but it was the pilot who drew her attention.

Her hand trembled as she reached for a brush and then changed her mind and set it back down. She had hoped, nay prayed, that she would never again see the Fire Wizard who had broken her heart. The shock turned to fury as the water in the bottles overflowed, as unrelenting as her memories...memories of laughter-filled days, passionate nights, and then the dawn of heartbreak and betrayal.

Her voice rising over the beat of her heart, Morgan

pulled Caitlin's gaze toward her. "How could you? You arranged for Rowan to meet with the leader of the Grey Council on the island during Bealtaine, when you knew we shared a past? A risky move! What if either one of them had realized it was you who cast a spell to bring them together?"

Caitlin's voice remained calm. "You and I would die. High reward requires an even higher risk. If we are to succeed, we need Rowan on the island where he can be contained and controlled."

"I have told you before, I want no part of your plan. It is madness to believe that you can kidnap the scores of young Wizards on the island. We might manage a few, but fifty?"

"We do not have a choice. Their training becomes more dangerous with each year that passes. Of the thirty Wizardlings between the ages of eight and sixteen that began training on Dragon Mountain last year, only five survived. Rowan's duty is to the Grey Council and the Talons. If he suspects our plan, he will move heaven and earth to stop us. You are the key. You must choose him during the Bealtaine Fertility Festival and then be-spell him. With the Wizards in a spell-induced sleep, we will take a few of the young Wizards to safety each night."

Morgan heard the moment Rowan's plane landed. Could she separate duty from painful memories and the ever-present ache in her heart? She concentrated on her surroundings to help focus her thoughts.

Candelabras lit the room, and a milk-white glow settled over the chamber like a shroud. The oval mirror in front of her was framed in antique sterling silver and encrusted with amethysts and diamonds. The beauty only made her feel more isolated, more alone. Her vibrant features looked pale, reflecting the veil-like quality of the room as though she looked at herself through a lens coated in pearl dust.

At thirty-five, she'd lived a longer life than most female Water Wizards. She should be grateful. Instead, she felt suffocated. A building resentment, viewed as traitorous by the Talons and Grey Council, brewed beneath the surface. What if Caitlin and her conspiracy theories were right? Caitlin believed that the untimely deaths were not accidental.

Reaching for the bracelets she would wear to the opening ceremonies, Morgan swallowed down the dark foreboding that had haunted her since she'd arrived on this island in the Canadian San Juans a week ago. Choosing emeralds to match her gown and rose quartz to enhance passion, she shoved the bracelets over her wrists. The cool stones only increased her apprehensions.

"Why don't you wear the jewelry your mother gave you?" Caitlin said, selecting a bracelet made from green Connemara marble. "There is strong magic in these stones."

Morgan snatched it from her friend and tossed it into a top drawer, glancing at Caitlin's reflection. Her features were crisp and clear. Waves of dark hair crested over the sapphire-blue cape she wore and framed a confident expression. Why did Caitlin keep insisting she needed Morgan's help? Caitlin had all the qualities necessary to lead a rebellion, not her. Morgan took a deep breath. "Why is the head of the female Wizards wasting her time with me? You should be preparing for Bealtaine."

Caitlin motioned toward the open drawer which

contained a leather-bound journal. "You must select Rowan. I've heard he will attend Bealtaine, and you are the only one strong enough to contain him."

Morgan glanced toward the journal resting beside her mother's bracelet, the journal where she had poured out her heart. Rowan was a powerful Fire Wizard, and the father of her child. He was respected. Honored. Feared. He didn't know he'd fathered their son. The law was as old as time, and she had honored its teachings. Male Wizards were not to know the identity of their children. A male Wizard's only allegiance was to the Grey Council and the Talons. Despite the law, she still regretted not telling him.

"I can't…"

Caitlin rested her hand on Morgan's shoulder. "You must. Our sisters are dying."

Morgan shrugged away from Caitlin and fastened a bracelet made from freshwater pearls. "When the Grey Council takes our boys to foster when they are four or five and our girls after the start of their first flow, the pain is unbearable. Our hearts simply cease to beat. I told you before. I am too old for your rebellion."

"Some say the older a female Wizard grows, the more wise and powerful she becomes."

"Myth."

"Or a truth," Caitlin said, "suppressed by those who fear our potential. Female Water Wizards thrive on change, abundance, and laughter. We are fluid, adventurous, and as free-flowing as a mountain-fed stream. We also have great power. Have you forgotten the children's poem? *Starve the fire and burn the wind. Steal the earth and boil the seas. Ashes, Ashes, they all fall down.* It was thought inspired by the Black Death in

Europe and considered a cautionary tale. We are stronger if we work together. Separated, we fail."

Morgan spun to face Caitlin. "It is too late for children's poems. We have already failed. I reject your description of our power. We are not fluid. We are stagnating, dying, relics of the past."

Caitlin motioned over her shoulder. "Is that why you have taken this human male to your bed? You want to feel alive again?"

"A distraction."

"A rebellion. Wizards are forbidden to join with humans. More to the point, does your human realize he is only a distraction? That you are using him to forget…"

"You go too far," Morgan interrupted, hands clenched.

"Such passion," Caitlin said, but her voice was as cold as ice. "It is about time it resurfaced. The Talons and the Grey Council set boundaries around us in the name of protection. Instead of prolonging our lives, they grow shorter with each generation. Do you really believe it is a coincidence we die so young while they live on and on and…"

Morgan stood, toppling over her chair as she headed toward the French doors on the opposite side of the room. She threw the doors open, exposing an inner courtyard that this time of year should have been bursting with signs of spring. But the cherry trees were bare, and the gardens were dry and cracked. Drought and the lack of sun had delayed the season. Again.

Two young female Wizardlings, Anne and Deidre, five and eight years old, played along the garden path. As part of their gift as Water Wizards, they sensed that the gardens needed water and had created tiny rivulets of rivers and ponds where they played with their small boats and tiny figurines. The streams pushed and shoved their way through the dry earth, dissolving and reshaping as they gained momentum and strength. The sight only darkened Morgan's mood. There was a time when she was like those young girls. No worries. No cares. Full of hope and possibility.

Morgan felt as though her heart had stopped beating. Her son was about the same age as the younger of the two Wizardlings when he had been taken from her. She pressed against her chest with one hand and held onto the railing with the other as thoughts of her son crashed against her. It was tradition for children of high-ranking female Wizards to be taken from their mothers and fostered. There was not a day that went by that she did not think of him. She wanted to believe that he was well cared for by the leadership. But what if that were not true?

She rubbed her temples, and when Caitlin joined her, Morgan pressed harder, moving near the railing. Her headaches had grown more frequent of late. Headaches were the first indication that a female Water Wizard's time on this earth neared its end. Most looked forward to the ten days of festivals leading up to Bealtaine on the first day of May. She alternated between dread and fear. "Leave me alone. I grow weary of your threats of impending doom."

"I do not warn of a possible threat, but one that is already upon us. We've learned that the human leadership, who still call themselves the Talons, have formed an unholy alliance with the Grey Council. I'm not sure how the Talons managed it, but they convinced our leadership to turn over the training of our

Wizardlings to them."

Morgan's temper simmered beneath the surface as she watched the young Wizardlings in the garden, laughing and playing as though the world was a safe place. In the beginning times, after a millennium of wars between humans and the magical community, a truce had been formed in the hope of achieving a lasting peace. Humans chose the name Talons, after the name of one of their founding leaders. But until recently, there had been a clear separation of powers.

She turned on Caitlin. "Humans training Wizards violates our laws."

"As does murdering female Wizards before their time."

"Caitlin, please. That is but a conspiracy. I am not convinced it is true."

"As the Latin proverb states, forewarned is forearmed." Caitlin nodded toward the children. "A few of us intend to take them from the island as soon as the festival is under way. All we ask is that you and those who remain keep the men distracted. If we fail, Anne and Deidre will need you. They all will."

"They will have to rely on someone else."

"There won't be anyone else."

Chapter Two

Storm clouds raged overhead, laced with veins of ebony and crimson, resembling an angry forest fire or a blood-soaked battlefield.

"Bad idea," Rowan said under his breath as he flew his twin-engine float plane over the Grand Vizier's private landing strip toward the public terminal on Galliano, a small island in the Canadian San Juans. He'd witnessed float planes brave the seas and winds with mixed results.

But this wasn't an ordinary storm. It was Wizard-made: Air Wizard, to be precise. If not for the two passengers who'd hitched a ride, and for the order he'd received to be on the island to investigate the recent murder, he'd turn around. For some reason, the Air Wizards were in a bad mood.

Maybe it was because they had been banned from this weekend's annual Fertility Festival. He'd heard that Constantine, the president of the Talons. had accused them of creating a hurricane that had destroyed his beachfront property in Florida. They'd denied the allegations, but it fell on deaf ears.

A bolt of lightning flashed close to the nose of the plane as though they'd read his thoughts and confirmed his suspicions.

Rowan swore under his breath, bracing for the thunder and the next gust of wind he knew was coming.

"Hold on," he shouted to the passengers. He'd flown in worse weather in the Middle East while being shot at, but this was still no picnic. While the Air Wizards could conjure a mean storm, they were no match for Mother Nature.

He'd not wanted to take anyone along, but somehow, they'd found out where he was going and offered him an insane amount of money. Everyone outside the magical community believed Wizards were rich, with the ability to conjure vast sums of money. Rowan wished. Consulting for Seattle's police barely covered the cost of magic wands.

The sky opened and hail the size of ping-pong balls pelted the windows. "Bloody hell!" The plane shuddered, and the right wing dipped. The clouds parted for a split second, exposing a narrow landing strip illuminated by running lights. Rowan released the landing gear and shouted above the storm, "We're going down." One of the passengers let out a shrill scream. "Sorry. Poor choice of words."

In the next instant, the plane touched the runway, rose slightly, and then touched down again. Not his smoothest landing, but he was on the ground. He taxied to a stop and turned off the engine. He thought about cracking a plane-crash joke to his passengers as he moved through the plane to open the hatch, but he doubted they had a sense of humor.

The first to disembark the plane was a six-foot-tall Earth Wizard, built like a rock wall—probably the one who'd screamed. The second was a Troll, tall for his kind, at a height of just under five feet eight inches and looking more human than most humans. Judging from how the Troll moved when he came on board and the steel-like expression in his eyes, he probably had the skills of a black belt and could shoot the stem off an apple. Trolls hadn't shapeshifted into their hairy-creature form in centuries.

Trolls were considered low on the magical food chain. There was a time when Trolls and Wizards fought side by side against common enemies. A centuries-old feud had changed the alliance. Rowan felt it was a loss for both sides. Trolls were deceptively powerful for their small stature, had short tempers, were fiercely protective of their females, and when they gave their loyalty, it was not just for life. Their loyalty spanned generations.

As Rowan peered out the hatch, two cars waited on the runway. Based on the signs the drivers held, the BMW was for the Earth Wizard. What didn't add up was that the white stretch limo was for him. Constantine was trying to impress him. Usually, he got a car headed for the junkyard. There was neither sign nor car for the Troll.

Rowan debated the impulse to fly the plane back to Seattle. There was only one way this day could go and that was downhill. He didn't like being summoned to the site of a fracking Fertility Festival like a common garden-variety Wizard. But he'd given his word and that still meant something.

He also didn't like Irish music, people who were cheery when they first woke up in the morning, and flying over water. The order to come to this remote rock to investigate death threats and murder as though he were the last great hope of the magical community was suspect. Although he liked solving a good mystery as much as the next guy, he wasn't the only Fire Wizard turned detective. But it must really rankle the Talons and Grey Council to know that he was the best.

"Get out of the way, creature," The Earth Wizard shouted, pushing past the Troll with typical chip-on-shoulder attitude. "Let your betters go first. Where's my luggage, pilot?"

Sensing trouble, Rowan stepped between the Troll and the rockhead, reaching for a duffle bag. If Rowan were a betting man, he'd bet everything he had on the Troll kicking the living shit out of the Earth Wizard, but it wouldn't end well for the Troll. Vlad, head of the Grey Council, and who insisted on being called "The Grand Vizier," was also an Earth Wizard. Vlad wouldn't take kindly to having a fellow Earth Wizard being bested by a Troll. And since the island literally overflowed with Wizards, all pledged to do Vlad's bidding, the Troll would be dead before nightfall.

Rowan caught a glint of rage as old as time in the Troll's expression and recognized the signs. The "creature" was poised to attack. Rowan picked sides. He tossed the Earth Wizard's duffle through the open hatch. As Rowan had hoped, when it hit the ground something inside broke. Earth Wizards were notorious for carrying breakable keepsakes with them as their good luck charms.

The Earth Wizard forgot his beef with the Troll and scrambled after his bag, examining its contents. A figurine of a turtle, the symbol for fertility and luck, had lost its head. Rowan would have gone with another symbol for the Fertility Festival, but that was him.

As the Earth Wizard tried to reattach the turtle's head, Rowan put a restraining hand on the Troll's shoulder. "Rockhead is not worth your trouble."

The Troll's gaze lost some of its heat. "Disagree, but it can wait. War is coming. Choose the right side, Fire

Wizard. The Troll took off on a dead run with speed that might make a cheetah jealous.

While the driver of the BMW had the good sense to distract the Earth Wizard with the promise they'd find him another turtle, Rowan grabbed his jacket and tried not to overthink what the Troll had said.

Rowan had had more experience in battle than most, and not the pretty, orderly kind where you knew your enemy by the uniform they wore. His battles involved the kind where comrade turned against comrade, an ambush could come at any time, and survival meant knowing your enemies as well as you knew your friends. One thing about Trolls, you knew where you stood with them. If they said they'd guard your back, they did. So what the hell was the Troll talking about?

Shouldn't be his problem. He should worry about why the Talons had asked him to the island. Rowan had built a solid reputation investigating crime and solving the unsolvable. Solving the pentagram murders with his friend Detective Lyons was the latest example. Rowan had the ability to walk in both the human and the magical world without dying.

The sky darkened again. The day looked more like deep winter than springtime, as though the seasons had turned upside down. Wizards were taking sides.

The limo driver held the door open for Rowan. The broad-shouldered young man was dressed like a young Merlin in a B fantasy movie, wearing a blue tunic and matching cape.

"You've got to be kidding me." Rowan shoved on his sunglasses. He'd forgotten about the Talons' obsession with anything medieval.

When he ducked into the back seat of the limo,

Rowan declined both the offer of Champagne and a soak in the hot tub on wheels. He wasn't in a celebratory mood, nor in the mood to wear a costume. Thankfully, no one had asked Rowan to bring his motheaten Wizard's cape.

For fifty-one weeks of the year, Rowan convinced himself he'd evolved. He'd worked to dispel the archaic image of how Wizards should dress and had adopted something more practical and less theatrical for his detective work.

It had taken years to perfect his appearance to blend in. Six feet-four in height, with an athlete's body and a day-old beard, he'd dressed casually in jeans, a T-shirt, and a travel-worn leather jacket he thought had been brown once. His only connection to his alter ego was the dark glasses he wore to cover his unusual eyes. Normally, they ranged from dark brown to black. When he was about to torch something, or someone, they went flame-red.

He'd wanted to change his name to something more vanilla sounding, like Tom, Dick or Malcolm. Rowan was a Fire Wizard with a tree name. His mother had had a twisted sense of humor, but she was a powerful Wizard in her own right, and the Talons and Grey Council refused his request to override the name she had given him at birth.

Rowan glanced out the window, wondering where the Troll had headed and why, for the life of dragons, was he here. The Troll had told him war was coming and to choose the right side. Rowan remembered something his mother had told him before she disappeared. She'd told them that Trolls could predict the future.

"Shit."

Chapter Three

A short distance away, behind the walls of the replica of an eighteenth-century castle, were the headquarters of Vlad, an Earth Wizard and the Grand Vizier of the Grey Council and the magical community. He sat at his desk and held a framed picture of a young woman in her early twenties. Her smile lit up his heart even after all these years. Her shoulder-length hair was a thick cascade of gold and her eyes summer-sky blue. She was the first woman he'd loved, and the last.

At the time, he'd believed he'd meet others to take her place, other loves that would exceed the strong passion he felt for her. He ended their relationship and told her not to cry. She hadn't listened. Her tears and the hate reflected in her eyes were the last thing he remembered.

He had been very young and very much a fool.

Deborah had wanted him to stay with her. He was tempted until he learned she had had a daughter. Back then he'd had no interest in letting her domesticate him and even less interest in caring for her brat. He was already on the rise in the Grey Council, he'd reasoned, and they disapproved of male Wizards who mated with only one woman. Besides there were so many women How could he be content with just one?

When he learned she'd died, he'd felt like a part of what was good in him had died with her. Like so many female Wizards, her heart had simply stopped beating. He ran his fingers over her image. "Deborah, you would not recognize the man you loved. I barely recognize him myself. I've done things…"

"Grand Vizier."

The monotone voice belonged to a male servant. There was a time when he would have known the man's name. He set the picture down over the latch that opened a hidden door behind his desk. After Deborah's death, a death he suspected was not accidental, he'd had the hidden door installed. "Yes?"

"President Constantine of the Talons is here to see you."

"He is late." He shook his head and turned Deborah's picture toward the wall. "Never mind. Show him in." Although Vlad didn't trust humans, and the president was no exception, the man had taught him the politics needed to survive. It was Constantine's idea for him to change his name to Vlad, the fifteenth-century ruler of Romania, after reading a novel on the life of Vlad The Impaler, thought to have been the inspiration for Dracula. Constantine had pushed for the Grey Council's approval of the name change and won. The tactic was meant to instill fear. It worked too well. Vlad was feared, but he was also mistrusted.

Vlad rose when the president's four bodyguards entered and, without permission, made a security sweep of the room. After a mind-numbing search, one of the men turned to another and made an all-clear sign.

The president's entrance was less dramatic than that of his guards. He was a study in controlled elegance. His dark suit was tailor-made; he had distinguished gray hair at the temples, a fit body, and sharp, angular features. He could fit into any Fortune 500 company.

"I apologize for the security check," Constantine said in an accent that hinted at a Cambridge education. "You know how suspicious the Talons are."

Vlad nodded. The Talons weren't the only ones. Vlad stepped around his desk to shake the president's hand, then motioned toward a pair of matching leather chairs by the window. They might as well be comfortable. Constantine never got down to business right away. He was a master of small talk, and Vlad, like most Earth Wizards, was a patient man.

Earth Wizards played the long game, unlike the unpredictability of Air Wizards, or the flash tempers of Fire Wizards. Earth Wizards were patient, very similar to the female Water Wizards. Maybe that was the reason Earth Wizards feared them above all others. Amongst the magical community, water was considered the most destructive of all the elements.

Vlad settled in the chair opposite Constantine's, then waved away the servant's offer of tea. The president's white shirt was open at the collar to show off a series of black swirls twisting around his neck. The tattoos were fakes that needed a touch-up and were Constantine's Achilles Heel. He envied Wizards and believed the thick black Celtic swirls made him look like one. They didn't.

Constantine looked around the room as though trying to figure out how to start on the topic he wanted to talk about. "I heard attendance has fallen for this year's Fertility Festival."

Vlad had had this conversation before. "We have the same problem as always. Too many men. Not enough women."

Constantine examined his fingernails, then looked up. "There is a solution. Let my people participate in the festival."

Despite his resolve to remain calm, Vlad's blood simmered. "You want me to allow humans to participate? This is a Fertility Festival. We are trying to preserve our species, not dilute it into oblivion with human blood. Or is that why every year the Talons suggest that ridiculous solution? They want the Wizards weakened so they can take over."

Constantine heaved a sigh. "You are being paranoid and growing too much like your namesake. Perhaps I merely envision a blended leadership, where both sides are magical. Or perhaps we ask because we just want to participate. You have to admit, you throw a hell of a party." When Vlad didn't respond, Constantine let out his breath. "Earth Wizards have no sense of humor. Forget I asked. I anticipated your position and brought my own entertainment." He snapped his fingers, and the doors flung open again.

Framed in the entrance was a petite woman. Vlad doubted she was more than four feet tall. Her hair hung down to the floor and there was a green cast to her passive features. She was dressed in a low-cut French court gown that would have made Marie Antoinette envious.

Constantine nodded to the guard, who pushed her forward. "She's quite a find. Looks more like a fairy than a Troll, and very rare. Not many of her kind left, or so I'm told."

Vlad gripped the arms of his chair. If anyone else had brought a Troll to the island, he'd have killed the man on the spot. He didn't trust people who couldn't be bought. "Why did you bring that thing here?"

Constantine patted the woman's hand. "Female Trolls are considered lucky."

"Only to other Trolls."

"Nonsense. I have it on good authority. Besides, I intend to participate in Bealtaine, and even if you had reconsidered and offered me a female Wizard for the festival, they always judge a man's performance. Female Trolls aren't as particular."

Constantine winked at the woman, while Vlad swallowed down bile. The creature's expression remained unchanged. Her lack of interest didn't seem to bother Constantine, Vlad noted. The president drew her to sit on the arm of his chair.

"She can't stay," Vlad said, through clenched teeth.

"On the contrary, I want her here. She relaxes me. I think it's all the soothing green. Anyway, she can't hear or speak." Constantine had a silly-ass grin on his face as he tucked the creature's hair behind a small ear that was shaped into a point on the tip. "Think of it. A woman who won't talk back. My dead wife would never shut up. Arranged marriages are a real crapshoot. I'm taking better care in the selection of my son's bride than my parents did in mine."

Vlad almost felt sorry for Constantine's son. Inbreeding was as common in the Talons as it was in Europe's royal families during the Middle Ages. Talons bragged they could trace their lineage back to the original seven founders. It also meant it weakened the humans' bloodline and made for a small pool of marriageable candidates. "Does it have a name?"

"I don't think Trolls have names."

Vlad studied the creature. "They have names. They

just don't want us to know them." The Troll sat on the arm of Constantine's chair with her hands folded in her lap. Her expression reminded him of a domesticated cat, which only added to his unease. It was said a cat was a witch's familiar, and some believed female Wizards used Trolls as spies or to carry out their summoning spells. He leaned forward until he was inches from her.

There was no emotion reflected in her eyes, and no response that she was in the presence of a predator. Was she aware of his powers? Perhaps she wasn't afraid because she considered herself as deadly. When it came down to it, he really didn't know much about Trolls. He sensed there was an underlying primal and unpredictable nature lurking under her calm exterior. Underestimating a cat could get your eyes scratched out. He wondered what the consequences were if you angered a Troll.

He sat back in his chair and shook his unease aside. She was just a Troll, he reminded himself. If she was ten times smarter than the male Trolls he'd interrogated, she'd still have the IQ of an earthworm. Or at least that was what he had been told.

Constantine took the female Troll's hand in his. "Satisfied?"

Vlad wasn't.

The president ignored Vlad's black expression. "Down to business. The Talons are displeased with the current training arrangement. First, there is the insistence of female instructors in the early stages of a young Wizard's training. It makes them too soft. More troubling is their survival rate once they reach the training fields of Dragon Mountain. Need I remind you that we need warriors, not men and women who can perform magic tricks. Fortunately, the Talons offer a solution."

Vlad shifted in his chair. Wizards were opposed to human interference, and although Vlad didn't care one way or another, right now he needed the magical community's support. There was an election coming up in a few weeks and he couldn't keep killing the opposition. Sooner or later, someone would connect the dots. "We have it under control."

"Clearly you do not. Need I remind you that a war is coming?"

Vlad thought about mentioning that the last one had never ended but decided against it. Cemeteries were filled with those who'd disagreed with President Constantine.

"We found an ideal facility in the Puget Sound area," Constantine said, as though the matter was settled. "It's an old school we acquired and renovated, complete with dormitories, classrooms and a staff of qualified teachers who are experienced at turning children into warriors."

"Human teachers?"

Constantine nodded.

Vlad glanced over at Deborah's picture. He remembered how adamant she'd been about her child being raised by female Wizards. Deborah would have been furious at the thought of humans taking over those duties. In fact, the whole magical community would turn against him. He'd met human women before. Some were all right, but no matter how they tried, they would never understand what it meant to be a Wizard, making it an even more difficult argument to win. It was too big a gamble, at least until he had more power. But he couldn't risk alienating the Talons, either. They were itching to replace him with one of their own.

"I'll consider the plan. Was there anything else?"

The president slid his hand under the Troll's gown and up her thigh. There was no change in the creature's expression. It was as though she was carved from green Connemara marble. "It's a small matter. At least, that's what we hope. The Earth Wizards have grown sloppy. We've heard a few of the Water Wizards are living a little longer these days, and we are not pleased."

Constantine leaned toward Vlad. "Are you aware of the theory that the longer a female Wizard lives, the more powerful she becomes?"

Vlad sat up straighter. Deborah had told him about the theory on more than one occasion. But he had discounted it as a mere legend."

Constantine continued. "In records dating back to the beginning of the alliance between Wizards and Talons and the Time of Dragons, female Wizards lived to an advanced age, longer even than their male counterparts. Some even held the position of Grand Vizier. Even now, I have heard chatter about rebellion. I know your reluctance during Bealtaine, but you must reconsider. More female Wizards must die."

Vlad tightened his grip on the arms of the chair again. The wood frame cracked under pressure. While he knew most male Wizards supported him, the female Wizards did not. They wanted more than one seat on the Grey Council and blamed him for not pleading their case. If they did gain a voice, he was certain they'd vote him out. He'd used the excuse that they died too young to take on such responsibility. But if they were allowed to live longer...

Constantine drew the female Troll toward him for a

kiss, then continued. "Some believe female Wizards have the power to control a person's thoughts as well as water. If those powers increased, even slightly, they could replace us all. Need I remind you that water is the most powerful of all the elements. It can extinguish forest fires, erode mountain ranges, create floods, change the course of rivers, and destroy towns. The most earth can do is contain it. Female Wizards aren't happy being confined and they aren't happy when we remove their children from their care. If they lived longer, they might have a chance to join together. Elect a leader. Formulate a plan. We've heard rumors. A few of the older female Wizards are speaking out. They must be stopped."

Vlad rolled his neck to ease his tension. A new threat. He glanced out the window toward the quarters that housed the female Wizards. "It's risky. If I was discovered…"

"It's nothing you haven't done before." The president let his words hang in the air. "Think of it as eliminating the competition. Something you're very good at, by the way. Normally we'd wait until after Bealtaine, but too many are asking questions. Under the circumstances, and with elections so close, I thought it best if you were involved."

Vlad didn't like the direction this was going. He slid his gaze toward the female Troll. She sat as passive as stone. What Constantine suggested would be considered treason in the magical community. Female Wizards were revered. Vlad lowered his voice. "Are you positive that creature doesn't understand what we're saying?"

Constantine rested his hand on the Troll's neck and pressed his thumb against the pulse point at the base of her throat. "If you do not please me tonight, my dear, I will kill you." He waited for a moment and then smiled. "There. You, see? No reaction. I'm told her capacity to understand is comparable to a human's domesticated dog or cat. She might catch a few words here and there, but that's about it. She lacks the brain cells to link words together into meaningful sentences."

The female Troll didn't move. Didn't blink. Her eyes still reminded Vlad of a cat's eyes and seemed to stare somewhere out the window in the direction of the landing strip. If she had a thought in her head, there was no indication. But Constantine's comparison to the understanding of a dog or cat hadn't given Vlad comfort. He'd known those animals to be more aware than people thought.

Although Vlad still didn't trust her, he agreed with Constantine that she was harmless. He also understood what the new president was asking him to do. Eliminating the eldest of the female Wizards was critical. One of an Earth Wizard's powers was the ability to accelerate or slow down a person's heart rate. When a female Wizard died, it was because her heart stopped beating. No one would suspect a Wizard would use his power to harm a female Wizard. The penalty for such an offense was death. He risked much. But once he was in full power, he trusted that the magical community would understand. And Constantine was correct. It wasn't Vlad's first time at breaking rules.

The solution was a simple one. Vlad couldn't permit even a small threat to stand in the way of his quest for more power. He'd achieved the role of Grand Vizier; the next step was not only to retain that position with the Grey Council but to change their constitution and take over as President of the Talons, as well.

He was glad he'd turned over Deborah's picture. Although he didn't believe the dead haunted the living, he couldn't face looking into her trusting eyes. "I will not stand in your way."

"One more thing." The president glanced at his watch. "Our meeting with the Grey Council is about to begin, so I'll be brief. There's a senator who has become an embarrassment. It's time she had a heart attack. Another issue is closer to home. The Fire Wizard known as Rowan is looking into a series of murders in the magical community. Because we trust his loyalty, I invited him here to help with the investigation. We have reason to suspect the murderer is on the island." Constantine reached into his jacket and pulled out a manila envelope. "Last night a male Wizard was found murdered. Grisly business. We managed to reach the scene only moments before the police arrived, so we're not sure what evidence they have. This will give you and Rowan a head start."

Vlad's temper rumbled in his chest. Someone had killed the Wizard ahead of schedule. A colossal blunder. The murder was not to occur until after the festival. Vlad was surrounded by incompetents, but that was the least of his worries. The president had summoned Rowan. The Wizard was like a dog with a bone. If Vlad didn't know better, he'd swear Rowan was part werewolf. Vlad accepted the envelope with a tight nod. Hesitating would draw unwelcome suspicion.

Constantine smiled, slipped his arm around the Troll's waist and gave her a wet kiss on the cheek before continuing. "What we've discussed regarding female Wizards must remain between us. Not everyone on the Grey Council understands the ramifications of female

Wizards living longer." He stood. "Do we understand each other?"

"Perfectly."

Chapter Four

Twenty minutes later, Rowan reached the estate owned by the Grey Council and operated as a school for apprentice female and male Wizards. Trees and dense foliage flanked the winding mile-long road and were decorated with hanging crystals, white lights, and strands of pearls. Each night there would be a fire on the shore lit by nine Fire Wizards, weapons dedicated, and new Wizards initiated. The real reason Wizards turned out in record numbers was because it was a sanctioned orgy where they could indulge in their wildest sexual fantasies. The place would be packed.

When he was younger, he'd never missed one. Now, he avoided them like swimming with sharks and commitments. It was one thing to say you weren't going to get emotionally involved with the female you mated with at the festival and another to keep your promise. Female Wizards had a way of getting under a man's skin. He didn't know if it was a result of the spells they cast, the brand they sometimes bestowed after lovemaking, or that they were the most mind-blowing, sexually creative and intelligent women ever created. Being here was also dangerous to a man's health. Jealousy and bloodshed were as common as naked bodies.

The limo drove through the gate and parked on the perimeter of a large practice field resembling a medieval movie set. Male Wizards were shooting arrows at defenseless straw dummies, engaged in hand-to-hand combat or brandishing broadswords. He figured the jousting matches and the event where Wizards rescued virgins from a tower were on tomorrow's program.

The limo driver who opened Rowan's door was a young male Wizard not yet qualified to participate in the festival. Rowan could tell by the lack of tattoos on his right hand and around his neck. The thick black Celtic symbols covered Rowan's back, shoulders, and right arm. The honor of participating in the festival was reserved for Wizards who'd achieved all seven degrees. Reaching the last degree could take years and was marked by the corresponding tattoo representing the degree achieved. Many never made it through the rigorous tests or survived tattoos more painful than a brand. The one on Rowan's back signified the degree, Master of Combat, and still burned from time to time. He didn't know if it was the tattoo or the circumstances that caused the discomfort.

Rowan had attended several festivals scattered around the globe, but this was his first time here. The estate had the feel of a European castle, replicated down to the smallest detail, complete with turrets, towers, moat, drawbridge, and a tiered garden flowing down to the shore. The stones looked ancient. Most likely a castle or manor house had been dismantled and rebuilt on the island.

Loud shouts cut through the air as a handful of Wizards cheered their victory over those they defeated. Rowan caught a glimpse of a familiar face. In the middle of the courtyard was his brother. Stryker fought two men at a time and, no surprise to anyone, Stryker was winning. A deadly opponent, Stryker was a man you wanted on your side, not fighting against you.

Stryker and Rowan were the same height and built, but Stryker's skin was darker. Although they'd had the same mother, they'd had different fathers. He and Stryker had achieved the seventh degree in record time. Capturing a dragon had placed their apprenticeship on the fast track to full Wizardry. Rowan and Stryker were dubbed the Dragon Brothers, a title Rowan suspected his brother took too seriously. Sometime later they learned that the dragon had disappeared, and to this day no one knew what had happened.

When Stryker saw Rowan, he ended the contest quickly, disarmed the men, sheathed his sword and jogged over. He clapped Rowan's hand and arm in a two-handed greeting. "Thought you didn't attend these anymore."

"I'm here on business, not pleasure."

"Lucky you. I'd rather face a horde of man-eating goblins, but the pull of Bealtaine was too strong this year for some reason."

Rowan laughed and pulled his brother into a warm embrace. Stryker was the only family he had left. He drew back, basking for a moment in the knowledge that their bond was strong. It was the one constant in his life. Rowan would give his life to protect his brother and knew Stryker would do the same.

A chorus of apprentice female Wizards walked by giggling. Stryker winked at them, causing the young women to blush and hurry away. Rowan kept his hands in his pockets, watching the exchange. Stryker was outgoing, friendly and a man you'd follow into the depths of Hades, but he fought the same demons as Rowan. Stryker just did a better job of keeping them hidden. They both blamed themselves for their mother and younger brother's disappearance and everything bad that came after.

Stryker turned toward Rowan, his smile frozen in place. As usual, the emotion never reached his eyes. "If you do stay, remember that once here few can resist the pull of Blood Passion. It's both the reward and the curse of being a male Wizard. A seductive woman chooses you for the express purpose of having sex and all you must do is remember to say thank you, treat her respectfully, and not kill anyone."

His brother had alluded to the dark side of Bealtaine. Male Wizards became obsessed with possessing a female Wizard. Women did the choosing, but if a male Wizard felt slighted, people died.

Rowan looked away. "It won't happen this time."

"Hope so."

****

Rowan entered the mahogany-paneled reception area of the castle decorated with both reproduction and authentic medieval antiques. There were two life-size mannequins dressed in full suits of armor dating back to the First Crusade. The only thing spoiling the effect, as far as Rowan was concerned, was the hum of computers and the conversational buzz of a half dozen office workers dressed in business grey.

Stryker's eyes grew darker than onyx. "This is as far as I go. Fraternizing with authority isn't my style. I prefer to run the show, not be run over by it."

"My brother. The philosopher."

Stryker shrugged. "Must be this place. It brings out my inner dragon. See you around."

And he was gone.

Bothered by his brother's comments, Rowan silently nodded his thanks to the unsmiling human receptionist who led him down a corridor to the Grand Vizier's office. Stryker had never been the same after they'd captured the dragon. A few years later, his brother claimed he'd discovered a dragon's lair like the one they'd found when they were boys. Just like the earlier incident, his brother had spared the dragon eggs and refused to disclose its location. Rowan shuddered as the recurring fear flashed around him.

The rule was to kill dragons on sight. Period. The rule was in place for a reason. There was a real possibility his brother had been infected by an ancient form of madness and obsession associated with dragons. But that was only part of it. If the infection ran deep, it could awaken the dormant dragon gene and turn a Wizard *into* a dragon.

Rowan tried to shake his apprehension as he entered the Grand Vizier's office. But it clung to him and wouldn't let go. Wizards had a rich legacy of legends and myths. Some were true, most were little more than creative bedtime stories. The ones involving dragons were somewhere in between.

A man with an easy smile and the look of a body builder entered from a side door. "Rowan. You're a sight for these tired eyes, old friend." He paused to sign a few papers his secretary handed to him.

The man was Vlad, the Grand Vizier, head of all the Wizards, undisputed king of the magical community, chair of the Grey Council and with an ego as big as his biceps. They'd met when they were apprentice Wizards. Vlad's name was William then, and he was learning how to control the power of earth elements, just as Rowan was with fire. William had changed his name to Vlad when he was elected to the Council, despite protests from the vampires. Or maybe it was because of them. No one took vampires seriously these days, so their concerns were ignored. It was the one-time Rowan agreed with vamps, and not just about the name change. Vlad couldn't be trusted.

Much like his namesake, Vlad had risen into a leadership role in the good old-fashioned way—through bloodshed and treachery. The Grand Vizier might have the expression and demeanor of a friendly lap dog, but the man had a thirst for power, a thirst equal to that of the Talons. It was no accident he was the Grand Vizier. No one crossed him. Wizards were at the top of the magical food chain. Their only real enemies were dragons, and according to the latest census, those were extinct.

Vlad dismissed his secretary, took the room in a few long commanding strides, and clasped Rowan's hand in a vise-like grip. "Glad you could come on such short notice. We have a record number of Wizards attending this year's festival. Most of them arrived late this afternoon, which might make what I'm about to ask more difficult."

"Constantine said it was urgent."

"Let's go out onto the terrace. There's an old saying, 'the walls have ears,' and I don't want to take any chances. I'll bet humans aren't aware the expression originated with Air Wizards who liked turning their enemies into castles."

"Probably not." Rowan wasn't buying Vlad's paranoia. The guy was living in a fortress and had routine security sweeps twice a day. There was another reason he wanted Rowan on the terrace. Target practice came to mind, with Rowan as the target. Or maybe Vlad wanted to make sure everyone knew Rowan was here.

Vlad surveyed the grounds like a king would survey his conquered domain.

Rowan walked to the edge of the terrace. He took his time responding because he knew it would piss off the Grand Vizier. It also gave him time to sort out why he'd been called to solve the mystery. Constantine and Vlad must be desperate. They didn't like what they couldn't control, and trying to control a Fire Wizard was a gamble few risked taking.

Rowan leaned against the iron railing. Vlad was being patient, which only made Rowan more suspicious. Two could play that game.

Late afternoon melted into dusk. A new moon was rising, and stars were hidden behind thick clouds. The Grey Council had chosen an ideal location for one of their compounds. The site was secluded. Secrecy was a main component for the magical community. At the height of the Wizard's power, when they numbered in the thousands, instead of hundreds, Bealtaine had been held out in the open.

Over the centuries, humans became jealous of magical communities, and they, along with the Wizards, were hunted and faced extinction. Then the Grey Council was approached by a human governing body who called themselves The Talons. They would offer protection, if the Grey Council agreed to their conditions. An uneasy truce was formed. It didn't take a seer to foresee that it was falling apart.

Vlad broke the silence. "Did President Constantine fill you in?"

"Constantine didn't say much, other than someone was murdering Wizards and making it look like a drug overdose. We have enemies and a lot of people who want us dead. What information do you have so far about the murders?"

"On each victim, the eyes were gouged out and an autopsy showed a high level of drugs in the Wizard's bloodstream. Each was overdosed. We think the murderer could be one of the Talons or a member of the Grey Council."

"That's a big leap." Rowan didn't like Vlad's assessment. None of it made sense. Vlad had blown by any thought one of their enemies could be a suspect. "Gouging out a Wizard's eyes takes away his power, making him as vulnerable as a human. Did you find out what drugs were used?"

Vlad reached into the inside pocket of his jacket, handing Rowan a clear plastic bag containing a white powdery substance. "This was found attached to the most recent Wizard, with a note."

"Cocaine?"

"I wish. Look closer."

Rowan held it near an electric sconce attached to the stone wall. Specks of crystals sparkled like they'd captured the Aurora Borealis. "What is that?"

"The note claims the drug is poison to Wizards. It's called 'Magic Carpet Ride.' "

"Do we know what whoever's behind this wants?"

"That's why President Constantine asked you here. He wants you to stay for the festival and see what you can find out."

"Why me? You have enough soldiers to invade and take over a small country."

"Actually, a continent would be closer to the truth."
Vlad laughed, a grating sound that reminded Rowan
more of tectonic plates rubbing together than
spontaneous humor. "But now is not the right time. Soon,
perhaps. Why you, you ask? Simple. Everyone knows
you don't trust either the Talons or the Grey Council, so
people will believe you if—no, *when* you find the
murderer."

Vlad might not be exaggerating about the size of his
army, his intent to take over the world, and his reasoning
for asking Rowan to take over the case, but he was lying
about his involvement. Rowan could smell it on him.

Chapter Five

Morgan stood behind a heavy red-velvet curtain on the Talons and Grey Council's island compound as a new resolve wove through her. She must not fail Caitlin's request to do her part. Morgan had learned that two female Wizards had just died of heart attacks a few hours ago, with their deaths declared a result of natural cause. Both were around her age. Thirty-five.

She gripped the curtain, fighting the impulse to rip it down. She had to trust that the plans would work for both kidnapping the children before they were taken from the island and helping her sisters escape not only the island but the threat of these premature deaths. No one knew if escaping the control of the Earth Wizards would prolong a female Water Wizard's life or shorten it, but Caitlin believed it worth the risk. The plan was to leave the women's compound on the island and seek refuge with the magical community.

As part of the plan, Morgan had taken special care with the Siren Glamour spell. It cloaked her identity and made her irresistible to any male Wizard she chose as her mate during the festival. Her task was to choose Rowan.

Each new dawn, male Wizards were initiated, the weapons and tools of their trade dedicated and blessed, and vows of loyalty given. But the seven nights leading to Bealtaine were devoted to lovemaking and was the only time a female Wizard could become pregnant. The consequences of the festival were too important for a female Wizard to leave to chance. They had to choose their mates wisely.

The marble terrace where she stood swept onto lush gardens with ponds decorated with Greek and Roman statues. Music from harps and flutes floated through the air like soft-flowing mountain streams. Its beauty was an illusion, created to reduce inhibitions and fuel passion.

She whispered another spell into the air to calm her nerves. Now her biggest challenge was getting through tonight's activities without drawing suspicion.

Morgan swept the curtain aside to gain a better view of the gardens and the participants. She and her sisters had used a summoning spell to call all available male Wizards to the festival. If the plan were to succeed, they needed as many as possible under their spell. The first phase had worked. More were gathered below than expected.

She should be excited at the prospect of waves of orgasms, each more powerful than the last. However, instead of feeling aroused, she'd broken out with bright red, splotchy spots. Creams helped, but the nerves causing the condition remained. Female Wizards were not allowed to fall in love with their partners during the Fertility Festivals. They were told that male Wizards were incapable of love, and the result would only bring heartache and despair. But she had fallen in love with Rowan, the father of her child, and even after he left her, she had never stopped loving him.

Emotional love was forbidden by the Grey Council, the governing body of the Wizards, and their human counterparts, the Talons. For that reason, powerful glamour spells were cast to assure the male Wizards never knew the identity of their lovers.

Would she be able to detach long enough to do what was needed? She must. She was the only female Wizard powerful enough to enchant Rowan. They needed Rowan, and the other male Wizards, under a spell-like sleep if their plan was to work. The fate of her sister Wizards and the children depended on her success.

She reasoned that if she concentrated on what he'd become, a loyal commander of the Talons and Grey Council, and thus her enemy, she could remain focused. He'd made his choice. Now it was her turn to make hers.

"Do you see the man you've chosen?"

Morgan tensed as she turned toward the young female Wizard who'd spoken. This was Zephra's first time in the position to choose a mate for the festival. Wide-eyed, eager, and flushed with excitement, Zephra was eighteen, tall, slender, with blonde hair that curled under at the ends. The older female Wizards had felt it unwise to bring the younger ones into their confidence until the last moment. There were too many lives at stake.

Zephra sighed dramatically. "I knew I'd have a challenging time choosing. They are all magnificent. A representative from the Grey Council told me that I could select a different man each night. Is that true? I thought multiple partners were discouraged, as the focus of the festival was to find a compatible match, with the hope of becoming pregnant?"

Morgan balled her fists at her side. Although becoming with child was the key reason female Wizards participated in the festival, whoever had instructed Zephra was mistaken regarding the need for multiple partners. "Did you inform Caitlin?"

"I couldn't find her." Zephra turned to talk with another female Wizard as Morgan fought for control over her rising temper.

Matters were worse than she and her sisters thought. Caitlin should have been consulted over Zephra's preparation for the festival. Why was the Grey Council interfering? It went against centuries-old customs and rules.

While a male Wizard and the outside world might view this festival as an excuse to satisfy sexual fantasies, this was serious business. The only reason for multiple partners was if a female disapproved of the temperament of her first choice, found their powers lacking, or discovered a flaw she did not want passed on to her children. Knowing how to select a partner for the festival should have been included in Zephra's training.

What was happening with the education of female Wizards? Caitlin was right to worry. Critical lessons were being neglected. The need to escape the control of the Grey Council increased. Their plan had to work.

Silence hung in the air like a heavy fog. Morgan slid a glance toward Zephra. In that moment, that split second of time, the secret unspoken horror shared by all female Wizards was exposed. After a successful birth, many, including herself, secretly used protection against pregnancy during Bealtaine.

After Morgan was forced to give away her son, she feared she would not survive the pain again. There were times when she suspected it was the reason she was still alive. The more children a woman had, the younger she died. It was believed their hearts couldn't bear the pain of loss. Morgan did not know where her son was, nor if he was happy or sad, alive or dead, or if he'd forgiven her or still cursed her for not fighting harder to keep him. Worse yet, for not telling him the identity of his father.

Morgan blinked away the gathering moisture and lifted her chin. She must stay focused. She motioned for Zephra's attention. "Choosing a male Wizard as your partner for the festival takes a great deal of thought. Outward appearance is only one of the factors."

Zephra lowered her voice to an excited whisper. Her face flushed bright red. "Is it true their skills as a lover are a major consideration?"

Caught off guard by the direct question, Morgan laughed aloud. The sudden outburst was like the release of tumbling water over smooth river rocks. It helped to restore her balance, but it caused many to cast her disapproving glances. This was a sacred time. Normally, only hushed and reverent whispers were allowed. Morgan disagreed, believing humor would help the younger female Wizards overcome their apprehensions.

Morgan smiled. "I asked my instructor the same thing. The fifth degree of male Wizardry is Master of Pleasuring a Woman. However, not all Wizards honor their responsibility. If their skill is lacking, or they are abusive or lack control, we call into question not only their intent at Bealtaine, but their commitment to their other degrees. Knowing how we feel, and that a negative report will spread, a serious male Wizard will take the role of a skilled lover seriously. The answer, is yes, Zephra, a skilled lover is a major consideration."

Zephra paused, her thoughtful expression a mirror of her inner growing awareness. "I have another question. Other than his reputation as a lover, how do you choose a mate for the festival?"

Morgan was impressed with the young woman's

curiosity and thirst for information, but it was tragic, too, how lacking Zephra's training had been. The Grey Council had assured Caitlin that they were providing competent teachers. Clearly that was not the case. Were other areas also overlooked? What about spell work. Power Recognition. Power Implementation... Was it possible that keeping female Water Wizards ignorant of their potential deliberate? But why?

Morgan smiled through her unease, trying to infuse life into her expression so as not to worry Zephra. "It is important to realize, when choosing a mate for the festival, that more than outward appearance needs to be considered. You must consider the male Wizard's power, and whether it will best compliment your own. For example, female Wizards have power over water, but in addition, some of us can also shift and change the thoughts of others, like a river has the ability to alter its course. If that is the case, joining with an Air Wizard will enhance those characteristics in your child. Other female Wizards are powerful healers, bringing life and hope where before there was illness and decay. For them, an Earth Wizard would be an excellent choice.

"When you are unsure, a Fire Wizard is always advised, because of his strength of will and integrity. A select few female Wizards possess all of the gifts I've mentioned. For them the choice is more complicated."

Zephra edged closer and whispered, "Like you?"

There was wisdom behind the young woman's eyes. Had Zephra heard the rumors? Few suspected the extent of Morgan's powers. In fact, her mother had made her vow she would keep their secret. The lie had become easy with years of practice, but Morgan struggled with the deception.

Her question forgotten, Zephra peered through the opening again, and a smile fluttered over her expression. "If it were me, with your seniority, I know who I'd choose. I'd choose one of the Dragon Brothers. Rowan and Stryker are considered the most powerful of the Fire Wizards."

"Few would argue. In the end, they are still just men." Morgan forced the air in and out of her lungs in an attempt to appear unconcerned. The mere mention of the Fire Wizard heated the air around her with anticipation. There were times in the past when she'd believed he was immune to her spells and only pretended that she had enchanted him.

Zephra sighed. "But men, indeed. They are so different from each other, but each possesses a banked sexuality which smolders under the surface. No wonder they're Fire Wizards. I'll bet sex with them is hot."

Morgan laughed nervously at the obvious connection and the ring of truth. "Hot" was an understatement. "So I've heard," Morgan whispered under her breath. Only a select few knew of her connection to the Dragon Brothers.

Her face warmed as she followed the young woman's gaze. Rowan and Stryker stood apart from the others, engrossed in a private conversation. It was how she remembered seeing them for the first time. They always kept to themselves. Even other Fire Wizards were cautious around them. Rowan and Stryker were tall and straight, like mighty oaks. They had powerfully built long legs, muscled, well-toned bodies, and features that looked like they were chiseled out of stone. Her heart rate increased until she feared its thunder could be overheard.

At that exact moment, Rowan glanced in her direction.

Startled, she took another breath. Rational thought argued that he was aware female Wizards were waiting on the stage but had no reason to suspect she was here. If he thought of her at all, he would expect she had died.

Despite her reasoning, his gaze seemed focused on her, turning molten and setting her senses on fire. A tremor of excitement shimmered over her like satin against bare skin. This moment, steeped in history and survival, was difficult to deny, and harder still to resist. She relished the moment, tasting each sensation as her breath quickened.

She gasped and pulled back. Her heart raced and fluttered like a caged bird fighting for release as she let the curtain fall into place. Her fingers clutched the silk folds of her gown to keep them from trembling. When she'd regained a small portion of her composure, she offered a weak smile. "Zephra, could you fetch Anne and Deidre and ask them to bring me some of the cream I was using earlier? It feels like my skin is inflamed. I need something to cool it."

She'd spoken the truth, but it wasn't nerves heating her blood—it was desire.

Zephra looked like she wanted to ask Morgan a question. Instead, the young woman did as she was asked and headed toward the dressing chambers to find Anne and Deidre.

Wave after wave of intense emotion crashed against Morgan. There were hidden dangers at the festival. Although male Wizards were forbidden to use their powers, in the heat of passion or jealousy it was not unusual for them to lose control. When that happened, a female or rival male Wizard could be accidentally harmed or killed. She'd only witnessed it once, but the memory was a haunting reminder that the festival was dangerous. They had one chance of rescuing the apprentice Wizards and escaping the island without the male Wizard's knowledge. Her participation in Bealtaine was the key. If Rowan learned of the plan, he would set the island on fire to stop them.

Calling upon the last reserves of her strength, she drew in a deep breath. She would let the others know the plan was in motion and confirm her intention of bringing Rowan under her spell.

A familiar phrase replayed in her thoughts.

"Easier said than done."

Chapter Six

Torchlight turned night into day, casting long shadows over the male Wizards assembled below the terraces. Fragrant gardens spread from the foot of the massive marble staircase, past triple-tiered fountains, and down to the shore. The area was transformed into a scene from Shakespeare's *A Midsummer Night's Dream*. There were fairies the size of hummingbirds, unicorns grazing in a meadow of wildflowers, and tents with identifying flags and banners crowding an open field.

Rowan was in hell. The last time he attended one of these Fertility Festivals he'd almost killed a guy. Over a woman. Fortunately, Stryker had come to the rescue and knocked some sense into him. Rowan had searched for the woman, to apologize, but she had vanished. That was the last time he'd attended a Bealtaine festival.

He ground his teeth together. A better use of his time was tracking down a suspected paranormal bottom feeder who was trying to make the killings of male Wizards look like a drug overdose. Detective Lyons had given Rowan the assignment to find those responsible. Rowan thought about turning it down, but when Constantine contacted him with the same assignment, and the same theory that the killer might be attending the Bealtaine Festival, it piqued his interest. People were going to a lot of trouble to make sure he made an appearance.

Just as troubling was that his brother was here. Stryker avoided Bealtaine as much as he did.

Good news: The opening night of Bealtaine was packed with murder suspects, from smiling but overworked caterers and waiters dressed in medieval costumes, to male Wizards waiting for the festival to begin. At least that would keep him busy.

Rowan took a long pull of the wine, made at one of the Talons' vineyards in Tuscany. It was too sweet for his taste, but the wine was an essential element of the ritual, and therefore critical. Abstaining would only draw unwanted attention. After all, he was supposed to blend in. That part was easy. He knew he looked like every other sex-starved male Wizard at the festival. For male Wizards, human partners were off limits, and female Wizards were scarce. He'd tried having a relationship with a female vampire, but it ended when they both realized they were each in love with someone else and only making themselves miserable.

He forced down another sip of wine. The icy wine was made from grapes harvested after an early frost and laced with a secret magical potion that dulled a Wizard's power and made it impossible for him to recognize any of the female Wizards. Both conditions were deemed a safety precaution. Male Wizards were jealous by nature, as well as volatile and unpredictable. Having full use of their powers during the festival added fuel to the fire. A deadly combination in one of his kind.

Stryker, like Rowan, had moved to stand by himself. His brother slid a glance toward him and nodded. Rowan returned the gesture, recognizing the silent meaning. Whatever happened tonight, no one would die at their hands. At least that was their hope. Fire Wizards weren't known for their restraint.

In theory, each man and woman would have multiple partners over the course of the week, magnifying the female's chance of becoming pregnant. Because multiple partners were involved, the Grey Council assured male Wizards that it was impossible to know if they had fathered a child. The explanation was meant to absolve male Wizards of any guilt they might feel for potentially fathering a child. The ploy worked for some, but not all. Rowan and Stryker counted themselves amongst those who wanted to connect with any children they might have sired.

Female Wizards, however, knew instinctively who had fathered their child, but were forbidden to disclose the information. In addition, with the spells and glamours they cast, a man never knew for sure if he slept with a different woman each night or the same one for the entire festival.

It bothered some—hell, it bothered him. When he was younger, he didn't care so much about who he bedded. But then he'd met a woman at Bealtaine, learned her name, broken rules to spend time with her after the festival, only to lose track of her when he was pulled away on assignment. He had been told she died. But if that were true, why, even after all these years, did he still feel her presence in the early morning hours before dawn?

Trumpets broke through the quiet hum of conversations. There was a heightened excitement vibrating through the throng of male Wizards crowded below the curtained terrace. No one spoke, and the silence added to the tension. The women had gathered behind a velvet barrier. Rowan wondered if they were as eager for the festival to begin as the men. Or was it duty, not passion, that drove them?

Duty. The word had a bitter aftertaste in Rowan's mouth. Everything he'd ever done in his life, every decision he'd made, was measured by the Grey Council's definition of that one word.

He took another swallow of the wine, downing the concoction like a small child might drink a foul-tasting medicine. The wine gave Rowan a headache. When the waiter walked by, he handed over his glass, declining a second.

Tonight, Rowan needed a clear head. He was not on the island for pleasure. He had a job to do. He had to catch a killer.

Besides, he reasoned, he was a late arrival and not likely to be chosen. Female Wizards took the selection process seriously. He felt a twinge of regret and shook the all-too-human emotion away. It must be this place and the wine. Bealtaine shut out the dark realities of the outside world. For the duration of the festival, a male Wizard could have his sexual fantasies fulfilled, experience pleasure and the illusion of love, all with the knowledge that for seven days he wouldn't be hunted by those who wanted to extinguish all magical creatures. Was this nameless, faceless organization behind the current Wizard murders?

****

A Celtic melody, sung by a chorus of young women, was carried on the fragrant air. It started low and seductive, blending the voices and the haunting notes of a violin in perfect harmony. All eyes focused on the massive arbor positioned on the edge of the stage. Entwined with roses, daises, lilacs, lavender, and ivy, it marked where female Wizards would pass through to the awaiting male Wizards below.

The men believed the selection process was not random and that the females knew before they appeared who each would select. Rowan suspected it was the magic property of the wine that heightened his anticipation. He reminded himself he wouldn't be selected, he was on assignment, but his core began to heat, nonetheless.

His mind was reason, his body primeval memories. Memories raced to the beginning times when Bealtaine and its success meant the difference between survival of the race or extinction. His frustration grew. The Fertility Festival had come full circle. It still meant the survival or extinction of his kind.

He'd thought he was immune to the festival's allure, but something had changed and that bothered him. He was aroused and couldn't deny the strong pull of Bealtaine. The power and magic were unmistakable. But this felt different from the times he'd attended in the past. There was something personal he couldn't explain, as though he'd received his own engraved invitation. The ceremony was drenched in Wizard lore and history. He tried to block out the hypnotic music and concentrate on duty. He was here to find out if the Wizard killer had infiltrated the festival.

A voice in his head whispered. *"It can wait."*

He rubbed his eyes with the heel of his hand, and although the voice was gone, the memory of the words remained.

The music invaded his thoughts again. He pushed the sound away and focused on his dual life to keep him distracted from the festival's seduction. By choice, he walked in two worlds. The first was as a soldier for the Talons and Grey Council, the second as an off-the-book undercover detective for Detective Lyons and the Seattle police department. He lived in Belltown and owned a vintage motorcycle he was restoring. Most days he enjoyed the work. Especially when he brought the bad guys to justice. But it wasn't always that simple. There were gray areas. Like the time a woman killed her long-time abuser. He hadn't brought her in and made an excuse that the murderer had escaped.

The music grew louder.

Drums rolled and thundered through him, drowning out his thoughts, reminding him that he was a Fire Wizard. In this time and in this place that was the only reality that mattered.

His blood simmered as the first woman walked through the arbor. The tempo of the music increased, and his pulse rate kept time. More drums were added, pounding in his ears, vibrating through him. The women descended the stairs in wave after wave of glorious color and surrounded by shimmering halos of light. He swallowed hard.

Each woman was dressed in sheer silk and gauze, ranging in shades from forest green, crimson, amethyst, and sapphire to silver or gold. He'd heard the shade didn't necessarily reflect the color of the gown but could be the female Wizard's dominant aura or a reflection of the spells in her glamour.

The gossamer fabric of their gowns pulled across full breasts and caressed long legs. Sweat beaded on his forehead and tendrils of smoke rose from the ground beneath his boots. He cursed under his breath. "Damn."

If he set the grass on fire, he'd be kicked out of the

festival, and the desire to stay blocked out everything else. The phrase "banned for life" popped into his head. He fought for control, and while he succeeded in keeping his fire powers at bay, his blood rolled to a boil.

The men grew restless. One young man broke rank and ran toward the closest female Wizard. Guards intercepted him before he reached his goal and dragged him away. Because of his enthusiasm he would be sent packing. Female Wizards demanded self-control, and this was one time the men listened. Two hundred years ago the Talons and Grey Council had defied the rules of Bealtaine and insisted apprentice male Wizards be allowed to participate, confident and arrogant their will would prevail. Male Wizards gathered for the festival. Female Wizards did not.

The Grey Council tried threats, then gifts, then literally got down on their knees and begged. In response, the female Wizards sent a tsunami to swamp the island. Negotiations ended that afternoon and the festival was cancelled. The female Wizards had sent a powerful message. The following year, only qualified male Wizards were in attendance.

With the eager young man whisked out of sight, the procession continued as though nothing had happened. Women srolled around the group of men in a wide circle as though there was no time constraint. Their movements were seductive; their glances filled with promise. Rowan was more certain than ever that he wouldn't be selected.

His disappointment rocked him to the core and caught him off guard. What was happening to him? Why, after all this time, did he still care about such things?

"Because you're male and breathing," he hissed under his breath.

A chestnut-haired woman, dressed in flame-red silk, turned from the line and, with slow and deliberate steps, walked in Stryker's direction. The drums ceased. Tension rose around the gardens. Fire Wizards were not known for restraint in any form. If she rejected Stryker, or worse, if he turned away from her...

It had happened before. The woman had killed herself in front of everyone. It had been a black day.

The crowd held its breath.

The female Wizard's focus was only on Stryker, her intention clear, yet also giving him the opportunity to look away. That would signal that he had rejected her. While a female Wizard did the choosing, a male Wizard could refuse. Sex was consensual.

Stryker showed no signs of turning away. He was focused on her as though she was the only person in his world that mattered. Stryker moved toward her. When she was within his grasp he hesitated, his body looked like it was coiled and waiting. The woman had to make the first move. Her smile spread, touching her eyes. She rested her hands on Stryker's shoulders, rose on tiptoes and kissed him, lightly at first, then deeper.

His brother responded as though his existence depended on her embrace, as though her touch was his salvation. He picked her up in his arms and headed for one of the tents located on the perimeter of the garden. Stryker was the first to be selected.

A roar of excitement erupted from the men. The drums renewed their beat, more urgent than before. With the first selection the festival officially began. Rowan clenched his hands at his side, praying for continued control. The emptiness within him, which he fought so hard to contain, grew darker, more intense, a physical pain only a woman's touch could heal. Each male Wizard fought the darkening, a consequence of living outside the healing caress of a woman's love for long stretches of time.

Another female Wizard, drenched in shades of a summer sky blue, brushed past him. Her beauty shone more radiant than a full moon and a hundred times more seductive. His breath quickened. He caught a glimmer of spun silver overlying the blue and could not pull away from her hypnotic allure. She shone more brilliantly than all the others. He could see only her. All colors faded away except for hers.

He was drawn to her and couldn't look away. Didn't want to look away. And then she turned toward him, her smile filled with enchantment and promise. He held his breath, waiting, hoping.

She moved toward him. The gentle sway of her hips was a promise. She paused, gazing up at him, laughter and desire blending in her eyes. Her tongue moistened the corners of her mouth. She sighed.

He clenched his hands tighter at his sides. The impulse to take her in his arms and kiss her roared through him like a wild forest fire. She had to be the one to make the first move. So intense was his longing for her, he knew that if she rejected him now, he would never be the same.

She placed the palm of her hand over his heart. The contact was like a jolt of electric current. Her eyes held his. The music floated away and the couples around him blurred. Only the woman who stood before him was clear, solid, intoxicating.

"*I choose you.*" She'd spoken, but he hadn't seen her lips move. The statement was in his thoughts. That was fine with him. More than fine. He wanted her. Wanted her more than anything or anyone he'd ever wanted before in his life. He paused. It was more than want. It was need.

The woman moved closer until her body touched the length of his, her form soft and lush and willing against his hard muscles. The world disappeared. Her full lips pressed his and he drank in her heady scent, kissing her deeply. The taste of her, with her exotic perfume, was vaguely familiar, laced with tropical sea breezes and orchids. He had an image of warm sand and star-dusted nights and a woman who'd fulfilled his every fantasy. A woman who had banished the darkness for a time.

The woman in his arms placed her fingers on his mouth as though she'd read his mind. "Think only of me. Of tonight," she whispered.

She had read his thoughts. There were rumors that a select few female Wizards had that power. But when her voice and her expression didn't reflect jealousy that he was thinking of another, he dismissed the theory as nothing more than a lucky guess.

Doubt and fear persisted.

He prided himself on the ability to block his thoughts. It had worked well on more than one occasion. But all he could think about was that if she could read his thoughts and see into his soul, she would deem him unworthy, change her mind, and reject him.

And he wouldn't blame her.

Her lips parted again and there was laughter in her voice, like rain caressing the first buds of spring. "I made the right choice."

Relief washed over him. He knew it was the spell in the wine, the glamour she wore, and this night, but it didn't matter. Whatever she wanted, or desired, it would be hers. He would find a way. Nothing she asked for would he deny. He would protect her with his life. Now and forever.

She drew his face toward her and kissed him with urgency and passion. Was it a thank you for his unspoken declaration? Or building desire?

"Yes," she answered against his lips.

He picked her up in his arms. The fabric she wore was as transparent as mist. The memory of another island tugged at his thoughts again but evaporated as quickly as a dream when her arms wrapped around his neck and her breasts pressed against his chest.

Her nipples were ripe and ready for his touch. Her lips parted again in an invitation he could not deny. Would not deny. He didn't know why he'd been granted such an honor, but he intended to enjoy and savor each moment. She was perfection and she had chosen him.

Chapter Seven

Morgan still wanted him, despite all that Rowan represented. He had not been born into privilege. His father was a member of the nameless, faceless outcast contingent who had dared to rebel against the establishment, which meant that his sons were sold into servitude. Rowan and his brother had had to fight for respect and acceptance. Not only did they succeed, but they also excelled.

And through it all, Rowan never lost his sense of fairness and decency. He helped those less fortunate and never lost sight of how far he had come. How could she not fall in love with a man like Rowan? She knew when she had met him those long years ago that he was the man she wanted as the father of her child. But she never thought she would see him again.

A massive tent was made ready for them. Perfumed candles illuminated the interior. Rose petals formed a path to the four-poster bed piled high with satin and silk pillows in red and deep purple. Nutmeg, cinnamon and lavender perfumed the air. Dark chocolate, red wine, succulent fruit, and oysters were spread over a cloth-draped table.

Rowan released her to the ground, placing a tender kiss on her head. She leaned against him, using his warmth to chase away the self-doubts racing through her. Could she do what was required?

Each woman planned to make sure all the male Wizards on the island were in a spell-induced sleep. If they succeeded, they would be able to spirit the young Wizards to safety. The children were not safe if they were on the island. But she and her sister Wizards had never tried something of this magnitude. It was a daunting task.

Rowan drew her against him, his strong arms wrapped around her waist as he leaned down, placing hot kisses on her neck and shoulders. She sighed and tilted her head to the side, letting the warm shivers race through her, bringing her body back to life. She'd underestimated her feelings for him.

When he'd first touched her, the overpowering desire for him caught her off guard. She knew that, when he awoke from the enchanted sleep, he would be furious with her. He would feel betrayed. She knew all too well the depth of that type of betrayal—that loss of trust. But she was not here to rekindle love. She was here for a higher purpose. The thought of the Wizardlings and apprentice Wizards kept her strong. Their lives depended on her and her sister Wizards remaining resolute.

She turned in Rowan's arms and rested against his chest, feeling the beat of his heart, the heat of his body, the deep sadness that held him in its grip. So concerned by anger and loss over losing her child, she'd never guessed Rowan still fought his own demons. He had never stopped grieving for his family and felt guilty over not being able to save them. There were words she wanted to say, comforting, healing, loving words. Instinctively she knew he was not ready to hear them.

This was one of the times that could break a female Wizard's heart. Female Wizards could sense the true nature of those they mated with, their regrets, their hopes. Morgan felt his pain, his great emptiness. For the duration of the festival male and female Wizards could chase away the darkening while in each other's arms, but the feelings would not last. Their time together would pass too quickly, and their fears would return. The oasis that was Bealtaine was the real allure. A haven where dreams came true, fantasies were realized, and you could pretend love lasted forever.

Time was an illusion, and love the only reality, or so her mother had promised. Seven days was supposed to kindle a love that would last a lifetime. It rarely did.

She was one of the lucky few. The realization was bittersweet.

Morgan rose on her tiptoes, pressing her cool lips against his warm mouth. He leaned into the kiss, his arms around her, lifting her until her feet left the ground. His strength and power took her breath away. His intensity surrounded her in waves of shimmering heat. She'd forgotten how strong he was, how loving, how warm. Mating with a Fire Wizard was like venturing too close to an active volcano.

The danger was exhilarating.

Not all female Wizards could endure the unrestrained raw energy of a Fire Wizard when he made love. They were passionate, and attentive lovers. While all women wanted to be with them, few had the power to survive the experience.

His kiss deepened, searing through her, awakening passion and something more dangerous. Memories.

He pulled away slightly, his breath hot on her face. "Why me?"

This man, this Fire Wizard, was the most powerful

and courageous man she'd ever known. Yet he thought he was not worthy of love.

The love she had hoped to deny poured from her voice. "How could I not choose you?"

"You give me great honor. Your beauty blinds me, and your fragrance is intoxicating. You have seduced me, body, and soul." He smiled, slowly at first, and then the smile spread across his features until it reached his eyes. His expression reflected the boy in the man. It warmed her with its radiant glow. He picked her up in his arms again and carried her to bed. "You are as light as a Highland mist."

She laughed at the playfulness in his voice, feeling the darkness around him lift, but the joy melted away like the Highland mist he referenced. Her intent had been to make sure he was in that spell-induced sleep while the young Wizards were safely spirited away. But to accomplish such a goal she must remain strong and remember that this man was her enemy. He stood between success and failure.

She forced laughter into her voice. "It is not that I am so small"—she smiled as he laid her down on the silken sheets—"but that you are so large and strong."

His eyes glinted with humor and desire. "Aye, very large indeed." For the first time his voice was laced with a heavy Scottish brogue. She rejoiced. It was part of his heritage and a sign he was letting down his guard.

She allowed her sheer garment to slip from her shoulders, exposing the mounds of her breasts. "Humor from a Fire Wizard. Most rare."

His voice lowered, rich and lyrical. His eyes reflected the banked heat of his passion. "Ye are the cause, lass. I'm enchanted and under your spell."

"And I yours," she whispered against his lips as he leaned toward her.

Rowan's hand rested on her stomach, the warmth igniting her. She arched toward his touch. Desire erupted within her. She had chosen him because she knew she had the best chance of keeping him under a spell.

That was not entirely true. She chose him because she wanted him.

Her plan was flawed from the beginning. It was she who was in danger of becoming enchanted, of losing her way and her heart. The longer they spent together the higher the risk. It was fortunate they would only have this one night. She faced the reality that she still loved him, still wanted him, and that changed everything.

Morgan did not fool herself. He did not love her. Male Wizards were incapable of the emotion. The ability to care for another living being for more than a few days was bred out of them. Their only long-term loyalty was to the Talons and the Grey Council. It was the enchantment and spells that caused the tender kisses, the caresses, and the heated look in their eyes.

But what if she were wrong and this inability to care was only a myth perpetuated by the Talons and the Grey Council? She pushed away the doubts. To hope was foolish…and deadly.

He did not love her. She repeated that message in her thoughts. More reason to leave him while her heart was still in one piece.

More was at risk tonight than her growing awareness of her true feelings for Rowan. To save the lives of her sisters and the Wizardlings she must be strong. She refocused, banishing the dark feelings threatening to overwhelm her.

Morgan pressed her lips against his, moving her tongue over the contours of his mouth. He groaned and deepened the kiss, cupping her breast with his hand, sending hot currents of desire rushing through her. She was swept away on waves of pulsating heat so intense she feared she would burst into flame. She held on, wanting more.

She felt him pull away, but it was only to gaze at her with a smile on his lips. His hot breath, a Fire Wizard's breath, caressed her skin, seduced her senses, igniting her passions. "You're the most beautiful creature I've ever seen in my life."

Morgan smiled and traced her fingers over his mouth, aching for the moment when she could touch all of him. "It is the glamour. The spells."

"'Tis not so. I see you clearly."

Her hand trembled as fear seeped, threatening the euphoria. "Not possible." A part of her hoped what he said was true. Hoped that the passionate way he looked at her was real. "Do you know my name?"

"Goddess."

She almost cried in relief...or was it regret?

He kissed her tenderly. "I wish I knew your name."

"Does it really matter?"

"I want it too."

Morgan knew her heart would break from wanting him. He was different than before, she knew, as the fire between them became more intense, more explosive. If he burned through the spells and recognized her, the plan would fail. She had one chance to rescue those in her charge.

She wove a silent spell in the air, sighing when she felt a shift in Rowan's gaze.

His voice filled with passion again as he winked playfully. "I have achieved the degree of Master of Pleasuring a Woman."

She welcomed the lighthearted mood. She had been dangerously close to telling him her name.

She moistened her lips. "There are many ways a woman can feel pleasure." She traced light kisses over his strong jaw. Her hands traveled under his shirt to the muscled planes of his chest. She wanted him naked. "Are you fond of your shirt, milord?"

"Do you mean to rip it off me, wench?"

She laughed. "First, I am a goddess, now a wench. Can't you make up your mind?"

"I'm hoping you are a little of both." He ripped off his shirt and threw it to the ground.

"In a hurry, Fire Wizard?"

"Aye." He moved toward her, his motions slow and deliberate. "Tell me, lass, how can I bring you pleasure?"

Hard muscles pressed against soft curves. Rowan's mouth was hungry as he gathered her in his arms and toppled to the bed of pillows, sinking into the silk and velvet. "You're wearing too many…clothes," he said between kisses.

"You always say that," she said as he unfastened the clasp on her shoulder.

He leaned away. "Do we know each other? I thought…"

She pressed a finger to his lips, weaving a hurried spell, strengthening her glamour. He should see a woman with waist-length golden curls, not waves of raven black, with blue eyes instead of meadow-green ones. She forced a smile and voiced a sad truth. "We do not know each other."

"But you said…"

She moved close, pressing against him, feeling his heat rise. "Men always want their women to wear as few garments as possible, do they not?" Before he could respond, she kissed him and felt his focus shift as he slipped her silken garments over her head.

His breath deepened as he bent to kiss her nipples. She held his head against her breasts as her own desire flowed through her like warm currents in a tropical sea.

She fumbled to remove his belt and the zipper that contained him. In a blur of speed, he ripped off his jeans and captured her mouth. She laughed. "In a hurry?"

Caught in the throes of Bealtaine's blood lust, he mumbled a reply. His mouth captured hers as he cupped her breast and pressed her against the silken bed.

She gave in to the desire. His warmth. His heat. She wove her arms around his neck and opened her body to him.

****

Torchlight filtered through the tent, but instead of a rosy glow it cast a pale imitation, like the onset of winter instead of the promise of spring. It reflected her mood. The ache in Morgan's heart threatened to crush her. Rowan lay beside her, his head turned away. She should go now, while he was still asleep. If he awoke, her resolve might crumble.

Why she believed she could keep her heart protected while she tried to capture Rowan's was an act of madness. The spells and glamours were working too well…on her.

She started to sit, but Rowan reached out to her. "Where are you going? The night is still young and I'm…" His smile froze. He rubbed a tear from her cheek.

"Why are you crying?" He sat up, running both hands through his hair. "What did I do? Did I hurt you? You must think I'm a monster."

"No! Of course not. You were… It's just…"

He shook his head. "I am selfish, that's what I am. Thinking only of my own lust, not your pleasure. It's been a while since…." His jaw tightened. "No excuses. You deserve better. Look at you. Sitting on a throne of silk. You should be worshiped."

"Really. It was fine."

"Fine." His voice fell an octave lower. "Ouch. I was worse than I thought." He cupped her face in his hands. "I beg you. Please. Please give me another chance."

The tenderness in his eyes reminded her so much of the time they'd first met that she melted against him. "I would like that very much."

He smiled against her lips as he brought her closer. "There's a legend that when a Wizard finds their soul mate, they will be branded with the sign of their life mate's Wizard power and need no other romantic love to sustain them."

Her heart vibrated against her chest as her breath quickened. It was not a legend. It was a dangerous truth. "A romantic notion. More likely a brand materializes if the couple has been particularly passionate. Those brands disappear after Bealtaine. But regarding the question of soulmates, you need not concern yourself. You and I just met. It is unlikely we are soulmates."

He toyed with a long strand of hair that grazed her shoulder. "You sound as though finding my soulmate is not my desire."

"There are laws…"

"Laws cannot tell us who we can love."

"My lord. Please. The Grey Council forbids strong connections between Wizards. If discovered, it is tradition that the female Wizard would be killed."

"If I was so fortunate as to discover that you were my soulmate, and we exchanged brands as proof of our connection, I would vow to protect you with my life." He leaned toward her, kissing the mound of her breast, then lifted to whisper against her lips. "If we were soulmates, you could not hide behind glamours or spells. I would know you the moment you walked into a room."

She touched his brow, easing the tension she felt beneath her touch. She wished the words he spoke were real. They were not. His passionate speech was a result of the festival's spells, and it saddened her more than she thought it would. Her love for him had not faltered over the years, it had grown.

She kissed him gently on the lips. "You are under the enchantments of Bealtaine, and what you feel for me will pass."

"And if what we have is more than a result of spells? What if the legend is true?"

"If we are truly soulmates, then one of the times when we make love, the brands will manifest. Or it will manifest if we are…"

"Energetic in our lovemaking," he suggested.

She laughed. "Well said."

He pulled her into his arms. "A night filled with lovemaking so passionate that it results in shared brands? Whatever the outcome, it sounds like a worthwhile goal."

Chapter Eight

Hours later, with Rowan sound asleep, Morgan was summoned to Caitlin's quarters. As she followed the young female Wizard down the corridor, she rubbed the brand over her heart: Rowan's Fire Wizard brand. Why, after all this time, had it appeared? True, they had been particularly... What was the word he'd used? Oh, yes, *energetic*, in their lovemaking. But she worried that the brand represented more, much more.

She closed her hand and forced it to her side. She would have to deal with that later. Right now, she sensed that something was wrong in the Wizard community. She could feel it. The unusual request worried her. The last time she spoke to Caitlin, they'd agreed not to have contact until the Wizardlings were safe.

Morgan sensed a shift in the air before she entered Caitlin's rooms. It was heavy and soaked with moisture, like the moments before a storm. Her breath caught. Her hand clung to the door jamb, frozen in place, afraid to move farther and learn what she already suspected. There was only one reason she would be summoned to Caitlin's quarters during Bealtaine. A female Wizard had died.

Caitlin's rooms had been transformed into a Weeping Room that celebrated a loved one's passing. There were at least a dozen female Wizards crowded into the compact space. Warm tears pooled in Morgan's eyes.

She grieved for whoever had died but knew in her heart that this much attention could only mean one thing. The leader of the female Wizards was dead.

Caitlin had embraced the old traditions and used meditation, subdued light and the gentle shades of rose pink, pale lavender, and spring blue to keep herself calm as she prepared for the grand expectations of Bealtaine.

Music that had caressed the atmosphere in the castle was blocked inside the room with a powerful ward. The closest of the female Wizards noticed Morgan and paused, grabbing the woman next to her and pointing toward Morgan. Caitlin's death wasn't their only concern. More women turned their wide-eyed gaze in Morgan's direction, as though all were pulled by the same invisible cord.

Then, as though a dam had broken, women rushed toward her, offering comfort and condolence for a lost sister and confirming Morgan's worst fear. Their thoughts were as gentle as the touches on her shoulders and their words a soothing balm. They all felt the loss deeply. Life was precious and all too short.

The tenuous grasp of strength Morgan had held onto crumbled. Her legs could no longer hold the weight of her grief. She had thought she would die before Caitlin. How could this have happened? Morgan slumped to the ground. She was the one who should die first, she repeated, not her friend. She, not Caitlin, was the one who'd lost hope. Caitlin was strong and confident.

Tears blurred Morgan's vision. "How…?" was all she could manage.

"Her heart stopped," said one.

"The Grey Council pronounced it death by natural cause," said another. The tone in the woman's voice was threaded with sorrow, and with something else.

Female Wizards had the ability to sense the day of their death. Therefore, Caitlin would have prepared and chosen her garments carefully. The garments and jewelry a female Wizard wore held great meaning to those who knew how to read the signs. The signs often were messages to loved ones or reflected anger or despair. Caitlin was not only a sister Wizard, but she was also their leader and had spoken openly about uniting female Wizards and demanding change. Their dreams died with her. What she chose to wear would have been of great significance.

Female Wizards died when they no longer had something to live for, or when the pain of losing their children was too great. Caitlin was not in that place of despair. What changed?

"Please. Take me to Caitlin."

In silence Morgan was led to her friend's body. Caitlin wore a hand-painted silk gown with the image of a cascading waterfall down the front panel and spring flowers entwined at the hem. Her dark hair was loose around her shoulders, and her hands were folded one on top of the other across her waist. Sacred symbols were painted on her arms in gold, and she wore diamond drop earrings and matching bracelets. Outwardly, Caitlin looked lovely, and her rich garments and jewelry chosen to reflect that she had been ready for death and that she had no regrets.

Looks were deceiving.

Caitlin did not look at peace. The lines around her mouth looked strained and pinched. When Morgan's mother had passed on, it was with full acceptance of her death. In contrast, there was an element of anger and frustration surrounding Caitlin. Her expression was severe, not serene.

An easy explanation, some would caution, would be that her death might have been painful. But the jewels were an odd choice for someone who knew Caitlin well. Diamonds were not her birthstone. Actually, she did not like diamonds. Then there were the designs and the initials of her name, Caitlin Olivia Drumquin—after the river in Ireland where she was born—that she had painted in gold on her arms. Instead of the Celtic symbols representing the stages in a woman's life being intertwined, they were separated and broken.

Whispers began, rising and swirling around the room, drawing Morgan away from her troubled thoughts. Someone asked if the festival should be canceled.

There were other whispers, darker, more ominous. Morgan was not the only one who had noticed the irregularities in how Caitlin had prepared for her death. Morgan concentrated on Caitlin, searching for guidance and answers. Then it registered why the symbols and lettering on her friend's arms bothered her.

Caitlin had written the initials of her name, COD, numerous times. That could not have been an accident. Like Morgan, Caitlin rarely used her full name, preferring to use her title of leadership, Caitlin of the Waters. Then Morgan sucked in her breath slowly and whispered, "Caitlin, you were not writing your initials but what you wanted us to do. Brilliant! COD can also stand for Cause of Death."

Morgan, pushing to her feet, raised her hand to get everyone's attention. "I believe Caitlin wanted us to conduct the Cause-of-Death test." The Cause-of-Death test had been outlawed by the Grey Council as unnecessary and cruel. They argued that it was better that a loved one be allowed to move on as quickly as possible rather than prolong the grieving process by concerning themselves on the hows and whys of a person's death.

The treasonous suggestion wove through them all until it crested into one word that shook the room in raw anger.

"Yes."

And in a matter of minutes the ceremony began.

A female Wizard knelt beside Caitlin and lit a small bundle of white sage. Slowly the woman allowed the smoke to trail over Caitlin's body. Sage was used to cleanse dwellings and people of evil and negative energy. When controlled with a spell, it had another use. Using sage to question the Grey Council's judgment was viewed as an act of treason, punishable by death. Nods of approval confirmed that everyone believed the test was worth the risk.

The pungent odor filled the air, combined with ancient words. All were riveted on the tendrils of silver smoke and its message. It could detect if a magical creature was deliberately harmed or murdered. If the smoke remained in its natural grey shades, the cause of death was as the Grey Council proclaimed. If, on the other hand, it sparkled with pulsating blood-red lights, the cause was more sinister.

Morgan eased down next to the female Wizard conducting the test, while one of the women went to guard the entrance to Caitlin's quarters.

The silence bore down, and as the smoke drifted around the room a loud gasp broke the silence. Directly over Caitlin's heart were pinpoints of light that sparkled and shimmered like a miniature fireworks display.

The female Wizard holding the sage spoke for the first time. "It is confirmed. Our sister was murdered."

A collective gasp was followed by a knock on the door. Tension crowded the room as Morgan spun toward the sound, holding her breath.

"A female Troll," the surprised woman guarding the entrance announced.

Morgan's mother had told her of such creatures, magical, gentle, and faithful allies of female Wizards. "Quick. Show her in."

Chapter Nine

The female Troll, who had arrived with Constantine, the president of the Talons, as his concubine, entered and touched her bowed forehead in respect. When she raised her eyes, her gaze was directed at Morgan, but her thoughts touched them all. *"I am known as Cassandra and seek your forgiveness for the intrusion during this time of mourning, but you are all in grave danger. Tonight, unless you can conjure a protection spell, the Grand Vizier will succeed in murdering more of your kind. I am here to help."*

Whispered conversation ebbed and flowed, building, growing, until there was a powerful undercurrent of controlled energy. All welcomed Cassandra. Once, in the time before the shift from female to male power, female Wizards, in alliance with others of their gender, were part of a warrior people. It was this long-buried spirit that shone in their eyes after centuries of absence.

Morgan made eye contact with each one in silent understanding. What they had learned concerning Caitlin's death had rocked them to the core. If someone could kill one of them, no one was safe. Morgan felt a renewed strength as though her friend's life force had passed into hers.

Morgan's deep sadness transformed with each breath she took, replaced by a new strength of purpose.

For too long she had stayed on the perimeter, ignoring the signs. With each year that passed, Vlad welcomed the dark side of Wizardry and pushed back the good. Emboldened, he had killed Caitlin and, no doubt, countless others.

She gazed at the sparkling lights still hovering above Caitlin's heart as Morgan's hands clenched at her sides. She fought the instinct to strike out in revenge. But even as her mind's eye plotted the attack, the light of reason took root. Vlad was well protected, and she knew her chances of reaching him to end his reign of terror would fail. She must assure the safety of the young Wizards first.

Morgan focused her thoughts on Cassandra, allowing them to travel to her sister Wizards as well. *"Cassandra, we are honored by your presence and willingness to help us. We accept your offer."*

Morgan raised her voice, taking on the mantle of leadership. "No one must learn what we have discovered. Extinguish the sage and cleanse the room of smoke. There is much to discuss and little time before they call us for the second day's ceremony. When the male Wizards are all under your spell and asleep, that is when you all will escape with the young Wizards."

A collective gasp and a hum of whispered conversations surged through the room like a river overflowing its banks. Morgan knew her words tested the beliefs of all her sister Wizards. They had been raised to rely on the male Wizards for their survival.

She raised her hand to still the growing unrest. "Someone killed Caitlin because she spoke out against the leadership and was of an age where no one would suspect it unusual if she died. The oldest among you and those who have spoken out in protest are the most vulnerable. Therefore, I advise that all of you should leave and take the young Wizards with you. But as is our custom, it is your choice to stay or leave. I have already made the decision to remain on the island to assure that our plan will succeed."

"Cassandra. Come with me. We have much to prepare before I must return to the Fire Wizard before he awakens."

Chapter Ten

After finalizing plans with Cassandra and bidding goodbye to her sister Wizards, Morgan was numb and felt as cold as ice as she entered the tent where Rowan slept peacefully. Candles had burned down, and a soft breeze pushed against the sides of the tent. It would be dawn soon, but first she had a task she must complete, and with it a new day.

Leadership had been thrust upon her at a time when she had believed she had nothing more to contribute. When Caitlin died, her first thoughts were to run and hide and grieve. Caitlin was their rightful leader and had been killed because she posed a threat to the Grey Council. She had been raised to lead and was calm under pressure. Morgan was not calm. All she wanted to do was find Caitlin's murderer and kill him. She could not. At least not yet. Her first duty, which would be her last, was to assure that the young Wizards and her sister Wizards escaped the island.

With new resolve, she slipped into bed with Rowan, and the moment she did, the Fire Wizard brand over her heart warmed. He must have felt hers as well, for he opened his eyes and gathered her in his arms.

Silently, she welcomed him, knowing that this would be the last time they made love. If he sensed her brand, she had no way of knowing and did not want to ask. Time slowed, and her heart ached with the gentleness of his touch as he kissed her and once more drifted back into a deep sleep.

Moments later, her eyes filled with unshed tears as she eased away from Rowan and the warmth of their bed. The frigid air hit her body like a physical blow as she dressed. Outside their tent, all was quiet. Even the music had stilled. The only sound was the breeze rustling through the trees. It seemed to whisper for her to hurry. She had spent more time with Rowan than she had intended. Leaving him was harder than she had expected.

She wanted to stay and bask in the fantasy that he loved her. She could not. Lives depended on her. Once the Talons and the Grey Council realized the female Wizards had escaped with the young Wizards, they would turn the island into a blood bath, looking for them.

Rowan stirred in his sleep. Murmured that he loved a goddess. The brand over her heart warmed in response to his voice. Memories of their time together flooded back like an erotic dream. She shouldn't be surprised he'd left his mark, the image of a rowan tree in the center of a circle of flames. When a Fire Wizard made love to a woman with whom he felt a connection, and she accepted that bond, he left his mark.

She had left her brand on him as well. Over Rowan's heart was her personal mark—three equal blue lines, representing currents of water, intertwined with Celtic symbols. Rowan had believed the legends that if a Wizard found his soul mate, he would be branded with her sign, and no glamour or spell would cloak her identity. A deluge of conflicting emotions threatened to drown her.

What would it be like for them to make love without the enchantments? She shook her head, trying to clear the thoughts from her mind. Rowan represented everything she and her sister Wizards were trying to escape. If she weakened, and remained with him, countless others might suffer for her selfishness. Besides, there was no way of knowing if her mark on him would fade over time. Perhaps it was only the heat of passion that had seared him, not the sign of a lasting love.

Morgan gathered her strength around her like a winter cloak. She'd woven a sleeping spell around him while they'd made love, but even she was not sure how long it would last. Rowan was a powerful Fire Wizard. What had proved to work for someone else was not as certain with him.

She finished dressing in slacks and a white sweater, denying herself the small pleasure of kissing him goodbye. She didn't trust herself. If he reached out to her in his sleep, drew her into his embrace again…

She ignored the seductive thoughts as she stepped out into the cool air. Dawn was a mere hour away. Shivering, she blew on her hands to warm them, already missing Rowan's touch and the heat of his breath on her skin as she headed toward the prearranged meeting place in a clearing down by the shore. Too much was at stake, too many lives counted on her leadership and clear thinking. Giving in to passion was a luxury reserved for the young.

****

A sapphire mist grew more concentrated as Morgan drew near the clearing. Fir and pine trees stood guard while magic illuminated the darkness. Her heart ached in response to what she'd asked of them. In the center, young female Wizardlings, ranging in age from infant to teenager, huddled together. Without a word of dissent, all female Wizards, young and old, had agreed to the mind-speak messages she'd sent. They trusted she knew what was best. She prayed their trust was well placed. Today she'd asked them to leave behind a world they knew, with the hope they would find one better.

Dressed to blend into the human world, they wore jeans, sweaters, and hooded sweatshirts. The older female Wizards flowed among the youngest, comforting, wiping tears, handing out stuffed unicorns and bunny rabbits, and giving hugs. All knew the dangers. Defying the Talons and the Grey Council was not tolerated and would be met with swift and merciless consequences.

Morgan noticed Zephra standing on the perimeter, her expression vacant. Morgan reached her side and clasped Zephra's hand in hers. "What is wrong?"

Zephra's voice sounded as though it was holding back a sob. "Vlad attacked the man I'd chosen, after we were in our tent, and drove him away. Then Vlad forced me to lie with him."

Morgan pulled Zephra into her arms. The young woman was still, her arms held stiff at her sides. Morgan's pulse quickened. How had this happened? Sexual assault was forbidden, an offense punishable by death. That the Grand Vizier, the leader of the Grey Council, had committed the heinous crime was chilling. It meant he felt himself above the law. Caitlin had been right all along.

Morgan shut her eyes against the horror. It confirmed their need to escape. "I vow we will avenge you."

Zephra's expression was as dark as an underwater cave. "When I realized Vlad was blocking my cries for help, I concentrated on reading as much of his thoughts as were open to me. Such an arrogant man! He thinks we're stupid and weak. I gave Vlad an exceptionally strong spell to keep him asleep. We should be the ones to rule, not male Wizards."

Morgan felt the deep revenge eating away at Zephra's soul and sent healing waves toward her. On a sigh, Zephra's clenched hands eased, and her breath became more even. Morgan squeezed Zephra's hand gently. "I want you to leave the island with the Wizardlings. I do not want you here when Vlad awakens."

Zephra shook her head slowly as she forced a smile. "Morgan, I know your thoughts and know you want to stay behind, but in your heart, you know you can't. You are our leader now. Your powers and wisdom are the most advanced. The hope of our survival as free women rests with you. I read in Vlad's thoughts that after Caitlin, he feared you the most. All are grateful to do their part. Do not fear for my safety. I might be able to learn more from Vlad that will be of help to us."

Morgan rubbed her shoulder at the base of her neck, but the tension did not subside. Unfortunately, Zephra's reasoning was sound. "I just hope there are enough left on the island to maintain the spells until dawn breaks. After that, the enchantments will dissolve and the men will awaken."

"Will seven be enough?"

"It will have to be." Pride for Zephra and her sister Wizards swelled within Morgan, while fear for their safety and doubt of her own abilities to lead them threatened to tear her apart. There was a real chance she would never see many of them alive again. She must not fail. Morgan rested her hands on Zephra's shoulders. "I pray I am worthy of your trust."

"There is no doubt in our hearts. You have given us hope." As the young woman turned toward the shore, her expression shone with a new inner strength and confidence. "The Grand Vizier's yachts are anchored in the harbor and his plane is on the landing strip behind the castle. The man I lay with before Vlad arrived was an Air Wizard, and he confessed that he and his brother Wizards are sympathetic to how we are treated. I do not believe they will attack as you escape the island."

Morgan glanced toward the sky. The weather over the past few days had been unpredictable. If Zephra's belief was correct, it would explain the unusual weather. The Air Wizards knew Vlad liked clear skies during the week of Bealtaine. But the weather had been fraught with high winds. Dare she hope that the Air Wizards were expressing a small rebellion?

"I hope you are correct. But we cannot take the chance. Using an airplane is too risky. Although slower, yachts are a safer choice. Water is a female Wizard's natural protector, while air is the domain of Air Wizards. Come. We must prepare the young Wizards for a boat ride. We leave immediately."

Chapter Eleven

Two hours later, the Grand Vizier's yacht sped over the glass-smooth waters of the Salish Sea as Morgan closed the window on the rays of the morning sun. Leaving the island with the young Wizards had gone smoothly but Morgan was not taking any chances. Until they reached their destination, they were not safe, and they would not let down their guard.

The voyage to Seattle was nearing its end, but their problems had only just begun. She wished she had the gift to predict the future, but then, with a smile, remembered her mother's teachings. The future was fluid. Predicting it was as challenging as trying to contain the currents of the ocean.

Morgan tucked Anne and Deidre into the king-size bed in Vlad's cabin with two other Wizardlings, all clutching their stuffed animals. Vlad's yacht was so large it accommodated all the young Wizards. She kissed each child on the forehead, thankful the gentle seas had lulled them to sleep. It had been a long night and would be an even longer day. There was comfort in knowing they were together.

Near the bed, Cassandra was using her lyrical voice to sing a restless babe to dreamland in a cradle of pillows and soft blankets. Morgan was grateful the woman had chosen to repeat what she'd overheard, confirming their fears, igniting them to action. The female Troll was proving to be a strong addition to their band of rebels.

Morgan covered a small child's foot with a blanket, still not at peace with Caitlin's death. Whoever had murdered her must have realized the risk of discovery. For that reason alone, Morgan knew no one was safe.

Cassandra's voice entered her thoughts, her lovely face lined with concern. *"I didn't want to mention this until all the Wizardlings were asleep. Some of them already show signs of being able to read my thoughts, and what I am about to say might frighten them."* She paused. *"A man follows us."*

Morgan crossed her arms over her waist, trying to ward off a chill of foreboding. *"We knew escaping would not be easy."*

Cassandra's eyes were downcast as she fingered a silver ring on her right hand. *"He was my betrothed and I loved him and thought he felt the same. I rejected him when I learned he intended to petition for more than one wife."* She lifted her eyes. *"Although I can read his thoughts, he cannot read mine, an advantage that has proved most helpful."*

Morgan shook her head. *"I am so sorry he broke your heart. The ability to read minds is the same with us, and a useful tool. Although of late a few of the male Wizards have found ways to block their thoughts. Please go on."*

Cassandra sighed as though the weight of the world rested on her shoulders. *"I confronted him and broke off the engagement. Eventually, he did apologize and vowed that I was the only one for him, but by then the damage was done. I told him I could not trust him to keep his word. Trolls are hardheaded, and he said he would not give up until I agreed to marry him. When he learned I'd been captured by the president of the Talons, he followed me to the island. The infuriating man has allied himself with a Wizard..."*

"For a Troll to try and form an alliance with a male Wizard takes courage. He sounds like an extraordinary man to risk so much to find you." Morgan pulled the covers over one of the children's shoulders as a plan took form. *"Vlad's hold over the magical community might be slipping. The proof is doubled—not only was your man able to ally himself with a male Wizard, but Zephra discovered the Air Wizards are not all as loyal to Vlad as he might hope. If we can prove that the president of the Talons and Vlad are abusing their powers for their own gain, others might join our cause."*

"What you suggest is dangerous."

"So is doing nothing. We cannot hide the Wizardlings forever. Alert me the moment you know when the Troll and the Wizard arrive in Seattle."

"Milady, there is a disturbance in the air." A young woman stood in the doorway, dressed in black, her hair pulled into a tight knot at the base of her neck, her eyes steady and calm, and the lineage of a warrior evident in her stance. The farther Vlad's yacht sped from the island, the stronger the female Wizards became, another indication the male Wizards' hold over their female counterparts was loosening.

Morgan was encouraged but knew they needed more time to reach their full potential. An attack now could be disastrous. *"Cassandra, if the children awake, please do your best to keep them from becoming afraid."*

Then Morgan motioned for the young woman to follow her into the hallway. She shut the door behind her, not wanting to wake the Wizardlings. "Una, how long do we have?"

"Not long. An Air Wizard was spotted moments ago."

Morgan tied her own hair behind her neck, fastening it with one of her elastic bracelets. "I want you to stay here and help Cassandra guard the children."

"Yes, milady. What are my orders if they get past you and the other female Wizards?"

"We are at war and the Wizardlings are our future. Defend the children at all cost. If necessary, protect them with your life."

Morgan hurried to the upper deck, sending a message via her thoughts to her sister Wizards that an attack was imminent. Pushing the door to the outside open, she was met with an explosion of wind. The blast was as cold as an Air Wizard's heart. She shoved against the gust and ran along the walkway, searching the sky.

Behind the mist rising from the sea, and the low-hanging cloud cover, she saw a dark outline of a ship heading straight for them. The cloud cover made it impossible to determine the number of Vlad's men onboard. Zephra believed the Air Wizards would help them, but all indications so far suggested that their loyalty remained with Vlad.

She sent another message, this time for the female Wizards to meet her on the forward deck and prepare for battle.

A hurricane-force wind threw her against the side of the ship, while a series of gusts of air tossed the yacht like a toy ship in a bathtub. Scrambling to her feet, she grabbed the railing to keep from being blown overboard. Her hair came loose, whipping around her face in the gale-force winds. Gathering the strength of the ocean, she pulled her way to the forward deck. Many female Wizards were already waiting for her, struggling to keep their balance.

The ship that sped toward hers was also blown off course. The windstorm was Wizard-made, but it was difficult to ascertain if the Air Wizards were helping the female Wizards or Vlad's men.

"Rhiannon, Etain, Sabrina, bring ropes," Morgan shouted. "Sisters, tie yourselves down, but remember—keep your arms free. We have spell work to do."

Etain slipped on the wet deck, crumbling in fear. Morgan helped her to her feet. She wiped the trail of tears from the young woman's ashen face and secured her to the railing.

The woman lifted her hopeful gaze toward Morgan. "Can we defeat the Air Wizards?"

Morgan infused the strength of Caitlin into her voice. "We must."

She then tied herself to the forward railing, tugging the rope securely around her waist. The bow of the ship where she stood received a punishing blast of freezing air. She shuddered, thoroughly grounded her resolve, raised her arms, and summoned the seas. Her sisters mirrored her actions.

Her voice rose to challenge the wind's fury. "Danu, patroness of female Wizards, we beseech you! Please help summon Cliodna, the goddess of the sea, and daughter of the Sea God, Manannán, and Aine, goddess of mermaids, to our aid us in this desperate hour."

Her sister Wizards repeated the words, and each time their voices gained in strength. Powerful water spells vibrated around the ship. The ocean began to awaken as though from a slumbering sleep and churned in response. Waves crashed against the ship, but instead of the action rocking it back and forth, they held it in place, as though in the protective palm of a mother's hand.

Morgan's voice grew louder, as female voices lifted with hers until the sound drowned out the storm raging around them. Spells rose in volume, matching the intensity of the gale-force winds.

The air, black as pitch, shimmered like mercury, as though trying to ward off the water-Wizard magic. Waves rose to join with the spells to form a solid wall of protection around the ship. Morgan sent words of encouragement to her sister Wizards to hold on and fight through their fears and the growing drain on their powers. She did not know how long they could hold on. Few would escape a full attack from an army of Air Wizards.

The sea churned and bubbled as it released an army of its own. Killer whales surfaced, circling the ship that was following them. A giant Kraken surfaced and grabbed the ship in its tentacles. Screams lifted on the air as Air Wizards dove overboard or took to the sky to flee the attacks.

Danu had answered their prayers. Morgan and her sister Wizards intensified their chants, their voices rising even higher.

Time lost its meaning. Each moment felt like a lifetime. Morgan said a silent prayer that her strength and the barriers created by their spells would hold. Then she felt a change in the air, a softening.

Suddenly, like the flip of a switch, the storm subsided to a gentle breeze. The army of the sea slipped into the water as Vlad's ship retreated, leaving only silence in its wake.

Shouts of victory crashed through the silence and flowed through the female Wizards.

"Our strength has defeated them," said one.

"We are safe now," said another.

Morgan held her hand up to silence them, keeping a watchful eye on the sky. "The Air Wizards have pulled back their attack. But why?" Morgan's voice was strong and unwavering. "Be vigilant, my sisters. Our journey has not ended."

****

After the Air Wizards' retreat, their journey under the protection of the water goddesses had held. For the remainder of the voyage to Seattle's inner harbor, the storm had passed and the sea remained calm, as though a reward for winning the battle.

Morgan stood at the railing as a ferryboat cruised past. Its passengers waved toward her from its deck as it headed for one of the over-one-hundred named islands and reefs in the San Juans. It struck Morgan that those people went about their daily lives unaware of the possibility of a war pending between Wizards and the magical community, a war that would forever disrupt the humans' way of life.

Gripping the rail at this serious thought, she watched the Seattle skyline rise before her with its iconic Space Needle. The city was a unique blend of financial centers and condominiums with garden rooftops, all folded around Pioneer Square and the well-known Pike Place Market. On the waterfront, piers were crowded with cargo ships bound for the Pacific and cruise ships loaded with tourists headed to Alaska.

Morgan closed her eyes and drank in the power of

the water as Vlad's yacht headed in the direction of the Ballard Locks, which connected Puget Sound with Lake Washington, where Cassandra promised they would be safe. She let her mind drift with the salt-sea breeze, knowing that once they reached their destination there would be precious time for herself. She was the leader of the female Wizards, and with the honor went great responsibility.

Morgan had no reason to doubt Cassandra's belief that the place she mentioned would be safe, but it was foolish to underestimate the determination of the Wizards to find them. One in particular came to mind as the yacht navigated the locks.

She pressed her hand over Rowan's brand, feeling a deep sense of regret for deceiving him. She'd had no choice, she reasoned. He was the Grey Council's most trusted Wizard. She had little doubt that he would have sided with Vlad.

A few nautical miles from the locks, mist rose from the depths of Lake Washington and shrouded their yacht. Cassandra emerged from below deck to take her place. She stood on the bow as the yacht glided toward a tree-lined shore. When she raised her arms, the trees parted, exposing a secluded inland waterway. Once inside the safety of the canal, the trees folded back in place behind them and exposed before them a world of enchantment.

Unicorns peeked out from behind giant cedar trees, dragons the size of hummingbirds played hide-and-seek with winged fairies, and beds of wildflowers cascaded down stone walls or wound around trellises.

A collective sigh of gratitude, acknowledging the beauty after the hours of uncertainty, settled over the yacht.

Morgan took a deep breath. It was different here. It smelled like second chances.

A few of her sister Wizards joined her on deck, each keeping their thoughts private, but from their expressions, Morgan felt they shared her concern. They were safe. For now.

Chapter Twelve

Rowan awoke with a start. Someone needed his help. In his dream an impenetrable barrier separated him from a female Wizard who was under attack. He felt he should know her. He remembered pounding on the barrier but no one would let him in. A blinding headache blocked out the nightmare.

He clenched his jaw against the pain and then he sensed a shift in the air. A male had just entered his tent. The energy surrounding a male Wizard felt darker and heavier than a female's. Rowan feigned sleep, trying to ignore the throbbing in his temples, stalling for time while his body regained its strength. The remnants of last night's magic and lovemaking clung to his body like a hangover. Spells and the intoxicating woman were a deadly combination. No wonder he was having bad dreams.

Dawn's grey light filtered through the tent, reflecting his mood. The place where the female Wizard had lain beside him last night was stone-cold, adding to his foul mood. Despite the passion they shared, she'd left without a word of farewell. The connection between them had been strong. That much he remembered. He'd thought that would be enough to keep her beside him for another night. He swore under his breath. He'd been wrong, of course.

For as long as he lived, he'd never understand

women.

Bad timing on the part of the intruder. Good news for Rowan. He could take out his frustration on the fool who'd invaded his space. It was Bealtaine. No one entered a male Wizard's domain without his permission, and whatever punishment Rowan delivered would be excused as justified.

Ready to crack the man's jaw, he rose from the bed. "Show yourself," he commanded.

A young man, dressed in a faded tunic and breeches, quivered near the entrance. "It's Declan, sir. I was told to find you."

With an effort, Rowan tamped down his desire to fight. The intruder was just a stupid boy. Rowan rubbed his temples. Justified or not, beating an innocent into a bloody pulp was something he didn't do anymore. "You're lucky I didn't kill you."

"Yes, sir—I mean, thank you, sir."

Rowan retrieved his clothes from the floor and dressed. There could be any number of reasons why this lad was sent to find him. None of them good. He lit a candle. Where the hell had he tossed his boots?

He found one under a floor pillow and the other in a corner of the tent. The young man stood exactly in the same place he'd been when Rowan first addressed him, as though afraid to move. Maybe not so dumb after all. Waking a sleeping Wizard was never a good idea.

Rowan shoved his boots on and brought the candle closer to Declan. Judging from the smooth face, Rowan guessed the boy was about twelve or thirteen years old. Too young for his true nature and powers to be determined with any certainty.

"What's so important, lad? Wizards don't like to be

disturbed. Or were you absent during that history lesson?"

Declan's expression reflected confusion as his voice cracked. "I don't know why my mentor told me to find you. All he said was to ask you to come to the courtyard as soon as possible."

There was a nasty gash on the boy's forearm, and he had a swollen eye. This was a dangerous age for apprentice Wizards. Only the strong and resourceful survived the constant trials. It didn't help if your mentor was incompetent. "How'd you get your injuries?"

"You weren't in the first few tents I checked."

Rowan could only guess what had happened. When a Wizard was surprised, he usually attacked first and asked questions later. "And yet you survived."

For the first time the boy's features relaxed enough to smile. "Yes, sir."

"Well done." Rowan liked the boy's spirit. If he lived through the trials, he might prove to be a capable Wizard. Rowan had heard that, of late, mentors were reckless with the lives in their charges. Their methods and training were ineffective, barbaric and out of date. He lifted the tent flap and motioned Declan outside. "A word of advice. Petition for another mentor."

"I can do that?"

"If you're strong enough to escape the wrath of the male Wizards during the festival, the Grey Council will pay attention. Let them know I was the one who gave you the idea. Now, if I were you, I'd have a healer examine your injuries." Declan's smile lit up his face, making him look even younger. An apprentice Wizard was rarely shown compassion. "On your way, lad. Report to your mentor before he sends someone looking for you."

Declan took off at a dead run. The boy had some serious speed. That ruled out Earth Wizard powers. Normally they moved at the speed of tectonic plates.

Rowan turned in the direction of the courtyard. He hoped Declan would take his advice and ask for a new mentor. If Rowan had his way, he'd cull the mentors, not the apprentices. But to accomplish that goal he'd have to accept the offer to join their ranks. There were moments last night when he'd considered the opportunity. Crazy thoughts. Of course, everything about last night seemed more a dream than reality, so it was no wonder his thoughts were scattered and unrealistic. Mentors, if they were to do it right, needed patience: a virtue he didn't possess. Then there was the unrealistic sense that he knew the female Wizard he'd slept with last night. Again, crazy thoughts.

But he couldn't deny that this morning he felt more alive than he had in years. The female Wizard had awakened emotions he'd buried and washed his soul clean with her caresses. Time would tell if the feeling would last past Bealtaine.

But when dawn broke, reality returned. He didn't believe in redemption for himself. He wanted his demons out in the open where they could serve as a cautionary tale of what happens when you let down your guard.

On the perimeter of the courtyard, Stryker intersected with him. His voice was low, meant only for Rowan. Stryker turned his back to the male Wizards straggling in from all directions of the compound.

"All hell's broken loose. Another male Wizard was found murdered around two or three this morning. The healers believe he was poisoned. What they're not sure of is if it was before or after the poor bastard's eyes were gouged out."

Fragments of Rowan's nightmare chased through his thoughts like wisps of smoke. "Damn."

"There's more." Stryker looked over his shoulder toward the castle. "Vlad's on a particularly vicious rampage. Even for him. And true to his namesake, he's calling for blood. Yours, mostly, and mine because we're related. You were the lone ranger he counted on to keep things safe. He took a sledgehammer to his office and turned one of the towers into rubble. Our esteemed leader has real anger management issues."

Rowan raked his hands through his hair. "I'll meet with Vlad. Tell him I'm on it. I guess this means the festival is cancelled."

Stryker shook his head. "You'd think so, but Vlad said he had the situation under control and ordered everyone to stay."

Rowan ground his teeth. Instincts shouted this murder wasn't going to be a simple case of who-done-it. There was an old saying: a mystery was a puzzle and a thriller, a nightmare. The way his day was going, he'd wager a year's pay he wasn't going to be getting much sleep.

"What's next?" Stryker said.

"I work alone."

Stryker shrugged. "Not this time, cowboy. This time the Grand Vizier wants you to form a posse."

Rowan cuffed Stryker on the shoulder. "What's with you and the Wild West references?"

"The woman I was with last night has a thing for outlaws. I guess I'm still in character. Look, Vlad's going to be a while. Why don't we go into town and grab a cup of coffee, and I'll fill in more of the details. My car is warmed up and ready to go."

The humor in Stryker's eyes dulled. "The murder isn't the only strange thing that happening. Everyone's on edge. I've heard rumors that most of the female Wizards, as well as the children and the female apprentice Wizards, have vanished without a trace. What about the woman you were with last night?"

"She left before daybreak without saying goodbye."

"Mine too. Think that's a little odd?"

"Very."

Chapter Thirteen

Stryker was a man of his word. His silver Jag was parked a few yards away. Rowan ducked into the passenger's side. "I'm disappointed, little brother. I thought you'd be driving a Jeep?"

"It's on order." Stryker revved the engine and headed toward the gate, braking to a dead stop to inform the guard they were going for coffee. Rowan wasn't surprised the man let them pass. Challenging two Fire Wizards was never a good idea unless you had a desire to be turned into a flaming tiki torch.

When they cleared the compound, Rowan rolled down his window. "Are you going to tell me the real reason for the sudden obsession with gourmet coffee?"

Stryker headed toward a winding road that bordered the ocean. He kept one hand on the steering wheel and turned on music with the other. The sound was a combination of electronic and classical Stryker had mixed himself, which fit into his computer-nerd persona. He attended comic book conventions in Europe, science fiction conventions in the States, and Renaissance fairs around the globe with equal enthusiasm. The Grey Council disapproved, saying he should keep a low profile. Rowan smiled, leaning back. His little brother didn't do low profile.

Stryker took a bend in the road without slowing down. "Ready for the really bad news?"

"Worse than finding out there's someone killing male Wizards and that the female Wizards vanished?"

"You be the judge. One of the female Wizards died before the start of the festival."

Rowan whistled under his breath, glancing out the window at the cliffs below. The waves foamed with angry white caps that beat against the rocks as though they meant to tear down the cliffs. That tracked. A female Wizard's power was water, and it appeared that the ocean was mourning the death. There was a shift in the atmosphere, and for some reason he hadn't picked up on it. Why hadn't he known—or at least felt—what was happening? It had to be the residual effects of the spells the female Wizards had created. No wonder he'd had such a powerful magical hangover.

He didn't like it when a Wizard died, but for some reason it was worse when it was a female. It wasn't that there were so few of them, it was that their essence helped create calmness in the magical community. With each death the world seemed to grow more volatile, more hostile, less safe.

"How old was she?"

"Her name was Caitlin, and she was thirty-five years old, so the Grey Council didn't break a sweat. The official word was that female Wizards usually die around that age. But get this—she was the female Water Wizards' leader. Then two more female Wizards died this morning."

Rowan felt a shiver ride his spine and balled his hands into fists as he remembered the woman he'd slept with last night. Female Wizards died young, that was the rationale for the Grey Council forbidding involvement. No one questioned *why* they died so young. Maybe it was time someone did.

Worrying that the woman he'd slept with had been one of those who died this morning, he kept his voice calmer than he felt. Rowan focused on another question. "Do they know their names or what they look like?" He almost laughed at his own question. She hadn't told him her name. He thought he'd recognize her if he ever saw her again but figured that was more wishful thinking than reality.

"Their identities are being kept secret, and their deaths are nothing that would draw suspicion. Like always, their hearts just stopped beating...on the same night female Wizards and children vanish. Quite the coincidence, wouldn't you say?"

"We don't believe in coincidences."

"No, we do not."

Rowan heaved a sigh. "I've never heard of a female Wizard dying during Bealtaine."

"Me either." Stryker tapped his fingers on the steering wheel in tune to the high octane beat. Percussion instruments folded into the melody as Stryker sped around another corner. "There's more. I awoke a little after midnight to a cold bed. The enchanting goddess who'd chosen me was standing outside our tent, talking to another woman. By her height and green aura, I guessed it was a female Troll. I heard yesterday that the president of the Talons has an obsession for female Trolls. The women didn't know I was awake, but I caught only random words and phrases. I was still under a heavy cloud of spells. Hard to tell what was real. What I *did* learn was that they believed all three women were murdered."

Stryker's comments hung in the air like silence

before a raging firestorm. Rowan whistled low under his breath, trying to remain calm and failing. "Why didn't they come to us? We would have protected them."

Stryker snapped off the music and slid a glance toward Rowan. Stryker's anger looked like it was boiling beneath the surface. "You've been out of touch for a long time, big brother. And female Wizards don't trust anyone with a cock."

Rowan nodded slowly, knowing his brother had hit the mark. His blood simmered. He and his fellow Wizards had failed to protect their women. "Did you ask the woman you were with about the conversation she'd had with the female Troll?"

"Of course, and then she started taking off her clothes and I lost my train of thought. I'm hoping she cast a spell over me to turn my brain to mush instead of my being a complete tool."

Rowan shrugged. "We'll stick with the spell theory. If they don't want you to know something, it stays that way."

Stryker shook his head slowly. "She hit me with another wave of spells. One minute we were making love and the next I was unconscious. When I awoke, I learned that of the scores of female Wizards attending Bealtaine, only seven have been seen. Vlad, in his colossal stupidity, ordered the remaining female Wizards locked up and interrogated, believing he could contain the situation."

Rowan watched the scenery blur past, like so many lost opportunities. "Let me guess—the remaining female Wizards announced they'd commit mass suicide if he so much as came near them. Any idea how the others escaped the island? The only way on or off is by boat or plane."

"Debris from Vlad's yacht was discovered in the bay. Our Grand Vizier believes they all drowned, pointing out how unpredictable the waters in the Salish Sea and Canadian San Juans are this time of year."

"That's insane. They're Water Wizards. Water protects them. They would never drown."

Stryker rolled his eyes. "Exactly. Earth Wizards aren't that bright. Fortunately, someone reminded him of your point. His abridged theory is that they smuggled on board two planes carrying a load of caterers and staff that took off before dawn."

"You just said they don't trust men. Why would they risk flying in a plane in the domain of Air Wizards?"

"Like I said, Earth Wizards are dumb as mud. Now for our real destination. Remember the male Troll who hitched a ride with you yesterday? Well, for some reason he trusts us and believes he knows where the women are headed. That's why we need your jet."

"He doesn't trust us. He just needs my plane. Female Wizards don't just vanish without a trace." Rowan hesitated. "Unless they want to disappear."

Stryker drove into the terminal and headed toward Rowan's plane. "My thought is that one death got them spooked. Two more propelled them into an all-out panic attack. According to the male Troll, there's a large underground magical community sympathetic to female Wizards. He thinks they only made it look like Vlad's boat sank to get the Grand Vizier off their scent, then headed for Seattle in another one of his yachts." Stryker grinned. "You've got to admire their style."

"I'm sure I will, when I'm done being pissed off. Great detective work, Stryker. I'm betting you're planning on defying Vlad's direct order and leaving the island."

Stryker parked the car and cut the engine. "That's what makes this fun. I told the guard we were going for coffee. I just didn't mention the coffee shop was in Seattle."

Rowan noticed a male Troll standing by his plane, the same Troll who had hitched a ride on Rowan's plane from Seattle, and he looked mad as hell.

He nodded toward the man. "Did he tell you his name?"

"Renegade."

"Fits. Does he trust us?"

"Pretty sure he doesn't, so watch your back."

Rowan got out of the car and slammed the door, frustrated the female Wizards didn't trust him. Who was he kidding? It bugged him the woman he'd slept with didn't trust him. For some reason, that one stung far worse. His anger ran like molten lava through his veins, and he did nothing to cool it down.

Stryker was right. Something must have really freaked the female Wizards, to cause them to run. His anger spiked and a cluster of bushes caught fire as he passed them on his way to the plane. Rowan let them burn. He planned to find out who or what it was that had pushed the women to desperation. But first he intended to find out where they were hiding and protect them, whether they liked it or not.

Chapter Fourteen

In the late afternoon, Seattle's waterfront warehouses buzzed with activity. The brick warehouse of Magus Stone & Gravel was no exception. Perched on the farthest pier, it reeked of wet rock and sea water. Large slabs of blue-veined stones, resembling granite, were loaded onto conveyor belts and crushed. The material was then deposited into containers and stacked in rows, in preparation for shipment.

The company, Magus, named for a Scottish Wizard from the ninth century, supplied landscape boulders, crushed granite, flagstone and river rock for pathways and gardens to the general public. The real money was in extracting arsenic, asbestos, mercury, lead, uranium and thallium and selling them to the magical community. These elements were among the key ingredients used in forbidden spells and potions.

In the corner office, overlooking the warehouse floor, Zacharias Phillips studied the profit-and-loss statements on his desk. He had the reputation of being a hard worker. When he was younger, he'd start his day with a run around Green Lake. Now he just went in to work. His dedication to his job had garnered him the approval from the leaders of the Talons and the Grey Council, and divorce papers from his wife of fifteen years.

The time on his cell flashed eight a.m. and, like

clockwork, his new assistant, Daffeny Schultz, entered his office to review the statements she had given him last night.

She was an improvement over his last assistant. Smart and attractive, she always wore dark slacks and a jacket, and according to her resume, she played volleyball in college and held a master's degree in business from Seattle University.

His former assistant was also pretty but was as dumb as roadkill. After his divorce, he'd wanted a little eye-candy to decorate his office. He was over that phase in his life now. Intelligence had become his main consideration. If he got both, that was a bonus. The most surprising of all was that Daffeny Schultz never flirted with him, even after she found out he was single and worth billions. He liked that about her—and the fact she always called him "sir."

Zacharias made a few notations on the statement and then handed it Daffeny. "Are you positive the count is off?"

"Yes, sir. We double-checked. Ten fifty-pound sacks of broken rocks are missing. Sammy verified it but said we still have enough product to fill our order with Northwest Landscaping. Should I ask him to double-check the count?"

Zacharias didn't like the implication of a discrepancy in the numbers. It meant there was either a thief or someone who couldn't count. He didn't like his choices. He kept the irritation out of his voice. No sense alerting his secretary to the seriousness of the problem. "Have Sammy conduct a recount, and this time bring someone else along to help him. Fifty-pound sacks of rock don't walk away without help."

"Very good, sir."

He watched her scribble on a yellow notepad. She was always making notes. He figured she was like those people who had to write everything down. He didn't care what she did to get the job done, as long as she kept her mouth shut.

Daffeny was the fourth assistant he'd hired in the last ten months. Finding competent people wasn't the problem. Zacharias could hire a law graduate with the salary he paid. The bigger issue for him was loyalty. The minute his assistants caught on to his black-market operation and showed signs they might share that knowledge with the authorities, they were replaced.

"Will that be all, sir?"

Daffeny's professional manner pulled him back. Yes, he hoped she wouldn't catch on for a while.

"Excuse me, sir, but there was one more thing. Your daughter called. She said her tuition is due."

Zacharias's mood lightened as he pictured Katharine. Except for her mother's exceptionally green eyes, Katharine was as plain and bland as English Yorkshire pudding. Maybe that's why he spoiled and indulged her so much. She'd never given him a moment's worry. She'd never partied like her mother had. Didn't do drugs, and earned straight As in the University of Washington's medical school. Even when her mother divorced him and then died of an overdose, Katharine remained unchanged, as though her mother had died years before. And in a way, she had. She'd accepted her mother's death as easily and as unemotionally as rain in Seattle. He'd never been more relieved. His only regret was that...

Daffeny cleared her throat.

"Sorry. I was thinking of Katharine. I'll call her myself and let her know that I'll transfer the money today." He could read the worry in his assistant's eyes. It was another trait he liked about her. She couldn't lie or bluff without him being able to read it in her expression. He'd know if she so much as stole a stapler or a box of paperclips. "Is there anything else?"

"There's a gentleman waiting to see you in the downstairs waiting room. I told him, per your instructions, that you weren't to be disturbed. But he was very insistent that he meet with you as soon as possible. He…he made me very uncomfortable."

Zacharias watched her fidget with a corner of her notepad. There were at least a dozen bodyguards patrolling his warehouse. He'd introduced them to Daffeny as custodians, despite the fact they looked more like pro wrestling candidates, or mercenary types in a B-rated movie. She seemed to accept the explanation. At the time, he'd been relieved. Her naiveté meant she could stay a little longer. It was a time-drain getting rid of assistants, disposing of the bodies, making their deaths appear accidental. Not to mention the inconvenience of interviewing new candidates.

He leaned back in his chair, glancing over at the drawer where he kept his gun. "Did the man give his name?"

"I apologize, sir. He refused. Should I call the police?"

Zacharias choked down an oath. The last thing he needed was the police snooping around. "No, I'll take care of it."

"Yes, sir."

She seemed to relax. But something else was

bothering her. Instead of bringing it up, she just nodded and left in a hurry. He made a mental note to ask her about it later today as he descended the stairs to the warehouse floor. There could be any number of people who would demand an audience. He would let Daffeny know she could call on the "custodians" to help her in the future. If all went as planned, she might need them in the next few weeks.

Satisfied he'd covered his base, he headed toward the waiting room. Like the warehouse and his office, it was stark and functional. He didn't believe in flaunting his wealth. It sent off too many red flags. So far, the IRS bought the explanation that people paid a high premium for imported rocks to decorate their yards and use them in their outdoor water treatments. It also helped that he had legitimate landscape companies on his client list. They wouldn't be as understanding if they found out the blue powder was used in illegal drugs, and in forbidden potions for the Talons and the Grey Council. He loved his little secrets.

He recognized the man in the waiting room. It was Vlad, the Grand Vizier of the Grey Council, and his specialty was surprise visits. Vlad had made himself at home and was drinking out of Zacharias's coffee mug. Zacharias made a mental note to throw it out as soon as Vlad left. He didn't like people touching his stuff.

Zacharias camouflaged his annoyance with a smile. "An unexpected pleasure, Grand Vizier."

Vlad held out his hand and offered a strong handshake that threatened to crush Zacharias's fingers. Either the man didn't know his own strength or he was making a point. A little of both was Zacharias's guess. "We're pleased with your progress."

Zacharias motioned for Vlad to take a seat and then sat down, ignoring the throbbing pain in his hand. One thing he'd learned from dealing with Wizards and the magical community was that it wasn't wise to show weakness.

He settled back in his chair and faked calm. "Thank you for the vote of confidence, Grand Vizier. It's easy when the product sells itself. The ingredient you suggested made the difference. We've named the product Magic Carpet Ride, or *MCR,* and it's an overnight success. I was concerned the side effects would discourage sales, but as you predicted, it only accelerated them. The kids are addicted to the danger in the same way people eat raw puffer fish or play Russian roulette. They believe the drug can provide them with temporary superhuman powers to give them the ability to jump off tall buildings and survive. Even the knowledge that the majority of people die or are crippled from the fall hasn't discouraged sales. It helped that we spread the rumor that a few people land on their feet and walk away. I'm curious. Is it true that the uncut stones are also an energy source, like the sun or wind? Any chance we might run out?"

"You have a lot of questions for a man in your position." Vlad set down the mug with such force it shattered. "None of that is your concern. I thought I made that clear. What concerns me, however, is that I suspect the drug is no longer under your control. Wizards are dead ahead of schedule."

Zacharias tried to regain his composure. He was shaken—not from the broken mug, but by the tone of Vlad's voice. Zacharias had met dangerous men before. He was surrounded by them. Hell, he *was* one. Vlad was at a different level. He swallowed. "Do you trust this Wizard?"

"Of course not, but I was pressured to get to the bottom of the murders, and it would have looked suspicious if I hadn't brought him in. I chose him because he would be easy to discredit if things got out of hand. One of the Wizards killed wasn't on the list I gave you. Explain."

Zacharias laced his fingers together, weighing his words carefully. Pissing off a Grand Vizier was never a good idea. He knew the Wizard in question, the one most recently deceased. The man was an undercover policeman who ventured too close to Zacharias's operation by cozying up to his last assistant. Naturally, both had to be killed. Vlad wouldn't like that excuse.

"I may have an explanation," Zacharias said. "As you know, a few Wizards have exhibited signs of addiction, which is why we set your plan in motion. Their deaths would be easily explained away. Unfortunately, dealing with drugs and the chemically dependent is never a stable cocktail. It's possible some of them stumbled onto our product by accident."

Vlad gripped the arm of his chair. The steel frame bent under stress. "Then explain to me, if you would be so kind, why the eyes were removed? The poison is all that is needed to kill them."

Sweat beaded on Zacharias's forehead. "I'm guessing whoever gave the Wizards MCR panicked. They wanted to make sure that if the Wizard survived, he would be helpless. Removing the eyes renders a Wizard helpless to use his powers."

"I know what it does when you remove a Wizard's eyes, you dolt. I'm the one who told you. I gave you my enemies list. Only the Wizards I designate on the list were to be sold Magic Carpet Ride by your drug dealers. Make sure you have control over all in your employ and that none have gone into business for themselves. I don't care how many humans buy it, but overdosing Wizards is another matter. Do I make myself clear?"

Zacharias nodded. It bothered him that on the exact day he'd found out a possible theft had occurred, Vlad appeared in his office. He couldn't ignore the possibility there was a spy in his organization. He wasn't about to let anything or anyone jeopardize his gravy train or his rise to power. Although he had a way to check if anyone was selling his product without his knowledge, ferreting out the spy offered a challenge.

"I assure you, I have everything under control."

"I don't want assurances." Vlad's voice rumbled, like the sound before an earthquake. "I want results. It is dangerous business procuring the stones needed to extract the elements for the new drug. Should I worry that you are not the human for the job?"

Zacharias noted the signs. Vlad was most dangerous when he perceived that someone had crossed him, or was not capable, and thus replaceable. In those incidences the person ended up in a shallow grave.

Zacharias kept his voice respectful as he lowered his head in submission. "I have never failed you. You can count on me to have this matter sorted out to your satisfaction."

Vlad nodded as he answered a text on his cell.

Zacharias forced himself to lean back in his chair and feign calm. Judging an Earth Wizard's emotion was an insight he'd learned from his wife. He'd fallen in love with her at first sight: Runway beautiful, with a compliant nature and generational wealth that she wanted to share with him to make his every dream come true.

It was only after the wedding that he learned she was part Fae and had used glamours and spells to entrap him. Her compliant nature hid a dark side. The wrong word, the wrong look, and she turned violent. But she was a woman of her word and had introduced him to the leaders of the Talons and the Grey Council.

He'd learned that Vlad was like many in the magical community he dealt with. Their inflated egos made them think they were experts on everything. Zacharias smothered his frustration. It was too soon to show his hand. All he had to do was wait. He blanketed his expression with a practiced smile and laced his voice with false humility.

When Vlad ended his text message, Zacharias resumed his line of defense. "It's true I'm operating numerous drug labs around the city, but it's standard operating procedure to have many going on at the same time. If the police shut down one or two, production isn't affected. I assure you, the labs will be checked out thoroughly."

Vlad stood, a clear indication the meeting was over. "So we understand each other?"

"Yes, sir."

Vlad headed for the door, pausing at the threshold. "You'll be receiving a large shipment by the end of the week. Can you handle the increase?"

The comment was a deliberate insult to Zacharias's competence. Vlad was treating him like an inexperienced punk kid. Zacharias smiled more broadly to hide the tightening in his jaw. "Piece of cake."

Zacharias waited until the Grand Vizier had left the warehouse and was in the parking lot before he was able to control his breathing well enough to make a call. When the person on the other end picked up, Zacharias snapped an order. "I have a job for you. One that you'll find to your liking. There's a rat in my warehouse. Find the bastard and exterminate him."

Chapter Fifteen

Across town, rain drizzled over the gray streets of Seattle as Rowan walked to his scheduled appointment with Detective Lyons. He'd landed his private plane a short time ago, parted ways with his brother and Renegade, and headed into the downtown area by cab. Meeting with Lyons was the last thing on his mind—the goddess at Bealtaine being the first, and the mysterious disappearance of her, the children, and the female Wizards running a close second.

But he owed it to the detective to fill him in on the deaths on the island. There was a connection, and Lyons might have learned more details while Rowan was gone. The man might not have a magical bone in his body, but his foster mother had been a recovering vampire who drank only synthetic blood. With this kind of mother, Lyons had been taught early in life about Seattle's underground magical community and how to navigate it without getting killed.

By this late on Monday afternoon, there were still no leads on the missing Wizards. Rowan was running out of options, so a meeting with Lyons was a long shot he was willing to take. After they landed, they'd all separated, Stryker to track down his leads, Renegade his. Or at least that was what Rowan hoped the Troll would do. The man was harder to read than a zombie's expression.

Rowan waited on the corner for the traffic light to change. It seemed to take longer than normal. Too early in the spring season for a power outage, but this was the Northwest and known for high winds, rain, and changes in weather. One minute the day was as grey as the underbelly of a dragon. The next the sun blinded, and he was the only one wearing sunglasses.

Rowan glanced at his cell. He was going to be late. His time on the island had changed the rules, and that made him very impatient. Forty-eight hours ago, his life was simple. Hunt down the bad guys. Catch the bad guys. Kill or arrest the bad guys. The latter outcome depended on his mood and the crime.

Three ravens dropped from a rooftop and perched on a trio of newspaper stands. People rushed past the birds as though they were the harbingers of doom in a fairy tale. The humans' instincts might be closer to the truth than they imagined. Most people couldn't tell the difference between crows and ravens. Crows were true scavengers, content to feed off scraps and roadkill. Ravens were hunters and protected their own. It was not uncommon to see them drive off an eagle who threatened their nest.

One of the ravens turned toward Rowan. For a split second its eyes looked human, and in that instant Rowan knew—they were Ravs, part raven, part human. Ravs were messengers, spies, snitches, protectors, and shapeshifters—which meant that, like the majority of the magical community, some were good, and some were evil.

The ravens lifted from their perch and disappeared down an alley. He couldn't tell if they wanted him to follow or... A horn blared. It seemed to shake the pedestrians on the sidewalk. Generally, Seattleites didn't honk horns. Must be a tourist, or maybe someone who'd just moved to Seattle from another part of the United States.

He swore under his breath. The presence of Ravs was never a good omen. It almost always meant a warning of some kind. What was taking so fracking long for the lights to change? Taking advantage of the sluggish flow of traffic, he jogged around the cars clogging the intersection and headed to the coffee shop.

It was in the middle of the block. Lyons sat under one of the café's large umbrellas, waiting for him. Rain had forced the less hardy indoors, which Rowan knew suited the detective. Lyons wasn't a people person. He sat at a table in the rainy drizzle as though it were a balmy day, wearing his grey wool suit like a superhero's costume. His college football career had ended with a torn rotator cuff. He felt his life was over, but in his senior year he learned that his foster mother had died trying to save an innocent, and her unselfish act had awakened a new sense of purpose. He was a rare breed and seemed surprised he got paid for doing something he loved.

Rowan joined Lyons, nodded hello and sat facing the street, accepting the black coffee that Lyons shoved his way with another nod of thanks. "Did the evidence you and I gathered on the Pentagram serial killer hold up?" Rowan said.

"Like glue. It's now in the court's hands." Lyons' grin lit up his face, minimizing the dark circles. "And thanks for the tip on the kidnapper. The guy was right where you said he'd be. The pond scum had the woman tied up in a deserted warehouse—lots of nasty-looking knives set out in neat rows on a table. Dried blood from previous victims smeared on the walls and floor. A real nightmare." Lyons rubbed both temples as though trying to erase the memory from his mind. The look in his eyes told Rowan he hadn't been successful. Lyons let out his breath and reached into his suit pocket for an envelope. "We never would have rescued the girl from that ghoul in time if it weren't for your tip."

Rowan accepted the envelope and tucked it away without counting the money. He knew it would be fair. Rowan was off the books and there was a silent benefactor at the department who paid him for tips or when he brought criminals to justice. "Glad I could help. Feels like more than usual."

"Consider it a bonus. The chief thinks you're a cross between a bloodhound and Houdini. I give you a sample of something belonging to the missing person and you find them." Lyons sat back and glanced over at the slow-moving traffic. "If I told them who you really were…"

"They'd throw you in a padded cell."

Lyons laughed. "I might enjoy the quiet time. I'm going to add fortunetelling to your job description. That's exactly what they'd do." Lyons stared into his coffee as though it was a crystal ball. "Think you'd reconsider starting a P.I. business with me? We can pick our cases instead of them picking us."

Rowan had received a lot of offers over the years. Working with Lyons held a unique appeal. He was the first human he had ever trusted. The global issues the Talons and the Grey Council dealt with took years, sometimes centuries, to accomplish. He and Lyons might be able to do a lot of good in the here and now. Besides, in addition to trusting the guy, he also respected him. He was one of the good guys.

Rowan finished his coffee. It had turned ice cold, but the jolt of caffeine was just what he needed. "I'll think over the offer. New topic. Any leads on the yacht, and the missing female Wizards and Wizardlings I mentioned over the phone?"

Lyons took out his notepad and flipped a few pages. "The only boats docking in the last twenty-four hours were cruise ships and ferryboats. Bad weather reports kept everything else tied up to a pier, but I'll keep checking. Want to tell me what this is about?"

"Would you like a refill on your coffee, Detective Lyons?" A tall blonde cliché batted her eyelashes and smiled, her teeth so white Rowan almost squinted.

Lyons didn't look up. "I'm fine."

She hesitated and then headed back inside.

"Interesting," Rowan said. "She acted like she knew you or wanted to know you."

"Don't. You were going to tell me the rest of the story."

Rowan rotated his empty cup. "Still trying to figure out if it's a mystery or a nightmare. Stryker is checking out his area of expertise, cyberspace, and I have someone looking into the magical community. Everything's as quiet as the tomb of a vampire in the daylight."

Lyons flipped another page and shook his head. "Still freaks me out sometimes that monsters like that exist. My foster mom…"

"…wasn't a monster," Rowan finished. "She loved you and was a good mother."

"Thanks for that. I miss her and still wish I could find the bottom feeder who killed her."

"We will."

Lyons nodded as he turned to another page. "Here's something that's weird. Almost didn't bring it up, but I know how you don't like coincidences, so it's better that I do. We found a floater a few days ago. A body washed to shore on Bainbridge Island. It scared the fillings out of an old lady who was walking her dog along the beach. Then the body disappeared from the morgue. Paperwork too. I interviewed the coroner, and he remembered a high level of hallucinogens present in the preliminary samples. But he couldn't remember the exact dosages or the composition of the drugs. He said because of the state of decomposition he almost missed the most interesting part. The eyes were gouged out of the scull. The coroner first thought it was the work of fish and parasites, but when he looked closer, he noticed cut marks around the eye sockets as though the eyes were surgically removed. He figured they were made by some sort of metal instrument and was going to do a more thorough exam. Then the body went missing. What do you think it means?"

"Nothing good." Rowan crushed his empty cup and threw it in a nearby trashcan. "Gouging out the eyes is an effective way of neutralizing a Wizard's power. After that, killing him is as easy as stepping on a bug. If this were a one-time thing, no problem. Stuff happens. A week ago, if you had told me this story, I'd say someone who was into dark magic stumbled onto the real thing and this was a one off. Unfortunately, that's not the case. This feels like the beginning of a turf war. I hope I'm wrong. If I'm right, Puget Sound and the lakes surrounding Seattle will flow red with human and Wizard blood."

For the first time Lyons looked older than his fifty

years. "I was afraid you'd say something like that. I had a bad feeling about this one. The missing body is the real mystery. Usually, this sort of thing happens at night, not in broad daylight. The coroner stepped out for coffee, and when he returned the body was gone."

"Blood work? Tissue samples?"

"All gone. Photos included. Everything we had on him vanished. Any ideas who could pull this off?"

"No one human would be my guess."

"Just so you know, it's not easy making these crimes appear the work of a sociopath instead of something from a horror movie. Any idea who could move around in the daylight and not be seen?"

"An endless list, but it might be the work of beings called Shadows. For the most part they're mercenaries, and impossible to catch. You might even start a conversation with one, thinking they were flesh and blood. The next minute you're talking to yourself."

"My foster mom never mentioned them." Lyons whistled low and looked uneasy. "But they sound a lot like what the kids strung out on the latest designer drug call Shadow People. Odd the name is so similar, especially with the drugs the coroner mentioned. Of course, with the kids, it's the drug that causes hallucinations, not the result of a paranormal being. Ever caught a Shadow?"

"Never, and you don't want to mess with them. Trust me. If you even think you see one, run. They're soulless, merciless, and deadly."

A cell phone rang, belting out Cher's "Gypsies, Tramps and Thieves." To someone who didn't know Lyons, the tune seemed dated. But the song was Lyons' foster mom's favorite, and he refused to change it, which earned Rowan's respect. Nothing was as it appeared. Probably one of the reasons they got along so well. Everything with Lyons had a double or triple meaning.

Feeling someone starting in his direction, Rowan glanced in their direction. The blonde was behind the counter, staring at Lyons. He couldn't tell if she was the one who'd called, but her expression was a little sad, as though she'd lost a puppy, or broken a nail. Rowan was bad at picking up on "woman-signals."

Lyons glanced at the caller ID. "Duty calls. I'll contact you if my sources discover the location of that yacht with the Wizards or learn about any new coincidences. Be in touch."

Rowan motioned inside. "Tell me about the woman."

"We had a moment."

"And then you found out."

He nodded. "And then I found out."

"Not all Fae women are psycho."

"Gotta go. I'll let you know if I find out anything."

Rowan nodded as Lyons headed for his car, a mint-condition cherry-red 1965 Corvette. Most people would keep such a valuable automobile in a locked garage under a custom-made tarp. Lyons wasn't most people.

Rowan didn't like this new wrinkle on the murders. It left a bad taste in his mouth. He glanced toward the sky, expecting to see Ravs circling around him, but there was only a thick blanketing of clouds. He felt like he was in a maze, with no clear path in sight.

What kept nagging him was the reference to drugs. Vlad had mentioned that he believed the drug Magic Carpet Ride was being used on Wizards. Not the first time an enemy had tried to poison a Wizard. But it had never been done on this scale. His guess was that whoever was behind the murders meant to eliminate as many Wizards as possible before war was declared. Had the female Wizards fled because they foresaw the danger?

Chapter Sixteen

The next day at Magus Stone and Gravel, Zacharias set the folder containing an employment resumé aside, savoring the moment. This was his favorite part in the whole tedious job interview process. The moment when he'd eliminated all the candidates except for a select few. The one sitting calmly in front of him was the best of the lot. It was too bad his last secretary, Daffeny Schultz, hadn't lasted, but stuff happened.

The newest candidate, Ms. Zollinger, was stunning. But that wasn't the reason she was in the top tier. She was a classic example of someone who didn't know what she wanted but was smart enough to realize she needed money while she figured it out. Ms. Zollinger had a lot of advanced degrees, and more importantly, a lot of student loans, no family, and no friends. His investigators said she had moved to Seattle from St. Louis, Missouri a month ago, after a bad breakup, and had run out of what little savings she'd brought with her. She was perfect. She checked all the boxes. Educated. Alone. Desperate.

He laced his fingers together on top of her file, already guessing the answer but wanting to see her reaction. "Your resumé and recommendations are impressive, Ms. Zollinger. I'm curious. Of all the opportunities for someone with your background, why seek the job as my assistant at Magus Stone and Gravel?"

She hesitated, focusing on where her hands gripped a small leather purse. When she lifted her gaze, it was steady. Even. Confident. "I'll be honest. I need the money. When I heard the salary range from the employment service, it made sense to apply."

He liked her honesty. Most of them lied and said something predictable, like, "I've always wanted to learn about rocks." He nodded and flipped open her file and reread the report. He also liked that she was single and the only child of parents who'd died in a private plane crash. His mistake with Daffeny had been that she'd had a family and a persistent boyfriend who'd asked too many questions about the odd hours of operation and the real purpose of the crushed rocks. In every incidence, nosey families and friends were the cause for eliminating assistants and warehouse workers. It was time for a new type of candidate. One with no ties.

He closed the file. "This is a demanding job, long hours, and a lot of weekends. My last secretary had a boyfriend who objected to the workload and persuaded her to quit and move with him to Alaska." He paused and sat back in his chair, letting this information settle in with the candidate. What he'd said wasn't a lie. Both bodies were buried in a toxic landfill somewhere outside of Anchorage.

For the briefest moment the muscles around Ms. Zollinger's lovely mouth tightened. He was curious. Perhaps he'd misjudged her. He leaned forward. "I know I sound harsh, but this is a pressure-cooker of a job. And although I'm not discouraging you to have a relationship, it will be difficult, at best, to have outside interests while you're learning the position."

The tension around her eyes and mouth eased when

she smiled. "There's no one in my life. I'm afraid my last relationship was a total mess. We were together for three years, and the whole time he was cheating on me with my best friend." She paused, then continued in a tight voice. "This wasn't my first misjudgment in character. I seem to attract lowlife scumbags, like the proverbial moth-to-a-flame cliché. I'm not looking for a relationship, Mr. Phillips. I'm looking for a job that will help me get out of debt."

"Why Seattle? Aside from the rain, which discourages people, it is one of the most expensive cities in the US."

"My boyfriend hates the Seahawks. He played football for the St. Louis Cardinals and a series of injuries ended his career. I thought it would annoy him that I moved here."

He chuckled, liking her answer. Her moving to Seattle was a form of revenge, an emotion he understood very well. "You have the job. Can you start tomorrow?"

She nodded, and her tense expression relaxed, replaced with relief. She rose from the chair and almost curtsied as she left his office. She wasn't as easy to read as Daffeny, but close enough.

Desperation and need were potent motivators he used to control those who worked for him. He also liked her slip regarding the ex. A beautiful woman might say she was done with bad boys, but they never were. They could never stay away from their addiction for long. For insurance, he'd play the matchmaker.

He picked up the phone and dialed a number by heart. He had the perfect man to keep a close eye on his newest hire. John Reynolds should be back from Alaska by now. He was an ex-NFL football player, soft spoken, with an easy smile and a way with the ladies. Zacharias chuckled at the irony as the phone started to ring. A hit man as a boyfriend. If Ms. Zollinger didn't work out, getting rid of her would be easier than all the others put together. Reynolds might even cut his normal rate.

Chapter Seventeen

Rowan's meeting with Lyons concluded, he was glad he was on foot, because Seattle traffic was worse than normal. Midafternoon, on the heels of rush hour, and the traffic lights still weren't working.

A few drivers used their horns, as though that would fix the situation. Traffic edged through the intersection from all directions. The area to his right was the real problem. Cars were perched on the crest of a hill, where visibility was nearly nonexistent for the drivers. More car horns joined in while impatient pedestrians moved to cross the street.

Brakes screeched over wet pavement as a sports car swerved, barely missing a woman and a black Labrador Retriever. Both were huddled together in the center of the crosswalk, where they appeared to be frozen in fear as a white sedan swerved around them. An impatient driver in a black pickup truck sped over the crest of the hill straight for them.

Across the street a man screamed to the woman to get out of the way as he hurried toward her. It happened like a movie played out in slow motion. Instinctively Rowan knew the man wouldn't reach her in time. A different kind of speed was needed.

Willing his core to overheat, Rowan took off in a blur of light. He sped around briefcase-wielding business types, parents pushing baby carriages, and teenagers attached to their cell phones. Racing past cars and people, his speed took on the power of a raging fire storm as though the world was standing still.

Rowan gathered the woman in his arms and reached for the dog. But the animal leapt out of the way and into the oncoming traffic. A truck swerved, trying to avoid the animal, but everything happened too fast. It struck the dog and plowed into a van.

Rowan spun clear of the chaos and sped to the curb, setting the woman down gently.

Silence hung in the intersection as Rowan scanned the faces of the crowd and recognized the confusion in their expressions. He knew they were trying to process what they'd seen happen.

He'd acted impulsively, something he hadn't done in a very long time. The Grey Council and the Talons wouldn't be doing a Snoopy Happy Dance in his honor when they found out. He'd risked exposure. Again. The Talons and the Grey Council only put up with these risks so long before they reacted. He'd never heard of them killing anyone, but banishment was always at the top of their list.

What was happening to him? He needed more sleep—or maybe less. One thing was certain. It was time to clean up the mess he'd made. Gone were the times when his kind could live out in the open. The witch trials, monster hunts, and purges had been a bleak reminder. Survival meant secrecy.

Rowan scanned the crash site for signs of the dog. The poor animal must have died when it was struck by the truck. He felt bad that he hadn't anticipated that the animal might spook if a stranger tried to grab him. The woman, her back to him, sat where he'd left her. She pulled the hood of her raincoat farther over her head, clutched her knees together, and rocked slowly back and forth. She looked like she was in shock, but there was nothing more he could do for her. Human hospitals were good at picking up the pieces and putting people back together. Or so he'd been told.

Regardless, she was no longer his concern. Mitigating the situation at the intersection was.

Removing his dark glasses, he cast a forgetfulness spell over the crowd. This method would distort the events of the last few seconds, leaving the crowd confused and unable to piece together what had happened with any certainty. It should be enough. A few might guess he was responsible for saving the woman, but the details of the rescue would be fuzzy, like the weather. Fortunately, humans had a way of adjusting what they saw to fit their perspective of the world and how they thought it worked. It was one of the main reasons the magical community had been able to co-exist with them without detection for centuries.

When he replaced his glasses, the deafening quiet broke and with it the traffic lights resumed their normal patterns. Maybe his spell had jolted loose whatever problem had caused the malfunction. Yeah, like thinking that if you threw you shoe at your flat-screen TV, it would change the outcome of a football game.

The accident forgotten, the crowd cheered in relief as cars moved through the intersection and people rushed to appointments. A few hurried toward the woman, offering help and comfort.

Hands in his pockets, Rowan crossed the street, wanting to be as far away as possible. Then he caught another distress call. The injured dog whimpered beside the totaled vehicles. The dog was still alive. He felt a ridiculous amount of relief and froze in place. If he was smart, he'd walk away. This shouldn't be his problem. He'd already risked exposure by saving the woman. Helping a dog would send the Talons and the Grey Council into fits of outrage.

The dog whimpered again; this time the sound was weaker. The animal wouldn't survive without help.

"Damn." Rowan let out his breath, turned around and headed in the direction of the animal's distress call. Aid cars and police and fire trucks were descending on the scene. No one took notice when he knelt and stroked the dog's matted fur. The animal's breathing was shallow and labored. "Easy, boy."

The dog's tail thumped once on the ground as though that was all the strength he had left. He was a beauty, with fur the same midnight black as a raven's feathers. But he didn't have a collar, and his ribs pushed against his chest. He looked like he hadn't eaten in days. Maybe the dog had followed the woman into the street, begging for food, or from a primal instinct to protect her.

The animal turned his gaze toward Rowan. The dog's brown eyes were filled with pain. Rowan glanced toward the crowd. Their attention was focused on giving their report to a police officer who'd appeared on the scene. Rowan would have to make this quick before the officer decided to include him in his investigation.

He pressed his hand over the animal's chest, transferring the healing warmth of his touch to the dog, hoping it would be enough. When he was younger, he'd healed his cat when she got into a fight with a racoon, and also a half dozen water sprites, three flower fairies and a baby Troll. His method didn't work on anything larger and resulted in giving the victim false hope. Healing humans or Wizards was not in his bag of magic tricks no matter how many times he'd tried to hone the skill. He'd learned that the hard way when he had tried to heal Lyons' foster mother after she was attacked.

The animal's breathing smoothed out and his heart rate grew stronger just as someone pointed in Rowan's direction. Rowan scratched the dog under his chin. "That's all I can do for you now, boy. Hope it was enough."

Rowan rose, and with his hands in his pockets, he headed toward a densely populated sidewalk. Disappearing into a crowd was one of his talents. Being identified as a hero complicated that objective. He'd read somewhere that the words "hero" and "tragedy" were linked together all the time. Made sense.

The Superman character was the perfect example. Like the man of steel, Rowan could move at the speed of light. But whether you donned a cape or put on the persona of a Fire Wizard, the outcome was the same. You were on your own.

A woman wearing a raincoat brushed his side. It was the human he'd saved. He tensed, catching her exotic scent. Why hadn't he noticed it before? Blurred memories roared past, each one more difficult to grasp than the last.

Her mouth tilted at the corners in a smile. He knew that smile. But how?

"Thank you, Fire Wizard."

He swore under his breath. There could be only one reason she'd seen him for who he was. She wasn't human. How had he missed it? Were the traffic lights, the damsel-in-distress, the dog, all an elaborate trap? He shook his head in self-disgust. And who was she?

He'd rushed right into the deception like a novice Wizard with a green wand and a heart filled with idealism. Someone must be laughing their ass off. In the name of all the scum-sucking bottom feeders he'd hunted down, why hadn't he known she was magical?

She stood there, waiting. Green eyes, heart-shaped face, hair piled in soft curls on top of her head.

He knew it fell past her shoulders and felt as soft as silk in his hands.

He knew she tasted like strawberries and honey and smelled like an ocean breeze off the coast of the enchanted Irish island of Hy-Brasil.

He knew how her naked skin felt against his, how the curve of her breast filled his hand, how her naked hips moved…

Without warning, the brand over his heart, the one he'd received during Bealtaine, started to burn. He took a ragged breath. "It's you."

****

One minute Rowan was on a busy street corner in Seattle, and the next he was in an alley, draped in shadows and heat. Only a distant hum of life outside the sanctuary managed to penetrate. Rowan wasn't sure how it happened. Didn't care. He held the woman from the accident in his arms as memories flashed back in a storm of light. He knew her name and every inch of her body.

"Morgan? What are you doing here?" he breathed against her lips, cupping the back of her neck in his hand.

"I'm glad to see you too." Her smile was intoxicating as she leaned in.

He pressed his mouth against hers and inhaled her fragrance, drowning in her scent. He'd never met a woman like her. She was everything. Every cliché he'd ever heard, every love song ever written. If he was a poet, he… But he wasn't.

He was a Wizard. And cursed to love forbidden fruit. Every fiber of his being screamed they were not meant to be together.

His thoughts blurred as though he'd been thrown into a cloud bank. He had a vague sense she was controlling his thoughts. Spell? Glamour? Then, somehow, they were naked. How had that happened? Did he care?

Hell, no!

He wanted something soft to lay her on. The alley was a poor choice for someone like her, used to silks and velvets. As soon as he'd expressed the thought, a bed of pillows appeared beneath them.

She lowered herself onto them and motioned for him to follow.

"You've enchanted me."

"Do you mind?" A soft shadow flitted across her face. He reached out as though he could brush it away. He couldn't stand to see her sad.

"Mind? I can't think when I'm with you."

She pulled him down. "Lust is a selfish mistress. Enough talk."

"Good. Because I'm out of words."

Chapter Eighteen

Rowan awoke to a headache the size of New York, a clear sign that he had been under an enchantment. He'd had the craziest dream. And what was he doing in an alley?

"Good afternoon."

He knew that soft, lyrical voice. Not a dream, then. He scrambled to his feet and checked to make sure he was wearing clothes. Relieved that he was dressed and not swinging in the wind, he spun around to locate her. She sat a short distance away, fully clothed, her knees pulled against her chest, her face lost in shadows.

She rose and moved toward him. Each liquid step was measured and slow, as though she were controlling time itself. After the day he'd had, he wouldn't be surprised if she was. Clouds parted overhead, creating enough light for him to see her clearly.

He stepped back. Her hair color, eyes, even the shape of her face were the same as the enchantress on the island, but there was a difference. Something familiar. A face he'd thought forgotten. Amendment. A face he'd tried to forget. He touched the brand over his heart. He remembered telling the enchantress on the island that if their connection was a blending of two soulmates, he would recognize her even if she used glamours.

But it was much more than a joining of soulmates. He'd known her before. Loved her before. And when they told him she'd died, it had nearly destroyed him.

Anger welled to deepen his voice. "Hello, Morgan."

Her face tilted. "How long have you known?"

"Just now. Always. Hell if I know. Pick one."

"You are angry."

"I'd have to calm down to just feel angry. They told me you died. Why did you trick me? I would have been happy to see you."

She arched an eyebrow, tilting her head. "Dead, you say? You must have been relieved. The Talons and the Grey Council snapped their fingers, and you left me for them."

He clenched his hands at his sides. "Now I remember why I left. You are the most infuriating woman. Wait. Why would I have been relieved?"

She waved away his comment. "It no longer matters."

He reached for her shoulders to turn her toward him. "Obviously it matters. All of it. Why did you leave Bealtaine without telling me? Why did you seduce me just now if I'm such a bastard?"

"You saved the dog, and I wanted you."

The air heated around him as he leaned toward her, a heart's breath from her full lips. "You want me?" He drew back. "Wait. A test? I don't know whether to be grateful or insulted. Because of a dog, you can trust me now?"

"It is a beginning. And you should feel grateful. I could as easily kill you."

He drew back even more. "It's all coming back, why we fought. And you could not trust me on the island?"

"There was too much at stake."

"Ouch."

"Do not play the wounded warrior. You do not trust me either. Come. We must talk."

"Whenever a woman says those words, the news is always bad."

She looped her arm through his. "This time won't be any different."

****

He tried to hail a taxi or an Uber as the steady stream of traffic edged past the sidewalk by the alleyway where Rowan and Morgan had made love. Morgan stood beside him, patiently waiting. She was giving him time to process. That was so like her. Morgan thought of others first, and her needs and wants last. Which meant that if she was here, instead of in hiding like the other female Wizards who had escaped the island, something was terribly wrong and she needed his help.

She would have known that seeing her again would be a shock that brought up painful memories. He'd dealt her an emotional blow as well when he told her he had believed she was dead. But he hadn't questioned the story they'd spun that she'd died. That was on him. It hurt that she had been right when she'd said that, in a way, he had been relieved. The reason he'd accepted the assignment that took him from her was that he needed the distance. He knew that if she had asked him to stay and give up working for the Talons and the Grey Council, he would have. At the time, that scenario scared him worse than facing a swarm of angry, half-human, half-bird Harpies.

Rowan slid his glasses down to rub the bridge of his nose. He had been young and dumb. Not one of his finer moments. His cell phone vibrated and he grabbed it from his inside coat pocket. "What?"

The voice on the other end laughed. "It's Lyons. Catch you at a bad time?"

"Understatement." Rowan glanced over toward Morgan. The Mona Lisa smile told him she might have read his thoughts. The possibility used to annoy him. Now he could see the advantages. He had never been good with words. "Do you have a lead?"

"Another dead body. Better come quick if you want to see it before its bagged and tagged."

"On my way." Rowan replaced his cell and focused on Morgan. "I have a lot of dead bodies and no clear answers as to how they died. I've heard female Wizards can determine the cause of death. Any truth to the rumor?"

"If I do this for you, will you help me solve the question of why my sisters were murdered?"

So that was what she was after. Had he hoped for something else? He gritted his teeth and pushed the thought out of his mind. She'd confirmed what he and his brother had suspected. Three female Wizards had died on the first night of Bealtaine. Rowan had a bad feeling that finding the killer was going to be easier than ferreting out the motive. He looked out over the flow of traffic. Everything appeared back to normal—normal gridlock, that is. Once he agreed to help Morgan, he was honor bound. There was nothing casual about a conversation with a female Wizard.

"To be clear about the ground rules, you'll come with me, tell me how the Wizard was killed, and I'll help you find your sisters' murderer." When she nodded, he continued. "I'll also need the location of the young Wizardlings you and your sister Wizards kidnapped."

"Rescued," she corrected. Morgan cinched the belt

of her raincoat tighter. "You're delusional if you think I'll turn over that information."

"Was that a yes or a no?"

She crossed her arms over her chest. "For the last few centuries, we have placed the care of our Wizardlings in the hands of the Grey Council and the Talons, with mixed results. Turning them over to you is not a consideration. In fact, if all male Wizards, you included, disappeared into a dark abyss of never-ending pain and torment, I would not shed a single tear. How is that for an answer?"

"Crystal clear." Rowan hailed a cab. "But a simple yes or no would have worked just as well. I'm assuming you set up this whole traffic chaos scene as a test to see if I'd save a human. The dog was a nice touch."

"Wiz is a shapeshifter friend of mine. We were divided on whether you'd risk defying the rules of the magical community and save a human. But if you did, it was Wiz's idea that we confirm that you still had a heart."

The cab pulled to the curb, and as though on cue, Wiz trotted over to Morgan and nuzzled her hand. She reached down and whispered something in his ear before climbing with him into the back seat.

Rowan climbed into the cab after her and Wiz and gave the driver an address. As the taxi merged into traffic, Rowan glanced toward the dog, who sat between Rowan and Morgan. "Why is it coming with us?"

"*He*," she said, emphasizing the word, "is someone I can trust."

Chapter Nineteen

A short time later, the taxi parked at the edge of Gas Works Park on the north shore of Lake Union. During the ride, Rowan kept his thoughts cloaked from Morgan, and his mouth shut. If Wiz was a shapeshifter, that meant he was also unpredictable. Black Labs might look all cuddly and calm on the outside, but, like all dogs, they were descended from wolves and had strong protective instincts.

Rowan was the first to exit the taxi, and after paying the driver, he headed to the crime scene while Morgan and Wiz took off in the opposite direction. He thought about asking them where they were going, but they disappeared before he had a chance. An annoying habit Morgan had, disappearing without a word. He'd told her once that she should tell him where she was going. Her simple reply was, "Why?"

Gas Works Park was the site of an iron structure that could fit into any apocalyptic movie with ease. Remnants of an industrial era, a world-renowned architect had arranged the towers, tanks and pipes as a monument to a different time.

According to Lyons, it was also the scene of another murder.

The irony that the murder had taken place in a popular tourist area was not lost on Rowan. The killer had sent a message. No place was safe.

The sun was setting over Seattle's skyline in ribbons of crimson and grey as members of the University of Washington crew team rowed past. A few broke their concentration and stared toward the crime scene.

Detectives and medical personnel swarmed over the park like locusts. Yellow police tape cordoned off the shore as they worked the dead body and surrounding area for clues. Someone took pictures, while media crews jostled for space around the iron sculpture. Even with the distraction, the rowing team didn't break their stride. The expression "life goes on" played over and over in Rowan's mind, but it didn't bring him any comfort.

A serial killer with a taste for Wizard blood was on the loose.

Although Rowan didn't recognize the victim, he knew two things. The victim was a Wizard who'd suffered the same fate as the male Wizard on the island. And second, the killer knew the best way to neutralize a Wizard was to remove the eyes. But how had the murderer been able to get close enough in the first place?

There were tattoos visible on the dead Wizard's neck and arms that chronicled the events in his life and told the story that the victim was a high-level Fire Wizard. Which meant the killer would have needed help on a supernatural level to get close enough to murder the victim. Yet, aside from the missing eyes, there were no signs of a struggle.

The medics said the body hadn't been in Lake Washington long, which would help make their identification easier, or so they thought. They were wasting their time. Wizards didn't have dental or medical records. To add to what was sure to become a media circus, someone had dubbed the serial killer The

Eye Doctor. The headline would get a lot of media attention, but the curiosity would turn to panic in both the world of humans and the magical community if the murders started to escalate. And he had no doubt they would. He needed to solve this case, and fast.

He sensed that Morgan had returned without Wiz and glanced in her direction. She was down by the shore, standing over the body. Lyons had secured the necessary security clearance. Medics and junior detectives were everywhere. They ignored her and the victim as though they were invisible.

Rowan wasn't sure how she was managing it, probably more spells. He didn't question her methods, and he wasn't sure she'd listen if he did. Every once in a while, she bent down closer to the Wizard, but other than that, she just stood there, alternating between glancing toward the water or down at the body. He could feel her strength and determination and power crackle in the air like an electric storm over water. This was a side of female Wizards he'd never witnessed before, or maybe he'd never paid attention. His brother was right. You had to admire the style of female Wizards.

A woman in a crisp dark suit emerged from a huddle of police and media. She slipped a yellow notepad into her oversized shoulder bag before heading in his direction. She was good-looking, for a human. Late twenties, early thirties, with an aura of self-confidence. When she drew close enough, she held out her manicured hand toward him.

"I'm guessing you're Rowan."

He stuffed his hands in his pockets, avoiding her outstretched hand. "Any leads?"

She seemed annoyed that he'd avoided shaking her

hand, but it couldn't be helped. Because he was so close to Morgan, his core temperature was somewhere between 120 and 125 degrees. The infuriating woman heated his blood just by her presence. In the condition he was in, his body temperature would freak out the human. No sense drawing more attention than he had to.

She furrowed her brows and looked over Rowan's shoulder. "Hello, daddy dearest."

Lyons nodded and handed Rowan a disposable cup of coffee. "Hello, AJ. You're looking good. Did I miss a lunch date?" When she assured him that he hadn't, he introduced her to Rowan. "I'd like you to meet my daughter, Alexandra Jordon Lyons." The tone in Lyons' voice was light and casual, but the pride and love shone through like a beacon. "How's the new job going?" Lyons said to AJ.

"Fine, and before you start, I was careful and used the name Mildred Zollinger, the same name I used in college." She leveled her gaze toward Rowan. "My dad insisted I use a fake name because he is paranoid his enemies would become mine. As a result, since all of my school records are in that name, I had to use it when I applied for my current job."

"Now, AJ…"

Rowan wanted to argue that his friend's daughter was being smart, but decided it was wiser to change the subject. He wanted no part of this argument, so he asked her, "Are you one of the detectives on this case?"

Lyons laughed and spat out a stream of coffee. "Hell, no! She's going to law school."

"Dad, that's your dream, not mine. I have a degree in political science as well as business, with a master's in psychology and one in ancient cultures of the

Mediterranean. Don't you think it's time I stopped being a professional student and got a real job?"

"I just thought…"

Rowan concentrated on his coffee, as the father-daughter argument escalated. Family drama was not his thing. He looked toward Morgan. Mistake. The way she moved should be outlawed. She wore a raincoat over a sweater and slacks that were a couple sizes too big, yet she managed to look like she'd stepped off a fashion runway. There should be a law.

He crumpled up his empty coffee cup and threw it into a nearby receptacle, afraid he'd set it on fire if he held it any longer. She was circling the corpse, her expression focused and intent. What was taking her so long? The argument between Lyons and his daughter had run its course and AJ was on to another topic. Rowan felt trapped.

"Dad, I have a favor to ask. That's the real reason I'm here. A friend from college called me late last night. You remember her, Sally Schultz. We roomed together my last year. Anyway, she knows you're a detective and wanted to know if we could help. Her sister, Daffeny, and Daffeny's boyfriend were found dumped on a landfill in Alaska, both dead of an apparent overdose."

Lyons' expression morphed from concerned father to patient cop who'd heard too many of these types of stories. "Overdosing is a tragic end and difficult for the family. I'm very sorry."

"Except my friend said that her sister never did drugs, nor, to her knowledge, had her sister's boyfriend. My friend said she and her sister were very close and a trip to Alaska had never been mentioned. Daffeny had just started working for a company along the wharf for an insane amount of money. But instead of being happy about it, Daffeny was really stressed and wanted to quit."

Lyons put his hand on AJ's shoulder. "In my experience, the family is either the last to know what a loved one is really doing or is in denial. As far as not liking a job…"

She shrugged out of his reach. "You're not listening. My friend Sally thinks her sister was murdered. The last text Daffeny sent claimed she'd discovered that the place where she was working made a substance linked to the drug Magic Carpet Ride. Sally believes her sister stumbled onto something she shouldn't have and was killed."

Rowan had been only half listening, but the mention of MCR caught his attention. And not in a good way. The coincidence was too strong. Vlad had shown him a sample of MCR on the island. Rowan exchanged glances with Lyons. The man looked pale and sick. He'd made the connection as well.

The detective spat out his words. "Don't tell me that you're working for the same company where your friend's sister was killed?"

The silence was deafening.

"AJ, stay out of this. That's an order! Let the professionals do their job."

"Too late," she said, matching his tone. "I've listened to you talk about your cases most of my life. I am not going to stand by and do nothing. I'm very careful. I created a whole backstory, complete with a fake boyfriend."

All the color drained from Lyons' face. "Holy crap! So you're a private investigator now? In this gun-crazy climate, when even computer programmers carry weapons, you won't last a month. You refused to learn how to use a gun."

"A month is all I need to prove that Daffeny was murdered." AJ opened the flap of her shoulder bag and exposed a .357 Magnum revolver. "I've been practicing and I'm quite good."

Rowan clapped his friend on the shoulder to hold him back from strangling his daughter. "Look at that," Rowan said in a sarcastic tone. "Your daughter has a cute weapon. Five or six rounds. She'll be perfectly safe in a gang war."

Lyons stood as still as a statue, his expression changing from anger to concern, then frustration, and back to full-on rage.

AJ latched her purse and slung it back over her shoulder like a messenger bag. "I thought we could work on this case together. I'm doing this with or without your permission." She snapped a perfect 180-degree turn and headed toward her parked car.

"AJ, wait! Alexandra?"

Lyons expelled a breath of air. "I screwed that up. She's bringing a toy gun to a war zone. Do you think she'll try to find out who's making MCR?"

"Guaranteed. You just threw down the gauntlet by demanding she leave it alone. She's your daughter. What do you think?"

"Did you catch the part about her not wanting to learn how to use a gun until recently?"

"Hard not to. If we're lucky, we'll solve the case before she gets up to speed."

"Hope so. Any bodyguards in the magical community? One that knows how to use a Gatling gun?"

"That weapon's a touch old-school," Rowan said,

"but I get your drift. I've a better idea. I'm guessing if either one of us shows up to shadow her, she'll bolt. I'll ask my brother to keep an eye on her. If she stumbles onto something that's connected to the Wizard killings, he'll be there to protect her."

****

Rowan finished his call to his brother in time to see Morgan head in his direction.

Just the anticipation of her drawing near raised his body temperature and singed the grass at his feet.

Lyons elbowed Rowan in the ribs. "She's an enchanting woman."

"Interesting choice of words."

Lyons winked and lowered his voice. "And the way you look at her should be R-rated. You two a couple?"

"Wizards don't play by the same rules as humans. No marriages. No taking the kids to football and swim practice. No happily ever after."

"Ever wish you did? You know, play by human rules?"

He felt the weight of hesitation. If he was honest with himself, the one thing he felt humans got right was when they created healthy, loving families. He didn't know if he'd ever fathered a son or daughter, and that pain was a constant ache. He would have liked to know, and even more, would have liked to help raise the child.

"Too much trouble," he managed, using the phrase he always used when asked. It sounded hollow even in his ears. When Morgan was only a few feet away, she turned a warm smile toward Lyons, who gave an almost imperceptible nod. Rowan narrowed his gaze. "How do you know each other?"

Before Lyons could answer, two policemen pulled

him aside to ask about another case. Rowan seized the opportunity to talk to Morgan alone and motioned for her to follow him toward an iron structure on the perimeter of Gas Works Park.

She folded her arms. "We are not doing this. To answer your glare, yes. Detective Lyons and I know each other."

"Define *know*?"

"I'll answer with a human expression that fits. Bite me."

Rowan counted to ten. He was behaving like a jealous lover and it annoyed the hell out of him. He gritted his teeth. "So what did you find out?"

"I couldn't find proof, but I suspect that the murders of my sisters are connected to that of the male Wizard here."

"My conclusion as well. Do you think it's a rogue Wizard, on a power trip or for revenge? There's also a drug that has been present in the case of the male Wizards. Maybe some kind of poison."

Morgan glanced in the direction of the shore where the body lay. It was being lifted onto a stretcher and wheeled to the ambulance, but Rowan had the impression she was looking beyond the crime scene.

"I wish it were that simple," she said. "Is there someplace secure we can meet later tonight? It would not be wise for humans to overhear our conversation."

"There's a restaurant in Pike Place Market. The Inferno. It's owned and operated by a member of the magical community, Colin, and he runs it like a neutral zone. But I'm not letting you out of my sight."

"Yes, you are."

Rowan reached for her arm, considering asking one

of the policemen if he could borrow a pair of handcuffs. He figured it was the one sure way to keep track of her. The woman had no concept of danger. He lifted his hand to get someone's attention.

Morgan smiled and put her hand on his shoulder. "I'll meet you there after midnight. You have my word."

Before he could respond, she parted her lips and kissed him, leaning into him, pressing her mouth against his. The brand she'd placed over his heart flamed against his bare skin. Desire burst through his blood like a flashfire and took him by surprise.

He deepened the kiss, tasting her warmth. The world fell away. His only reality was the woman in his arms. He filled his senses with her fragrance. His blood heated. His thoughts blurred…

Seconds later Rowan heard shouting.

Someone was yelling his name, over and over like some ancient Gregorian chant. He opened his eyes and wished he hadn't. Light blinded him.

Lyons held a flashlight as he helped Rowan to a sitting position. "Are you all right?"

Rowan cradled his head in his hands. "Stop shouting. I'm not deaf."

What was he doing on the ground? His head pounded like the god Thor had hit him with his hammer. He pressed the palms of his hands against his temples. Damn. She'd done it to him again. She'd cast a spell over him. She was driving him crazy. He lifted his gaze and saw a taxicab disappear around the corner. It would be pointless to chase after her. She'd made it clear. She didn't want his help. Fine. He got it. She said she could take care of herself.

Bullshit.

Lyons helped Rowan to stand. "What happened?"

"Morgan happened. Remember when I told you Wizards don't do relationships? Well, this is why. There's no reasoning with a female Wizard. If they disagree with you, they lull you into a false sense of security, then zap you with a spell." Rowan paused. "Lyons, what the hell are you grinning about? This isn't funny. And how do you know her?"

Lyons held up his hands and backed away. The grin spread over his face and crinkled the laugh lines around his eyes. "I've never seen you like this before, that's all."

"Like what?"

"Besotted."

"Who uses that word anymore? And you didn't answer my question."

Lyons shrugged, taking his car keys out of his pocket. "Do you want a ride into town or not?"

Chapter Twenty

The drive to the Trolls' compound passed in a blur as Morgan touched her fingers to her lips. She could still feel the effects of Rowan's kiss and the way his hard body felt against hers. She took in another ragged breath of the night air to quiet her racing heart. Only a few minutes ago, the cab driver dropped her off at the gate obscuring the compound's entrance near the shores of Lake Washington. The lands had been a gift to the Trolls from one of the local tribes, but no one, least of all the female Wizards, knew which one, why or when.

Both the magical and human world viewed this waterfront home and the acreage surrounding it as nothing out of the ordinary. It was just another waterfront property where the reclusive and eccentric built their homes. Overgrown with rhododendron bushes, wildflowers, cedar, maple, and birch trees, nature was doing its part to camouflage the compound from the curious. No one would suspect it hid a world where time was suspended.

She took her time to cover the short distance along a cobblestone road that led to the ivy-covered mansion. She must learn to control her emotions. No one must guess her true feelings for the Fire Wizard.

When Rowan had gathered her in his arms in the alley, she had welcomed his embrace, his touch, his kiss and the silent promise in the way he breathed her name.

For a precious few minutes, she had forgotten she was only pretending she felt something for him. The moment her lips sought his, the hunger for his touch was almost unbearable. And at Gas Works Park she'd kissed him again. It had taken all her strength to pull away and cast a spell so she could escape.

She was playing with fire. Literally.

Too soon she reached the oak-paneled double doors. She shut her eyes against the emotions raging through her. She sensed Rowan was as confused as she about the depths of their feelings for one another. But if she let herself dwell on those troubling thoughts, more would be lost than her fragile heart. Rowan was a powerful distraction. She must learn how to control her emotions or everything would unravel. She needed all her resolve to find a permanent safe haven for the female Wizards and Wizardlings. They were depending on her.

The double doors opened of their own accord, flooding the porch with shafts of golden light. Morgan passed through the entrance and crossed to the front room. She was not alone. Completing the welcoming atmosphere, an old woman sat in a rocking chair by the fire, knitting.

The Victorian-style home on the Trolls' compound held the charm of an old-fashioned greeting card. Dark wood, overstuffed chairs, and lamps dripping with crystals and bright beads decorated the rooms. Forest green drapes were drawn against the deepening shadows, while the gentle smells of baking bread and sweet rolls drifted into the great room from the kitchens. It was easy to imagine how the stress of life's difficulties could float away on the cinnamon-and-nutmeg-scented air.

The temptation to ignore the dangers closing in on

her was hard for Morgan to resist. But Wizards, both male and female, were being murdered. How could she stop the carnage? This task felt beyond her power, beyond her strength. She shook her head, trying to sweep the web of doubts from her mind.

As she sat down in a wingback chair, she smiled at the gentle-faced woman who glanced toward her. Before Morgan could engage the woman in conversation, though, she heard a rustle of laughter, and Anne and Deidre rushed into the room, calling out her name as they jumped onto her lap. Their cheeks were coated with flour and pink, green and blue candy sprinkles. Morgan pushed the self-doubts away as she hugged them to her and let their childlike excitement wash over her.

"It is wonderful to see you, my Wizardlings. Are you well?"

Deidre nodded, her eyes bright with laughter. "Oh, milady, we are having the best time! Cassandra is teaching us a spell that will make us look like big hairy creatures with sticky green slimy drool, bulging eyes and foul breath. Cassandra said humans will think we're Trolls from their faery tales. Isn't that wonderful? Can we stay?"

"I want to stay too," Anne added with the same enthusiasm. "They have baby unicorns in the forest, fish that will eat out of your hand, a man who can juggle with his feet, a mermaid with long golden…"

A gentle clatter of dishes and the sound of a door being pushed open on well-oiled hinges announced Cassandra. She entered laughing and carrying a silver tray that held a rose-patterned tea set. "My darling children, can't you see how tired milady is after her journey to the city? Seattle has become so toxic of late that I wager it could sour a sugar cookie. Milady and I need to talk while she relaxes. There's plenty of time to tell her all about your new adventures." Cassandra set the tray on a table beside Morgan, prepared a cup of tea, and brought it over to the old woman, who nodded her thanks with a warm smile. Cassandra turned toward Anne and Deidre, her voice a blend of laughter and smiles. "Off with you, my budding Wizards. If you hurry, Fiona will let you help with the preparations for our festival next week."

Anne and Deidre squealed with delight, gave Morgan another hug, and chased each other down a long corridor. Their innocent laughter was like sweet music in Morgan's ears, a strong reminder of what she was fighting for. The children were happy here. Their confidence grew with each passing day, knowing they were cherished, nourished, protected and encouraged to follow whatever path they chose. Bringing the apprentice Wizards to this enchanted wonderland had been a good decision. Too bad they could not stay.

The Trolls' compound had existed undetected for hundreds of years and its location shared by only a select few. Yet as long as Vlad searched for the missing Wizards it risked discovery. It was a cherished sanctuary that Morgan vowed to protect.

She eyed the lovely Troll who sat down across from her. She realized for the first time that not only had Cassandra exchanged the hideous gown she'd worn on the island for a long flowered skirt and lavender sweater, but she'd spoken out loud. If possible, Cassandra was even more radiant than on the island. Clearly, Wizards had spent at least a millennium underestimating these unique people.

Morgan poured herself a cup of tea. "I was taught female Trolls could only communicate with their minds."

Cassandra added cream and sugar to her own tea, eyes sparkling over the rim of her cup. "You are learning many of our secrets. I'm sorry we felt the need to keep them from you all these long centuries. The most important, of course, involves speech. A long-established habit, I'm afraid. All the women of our tribe share the ability to speak with their minds as well as with their tongues. The gift has kept us safe for centuries. Once we reached this compound, there was no longer a need for the pretense. We are protected here by powerful warding spells."

Pretense. The word stuck in Morgan's throat. She'd told Rowan she needed to leave to evaluate her findings regarding the Wizard found at Gas Works Park. Another pretense. She knew the cause of death. Rowan's suspicions were correct. The Wizards had been poisoned with a powerful enchanted potion that weakened them enough that their eyes could then be removed. What she needed to do was find out the source, who was making it, and if there was an antidote—and a motive. The questions weighed her down, nearly crushing her, and her hand trembled, clattering her cup in its saucer.

She set her tea down, and sank back against the soft contours of the chair. "How can you swallow all the intrigues, half-truths and lies? They threaten to choke me."

"Like all women, surviving and protecting our children is our reward," Cassandra said, her voice steady and sure. She raised a delicate eyebrow. "Were you able to learn anything from the Fire Wizard?"

At the reference to Rowan, Morgan sat forward and drew in a breath of air, composing her thoughts. She heard the old woman set her knitting needles on a side table and reach for her tea. Morgan lowered her voice and tilted her head toward the woman. "May we talk freely?"

"Only friends dwell here," Cassandra responded with a smile.

Morgan leaned closer toward Cassandra, with only the table separating them. "It is far worse than Caitlin or I first thought. At first, we believed Vlad was targeting only the female Wizards for reasons known only to him. After today, I suspect his plan is much more ambitious. I believe he targets anyone who speaks out against him." She hesitated. "I recognized the Wizard who was murdered. Finn McDougal. Caitlin spoke of him often as a friend to female Wizards and an outspoken critic of the Talons and the Grey Council."

Cassandra's hand trembled and her cup clattered on the saucer. "I know him as well, and he and Caitlin were more than friends and advocates for change." She set the tea on the tray. Her gaze drifted over to the old woman, whose cup was poised halfway to her lips. Cassandra continued, her voice quivering. "He and Caitlin spent time here last summer."

Morgan straightened, piecing together the bits and pieces of comments she and Caitlin had shared over the course of the last few months. Morgan had been so absorbed in her own thoughts and pains she had not recognized what Caitlin was trying to say. She swallowed. "Finn and Caitlin were lovers. I should have known."

Cassandra reached over and patted Morgan's hand.

"Do not blame yourself for not realizing what was happening between them. She didn't want you to know. They shared a dangerous secret. Consummating love outside of Bealtaine is forbidden. Finn was a gentle soul, a friend to us all and vocal in his distrust of the Grey Council, the Talons, and especially Vlad. He will be missed. We will see he is buried with honor. Have you told the Fire Wizard your suspicions that Vlad might be responsible for the deaths, even as he claims to be searching for the killer?"

Morgan shook her head slowly as she tried to reconcile the secret Caitlin had kept from her. "Not yet. It is possible Vlad is not acting alone. To accuse him now, without proof, could drive the real mastermind underground. We must discover the motivation and how many are involved."

The old woman coughed, and Cassandra rushed over to her, rubbing her shoulders and talking to her in whispers.

Morgan rubbed her own forehead, knowing the throbbing pain she felt was the weight of the responsibility she'd undertaken and the realization she'd failed her best friend. She reached out to her tea but drew back. She'd lost her taste for the warm beverage, and her taste for the woman she had become. She should have done more.

The Trolls, Caitlin, and Finn had all recognized the fight they faced. They had spoken out against the evil and been murdered. The female Wizards' deaths from heart attacks were difficult to prove as foul play. Finn's, however, was a different matter. If her theory was correct, the substance used to poison him—and make it look like the work of a Rogue—must be located. No excuse could be given for using a poison powerful enough to harm a Wizard. Even the Talons would show no mercy when the crime and its architects were exposed. Or that was her hope. Was it a false hope?

She was raised to believe that the Talons and the Grey Council existed to keep the peace between the factions of the magical community as well as to protect female Wizards. What if she had been wrong all these years?

The only way to double-check her theory was in her library in Ireland. Perhaps that was the answer. Being in Rowan's company had proved harder than she'd anticipated. She would be able to think more clearly without him distracting her.

Cassandra rejoined Morgan, refilling her cup. "There is something else that troubles you, milady, I can feel it."

Morgan met Cassandra's gaze. "I overheard a detective I know discussing a compound that was laced in a substance that might have been used to poison Finn. If it is what I fear, I believe Finn was poisoned by an ancient substance Wizards believed was destroyed centuries ago. If I'm to find an antidote, I'll need to leave for Ireland immediately. All my resources are there."

"You may not need to go so far, milady. As you know, Wizards once used my people as their personal servants and scribes. One of our many duties was to duplicate your records." She winked. "We always made secret copies for our own use. There is an extensive library on our compound, and you are welcome to whatever you need."

"Thank you." Morgan forced a smile, battling the dark shadows and disappointment that crashed against her. Cassandra's offer derailed her excuse to run, to retreat to Ireland with the pretense of searching for an antidote. She was pathetic. Not worthy of the title of "milady." Not worthy to be anyone's leader.

She stood and moved toward the window, easing the drapes aside. The full moon drifted between the clouds and a chill wind swept over the dark waters of Lake Washington. There were strange forces in the atmosphere. She was not the only life force feeling unsettled and uncertain.

She did not want to believe the deaths of the female and male Wizards were linked. Yet every instinct pointed to that as a definite possibility. She would help Rowan discover the truth. When all was accomplished, she would appoint someone to replace her as a leader and retreat into seclusion.

Thinking of Ireland reminded her of how much she had loved and lost in the Emerald Isle. It was there, during one of the Wizard's Fertility Festivals, that she and Rowan had met and fallen in love. They defied the rules and met secretly on the magical island of Hy-Brasil, off the coast of Ireland, that appeared only once every seven years. It was there she had learned she was pregnant with Rowan's child.

Cassandra touched Morgan's shoulder. "I'm a good listener, milady."

Morgan squeezed Cassandra's hand. "Perhaps later. First, I'd like to visit the library. I have a mystery to solve and not much time for doing so."

Cassandra's smile spread over her delicate features as she motioned to the old woman who sat beside them. "Then I believe you will need more than the resources in our library. Milady, may I present the oldest living female Wizard, Danu of the Waters."

Chapter Twenty-One

Later that evening, in Seattle's Capitol Hill neighborhood, Stryker leaned against his car across the street from Lyons' daughter's ground floor apartment. Stryker was on protection duty and not happy about it. He got the importance of it, yes. But still…not happy.

Clouds blanketed the night sky, shutting out the stars and moon. A lamppost sputtered and flickered on and off as though it couldn't make up its mind. He sympathized. He stared at it with disgust. Indecision, of any kind, was not part of his DNA. His first instinct had been to barge into the apartment and tell Alexandra Lyons that she was out of her depth. But then her father had filled him in on his daughter. Under Lyons' frustration Stryker could hear the pride and fear in the man's voice, and the worry that Alexandra wouldn't back down. Stryker respected the woman's grit even if he didn't like the setup.

According to Lyons, Alexandra liked championing lost causes, cheering for losing teams, jogging at three in the morning, and eating rocky road ice cream out of the carton. She also preferred to be called AJ instead of Alexandra.

The one thing, he, Rowan and Lyons agreed on was that Alexandra was in over her head and would likely get herself killed. What they hadn't agreed on was how to keep her safe. She'd bolt if she saw either her father or Rowan. She needed someone who had the protection gene in his DNA and wouldn't back down from a fight.

That's where Stryker came in. He ran a successful protection service for high-powered executives, royals and celebrities that spanned the globe. Having Wizard skills that gave him lightning quick reflexes, the ability to see in the dark, superhuman strength and a reputation for keeping his clients safe provided his edge on the competition.

There were two ways he could play this. The first was to follow Rowan and Lyons' advice and track her like a bloodhound, lurking in the shadows and running for a place to hide every time she turned around, with cold coffee and colder takeout. Or he could do it his way.

Tell her the truth.

He pushed away from his car and dialed Lyons' number.

The anxious father answered on the first ring. "Is my daughter okay?"

"She's fine. I want you to telephone her and tell her who I am and why I'm involved. I'll do the rest. You have exactly thirty seconds before I knock on her door." Stryker ended the call without giving Lyons a chance to respond as he headed toward Alexandra's apartment. He checked his cell for the time, pissed he hadn't allowed for time to get coffee.

Her door flew open. She stood framed in the doorway, wearing a navy suit that fit her curves like silk on bare skin. A tumble of black curls traveled past her shoulders. Her hands were anchored on her hips and her blue eyes looked like they were on the verge of bursting into a rage-filled flame. Under different circumstances, he'd ignore the rule about no sex with a human and start planning a trip to a remote mountain retreat or the tropics.

Her voice was even and clipped. "I suppose you're Stryker. You look the part. All brawn. No brain. I told my father on the phone I didn't need a babysitter. Go away."

"Should I be offended that I look the part of a bodyguard?"

"You should."

She was something. Too bad she was off limits. "I've made the command decision that it will be easier to protect you at my house. Can you cook?"

"Is your brain as muscle-bound as your biceps? I told you to go away. I don't need a bodyguard. I'm perfectly capable of taking care of myself."

"And I don't need a pain in the ass, but we don't always get what we want. Grab a coat. It's going to rain. You'll need enough clothes for two to three days, women things, and a toothbrush. I don't share my toothbrush. It sends the wrong message."

She crossed her arms under that ample chest and glared. "Let me guess. You don't like relationships."

"Look at that. We're bonding." He stepped around her and cased her apartment. Neat and tidy, in shades of white and chrome. He admired the simplicity. "You have ten minutes to pack."

"I'm not going with you."

He turned toward her, noting the change in the slump of her shoulders and the shade of her eyes. Fear had replaced bravado. A part of her realized that she was in danger but was too proud to admit it. He changed tactics.

He moved toward a cloth sofa that probably looked the same as it had the day it rolled off the assembly line.

Sitting, he draped his arm over the armrest. "Okay. New plan. You can stay where you are. Think of me more as your shadow rather than a bodyguard. Where you go, I go. Which means I'll have to stay here. Your father considered offering his place, but people know where he lives and it's too dangerous. Your place is not safe either, but it's better than his and I can make it work. Your father is worried, and cops only get worried if there's a reason."

"My father trusts you?"

"I wouldn't be here if he didn't."

Chapter Twenty-Two

Pike Place Market after midnight was like visiting another planet. The tourists were all tucked in their hotel rooms or on the cruise ships bound for Alaska, and the less adventurous of the locals in their homes. Urban legends had spread that the Market was frequented by magical creatures, and because it brought in the curious tourists, the business owners only fueled the fire.

Rowan arrived at the Market ahead of schedule. He didn't expect Morgan for another hour. There was time to meet with the informant he had talked with over the phone. He and Lyons had used the man before. His fees were high, but the man's information was reliable. Rowan walked past closed fish and produce stands, heading down a staircase that would take him to the lower levels and The Inferno Bar and Grill.

Retail shops wove through the block-long building like underground rabbit warrens and ranged from high-end pottery and clothing shops to used bookstores, souvenir shops and tables for tarot card readers. But this was after hours, and everything was shut down tight except for the tarot card readers. Their business was twenty-four-seven, accompanied by the throbbing of electronic music on the lower levels.

The pulsating music originated from The Inferno and was loud enough to break a human's eardrum, which was the point. When the clock struck midnight, the restaurant was off limits to humans. Rowan opened the door and found an empty booth near one of the back exits.

The Inferno enjoyed a turbulent past. At the turn of the century, it was the site of illegal boxing and gambling, and during Prohibition it became a speakeasy. The name of the club's owner changed from time to time, but it was always the same immortal Scotsman. Colin McIntosh had been kicked out of Scotland in the seventeenth century for reasons never made clear. There were rumors he'd killed someone or slept with the wrong woman. Probably both.

During the day, The Inferno was a typical Seattle seafood restaurant. After midnight, it took on another persona. The light green haze had nothing to do with tinted smoke, and the pinpoints of white light weren't the result of electricity. The anomaly was supernatural and pulsated off the club's inhabitants.

This was one of only a few places around the area considered neutral territory for the magical community. The only restriction was the use of black magic. Wizard, Vampire, Werewolf, Fairy, Troll and Half-Blood could all co-exist without fear of attack. Colin dealt with violators personally and no one asked what he did with the bodies.

The curl of cigarette smoke blew toward Rowan. Standing near an exit, a short distance from his booth, was a slender woman. She was six-foot-three-inches tall and dressed like a fashion model in thigh-high boots, a gold sheath dress, and raven-black waist-length hair. Her smile was seductive and all too familiar.

Without waiting for an invitation, his ex-girlfriend joined him, taking the seat opposite him in the booth.

"Hello, darling. Long time."

His first impulse was to respond that it wasn't long enough, but she didn't deserve the snide comment. Their split was mutual. "Hello, Sorsha." It always surprised him that her looks never changed. He figured it was part of being a vampire. She'd never embraced the Goth look or had the chalk-white skin common with others of her kind. She looked more like one of those porcelain-faced Glenda the Good Witch dolls in toy stores. Lovely to look at in their own way, until she bared her fangs…or you got to know her.

"You're looking well," Rowan added. "Must be your new diet. I hear you went vegan." Vegan in a vampire's world meant that they drank only synthetic blood, like Lyons' foster mother had.

Her thick eyelashes fluttered over dark ebony eyes. "Not quite, but I only drink the blood of a vegan, darling, much better for the complexion. Does that count?"

"You know it doesn't."

She flipped her hair over her shoulder. "I'm a work in progress. Anyway, you, on the other hand, look as though you haven't slept in days, but that's to be expected. I'd heard you were attending Bealtaine." She leaned closer and blew another ring of smoke in his direction. "If you were horny, all you had to do was scream."

And there it was; his history with her. A destructive time in his past when he'd believed the best way to forget one woman was to take up with another. "Haven't you heard; smoking cigarettes will kill you?"

"Promise? What are you doing here instead of on the island?"

"Someone is killing Wizards. I'm trying to find out

why and stop them."

She took another puff of smoke. "You're back to being the hero. How boring." She took another puff on her cigarette, then ground it out in the amber ashtray on the table. "It's all over the street," she continued. "The talk is that someone found a way to murder Wizards and make it look like a bad acid trip. I can see why they would target my kind, but Wizards are the beloved." She said the last as though the words left a bad taste in her mouth.

"Hunting vampires might change if you all agreed to stop sucking blood out of humans as well as some in the magical community," Rowan said in a flat tone.

"Addictions like smoking and drinking are hard habits to break."

"The comparison is not even close, and you know it."

She pressed her lips together and looked toward the center of the restaurant where tables were being cleared to welcome more customers. When she turned back, she had plastered a smile on her face, if you could describe a thin line across a plastic-looking face as a smile. "I don't want to argue. I'm here to tell you what I know about the murders. There's talk on the streets that the Talons and the Grey Council are behind the attacks. But I don't have a name, and I don't give the rumor much weight. After all, darling, Wizards help the Talons and the Grey Council save humanity from themselves. You're their foot soldiers, their knights in rusty armor. It makes no sense that the Talons and the Grey Council would want to eliminate you all."

"Well, someone wants us dead. I'm guessing a power play. Just not sure of the end game. Can you ask around?"

She glanced in the direction of a group of partygoers entering the club. She looked distracted, or maybe she was contemplating her next meal. Time oozed by as he waited for her response. A drawback with talking with a vampire. Time meant nothing to them. But she was an important member of her community. The next in line to take over and the first potential Queen in over three hundred years. If she agreed to help him, he might be able to discover not only who was behind the murders but a few other things.

Her red lips curled up in a mischievous grin. "If I agree to help you solve this mystery, you need to give me something I can bring to my people."

"That's fair. But if someone is really making a power play in the magical community, do you think they will stop at murdering Wizards? My guess is they'll eliminate anyone who opposes them. You can take that to the blood bank. Coincidentally, three female Wizards died the first night of Bealtaine."

She snapped her head around. "You should have led with that news flash, Wizard boy. No way was that a coincidence. We've had a longstanding truce with female Wizards. We watch out for each other. If whoever is behind this is also targeting them, we're in."

"Didn't know about the truce."

She slid out of the booth. "And for good reason. "I'll investigate. Call it a freebie for old time's sake. Looks like your informant is here." And she was gone.

Sure enough, Walter Billowry was seated in a back corner of the restaurant, eating a meal large enough to feed an army. Rowan had given up wondering how Sorsha knew the things she knew. She had her finger on the pulse of Seattle, and he trusted her to do her best to keep the other vamps in check. At the end of the day, she walked a fine line. He knew her kind's secret wish was to watch as Wizards destroyed themselves, leaving control of Seattle to whoever was still standing. Except, it seemed, when it came to female Wizards. Now, that was a new wrinkle he wasn't certain was a good thing. The deeper into this puzzle he dove, the more pieces kept appearing.

Rowan glanced at the time on his cell. Morgan hadn't planned on meeting him for another thirty minutes or so. Time to have a chat with his informant. He paid his tab and moved toward Walter's booth.

According to rumor, Walter Billowry's ancestors were descended from the giants that roamed Ireland before they were defeated. Walter bragged that he also had a touch of Wizard blood in his DNA. Linebacker large but without the athletic ability, he felt more comfortable around other magical creatures than in the human world.

Walter was busy devouring a meal of steak and potatoes smothered in thick white gravy when Rowan approached.

"Hello, Walter."

Walter nodded, his mouth full of mashed potatoes. He swallowed it down with a Guinness and cut into his steak. "Saw you talking to the vamp and didn't want to disturb. Plus, I couldn't wait. Blood sugar drops like a dead toad on hot pavement and makes me real mean."

Rowan sat down opposite Walter, refusing to comment. Rowan had never seen the man in a good mood.

The waitress, a young woman of delicate features,

wearing black jeans and an over-sized long-sleeved shirt, with matching green lipstick and chipped nail polish, wove toward them. There was a slight point around the tips of her ears and soulful brown eyes, and according to her badge her name was Holly.

Rowan guessed she was a half-blood. She had the look of a fairy, but without the white aura that accompanied them. It made sense she'd work here. It was probably the only place she felt accepted.

She flipped open her pad, arched a thin eyebrow and glanced in Rowan's direction. "Dinner or drinks?"

"Just coffee. Black."

Walter rubbed his eyes with the heel of his hand, and pointed with his other to his empty mug, indicating he wanted another beer. "The last Guinness tasted off. Tell the bartender to take his time. Guinness requires a proper pour. If he needs instruction, I'm his man."

The young woman nodded, nervously, and left as quickly as she'd appeared.

Walter bent his head and scooped up a mouthful of steak with his fork and knife before he shrugged. "Colin must have hired a new bartender. What's our question?"

Rowan spread on the table the photos Lyons had given him of the body at Gas Works Park. "You said you might have a lead?"

Walter wiped his mouth with his napkin, pulled one of the pictures closer to him and squinted. "Where's the body?"

"City morgue."

"Mind if I keep these? I'll check around some more, but I don't think you're going to like what I find. As I told you on the phone, I have already made a few inquiries. Someone's found a way to kill Wizards and make it look like the poor sod got mixed up with drugs and shit. No one cares if a druggie dies, or that's the theory making the rounds."

The waitress returned with Rowan's coffee just as Renegade slid into the booth beside Walter.

Renegade nodded to the waitress, adding a warm smile as though he'd sensed she needed a small measure of kindness. "Could you bring me a coffee as well, love?" Her dark expression seemed to lighten for a moment, before she turned to wait on another customer. Renegade shoved a cell phone toward Rowan. "A present from your brother."

"I already have a phone."

Renegade shrugged. "Stryker said your cell service either sucks or has been hacked, or else you've been avoiding returning his calls. Anyway, it's yours. He told me to make sure you got it. If you have a problem, take it up with your brother."

"Did Stryker say if he'd found out anything?"

"He's complaining about having to babysit Lyons' daughter and running into dead ends. Then one of his computers crashed. You'd think the world had spun off its axis. Is he always like that?"

"Always." Rowan slipped the phone into his coat pocket as the waitress brought Renegade his coffee.

When she'd left, Walter cut into his steak again. "Too bad about the waitress," he said, nodding over his shoulder. "Her name's Holly. Sweet thing. Tough breaks. Colin did a good thing hiring her." Walter cleared his throat and hailed the waitress back to their table. "My throat feels as though it's on fire. Why is it taking so long to build a proper Guinness?" he said loosening the top buttons on his shirt. "I'm dying of thirst."

Renegade leaned forward. "You don't look so good."

"I'm fine. Nothing a drink won't cure. You're not the only ones been asking about the murders. The magical community is walking on eggshells and scared as shit. Received a few deaths threats myself, and I'm pretty sure I was followed. Couldn't wait to get to The Inferno where I feel safe. No surprise you're here about the murdered Wizards."

Renegade nodded. "I overheard you say someone discovered a way to kill Wizards and make it look like a drug overdose."

Walter cleared his throat, setting his fork down. "Yeah," he said swallowing again. "The rumor is it's a nasty poison that causes humans to hallucinate but can be fatal or do real damage to anyone with an ounce of magical blood."

Holly set Walter's Guinness on the table, with a shaky comment that she hoped this one was more to his liking. Walter gave her a jerky nod of thanks, then reached for it, spilling foaming beer down his shirt as he raised the mug to his mouth. He downed half of its contents in one gulp, then gasped and grabbed his throat.

Spiderweb-like veins spread over Walter's face and hands, turning his skin an indigo blue. The condition of Walter's skin matched the body at Gas Works Park.

"You've been poisoned!" Rowan shouted to the waitress, "Quick! We need a medic over here—now!"

Walter reached for Rowan's arm and grasped it in a vise-like grip. "Too late for me..." His voice sounded pained, hoarse, as though he had a mouthful of razors.

Walter's eyes bled, widened, then dulled as his head

slammed down into his plate of food.

****

The Inferno continued, unaware of Walter's death. The roar of loud conversation mixed with the electronic music as people crowded the dance floor. The celebratory mood would change the moment Walter's body was discovered.

"Walter blamed the waitress," Rowan said with dead calm, getting to his feet.

Renegade nodded and did the same. "The bartender could also be involved."

Rowan scanned the room. Holly was near another table. Her eyes were locked on his. Guilt flashed in her eyes as her tray slid from her grasp and crashed to the floor. Rowan turned toward Renegade. "Inform Colin. I'll take care of the bartender and then capture Holly. We need answers. Watch the front entrance. Stop anyone with an itch to escape, and if Morgan arrives, don't let her leave. I'm going after Holly."

"Milady is meeting you here? Are you certifiably insane?

"Just make sure she doesn't eat or drink anything. Can I count on you to keep her safe?"

"You don't have to ask."

Rowan heated his core and reached the bartender while the man was in the process of filling cocktail orders. Like the waitress, he was a half-blood Fae, an easy target for a Wizard to disarm. With one punch Rowan knocked the man unconscious and looked for Holly.

She had paused to glance over her shoulders in his direction, then bolted through the kitchen's swinging doors. He reached the kitchen in time to see her disappear out the back door. She was fast, but no match for his speed. He raced past cooks and servers, overcoming her before she reached the steps leading into the alley.

He grabbed her arm and slammed her against the building. Walter had been poisoned and died before he could share his information. This case had as many twists and turns as an old-fashioned labyrinth. He hated labyrinths, mazes, winding paths through gardens— basically, anyplace he couldn't control, anywhere he couldn't see the enemy approach.

The young woman's fear was so heightened he smelled it in the wind. It would be a beacon to whoever might have ordered the kill. Which meant they'd likely kill Holly next. Killers didn't like loose ends. He'd have to act fast.

He pinned her against the wall in the alley.

"I know what you want. But I'm dead if I talk to you," she whispered.

"You're dead even if you don't. Who ordered you and the bartender to poison Walter?"

She seemed to weigh her chances. He doubted she'd last long on the streets, but sometimes a person measured their life in days, not years. He figured she'd been on borrowed time ever since she was born.

She glanced over his shoulder, blinked away a tear, then focused on Rowan. "The bartender wasn't involved," her voice was as thin as mist as her words tumbled out. "I didn't want to do it. Walter seemed a nice sort. He's never tried to grab me, and that makes him different from those who think because I'm one of the Fae it gives them the right. They have my sister. I didn't have a choice."

The rustle of leaves. A flash of silver. In the next breath an arrow lodged in the base of her neck. Her eyes widened and then narrowed as she slumped forward into Rowan's arms. He knew the weapon would be tipped with a fast-acting poison. She was dying. He scanned the rooftops. The assassin was gone. No need to stay and check if his victim died. Assassins in the magical community only used poisons that didn't have known antidotes. The unanswered question mark was why the mercenary hadn't shot him too.

He carried Holly a short distance away. She was lighter than he expected. A walking skeleton, made to look substantial by the layers of black clothing she wore. He guessed her age to be around twenty-one or twenty-two. A young woman who had never had the chance to grow and mature, and now she never would.

There was nothing he could do. He'd been able to save the dog, but a member of the Fae was different. Descended from pure light, they were uniquely vulnerable to poisons in the atmosphere, which was the reason the Fae's numbers had reached extinction levels. Once a poison entered a Fae's bloodstream, there was nothing anyone could do.

Already it was apparent that it had spread through her body, shutting it down. The good news was that it looked like she wasn't in pain. The poison was as merciful as it was lethal.

Her breathing was shallow, her eyes unblinking. If she'd been larger, the poison would have taken longer. By the color of her skin, she was losing ground fast.

The time for pressing her for information was past. She'd already told him that she had been forced to harm Walter to save her sister. Rowan wouldn't tell her that he doubted the people who had coerced her into murdering Walter would honor their vow and release her sister.

He would give her the dignity of dying in peace. He was not going to press her during the last seconds of her life. Besides, there weren't that many in the magical community who used poison, and fewer still who would be bold enough to use it in a public place christened a neutral zone. Someone was feeling desperate. And desperate people made mistakes. He vowed he'd find those responsible.

Holly grabbed his shirt. "I'm dying." It was not a question. She had stated a fact, and he would not lie to her. She swallowed as her eyes widened in fear. "I didn't want to hurt your friend. They didn't give me a choice."

"I know. Save your strength."

The humans and the magical community liked to debate the concept of what a person should do if they were in Holly's situation. There were strong opinions on both sides. Some felt magic or circumstances could force a person to do something against their will, against their moral code, no matter the consequences. Others felt the opposite and he didn't judge.

But what he did know was that everyone deserved another chance to get it right. If not in this world— maybe in the next. A thin grayish film clouded over her eyes, so he wasn't sure if she could still see him, but he formed a gentle smile all the same. The effort felt rusty. Whether he agreed she'd had a choice or not didn't matter.

He bent over her to make sure she could hear him. "I don't blame you." He added the words; "*May your journey be swift, and your welcome in the next realm joyous. When we meet again, let us embrace as friends.*"

It was the blessing said over the graves of those in the magical community who'd lived a full and respected life. Some might find it blasphemous he'd said this to her. He didn't care.

The thin smile that spread over her face told him he'd made the right decision. She pressed a cobalt-blue glass container the size and shape of a sugar packet into the palm of his hand. Her voice was feather soft as she struggled to draw her last breath. "Banshee."

Chapter Twenty-Three

An explosion blew the alleyway door to the restaurant off its hinges. Shards of glass and wood, along with a cloud of stinging, blue-colored dust, ejected through the opening. Rowan grabbed the lifeless young woman in his arms, shielding Holly from the falling debris as a stony silence hung over the dark alley like the calm before a rising storm.

When the dust settled, Rowan eased his hold on her and listened. Silence spread over the once-lively restaurant. No doubt people were processing what had happened. He heard nervous laughter, and someone shouting that the explosion had been caused by a kitchen fire. Then more shouts for the band to resume playing music. The restaurant had returned to normal as though nothing had happened.

A kitchen accident? Unlikely. If Walter hadn't died suddenly, or he wasn't holding a dead woman, he might believe in the possibility of exploding potatoes. More plausible was that the killer had set off a device to destroy evidence that what Walter ate or drank had been poisoned.

Rowan slipped the glass container Holly had given him into his jacket and stood. He'd ask someone in the restaurant to start making burial arrangements for her while he hunted the assassin. With any luck, the killer might still be lurking around to make sure his plan to cover his tracks had succeeded.

This wasn't just a cover-up of what had poisoned Walter. The restaurant was under attack. It made no sense. The Inferno had always been declared a haven for members of the magical community. Attacking it risked igniting the wrath of those who usually remained neutral during Wizard Wars.

But inside The Inferno, laughter turned into screams and seconds later its occupants flooded into the alley. Bleeding, with wide-eyed horror etched into every breath they took. Some collapsed to the ground like ragdolls, blocking the exit, while others jumped over the dead bodies in a frantic race to escape.

His mind raced to Morgan. Had she arrived while he was in the alley and been trapped inside? He had no way to reach her. The bloody woman didn't own a cell. He cursed himself for getting her involved and letting her out of his sight. He was slipping. If it had been anyone other than Morgan, he'd have hauled her sexy ass back to the island the first time he saw her.

The dense, never-ending flow of those fleeing prevented him from making any headway to the back door. He'd have to find another way inside.

Tapping into his speed, he draped the waitress over his shoulder and jumped to the fire escape. Waves of crazed restaurant-goers funneled into the alley as he climbed above the chaos. Part of him rationalized that he was saving the young woman from being trampled. Another part considered her a clue, a possible link to the mystery. Either way, he was not going to leave her behind.

He reached the third floor and kicked the door open to another level of retail shops. Muffled, panic-laced screams permeated through the floor below as people fought their way outside. Thoughts of Morgan trapped in The Inferno played repeatedly in his mind, fueling his rising concern, feeding his guilt.

In one fluid moment he laid Holly on a bench outside a pottery store and raced toward the stairwell he knew led to the restaurant's delivery entrance.

He sped to the restaurant, where he found bodies littering the floor. Tables and chairs were overturned, some smashed beyond recognition. A few people, frozen in terror, stood sobbing, while others pushed their way toward the exits.

Renegade jogged around smashed glasses and plates and pulled Rowan back into the stairwell. "Rowan," Renegade shouted. "Thank the goddess! I thought you'd been caught in the nightmare."

"Morgan?"

"So far, she hasn't arrived. As you know, Morgan doesn't have a cell, so I sent a text to a contact of mine to tell her that it's not safe to meet us. Just waiting to make sure she got the message."

Knowing she was not in the restaurant brought only momentary relief. At that moment, he made the decision to find Morgan rather than track down whoever had caused the carnage in the restaurant and killed Holly. This scenario was exactly the sort of thing the Talons and the Grey Council forbade. Attachments clouded duty. How many times had he heard that phrase? Hundreds of times? Thousands?

Bugger it. He would find Morgan first. It felt as though his very life depended on seeing for himself that she was okay.

Frustrated, he ground out his question as he

motioned for Renegade to follow him back up the stairwell to where he'd left Holly. "Do you know what happened?"

"It's a deathtrap downstairs. The smoke from the explosion triggered the sprinklers. I'm guessing the water was laced with poison, although it's anyone's guess what happened. When we first heard the sound, everyone froze, then an Earth Wizard made a joke about how a little smoke and water couldn't kill immortals or the long-lived. Everyone laughed. Female vampires bet on how long it would take for the good-looking, tasty, firemen to arrive. Wizards complained. Standard stuff. Not much scares the magical community these days. They think they're invincible."

As Rowan climbed the stairs, he removed his glasses, cleaning dust from the lenses with his sleeve. "That's our weakness. No sense of mortality."

"That's all changed now. A few seconds later there was a shift of some sort. Wizards started clawing at their eyes like they wanted to yank them out of the sockets." Renegade shoved his hands in his pockets and shook his head slowly. "I've never seen anything like it. When several of them dropped dead where they stood, the laughter changed to panic. I tried to reach the alley and look for you, but I couldn't get through the crowd. That's when I decided to use the delivery stairwell and go around and check to make sure you were still alive."

Rowan reached the third floor and held the door for Renegade. "Weird about the eyes, but one thing's for certain. This was a well-planned attack, a declaration of war. The end game is a question mark, as is the person or persons behind the attack. My guess is that if we find out who is behind it, we'll have our motive."

"This was a targeted attack. Only those with Wizard blood were affected. That's why the vamps and other magical people, and I, weren't harmed. Was the waitress any help?"

"She was killed with a poisoned silver arrow and died before she could tell me much. She gave me a packet of the poison. The last word she spoke was 'Banshee.' I laid her down over here."

Renegade whistled low as he followed Rowan. "Holly was Fae and Irish. They claim they see the banshee of death before they die. Might not be connected. The assassin could be an Air Wizard. Arrows are their trademark weapon."

"Or a mercenary. Or someone wanting to frame Air Wizards."

"I don't like any of the choices."

"Me either." Rowan reached the place where he'd left the waitress. The bench was vacant. He swore under his breath. "She's gone."

"Are you sure she was dead? She could have been a Phantom of some sort, masquerading as Fae."

"You saw her. She was flesh and blood. Holly died in my arms, which makes this personal. I couldn't save her."

"Fire Wizards can't save everyone."

"In case you haven't noticed, other than a shapeshifting dog, I haven't saved anyone. The bad guys are winning."

"No wonder you're in a bad mood. It's obvious that whoever is calling the shots didn't want any loose ends."

"I've heard Trolls are good trackers," Rowan said. "Any clues who took her? She might have left a residual signature."

Renegade knelt and placed the palm of his hand flat against the iron bench. "A female was here, all right. The essence signature is faint, almost nonexistent. Not a Phantom, like I thought. But she had mixed blood along with the Fae. That's interesting." He lifted his gaze toward Rowan. "It's faint, but she has a trace of Wizard blood in her DNA."

Rowan swore under his breath. "We're back to targeting only Wizards. Anything else?"

"There is also a trace of human blood, which would explain the lingering imprint. Human souls stick around longer when they've been murdered. It's one of their more endearing qualities. They never give up. However, the trail ends here. Whoever snatched the body did a good job of cleansing the air around it. But the person or persons running this show made a tactical error."

"How d'you figure?"

"This is no longer just a war against your kind. It's against anyone with even a trace of Wizard blood. The potential size of your army just increased."

"Half-Bloods aren't easy to control."

"I said your army increased. I didn't say it was a good thing. What's our next move?"

"Find Morgan." Rowan headed back toward the exit. "She was supposed to meet me here tonight." He hesitated, knowing his voice sounded too concerned. "It's a simple business arrangement," he began again. "She's helping me with this case, and in exchange I agreed to find out who killed the female Wizards on the island."

Renegade chuckled. "Spin your story to a human and see if they believe the fairy tale. You know as well as I do that where our women are concerned, it's never a simple business arrangement. You should have asked me sooner. I have a pretty good idea where she's hiding."

Rowan paused, his frustration rising to a new level. He was starting to feel like a guy in a rowboat with only one oar. Rowing a boat with only one paddle meant one thing. You ended up rowing around in circles or taking a long time getting to where you needed to go. "And why are you just now sharing this choice tidbit? You knew I was looking for Morgan."

"If I told you where she was, the lady I was betrothed to would have me drawn and quartered, and I'd never have another chance to ask her to marry me. Like I said, where our women are concerned, it's complicated."

Rowan shoved the door open to the outside, hoping the assassin had circled back and was standing behind it so Rowan could vent his frustration and slam him into the next dimension. "And they say women are the weaker sex."

"You're talking about a myth perpetrated by men. Women, whether human or magical, aren't weaker, they're just more subtle in how and when they use their power."

"Amen."

****

Three in the morning, and The Pike Place Market looked deserted. The street in front of the Market was a different scenario. Traffic resembled rush hour. Horns blared, people hailed cabs or ran from the market while fire trucks and police and aid cars jammed the narrow streets. All that was missing was a man with a beard down to his navel, carrying an eerily prophetic poster that read "Repent. The End Is Near."

Renegade pointed toward a cab parked on the corner a short distance away. "Looks like I'm not going to have a chance to show off my tracking skills after all. There's milady. My guess is that Morgan either didn't receive my message to stay away or ignored it.

Morgan stepped out of a checkered cab and paid the driver as she waited for a file of cars to pass so she could cross the street. The dog Rowan had saved bounded out of the back seat and took his place next to Morgan. Wiz stared in Rowan's direction as though waiting for the order to rip out Rowan's throat.

Rowan might have saved the shapeshifter's life, but Wiz's first loyalty was to Morgan. Rowan begrudgingly admired him for it.

"Question. You keep referring to Morgan as 'milady.' Why?"

"I thought you knew. Caitlin, the female Wizard who died on Bealtaine, was the leader of the female Water Wizards. When she was murdered, Morgan was next in line to become their new leader. Caitlin's murder triggered an old alliance between female Wizards and Trolls. Simply put, if you tried to harm a hair on Morgan's head, I'd kill you without a moment's hesitation."

"And here I thought we were pals."

Renegade grinned when they reached the cab. "That was almost funny. I was told you didn't have a sense of humor."

In a lull in traffic, Morgan crossed the street and headed toward him. Her appearance hit him like a bolt of lightning. He swore the woman was more beautiful each time he saw her. She was dressed to blend in, wearing light-colored slacks, a cream sweater and a trench coat.

Her efforts to blend in failed in spectacular fashion, if the appreciative glances cast her way were any indication.

Sensual images of their brief time in the alley and their night together scrolled through his mind, heating the air around him. What he wanted to do was forget the events of the last few hours and pull her into his arms and make love.

Instead, he forced a neutral tone into his voice, congratulating himself on his restraint. "This place is too dangerous and congested. I'll fill you in when we get somewhere safe. My apartment is a short walk from here. I think it's time we regrouped and started sharing information."

Morgan glanced beyond Rowan and Renegade to the congestion at Pike Place Market. "Where is your brother?"

"Last I heard, he took AJ back to his place. Why?"

"I told him it wasn't safe there and to meet us here."

"It wasn't safe here either, but here you are," Rowan said under his breath as he felt all the air rush out of his lungs. "Wait. How do you know my brother?" Reality dug in as he spun toward the Market and the destruction of the attack. Was his brother trapped inside?

Renegade put a steadying hand on Rowan's shoulder. "He wasn't inside. Believe me. Your brother's not someone who goes unnoticed."

"Except when he doesn't want to be noticed." Rowan reached for his cell phone and dialed Stryker's number. He'd found out the hard way that Morgan was a seer. If she said you were going to be hit by an oncoming truck, you'd better start making funeral arrangements. "My brother's not answering." Rowan couldn't breathe.

"Use the cell your brother asked me to give you,"

Renegade said.

Rowan felt ice-cold as he retrieved the phone and punched in Stryker's number again. It went straight to voice mail after the first ring, but the greeting sent chills down his spine.

"Dragons are coming."

Rowan clicked off the phone. "I must go. Morgan..."

She laced her arm around the Troll. "Renegade will take me to your apartment. I'll wait for you there."

His core heated, Rowan raced toward Stryker's house on Bainbridge Island. *Dragons are coming* was their code phrase for danger.

Chapter Twenty-Four

In a blur of white-hot speed, Rowan raced past downtown Seattle's office buildings toward the Kitsap Peninsula and the Agate Pass Bridge that connected Seattle and Bainbridge Island. Most people took a leisurely ferryboat ride, but he wasn't like most people, and he was in a hurry. Stryker had to be okay. His brother was fearless, invincible. No one messed with him.

No one messed with him and lived, Rowan amended.

Stryker lived on Bainbridge, less than a dozen miles from downtown Seattle. Last summer he had talked Rowan into building a large pier and boat house to overcome their fear of the water. Rowan wasn't sure the physiological exercise had worked, but the pier was big enough to moor a sixty-foot yacht. Flying on a plane or living near the water was one thing. Traveling on a boat that could sink at any moment was a dragon of a different color.

It all had to do with the theory that if Fire Wizards were submerged in water for too long, their inner core would flame out and they would die. Rowan's guess was that this was based on a superstition that arose after a Fire Wizard had drowned. Swim lessons might be the answer, but Rowan wasn't about to sign up to be the first guinea pig.

In a matter of minutes, Rowan reached the winding,

tree-lined gravel road leading to Stryker's home. Even the air was still. Nothing moved or breathed. It felt like the night their mother and brother had disappeared.

The door to Stryker's house was ajar, adding to Rowan's apprehension. His brother rented out the basement mother-in-law apartment of his house to college students, and although Stryker was willing to help the kids with cheap rent, he didn't want them coming into his living quarters unannounced. Thus, the separate entrance, double-bolt locks, and warding charms. Right now, however, everything was wide open, unlocked, and un-charmed. If there had been students living downstairs, they were long gone.

Rowan removed his glasses as he entered. There was an odd smell in the house that made his eyes water, but it was the sight that greeted him that turned his blood to ice.

In addition to his five-star-rated bodyguard business, Stryker was a successful freelance game designer, had the latest electronic gadgets on the market, and was a compulsive neat freak. Rowan was pretty sure his brother alphabetized his cereal according to fiber content.

But instead of a room so clean you could eat off the floor, chaos reigned free.

What hadn't been smashed was destroyed beyond recognition. It looked like a war zone. Papers were scattered as though caught in a tornado or a spin dryer, and Stryker's black leather furniture, chrome tables and computer equipment were twisted together in a tangled mass of wire, metal, and glass.

Rowan felt as though someone had sucked all the air out of the room. "Stryker," he yelled, his voice cracking.

He forced air into his lungs. "Stryker? Where are you?"

A faint moan and the whisper of a voice invaded the silence. "Rowan."

The image of the dead body Rowan had seen at Gas Works Park this morning flashed before him as he headed toward the front of the house. Stryker lay on the floor, his body turned toward the sliding glass doors. Guilt haunted Rowan's steps. He'd brought his brother into this case without really knowing what they faced. Overconfidence had made him reckless with his brother's life. He was no better than the victims in the restaurant who'd laughed in the face of death. Everything died.

He dropped to his knees beside his brother and felt for a pulse. It was weak and thready. Stryker's eyes were intact, but there were bloody scratch marks around them. Rowan shuddered and his mind recoiled at the words repeating over and over in his mind like the screams of a banshee foretelling death: *Your brother is dying.*

Rowan eased Stryker to a sitting position and kept the fear from seeping into his voice. "Can you travel?"

Stryker nodded, but his voice sounded like he was chewing marbles. "Dragons."

The word elevated Rowan's fears to a new level. His eyes blurred. "You're coming with me, little brother."

Stryker moaned an affirmative. "Need to bring AJ. When it started, I locked her in the wine cellar." He paused, coughing up blood. Stryker's hand trembled as he wiped his mouth with the back of his hand. "Morgan left a message. Said to get out of the house. Meet her at the Market. They came just as AJ and I were leaving."

"Save your strength. I'm getting you out of here."

Stryker held his arm across his stomach and

groaned. He took a few shallow breaths. "AJ…"

"I'll bring her too."

"If I die…"

"You're not going to die. I'm taking you to a healer."

"Morgan's a healer," Stryker managed.

"Yeah, I know."

"Probably not a coincidence she called me," Stryker said, coughing up more blood.

Rowan spoke through the layers of black fear that threatened to swallow him whole. "Probably not."

****

Rowan had sent a message to Renegade to contact Morgan and meet him at his apartment. He'd then carried both his brother and AJ from Bainbridge to Seattle in what had to have been a personal land speed record. Lyons' daughter, AJ, was right where Stryker had said she would be. She was unconscious, but alive. His brother was alive as well, but barely.

Rowan kicked open the door to his Seattle studio apartment, setting his brother down on his bed and AJ on the sofa. On the short journey, his brother had lapsed into a coma-like sleep and Stryker's throat rattled with each breath he took.

AJ's breathing, on the other hand, was strong and even, but she was still unconscious.

He was grateful for the small favor. He didn't know much about her. Normally, humans were unpredictable when they encountered the paranormal. They either became hysterical or viewed the phenomena like a kid discovering there really was a Santa Claus. Both scenarios were annoying.

Rowan would call Lyons and fill him in, letting him

know the location of his daughter and that she was in good hands.

What was taking Renegade and Morgan so long?

Pacing, he took a calming breath. If only his brother hadn't talked about Dragons.

Before their mother's and younger brother's disappearance, she'd sent them out in search of Dragon eggs. Boys of eight and six were ready to believe in the possibility that not only were there Dragons, but that they lived in Northern Ireland.

After a day and a half of fruitless searching, they found a cave and hurried home to tell their mother that they'd discovered what they believed were dragon eggs. But their house was deserted, and their mother and brother had vanished. When they were fostered, their stories were dismissed as visions induced by hunger and shadows,

In the years that followed, he and Stryker debated their mother's intentions. Had her request been a ruse to get her children away from the house while she finished her chores? Or had she had another motive in mind? Adults in the magical community believed that dragons were extinct and explained sightings in the same way as the skeptics explained UFOs.

But the last words their mother said before she disappeared became their code for danger. She'd said, "My sons. Dragons are coming."

Stryker coughed up blood, moaning as he thrashed on the bed as though fighting demons. Rowan pulled his cell from his jacket and dialed Renegade. "Where the hell are you?"

"Outside your door," came the curt answer.

Rowan sprinted to the door and yanked it open.

"Why didn't you knock?"

"About to. Get your brother and I'll carry the woman. Your apartment's been compromised."

"Where are we going?"

"I'll tell you on the way."

****

Across town, elevator doors opened onto the top floor of an apartment building with views of the Seattle skyline, Puget Sound and the Space Needle. The faint pungent odor of sage hung in the hallway as Renegade directed Rowan to follow him. The sage confirmed Morgan's presence and brought back bittersweet memories.

When he and Morgan had lived together secretly, knowing that their relationship was forbidden, she was in the habit of burning sage. She said it was to clear the room of unfriendly spirits, or the possible negative thoughts left behind by previous guests. He suspected she also laced the sage with protection spells.

Even setting aside that they'd ignored the Talons' and the Grey Council's ruling that Wizards were forbidden to have long-term relationships, he should have known any kind of Happily Ever After scenario was doomed from the beginning. A Fire Wizard's purpose was to serve and destroy. A Water Wizard healed and brought life into the world.

At the end of a long corridor, the door was flung wide and a cloud of sage-filled smoke pushed against him. And, right on cue, the brand over his heart flamed against his skin. He bit off a litany of curse words.

As soon as Stryker was well, he'd figure out a way to have it removed. He knew he was as much to blame as she was for the brand. It only happened with the full consent of both parties, which only made him more frustrated.

Spells on Bealtaine freed the barriers of the subconscious, allowing Wizards to follow their hearts.

He swore under his breath. Bloody hell. Why now and not all those years ago when they were young? The timing was terrible. Fate had a twisted sense of humor.

Maybe Lyons was right when he'd suggested Rowan was "besotted" with Morgan. No, that still wasn't the right word. "Obsessed"—now, that was a word.

"The room is prepared," Morgan whispered, interrupting his train of thought. "Please lay your brother on the bed in the room closest to the kitchen and AJ in the second bedroom."

Thankfully, the brand calmed to a mildly annoying throb as Rowan did what she asked. He stepped out of the way. Letting her take over Stryker's care was a relief. If anyone could bring him back, it was Morgan. She was able to wake Stryker enough to give him a drink of something purple and bubbly. She gave AJ a different concoction with pink and grey chunks.

Rowan rubbed his nose and moved to open the window. "What is that stuff? It smells like rotting garbage."

She brushed hair off Stryker's forehead, ignoring his comment. "I suspect the poison your brother was exposed to at his home on Bainbridge is the same that was used at The Inferno and on the Wizards who died recently."

Rowan felt helpless as he stared down on his brother and forced out the words he'd been afraid to say out loud until now. "Will he live?" He could hear the anger in his voice and the bone-chilling fear.

Morgan dipped a wet rag and bathed Stryker's forehead. "The antidote has never been tested, and I cannot be sure if there are any side effects." Her hand trembled as she pulled the blanket over Stryker's shoulders. "One more thing. If I'm right, the poison used is fatal. Your brother shouldn't be alive." She held Rowan's gaze. "I know this question is harsh. But I must ask. Do you have any idea how he managed to survive?"

Rowan clenched his jaw to fight back old fears involving legends, myths, and dragon possession. Until he had proof, he didn't want to voice his fear out loud, even to Morgan. When they were children, Stryker had repeatedly returned to the cave where they first thought they had found dragon eggs.

One day, Stryker told him they'd hatched. At the time, Rowan didn't want to believe his brother and dismissed his claim. If it were true, however, and Stryker had witnessed the birth of dragons, they would have imprinted on him. Such an honor had a reward as well as a cost.

Rowan cleared his throat. "A theory, but I'd rather not say until I'm sure. How did you know my brother was in danger?"

She whispered a few words that sounded like the form of an ancient Celtic prayer and sprinkled dried herbs over Stryker's eyes. When she'd finished, she laced her fingers together, her gaze locked on Stryker. "I'm not your garden-variety female Wizard and healer, Rowan. As you know, I'm also a seer. Or did you forget?"

Her voice sounded strained, and he knew it stemmed from her frustration and worry over Stryker's safety.

"No, I didn't forget." He'd forgotten a lot of things,

but not that. "Why didn't you contact me? Warn me?" His voice was now the one that was strained, and he was as mad as hell.

This wasn't supposed to happen. Stryker played by the rules, most of them anyway, and kept under the radar. Rowan was the one who was always pissing someone off. He balled his hands into tight fists to keep from tearing the place apart or setting something on fire.

She turned toward him, and her expression held deep concern and something he refused to identify. "I tried to warn you, but your mind was closed to me. All I could discern was that your brother was in danger, but not when, why, how or from whom. That is why I called him and told him to meet me at The Inferno."

She moved to light a white candle on the table beside Stryker.

"Morgan?"

"Yes. It is very serious. Stryker is so cold. I'm worried. He's not responding the way I'd hoped."

Rowan's knees buckled. He kept his balance only with iron will power. He had pinned his hopes on Morgan finding a cure. "What can I do?"

"Go back to your brother's home and see what you can find out. Maybe there's an empty glass container left behind that will confirm the poison."

"Stryker can't die," Rowan said, his voice deepening. "He's a Wizard."

Morgan was beside him, her gentle hand on his arm, the expression in her eyes begging him to remain calm. Her touch almost undid his resolve to stay strong and detached. He wanted to take her in his arms, let her comfort him, listen to the lies that his brother would live, but he held back.

He always held back.

Chapter Twenty-Five

Vlad shouldn't be in this position. He was Vlad Sinclair, the Grand Vizier of all Wizards, reduced to making an unholy allegiance with humans because someone had discovered a way to kill Wizards. Now the Talons threatened to kill all Wizards, not just Fire Wizards, if Vlad didn't do as he was told.

Vlad stared at the flames in the fireplace in his office while the president of the Talons sat behind him, waiting for his response. This plan was supposed to be easy. Instead, it had turned into a cataclysmic disaster, and the latest casualty was Bealtaine. The festival was suspended until the female Wizards had returned and the murders had been solved. He'd tried to forestall the Grey Council's decision but was overruled. The aging members believed in majority rule.

That would change when he took total control and obliterated the council. But to do so, he needed the Talons.

As he watched, the once robust fire turned the oak log to a blackened core and stone-grey ash. He felt like those poor bastards during the Middle Ages whose arms and legs were tied to horses and their bodies torn limb from limb. Helpless. The emotion was new and unwelcome and raw. He could well imagine the president of the Talons and his henchmen volunteering during the burning times of the Middle Ages.

It would be a pleasure to take them all down.

Vlad faced Constantine and purposely raised his voice enough to cause the pictures on the paneled walls to clatter. "How can I trust that you will keep your word after the recent series of blunders?"

Constantine looked uncomfortable, his eyes darting to the pictures on the wall. The president of the Talons, dressed in a dark wool suit and vest, sat in Vlad's favorite chair, pulling at a loose thread on his sleeve. Vlad knew Constantine's nervous behavior had nothing to do with Vlad's outburst. Something—or someone—else had him worried.

Constantine adjusted his tie. "The man in charge assures me the deaths were necessary. You must admit the way we neutralized the press, suggesting the murders were the work of a serial killer, was inspired."

"Must I?" Vlad edged closer until he towered over Constantine. His voice was deceptively calm. "And how do we explain the death of twenty-three people in The Inferno restaurant in Pike Place Market? Gas leak?"

"Precisely." The Talon president's voice sounded unsteady. "The report is on its way to the media outlets as we speak. We discovered an informant and made the decision to have him, and those he might have contacted, neutralized."

"Ah, well, that makes me feel so much better."

Constantine pulled on his loose thread again, this time snapping it free from his sleeve. "We have another problem. The vamp Sorsha is snooping around. We managed to convince her it was not in her, or her people's, best interest to interfere, but I don't trust her."

Vlad almost laughed at Constantine's comment. Thinking you'd convinced a Vampire of anything was foolish and often fatal. But like Sorsha, Vlad walked a fine line. Things were getting out of control. With the Grey Council and the whole magical community in a panic, it wouldn't take much to tip the scales. Vlad would present evidence that the Talons were involved in ethnic cleansing for their own gain. Until then, he had to appear to cooperate with the Talons a little while longer. He was close to achieving a lifelong dream. But he hadn't expected so many deaths or resistance. He shut his eyes for a moment to collect his thoughts.

The Talons and the magical community liked to joke that Earth Wizards were as slow to respond as a mountain rising out of the ocean. The myth worked to his advantage. When he accused the Talons, everyone would believe it was after a long and thorough investigation.

Constantine cleared his throat. It was evident the human was uncomfortable. The man's hatred of Wizards ran deep. His first wife had left him for an Air Wizard. But like Vlad, Constantine valued power and needed Vlad in the same twisted way Vlad needed him.

Vlad nodded for Constantine to continue. Like most humans, the man never seemed to run out of words to say.

Constantine shifted in his chair. "We have a problem. Rowan was seen talking with the vamp Sorsha. We are concerned she might betray us and convince him there is more to the murders than the work of someone out for revenge."

He really was surrounded by fools. "Sorsha is Rowan's ex and might have resumed their relationship. Nothing more. She cares only for her people and would like nothing more than for us to destroy ourselves. I'm more concerned about your failures. I ordered Rowan to find who was killing Wizards, and you were tasked with leading him down a false trail. If he gets too close to the truth, that's on you. Fix it."

"We have it under control. We planted evidence that will lead Rowan to Zacharias, who is the man supplying the poison-laced MCR. Rowan will believe he solved the case. To give him an extra added incentive, the latest victim of the Wizard poison was his brother Stryker."

Vlad erupted from his chair. "You fool! You truly believe Rowan won't burn the truth out of this Zacharias? And when he does, you'd better start digging your own grave. By killing his brother, you haven't stopped him, you've set him in motion. His brother is the only family he has."

Constantine steepled his hands and shrugged. "Rowan is one man. I have hundreds at my disposal. If he comes after me, we'll be ready. That is what's wrong with Wizards. You believe they are better than us."

Vlad thundered toward Constantine, grabbed him by the neck, and lifted him off his chair. "Rowan is no ordinary Wizard, you sniveling lump of clay. Rowan and his brother were from the working class. When Rowan was sixteen, he bargained with his master that if he could take out a faction of mercenaries who had been terrorizing a neighboring village, he could gain freedom for himself and his brother. It took him less than thirty minutes."

"I can't breathe."

Vlad released his hold on Constantine and let him drop to the floor. "Oh, and did I mention that it was rumored that Rowan and Stryker's mother was descended from a dragon? You want Rowan as a friend, not an enemy."

Constantine gripped the arm of the chair and struggled to his feet. He rubbed his neck, eyeing Vlad. "What do you want me to do?"

Vlad used his inner strength to curtail his simmering rage. What he wanted to do was have all humans die. Especially those of mixed human and magical blood. Those he wanted dead first. They were an abomination, but to accomplish his goal he had to play nice with the Talons. He didn't mind that the Talons were killing Fire Wizards. It was that they were killing too many, too fast. His plan had been to solve the mystery of the murders by blaming the Talons. He would be the hero, so that when he asked for more control, all in the guise of protecting the magical community, it would be like a walk in the park.

There was still time to salvage the Talons' mistakes. He tossed another log onto the fire and waited until it was seated and the flames caught. "If your plan is to blame Zacharias for the murders, you must make sure he and Rowan never meet. Another topic."

Vlad rested his hand on the mantel. "Any word on the location of the female Wizards and the Wizardlings they kidnapped from the Fertility Festival?"

"We're still working on it, but so far, we can't locate them. It's as though they've vanished off the face of the planet. Shame. My Troll disappeared the same night." He sighed. "I miss her."

Vlad hid his disgust for Constantine's attachment to a female Troll. It was disgusting. Vlad forced his voice to sound sympathetic. "There will be other women. Regarding the female Wizards, keep searching."

He could be patient. Patience and restraint were the

Earth Wizard's greatest strengths. That and burying anyone who stood in their way. He vowed the first to feel his wrath would be the female Wizards for their rebellion.

Chapter Twenty-Six

An eerie stillness settled over Stryker's house on Bainbridge Island as Rowan entered. Hours had passed since he'd found his brother and left him in Morgan's care...or was it days? It seemed like a lifetime. He'd remembered the mess in his brother's house, but not the odd smell. Perhaps it had been there and, in the chaos of searching for his brother and Lyons' daughter, he'd missed it.

Stryker's furniture, computer equipment, and kitchen items were scattered around the rooms like neglected tombstones in an ancient cemetery, but it was the smell that drew his attention. How had he overlooked the veil-like haze that clung to the air inside Stryker's home, or the rancid fumes? The odor smelled like rotting flesh in a plague-ridden city, making it difficult to breathe.

The vapor seemed to sweep up from the floor vents. His eyes watering, he rubbed them with the palm of his hand, but the pressure only made it worse. His eyes felt like something with razor-sharp claws was crawling into his eye sockets, ripping and tearing at the vulnerable soft tissue and blurring his vision. He reached up to rub them again and paused as a shudder rode his spine. Stryker's eyes had been bloodshot and the area around them bruised, as though he'd rubbed them also.

Ignoring the impulse to touch his eyes, he threw

open the windows and the double doors leading to the back deck. A gust of fresh air billowed the drapes aside and rustled the papers strewn over the floor.

Exposed to the fresh air, the toxic fumes lost most of their potency, but the shooting pain behind his eyes remained. Blinking to clear his vision, he rushed to the kitchen sink and ran cold water over them. Shuddering from the steady icy flow of water, he gripped the sink until the pain in his eyes eased.

Turning off the faucet, he slipped his dark glasses on, confirming his suspicions. The air was poisoned, but with what? And how? Scooping his wet hair off his forehead, he took another look around. If the vapor was coming up from the floor vents, it was reasonable to assume the source originated downstairs. The deduction was obvious, as well as the fact that he was no Sherlock Freaking Holmes. So why had he missed it the first time? Well, he was certainly aware of it now.

The door to the downstairs mother-in-law apartment that Stryker rented out was ajar and the place looked like whoever had been living there had made a hasty retreat. The smell was stronger and the odd sensation he'd experienced upstairs returned. He winched as the discomfort behind his eyes built again. He couldn't stay here or he'd end up in the same condition as his brother. He made a quick assessment of the area.

Dirty dishes clogged the sink, clothes and towels were piled in a corner, and a fine coating of white powder blanketed the linoleum floors and carpet. Industrial-size containers of antifreeze, drain cleaners and duct tape, fuel cans and red-stained coffee filters were stuffed into oversize trash bags.

The hair on the nape of his neck bristled. In

disbelief, he checked off the discarded items in his mind again and again, comparing it to his experiences working with Lyons. But no matter how he rearranged the contents of the apartment in his mind, the conclusion was always the same.

"Meth lab." He said the words out loud, words that brought with them a life that held no happy endings. Stryker had tried to help struggling college students with a place to live—and they had betrayed him by building an illegal drug business.

But how had his brother missed the illegal activity? Stryker knew the exact number of paper clips he owned. The setup must be recent. His brother had told him he'd been away on an assignment and only recently returned. A meth lab explained the fumes, but not why his brother lay in a coma, fighting for his life. This was no accident. Nothing created by the human hand could kill a Wizard. Was the meth lab a cover for something more insidious?

Rowan found a plastic sack in the kitchen and scooped some of the powder into it with a knife, careful to avoid contact with his bare skin, then headed outside. Finding a garden hose, he flushed his eyes again until the pain dimmed to a manageable throb.

Gasping for breath, he sank back on his heels. "Frack the living hell. What is that shit?"

But even as he asked the question, he knew. What he'd found had to be the drug that was killing Wizards— Magic Carpet Ride.

He pushed to his feet and held the plastic sack to the porch light. The powder sparkled like crushed gemstones, the same as the sample Vlad had shown him on the island.

His symptoms, his brother's condition, the deaths at

Gas Works Park, the restaurant, and others, and the way the powder caught the light, all tugged at a dark memory. Both Vlad and Lyons had referred to the stuff as Magic Carpet Ride, claiming it described the acid trip the users felt when they took the drug. Interesting name, pulled from the lyrics of an old song. But there was more to it than a catchy name. The name fit, especially if his suspicions were correct.

He shook his head, dismissing the theory. Not possible. The Talons and the Grey Council had vowed the granite-like rocks were no longer a threat. He had to get back to Morgan. She would know what this was and tell him he was conjuring demons from snowflakes.

His cell phone rang as he prepared to leave. "Lyons, tell me you have good news. I could use some."

Lyons' voice sounded tired. "Just finished visiting AJ. She's still asleep, so I didn't want to wake her. It's clear your brother saved her life." There was a long pause. "Our loved ones always seem to get caught in the crossfire, no matter what we do."

"Your daughter is going to be all right."

"Yeah, yeah, but it keeps me awake at night. The other reason for the call is business. I think you're going to want to join me at a stake-out in West Seattle. My informant might have found a connection to the serial killings."

"I'm on my way. One more thing. I found what looks like the makings of a meth lab in my brother's basement apartment. Could you ask your people to check it out?"

"Sure thing. See you soon."

****

It was a typical neighborhood in West Seattle.

Homes facing Puget Sound looked as though they were leaning forward or standing on tiptoes to capture the best view of the water. They stood proud, hoping those passing by would look at them with envy. The less fortunate homes slumped on the opposite side of the street looking resigned and invisible in comparison.

It was by this aura of invisibility that Rowan knew the occupants of the house he was staking out with Lyons craved more than a prized water view. And it had worked for a while. But the educated people of Seattle were beginning to recognize the signs.

The windows of this brick rambler were covered in blackout curtains. Neighbors had reported an unusual amount of traffic and visitors at odd hours of the day and night. After a windstorm that knocked over trash cans, a neighbor reported to the police that he'd seen suspicious garbage. Industrial-size containers of antifreeze, drain cleaners and duct tape, fuel cans, and coffee filters stained red. The conclusion was simple: meth lab.

Rowan watched from the driver's side of his car. Ignoring the throbbing pain in his eyes. They still ached like they had at Stryker's house. When this business was finished, he would wash them out again. Lyons and two undercover detectives were in an unmarked car a few car-lengths behind him, waiting for a warrant.

The door of the house opened. Two men emerged, stood on the front porch, lit cigarettes and talked in low voices. Even at this distance, the rod-thin, hollow expressions and jerky body movements of the two men marked them as addicts. When they were finished, they flicked their cigarette butts in the direction of a pile of blue rocks. One of the men picked up one of the stones and tossed it to his companion. They both laughed and retreated inside.

Rowan thumbed on his steering wheel. What kind of rocks were blue? He went over the types of blue rocks in his head. Then that same bad feeling he'd had at Stryker's place edged up his spine.

Wizard lore told of a type of rock, called Oculist stone, that was found in the polar regions in ancient times and possessed magical properties. As a crushed powder, it could weaken or kill Wizards, but when used in its solid form, it could power cities. When there was peace between dragons and Wizards, the dragons agreed to oversee the handling of the stones and protect them from the Wizards' enemies. Then the truce fell apart, and a war broke out.

When the Wizards defeated the dragons, they demolished the mines, fearful the stones would fall into the wrong hands. Rumors persisted among the Fire Wizards that not all of the Oculist stone deposits were discovered and destroyed.

Rowan focused on the pile of rocks again with renewed interest. The glow from the streetlamp turned the rocks indigo blue. He'd seen the same blue haze when The Inferno was under attack. His unease kicked into high gear. If he was right, an old enemy planned to release the powder on the world. But who? The enemy list was endless.

The powder made from the rocks was relatively safe to humans, giving them a psychedelic high that rivaled anything on the market today. The irony was that humans would survive. Anyone with even a trace of Wizard blood would not. Disguising the Oculist powder as a new designer drug called Magic Carpet Ride was brilliant.

Superman's Achilles heel was Kryptonite. A

Wizard's fatal weakness was oddly similar. The blue rocks were remnants of a meteor responsible for the mass extinction of the dinosaurs. Some speculated that an ancestor of the dinosaurs survived and became the dragon of myth and legend, capable of breathing fire and flying at dizzying speeds and heights.

The warrant to enter the house took too much time. And if his suspicions were correct, time was in short supply. If those inside suspected they were surrounded, they would bolt.

Rowan got out of his car and crossed the street. Someone inside drew aside the window curtain and peered out. He could hear muffled arguing over whether he was a customer or a cop. The heated arguing went silent, and he knew they had made their decision.

A gunshot punctured the silence. Then two more rang out, followed by an explosion.

Chapter Twenty-Seven

In the rooftop apartment in Belltown, a water glass slipped from Morgan's hand, dropping to the floor and shattering. It was the third glass in as many hours. Dawn was moments away. She hadn't been able to sleep. She'd had a premonition. And this one connected to Rowan. No, not quite a vision of the future. More a feeling of something that was happening in the present.

Across the room, Wiz lifted his head off his paws. He barked and his tongue hung out the side of his mouth. His expression was piercing, as though trying to will her into action. It was as though he could read her mind, her concern.

Morgan reached for a dustpan and broom in a closet beside the sink, to sweep the glass. She knew so little about his kind. She knew he was a shapeshifter but had never seen him shift into human form. She also knew he was loyal to female Wizards but not why. Perhaps it didn't matter. Some secrets deserved protection.

Was that how she classified her keeping the truth from Rowan that he had a son? Was her secret one that must be safeguarded? But who was she protecting? Certainly not Rowan.

It was baked into male Wizards by their leadership that they must not worry about such mundane matters as parenthood or raising a child. Their focus must remain on preserving the continuation of their species.

Neither did her secret protect her child. He had been taken from her to raise as a warrior, and she did not know if he was alive or dead. In the early years she had tried to search for him, but he had disappeared without a trace.

She cut her finger on one of the shards of glass as she dumped the broken pieces into the wastebasket under the sink. Red blood dripped into the sink as she gazed out the window at the awakening dawn. She knew who she protected.

She was protecting herself.

Her biggest fear was that he had wanted a child and would blame her for not telling him. Would he want to search for their son or tell her that their child was better off where he was?

Morgan stopped the blood on her finger with a thought and slid Wiz a glance. There were times when she could almost feel what he was thinking. She felt a wave of comfort advising her not to judge herself too harshly. "Wiz. Was that you?"

Wiz only blinked and rested his head on his paws once again.

Or perhaps her inner strength was growing and had made the suggestion subconsciously. Danu of the Waters had said that might happen the more her powers grew. She prayed her power of healing grew as well. She would need it in the coming days.

Stryker's condition had worsened. He was not responding as she'd hoped. He lay on his back as still as a likeness of a medieval knight on the top of a marble casket, a grim image with only the slight rise and fall of his chest as an indication he was alive.

AJ fared better. The sleeping aid Stryker had given her before he'd been poisoned was wearing off and there was color in her cheeks and an easy, strong rhythm in her breathing. When she regained consciousness, Morgan hoped AJ could shed light on what had happened to them. Until then, all Morgan could do was wait. She'd always believed she was patient. Rowan was the one with a short fuse. Not anymore. Somehow their roles had reversed.

When she'd broken the last glass, she knew the real reason her nerves were so frayed. Rowan was in danger, and she was powerless to help him. His mind was closed to hers and there was no way she could warn him or find out if he was all right. The only reason she sensed danger around him at all was that the brand he'd placed over her heart, and hers over his, enhanced their connection.

His was the image of a rowan tree in the center of a circle of flames and hers was three curved blue lines representing the currents and power of water. Water and fire should not be compatible except during the Fertility Festival of Bealtaine, or so she'd always believed. Was this another one of the lies they'd been taught as children?

Rowan's brand began to warm against her skin. Morgan placed her hand against it and received an instant jolt of heat. She turned toward the door as her pulse quickened. He was coming.

Wiz rose from a sitting position and barked.

AJ stirred in her sleep, curled into a tighter ball, and settled in a more comfortable position, but Stryker remained stone still.

Rowan's name on her lips, Morgan flung open the door.

As he stood framed in the doorway Rowan was covered with gray ash and soot, his clothes torn. When his gaze locked on hers, his disheveled appearance paled in comparison to the condition of his eyes. He was in pain. A pain that went beyond the flesh. Pain that was heart deep. Her breath faltered. Tear-like trails of blood etched down through the hollow expression on his face.

"What has happened?"

He winced and gripped the door jamb. "Explosion. Evidence destroyed," he said as he collapsed in her arms.

****

Rowan was alive. That was all Morgan cared about. But his eyes… Fear closed around her heart. They resembled the condition of Stryker's eyes. "Please, Goddess. No!"

Morgan pulled him into the room and over to the sink, ripping off his shirt and flushing his eyes with cool water. There were minor cuts scattered over his chest and shoulders. They would heal. She was not so sure about his eyes. Only when the redness around them dulled did she turn off the flow of water and guide him over to the sofa, pouring the strength and force of her healing touch into and over him.

When she felt she'd purged the worst of the poison, she relaxed enough to speak. "What did you learn at Stryker's house?"

He eased her hands away gently. "Nothing good. Stryker's house reeked with poison. The smell and the blue fog were everywhere. That's what burned my eyes. But the house that was destroyed wasn't Stryker's," he said, his voice strained. "I was with Lyons. We were investigating a lead on the Eye Doctor serial killings and about ready to make an arrest when the house exploded."

Morgan's hand trembled as she slipped her hand into his. She didn't want to ask about the poison in

Stryker's house. She sensed he was circling around the topic because he didn't want to face the truth head on. She kept her voice low and gentle. "Is Detective Lyons all right?"

Rowan squeezed his eyes shut and gripped the arm of the sofa as though fighting off a wave of pain. "Not a scratch. He and his men were still in the car. The only people killed were those in the house. We're back to square one." He kissed the back of her hand. "Thank you for your healing touch. My eyes are better," he said, trying to stand. "Need to get back…"

His eyes weren't better. She knew it and he did as well. The redness had only dulled. Whatever was poisoning him was pushing back. His whole body shuddered, and he would have pitched forward had she not been close enough to hold him still. Placing her hands on his shoulders, she guided him to a reclining position. She refocused and summoned her inner strength, praying for guidance, calling on the force and power of water to prevail against an unseen enemy that was poisoning his body.

Morgan wished she knew more about the poison. She felt lost in a dark forest without the stars to guide her. Seconds folded into minutes. The effort to heal him drained her strength but she persisted. She would not let it win.

Wiz padded over, turning first toward Rowan and then Morgan. He settled by Rowan's head, keeping his eyes trained on Morgan. A surge of power passed between her and Wiz. He had been with her when she had ministered to Stryker. At the time, she had felt a surge of power as well but had not made the connection that it had originated from Wiz.

Morgan breathed in the energy Wiz offered and, lifting her arms, continued to pull the poison from Rowan's body.

Time moved slowly as dawn's awakening light strengthened to welcome the day.

An hour later, she felt the cold tendrils of the poison's hold weaken, retreat, and finally dissolve, and she sank to her knees with words of thanks on her lips. Her gaze traveled over his bare chest.

Thick bands of Celtic spirals circled his shoulders. Ogham lettering, in neat, even rows, spread over the right side of his chest, retelling a history of battles lost and won, and the dates he'd accomplished each stage necessary for becoming a full Wizard. His accomplishments mirrored those of a decorated soldier, yet it was the brand she'd placed over his heart that held her attention. It pulsated with an iridescent silver-blue, a stark contrast to the ebony-black tattoos covering his body.

Morgan reached up to touch it, but Rowan opened his eyes and entwined her hand in his. His smile resembled a small boy's who was caught in mischief. "I'm burning for you, even when I'm on the brink of death."

She turned away before he could see the fear mirrored in her expression. "Do not speak of death. You are too stubborn to die. And I'm too stubborn to allow it." Morgan slipped her hand from his and reached for a jar of ointment on the table beside the sofa. She needed a distraction from her thoughts.

Sexual attraction was not the only reason for the brand's glow. Did he know what else it could do? Her hands trembled, making it difficult to open the lid.

He reached for the jar and opened it, handing it back. "You saved my life and all I can think of is taking you to bed and making love."

His gentle tone warmed her heart and reminded him of the man she had fallen in love with all those years ago. "Hold that thought. But I would not be a good healer if I encouraged you to overtax yourself. For now, you must rest." She gave him a nod and forced a smile while she concentrated on the ointment. She struggled with the warring emotions of relief that he was recovering and regret that there were so many secrets between them.

She applied the ointment over the lids of his eyes. Could she tell him? Would he believe her if she did? Or would he resent the connection between them even more if he knew of the child they'd created in love. Or the hidden secrets of the brand she placed over his heart? Male Wizards were fiercely independent. How would he react, knowing there was a possibility her brand had protected him until he could reach her? She was drowning in secrets.

"You should have come straight here from Stryker's house," she said under her breath, leaving an ocean of words left unsaid. She couldn't tell him. Not yet.

Rowan tucked a strand of hair behind her ear. "You are a woman of contrasts. Gentle as well as strong. I wanted to come, but when I received Lyons' call saying it was urgent, I made a choice. What I found out was worth the risk." He paused, and his glance traveling toward Stryker's room. "Oculist stones still exist. They're the main ingredient in the poison."

The jar of ointment slipped from her hand. Rowan caught it before it hit the floor and set it on the table.

She glanced toward Stryker as Rowan had seconds

before. "The Talons and the Grey Council told us—*promised* us—that the Oculist stones were destroyed."

Morgan studied the jar, remembering the story. An alchemist in Atlantis had created a substance from a meteor he believed would enhance a male Wizard's power. Instead, the poison almost wiped out the male population before the poison was secured and destroyed. Caitlin had been among a small group of female Wizards who believed the Oculist stones were never destroyed. But why would their leadership lie about something so dangerous?

She shuddered as a new fear vibrated through her.

Rowan drew her beside him on the sofa, wrapping her in his embrace. "How long have you suspected?" His words were not an accusation.

She welcomed his warmth, his heat, his strength. "Caitlin tried to warn me of an impending danger, but I wouldn't listen. Even when I witnessed your brother's symptoms, and then yours, I hoped I was wrong. Healers can minimize the effects of the Oculist stones if caught early enough and if the dose is weak, but even then we do not know the long-term effects. You could still…"

He stroked her hair, silencing her unspoken fears with the touch of his hand. "I have a confession to make. Although we were told that the mines were destroyed, Fire Wizards weren't convinced. I think it's our distrusting nature." He pulled her closer. "They lied to us, and now someone is harvesting the stones and killing Wizards."

Morgan felt the deep pain and loss raging through him. He had dedicated his life and loyalty to the Talons and the Grey Council, and they betrayed him. She glanced at his profile. His jaw was set, his eyes stone cold. She longed to bring life back into them. "What can we do?"

"The only thing we can. Destroy the Oculist stones before they destroy us."

Morgan shuddered, knowing he was not talking about just the stones.

Chapter Twenty-Eight

The Dragon awoke.

Awakened by a near-death experience, the dragon spirit in Stryker stirred. He stretched, listened, and learned. He had been dormant for what seemed centuries. Now, he was awake and knew he was alive. He knew because of the incessant voices buzzing around him. If he was dead, there would be a dark void of nothingness. The curse of being a dragon that did not die in battle was to experience an eternity of loneliness.

He was also aware of his surroundings. He knew he was in the bedroom of a rooftop apartment. He knew he had a strong connection to the Wizard called Stryker. The two were one. Had always been one, since that day when the boy Stryker had saved a dragon's egg from a predator.

But now it was time for the dragon to take control. He smelled salty air, heard the sound of traffic and the squawk of seagulls as they searched for food. He was starving. Soon, he cautioned. Soon.

He heard voices in the next room. Through the strong connection with his human side, he knew their names were Rowan and Morgan, but little else. They had been carrying on a nonstop conversation. His survival instincts told him they were Wizards and thus his kind's sworn enemy. A Wizard's young were not so bad, curious mostly, but fully grown they killed dragons on sight.

He needed peace and seclusion while he adjusted and recaptured more of his memory of both his human side and his dragon side pasts. There was a way to silence Rowan and Morgan, of course, but even as he knew they were Wizards, there existed something inside him cautioning that they meant him no harm. Their concern for him, however, would shift the moment he recovered. Most likely they would view him as an oddity to study and dissect.

Like so many who did not fit into a preordained set of rules, his kind had been hunted to near-extinction, their ability to adapt and shapeshift their only salvation. Taking human form was just one more of their many skills. This world, this reality, killed what was different or what they did not understand.

He risked opening his eyes, the better to identify his captors and his prison. The bedroom was small, but functional and near a source of food. There was a door to his left and an open window directly in front of him. A large dog sat on his haunches, staring in his direction. Dogs were aware of dragons in whatever form they took and considered them allies. The animal posed no threat. He might even prove useful. Their gazes met, and in that instant, he knew the dog's name was Wiz. The animal leapt on the bed and settled beside the dragon Stryker's feet.

"Stryker's awake," Morgan said, rushing into his room.

Rowan entered with Morgan and rested his hand protectively on the woman's shoulder. The tattoo of flames curling around a tree was visible on the back of his hand and marked him as a Fire Wizard.

There was something familiar about the brand. He shoved it into the dark recesses of his memories to consider later as Morgan sat down next to him on the bed and touched his arm. He tensed, but caution warned against the impulse to strike. No one was allowed to touch him without his permission. His weakened condition advised patience. There would be another time, a time of his choosing, to take his revenge for his kind's centuries of persecution.

She leaned closer. "How are you feeling?"

Rowan reached out and drew her back. The dark glasses he wore could not hide the man's growing wariness. Had Rowan sensed that a dragon had risen?

The Fire Wizard's voice was tight and low. "Morgan, let him rest."

"But Rowan…"

The Fire Wizard silenced her with a gesture of his hand and guided her to the far corner of the room. Their voices dropped to whispers. They needn't have bothered. Stryker's heightened sense of hearing heard every beat of their hearts, the tension in their voices, and the words they spoke.

Morgan was the first to speak. "Rowan, what is wrong with you? Stryker is awake. We should be with him. He must be very confused."

"Something's not right."

"You are impossible. Do you realize how close Stryker came to dying in the last twenty-four hours? There were moments when I almost believed he had, and now you're telling me you think something is wrong with him. Of course something is wrong. He almost died and is in a weakened state while his body heals."

"Morgan, there's something different about him I

can't quite place."

The woman's voice sounded unsure, as though trying to convince both the Wizard as well as herself. "Of course he is different. He has been at death's door since you brought him to me. He survived the Oculist poisoning, when those at the restaurant died a horrible death. Give him time."

The Fire Wizard clenched and unclenched his fists, reflecting the uncertainty in his voice. "I hope you're right, but didn't you notice his eyes?"

"Now you're being paranoid. Again, there could be any number of reasons for the change in color. We don't know that much about the side effects of the Oculist poisoning. His true color might return as he grows stronger. Stryker needs our help, and you're concerned about the color of his eyes? You're impossible."

"Then you saw it too. I've only seen that shade once before." His voice trailed off, the silence suspended in the air, ticking off the seconds. The Fire Wizard's voice dropped even lower. "His eyes are a fluorescent green, like the scales of a…"

Morgan interrupted with an exasperated sigh and glanced toward the bed. "As usual, you are jumping to conclusions. Sometimes I believe you are the one obsessed with dragons, not Stryker. Besides, you can see for yourself that Wiz likes him, otherwise he would be barking nonstop rather than snoring peacefully. We're finished talking."

Morgan started to leave, but the Fire Wizard stepped in front of her, blocking her path. "I don't want you going near my brother until I can get help."

"What are you talking about? Help for what?"

"I want him restrained. Watched."

Stryker pulled his concentration away from their conversation as they left his bedroom and continued arguing in the living room. He had heard enough. He was not safe here. The Fire Wizard called him his brother. How was that possible? Unlike dragons, Wizards of Rowan's stature did not mate for life, nor stay to help raise their children. They did not have families and would be unaware if they had a sibling. Was the Fire Wizard lying? But for what purpose?

Morgan made references to the Oculist stones, believing he had been infected by them.

Dragons were immune to the Wizard poison. Was that the reason his dormant state had awakened? Regardless, he'd heard enough.

It was time to leave.

One of the most important weapons in a dragon's arsenal was harnessing the gift of invisibility. It was the first thing young dragonets learned how to master. As long as his kind drew breath, they could summon this unique power. On the moment of their death, however, they turned to ash. Yet another protective measure developed over the millennia.

Enchanted words were all that was needed to trigger the power to become invisible. Their belief was that one day they would regain their place of honor and respect, before ignorance and misunderstanding had reduced them to fugitives in their own land.

Wiz lifted his head as the dragon Stryker moved from the bed, then paused to scratch Wiz behind the ear. "Thanks for keeping my secret, Wiz. I owe you."

Making sure Rowan and Morgan were still engaged in their heated discussion, he headed to the kitchen area and hoped he had enough strength to bring forth the gift of dragon invisibility. He whispered the sacred words: *"Forever together. Forever at peace."*

Light dimmed, casting the room in shadows that elongated over the walls, curled around corners and spread over the floor like a velvet shroud. Just when he felt his body change, he saw a strange woman enter the kitchen. Her black hair shone like polished ebony and her aura molded around her in shades of blue, green and white as she worked. The dark-haired beauty glanced over in his direction and started to speak, but whatever she was about to say dissolved into screams.

He knew by her panicked expression that she'd witnessed him disappear into thin air. Relieved his strength was returning, he moved toward the open window. Humans rattled so easily. It was one of their charms.

As expected, the Fire Wizard rushed in and scanned the room while Morgan comforted the woman. The Fire Wizard was wasting his time. Stryker had already slipped out the window. The most that was left behind was a thin haze of shadows. Suspended in the air, Stryker's next greatest gift took hold.

The ability to fly.

Chapter Twenty-Nine

Rowan backed away from the window and fought the hot currents of fear rushing through him. "My brother's turned."

"I saw him disappear." AJ was on her feet, her eyes wide. "You said he turned? Exactly what does that mean? And his eyes..." She swallowed and wrapped her arms around her waist as her voice shook. "Who are you people? My father used to tell me tall tales about the people he dealt with in Seattle's underground, but I dismissed them because he was overworked."

Morgan placed an arm around AJ's shoulders and eased her down into a chair. "We have a logical explanation."

Rowan arched an eyebrow. "This I've got to hear."

Morgan shot him an exasperated glance. "Not helping."

AJ shrugged away from Morgan. "What's going on?"

Rowan removed his glasses and wiped a nonexistent smudge from the lens. "Nothing much. My people are dying by a substance that was supposed to be contained eons ago. Fear is driving monsters into the open. There's a war coming."

AJ cleared her throat. "I'm having a nightmare, and when I wake up, I'm going to do as my father suggested and go back to school."

"I'll tell your father the good news. My advice, choose a university that's located on Mars, because Earth is not safe." Rowan shoved his glasses back in place.

"Rowan! This is not the time for sarcasm."

He looked at Morgan over the rim of his glasses. "I was being serious. In case you hadn't noticed, my brother disappeared in plain sight, which confirms my suspicions. He's a shapeshifting dragon."

AJ clamped her hand over her mouth, her eyes widening into twin orbs of fear.

"We have to trust that we will get through this," Morgan said.

Rowan leaned against the window, searching the street below. His laugh was hollow. "Trust is the reason we're in this mess."

Morgan reached for AJ's hands. She glanced at Rowan over her shoulders and glared at him. "Let me handle this." She drew AJ over to the sofa and motioned for the young woman to sit beside her. "Everything your father told you was true. Rowan is being dramatic, but it might be best if you and your father left Seattle for a while. We are trying to find a way to avert it, but we believe there is a war coming between the magical community and those humans who want to eliminate people like us who have certain…abilities."

AJ rubbed her temples as though struggling to understand the unexplainable. "Like the ability to shapeshift into a dragon."

"Precisely. Although until just minutes ago, none of us believed that was still possible. We believed dragons were extinct."

Rowan focused on the view from the window, watching a ferryboat pull out into the open water on its journey to one of the islands in the San Juans. Dragons were the least of his worries. The clues had been right in front of him the whole time. The fact a Wizard's eyes were removed, why female Wizards had felt the urgency to run, taking the Wizardlings with them, all played on his guilt. Then there was the ease with which the poison had killed the Wizards at the restaurant. Some detective he'd turned out to be. If he had been doing his job, his brother might still be a Wizard instead of something in between. "If you tell anyone what you've just witnessed, you will be killed."

"Rowan, stop it. You're frightening her." Morgan smoothed the hair off AJ's forehead. "What Mr. Tact is trying to say is that what you've seen and what we're talking about is very serious. The knowledge might put you in danger. The old saying 'Ignorance is bliss' applies. We can call your father, and you can go about your day."

AJ shook her head, leaning forward. "No, I want to know all of it. You said there are humans involved who are trying to hurt your kind. Let my father and me be the humans who are helping you."

Rowan narrowed his gaze. "You're like your father. You don't back down from a fight. No wonder he was worried about you. Well, the first thing a Wizard learns is that Oculist stones from Atlantis can kill us. There is no known antidote. What happened to Stryker is something else. Dragons are immune to the Oculist stones' fatal blue powder. I still don't understand why he shapeshifted, but I am grateful he did. His connection to dragons probably saved his life."

He took a deep breath, tamping down a growing fear of his own. He and his brother had used whatever spare time they had exploring old dragon caves. Partly because it was a fun pastime, but mostly because they'd overheard their father say their mother was descended from dragons. Did that mean he might end up like his brother? A man but caught between two worlds?

AJ took the cup of coffee Morgan offered and gave her a nod of thanks. "Remember my saying that my friend thought her sister Daffeny and her sister's boyfriend were murdered? She believed there was a connection to a warehouse on the wharf."

"We were going to check it out, but haven't had time yet," Rowan said. "Didn't you mention that you took a job there to investigate if your friend was correct about the murders? Your father was really steamed."

She took another sip of coffee. "Yes, and yes. The stones you describe look like the ones at the warehouse. Just saying."

Rowan pushed away from the window. This was the first good news he'd had in days. "How soon can you get me into your boss's warehouse?"

Chapter Thirty

In the Talons' copper-domed headquarters on the island, Vlad paced in the chrome-and-steel waiting area. The Talons and the Grey Council had called an emergency meeting. This was the third since the Bealtaine debacle. The female Wizards who remained on the island had offered suggestions for where their sister Wizards had taken the Wizardlings, and to no one's surprise, the clues were dead ends.

Vlad had wanted to use more persuasive methods of questioning, but the women were being watched too closely by male Wizards who would rebel if so much as a hair on any of their heads was ruffled. At present, the only options left to him were asking the Air Wizards and the Talons for assistance. As soon as the female Wizards were found and he'd consolidated power, he would deal with those who'd defied him.

Rowan was at the top of his list. He was becoming a problem. Something had happened at Bealtaine, something that changed Rowan's focus.

Until recently, Rowan had always been loyal to the Grey Council. Which was the reason he had wanted Rowan to be his eyes and ears, and report to him on the findings regarding the murders. In that way Vlad believed he could control the narrative. Then the idiot Constantine had to go and order that his people poison Rowan's brother. Fools.

Yes, things were getting out of control, but the Talons' miscalculation might prove to his advantage. With the Grey Council and the magical community both in a panic, Vlad would present evidence that Constantine and Zacharias were behind the ethnic cleansing and toss the humans literally to the wolves. Until then, he had to appear to cooperate with Constantine and the Talons for just a little while longer.

He glanced at the digital time on the wall, annoyed that he'd arrived early. When he was in charge, he'd make others wait for him. *Be patient. Your time will come*, he told himself. To quiet his nerves, Vlad looked through the locked glass doors toward the conference room. The chamber was circular, with a private waiting room for each member of the Talons and the Grey Council. In the center was a massive round wooden table, who some claimed was used by King Arthur and his legendary knights. He didn't believe the story. Most likely the table was a reproduction. It didn't matter. The round table was a strong symbol and reinforced their ideals.

Vlad shared his colleagues' belief in honoring the old ways. Five hundred years ago, when the alliance between the Talons and the Grey Council was created, it drew upon the themes of Camelot to create a better world. Those goals were needed now more than ever. King Arthur wouldn't have hesitated to eliminate those who threatened his kingdom, and neither would he. In his opinion, the world had reached a critical turning point. Self-proclaimed human mages spoke of things like Armageddon, the Rapture, and End Times. The visionaries were not that far off in their predictions, just in identifying the person who would save their kind from extinction.

At twelve, the glass doors in Vlad's waiting room opened simultaneously with the corresponding waiting room doors. Members of the Talons and the Grey Council filed into the conference room and took their seats at the round table. There were seven members of the Talons, representing the original seven founding families. One member represented the magical community, and the Grey Council was made up of a representative from each of the Wizard clans of Fire, Air and Earth. The chair for Water was vacant and would remain so. Two honorary, non-voting members were Danu of the Waters, and Old Man, who were the keepers of their history.

When Caitlin, the female Water Wizard died, and with Danu of the Waters missing, the Council had decided it was best to leave the positions vacant until replacements were announced. In Vlad's opinion, running the world was a man's business anyway. The remaining seat was reserved for Old Man, the keeper of their history.

Vlad took his place beside Constantine, who greeted each member in turn before addressing the business at hand. "War, when properly supervised," he began, "has its purpose. It cleanses much like a controlled field fire at the end of planting season. But when allowed to rage unattended, its destruction far outreaches its benefits. It's time we step in and extinguish the world's flames." He distributed black folders to each of the members and then waited for each man to open and glance at the contents.

Constantine placed the palms of his hands on the ancient wood of the round table and leaned forward as he continued, "The way human nations run their wars hasn't changed over the centuries. In the past, to bring order out of chaos we often simply assassinated their leaders, and the will of the people would collapse. In other instances, it was necessary to take out key politicians or generals, which achieved the same result. I propose that we renew that strategy." He paused to let everyone open the files before continuing. "Are there any questions?"

Connor O'Hara, a shapeshifting werewolf with silver hair and eyes, and the representative for the magical community, was the first to speak. "President Constantine, with all due respect, I disagree with your proposal to order killing the world's leaders. Need I remind you that not only will you be murdering human leaders, but there are also members of the magical community who hold high office. "Diplomacy is needed. Not murder."

The president waved away Connor's question as though it was not important. "Humans have no taste for diplomacy, and if I may be so bold, neither do certain members of the magical community. If there are no further questions, we will vote."

Connor stood and growled low. This time all turned in his direction. He was a man dedicated to peace, yet capable of calling upon his darker side. He was not a man to cross. His voice turned low and deadly. "The magical community will not condone these kills. This council of leaders was created to help humanity, not murder innocents. Further, we demand the Grey Council fill the position left vacant by the death of Caitlin, the leader of the female Water Wizards. Although many of the female Wizards have fled, there are several of them still on the island. I recommend we ask them if they could vote for someone to represent them here. A balance must be maintained in the world, and it begins at this table. Our first order of business can't be to declare war. It must be to discuss why the female Wizards left, taking our future with them."

Low murmurs rippled around the chamber. Other voices joined Connor's, shifting from Constantine's proposal to the debate on restoring the female Wizards' position on the board with the theory that the gesture might entice those missing to return.

Vlad and Constantine exchanged glances. Vlad ground his teeth together. The meeting was getting out of control. Connor was stirring up trouble and would need to be eliminated.

Always the diplomat, Constantine rose, raising his hand to silence the heated words. "We agreed that it was the right decision to keep the female Water Wizard position vacant until our women returned. It was further discussed that perhaps we should take the burden of board responsibility from their shoulders, to lessen their stress. At the time, Connor agreed with our assessment. We also considered the possibility that our female Wizards left of their own accord but dismissed the theory. Why would they? They were revered and given all a female could desire. We must consider the possibility that one of our enemies kidnapped them."

Vlad nodded at each remark Constantine made, marveling at the man's ease in turning around this potentially volatile situation. Deflecting the blame to someone else was Constantine's specialty. Constantine had presented the opportunity to openly wage war against an enemy of their choosing. The man was a genius.

Old Man, with a gray beard that hung past his waist, and wearing a midnight-blue tunic, spoke in a voice brittle and cracking with age. "Perhaps, esteemed President Constantine—perhaps. But even if one of our enemies kidnapped the female Wizards and our Wizardlings, we must entertain Connor's suggestion. Our ancient texts speak of how female Wizards are capable of flourishing without us. These same texts, state, bluntly, that without them to temper our violent nature, we will kill each other and vanish as though we never existed. I am not suggesting that we discount the possibility that they might have been kidnapped by our enemies, but neither rule out that they left on their own accord for reasons known only to them."

Frustrated with Old Man's interference, when Constantine had so expertly given them a reason to quell the heated discussion, Vlad pounded his fist on the table, with the desired results. All eyes turned from Old Man to him.

"I respectfully disagree, Old Man. Neither one of our kind will survive without the other. Female Wizards need our protection. President Constantine offered a reasonable explanation for the female Wizards' disappearance, and we have to heed his wise words."

A murmured discussion traveled around the table. Old Man had spoken of an ancient text that dated back to the time of Atlantis. It had never sat well with male Wizards. They did not want to believe that female Wizards could survive without them.

Old Man had gone too far, and that pleased Vlad very much.

Vlad smiled to himself as he developed an idea that might appeal to any who did not agree with

Constantine's plan. One that could solve all his problems, bringing the female Wizards and the Wizardlings back to the island and Morgan within his grasp. Zephra, one of the female Wizards who had stayed on the island, had let it slip that Morgan had been appointed leader after Caitlin's death. She had said it with pride, and a touch of warning in her voice. At the time, Vlad had kept silent, guarding his reaction, but that was before he realized that the female Wizards were more organized than he had first thought.

He raised his hand to still the murmurs of unrest. "Old Man is wise, and his words have given me a possible solution. I don't know if the women left of their own accord, but I have an idea that might prove once and for all if they are able to return of their own free will. If they do not return, then it supports President Constantine's theory that they were kidnapped, and we must prepare accordingly. With your approval, I propose we fill the vacant position." He paused just long enough to let his words settle over the Talons and the Grey Council. The tension in the chamber eased, proving how right he'd been that he and the president were in danger of losing their hard-won control.

With a great effort, he forced a smile onto his lips and a gentleness in his voice. "Zephra, one of the female Wizards who remained on the island, shows leadership skills. I propose we nominate her to fill the vacancy. The nomination will have to be confirmed by the female Wizards on the island, of course, but I'm sure they will agree. Female Wizards always have ceremonies to celebrate such things. I propose, as an offer of good will, we invite Morgan, who we know took over leadership after Caitlin's death."

Connor's voice was measured and his eyes cold. "I have met Zephra. She is respected and devoted to her sister Wizards. A fine choice. I second the nomination. I also approve of inviting Morgan, but this feels like an empty gesture. How do you propose we get this message to her, and what makes you think she would return? I share Old Man's concern that the female Wizards had strong reasons for leaving."

Vlad held onto a tight smile. "Female Wizards are known for their ability to compromise and seek peaceful solutions. I am confident they will consider Zephra's nomination as an olive branch and the beginning of a new and better relationship. We will enlist the help of the Air Wizards and the magical community to spread the word of our decision. This serves another purpose. If the female Wizards are free to come and go as they please, we will know they left of their own accord. If not, then we must seek out their kidnappers."

Vlad broke eye contact with Connor as they voted. He was certain Connor had seen through Vlad's deception, but it didn't matter. By the time Connor had proof that Vlad used nominating Zephra to a position on the board as a ruse to learn where Morgan and the other female Wizards were hiding, it would be too late. With Morgan under his control, he would deal with her treason and anyone else he considered a threat.

Chapter Thirty-One

Under a crescent moon, beneath a Seattle viaduct, sandwiched between Zacharias's warehouse and the ferry terminal, Rowan waited for Morgan to arrive. He was early. According to AJ, they needed to wait until after midnight, when the guards on duty became lightest.

They'd asked AJ to stay behind. This was no place for a human if their plan went sideways.

It should be easy. They'd break into Zacharias's office and search for incriminating evidence. A non-issue if the man was an ordinary businessman importing his product from the same approximate location as Atlantis. It would be nothing more than an unfortunate coincidence. Which meant the location of those harvesting Oculist power would remain unknown.

But if Zacharias was connected to a rogue element of the Talons, the Grey Council, or an unknown enemy, Rowan should have asked for more backup. In any one of those scenarios, the men guarding the warehouse wouldn't be your garden-variety security guards. Like Rowan, they'd possess paranormal powers.

Too late now for "what if."

He felt Morgan arrive before she came into view. The brand over his heart reacted like an overexcited puppy when its owner arrives home from work. Rowan's blood began to simmer as Morgan headed toward him at a brisk pace from the direction of a dock on the far side of Zacharias's warehouse. The raincoat she wore instead of adding more substance to her only made her appear more fragile, vulnerable. He should never have allowed her to come along. Female Wizards had power over water, but the fight they faced was on land. If anything happened to her, he didn't know what he would do.

He waited until she was close enough to touch, then clenched his hands at his side, fearful he'd give in to the impulse. "I've changed my mind. I can't solve this case if every time we're together I'm—"

"Turned on?"

Rowan frowned. The woman was driving him crazy. "Distracted," he corrected.

She turned her gaze toward the docks. "You are not the only one who suffers. I feel it too."

The dark shadows lengthening below the viaduct couldn't hide the conflicting emotions passing over Morgan's expression. Regret. Sadness. Fear. When she lifted her eyes to meet his gaze, the fear in her eyes remained.

Morgan placed her hand on the brand over his heart. Her voice was so low it sounded like the waves as they gently lapped against the pier at the nearby ferry terminal across the street. "You have asked that I remove my brand's symbol, and according to our laws, I agree." Again, those beautiful eyes filled with deep sadness. "But there is no guarantee it will work after this length of time. I will need to consult the elders."

Rowan fought the urge to place his hand over hers, draw her into his arms, and tell her he'd changed his mind. As aggravating as it was to know that she was near, it would be worse not knowing if she was okay. Being this close to her without touching her tested his resolve, which proved his point. He needed a clear head to fight what lay ahead, but it didn't sound like removing the brand was as easy as he'd hoped.

"I thought you could just say a few words and we'd be rid of the connection." He regretted the hardness of the words he'd spoken the moment he'd said them. "I didn't mean that the way it sounded."

Her voice tight and controlled, she secured her tangle of long hair with a silver ribbon and tied it at the nape of her neck. "The type of brands we have are rare. They are granted to a select few, and thus more difficult to remove. Were you expecting I would take you out to a spring-green meadow sprinkled with morning dew and wildflowers while I danced naked around you? Then, *poof*, you would be rid of me?"

He did not want to be rid of her. That thought screamed in his thoughts, louder than the roar of a raging forest fire. He took her hands in his, hoping to banish the sadness from her eyes. "I find that I do not want to be rid of you, but I do like the idea of you dancing naked in the woods. It's a better idea than consulting a group of white-haired elders. Can we try that first?"

He smiled at the image of them in the forest, wanting to undo her hair and watch as it tumbled over her bare skin. He wasn't so interested in the meadow and flowers, but the naked part sounded pretty good. She was beautiful and quick witted and a woman who would never need spells or potions to hold a man entranced. He wondered if she realized the potency of her appeal. No man breathing was immune to her charms.

Under the watchful gaze of the moon, her cheeks blushed, and her mouth turned up at the corners in a smile. "You are incorrigible."

His smile broadened. "And you are reading my mind again."

"It is hard not to. It is shouting."

Not wanting to let go of their easy banter, he leaned toward her, taking in her unique fragrance, a mixture of sun and surf. When she was near, the world seemed a kinder, gentler place, full of hope and possibilities. "Could we do that? The dancing naked part?"

"Maybe. If I liked you. Which I do not." The sparkle in her eyes told him she was lying through her perfect mouth.

He fingered one of her curls that had already fallen loose from the ribbon. "Why haven't you asked me to remove my brand?"

Her lips parted. "I…" Her response was cut short.

He sensed something or someone moving toward them.

Morgan glanced toward the shadows behind him. "We are being watched."

Rowan shielded her as he turned to face the intruder. "Show yourself."

Sorsha emerged from around a parked car, moving with the grace of a runway model. Although he'd asked Sorsha for help at The Inferno, this wasn't exactly what he'd had in mind. He wasn't surprised she'd found him, though. Her network of vamps always knew the whereabouts of everyone in the magical community.

Sorsha gasped, and her velvet black eyes widened in surprise as she dipped her head in reverence. "Milady. I didn't know you would be here. I see clearly the connection you and Rowan share, and if you heard that we… It was a long time ago, and Rowan means nothing to me. Less than nothing. A mistake. He means less to me than a dung beetle. A diseased rodent."

Rowan interrupted Sorsha's litany, holding up his hand in surrender. "I get it. I'm pond scum."

Morgan winked at him before turning toward Sorsha. The quality of her voice embraced the calm and even timber of a leader. "Sorsha, your relationship with Rowan is in the past and I was pleased to learn that it ended amicably. Cassandra has told me of your efforts to bring stability in your community. You are a strong and capable leader. It is an honor to meet you at last. We appreciate your willingness to help us."

Sorsha inclined her head. "I thank you for your kind words. We fight the same enemy. Vlad has never hidden his desire to see my people exterminated. We were honored when Cassandra asked for our help."

Morgan placed her hand on Sorsha's shoulder. "Whatever we find out, know that the female Wizards will not desert you. We are in this together. You have my word." Morgan's voice was framed in light humor. "If you change your mind about Rowan, know that he is not mine to lose or keep."

"Are you kidding me?" Rowan stepped between the two women, a dangerous move, but he felt he didn't have a choice. "Unless I'm mistaken, we're not at a Bealtaine Fertility Festival. Which means I'm the one who chooses, not you."

Morgan lifted a perfect eyebrow as her red lips curled into a seductive smile. "Male Wizards are so adorable when they're talking nonsense, don't you agree, Sorsha? The choice was mutual."

Morgan was right, of course, but Rowan considered pointing out that vamps rarely gave their victims a choice, but now was not the time to make that distinction.

If Sorsha was to be believed, she was trying to rectify that scenario. Plus, Morgan trusted Sorsha to fight alongside them against Vlad, and Sun Tzu's statement that "The enemy of my enemy is my friend" was as true today as it was over four thousand years ago.

Rowan let out a breath. "We are here to find out if there is a connection between Vlad and Zacharias's warehouse. According to AJ, there is a change of security guards at midnight. For added measures, she also hacked into Zacharias's security system and programmed it to shut down. I don't know how long it will take to find evidence Zacharias is working with Vlad. If it gets too close to sunrise, we'll understand, Sorsha, if you must leave."

"As I told milady, this is not just your fight anymore, Fire Wizard. Since the truce, many of my people have mated with Wizards. Their children are targets of this insidious poison as well. My people and I will take care of the security, and before you ask, we won't kill them, just render them unconscious. As far as sunrise is concerned, we'll help you as long as we are able. Happy hunting."

****

Rowan always cringed when a vamp said, "Happy hunting," but he didn't have a choice. He'd have to trust that she was a vamp of her word and her people wouldn't murder innocents.

Morgan beside him, they used AJ's keys and the directions she'd given him to unlock the front door and enter the warehouse. Before continuing, he paused. "Morgan, are you sure you still want to do this? There's no reason for you to try to find the files. You could wait outside with Sorsha."

"It will go faster if we both search."

Logic and courage in a beautiful woman were as irresistible as they were annoying. "What if I can't protect you?"

"I'll let you know when I need protection." It was not so much a rebuff as a statement.

She was his equal. He was not sure how he felt about that. Yes, he did. He gritted his teeth, fighting the impulse to kiss her. Instead, he headed toward the staircase and Zacharias's office.

Rowan clicked on a small pinpoint flashlight to guide their way up a metal staircase, climbing slowly to keep their steps from echoing over the vacant warehouse.

Zacharias's office wasn't what Rowan had expected. Instead of mahogany, brass and priceless artwork, there were used metal filing cabinets, a desk that looked like it had been purchased at a garage sale, and mismatched chairs. The view out the office window was of a seedy-looking parking lot instead of Puget Sound or the Cascade Mountains. The scene painted the picture of a struggling business, and AJ had said there were inconsistencies in the accounts.

On paper it looked like Zacharias's company was barely making its payroll. Rowan believed that Lyons would be proud of his daughter. From the details in the information she'd collected in a short period of time, it was obvious she'd paid attention to how her father investigated cases.

In AJ's undercover work, she'd learned Zacharias might not spend his money on his office space or expensive suits, but he liked his toys. She'd overheard him bragging about the yachts, the seaplanes, and the sports cars he kept in his daughter's name. Either his business was more successful than it appeared, or he had something on the side, something he didn't want exposed.

It was tedious work and a mountain of files to sort through. Rowan checked Zacharias's desk and Morgan started searching through the filing cabinets. Hours after they'd started, scarlet rays of sun stole through the blinds, announcing the dawn. They were running out of time. Sorsha would have to pull her people from their posts any minute now. He tried the bottom desk drawer. It was locked. Reaching for his knife, he pried it open. Jammed in the drawer were files with handwritten labels.

Without warning, the office door banged open. Three armed men dressed in black rushed into the room, pointing automatic weapons. Why hadn't Sorsha taken care of these thugs, or at least alerted them? Had she been overpowered as well?

Rowan had suspected that if Zacharias was working with Vlad, they would have hired paranormal mercenaries who could overwhelm the vamps. Rowan didn't want to consider the possibility that the vamps might have betrayed him and Morgan. He needed to start trusting.

The security guards opened fire, showering the room with metal rain.

Rowan took a bullet in his shoulder as he dove toward Morgan, cradled her in his arms, and pulled her behind the desk. "Stay here."

"You are hurt."

"Stay," he repeated.

Like a fire that erupts from an explosion, Rowan rose from behind the desk, sending a wall of flames toward his attackers. They screamed and fell back, but they kept firing. The sound of the bullets melded with that of more footsteps on the stairs—Zacharias's reinforcements were on their way.

He could hold them off, maybe even defeat them, but risking Morgan's life was something he wasn't prepared to do.

She was pulling the files out of Zacharias's desk drawer and stuffing them into her jacket. "What's the plan?" she said over her shoulder.

"I'm working on it."

An explosion blew the windows out as flames ravaged the warehouse.

Sorsha, the side of her face burned, and her clothes torn, burst into Zacharias's office with two vamps at her side. "What the hell are you two still doing here? We have the warehouse timed to blow in a matter of seconds."

Morgan touched Sorsha's face. "That looks painful. What happened?"

"Got too close to the sun when I was downstairs making sure none of Vlad's goons escaped. Now, unless you and Rowan can regrow body parts that are ripped from their sockets, I suggest you run for your lives."

There was not a trace of fear in Morgan's voice. "I like your plan."

In one fluid burst of speed, Rowan grabbed Zacharias's chair and hurled it through the window. He shielded Morgan with his body as glass blanketed the room. The surprise tactic worked, stunning the guards for a split second, giving Rowan the time he needed. He caught Morgan's hand and they raced for the opening and jumped through the window to the ground.

Chapter Thirty-Two

Escaping from Zacharias's security guards was easier than Morgan had thought. She'd forgotten how fast Rowan was when he summoned the power of his Wizard fire. The more pressing issue lay ahead. Had they been followed to Sorsha's house on Capitol Hill?

Before entering the warehouse, Morgan had shared her concern with Sorsha about a safe house in the event they were attacked. She hadn't wanted them to return to her apartment, as she was afraid of being followed, placing AJ in danger. Sorsha offered her place, and since the sun was up, the vamps were underground.

She set her tea down on the large mahogany table in the center of the bedchamber where she had brought the injured Rowan to tend his gunshot wound. He was resting comfortably, but her concern remained. He took too many chances with his life. In many ways he was as reckless as the immortal vampire Sorsha.

A breeze from the open window disturbed the crystals of a solid gold chandelier that hung from the ceiling. Floor-to-ceiling windows opened onto a parklike garden where a pair of peacocks unfurled their feathers. The birds were an expression of Sorsha's wealth. She wasn't just wealthy; she was easily in the top one percent of the world's richest.

"Where are we?" Rowan asked, pushing to a sitting position on the four-poster bed and lightly rubbing the bandage over his shoulder. "The last thing I remember is entering a mansion that looked like it had been built by one of Seattle's founding fathers."

"Make that one of the founding mothers. Sorsha has lived in Seattle for a while. You passed out soon after we arrived. You are a Wizard with superhuman abilities to heal quickly, but the amount of blood you lost from the gunshot wound took its toll. I've cleaned and dressed the wound, but you should rest."

"Any word from the vamp? She said she'd take care of Zacharias's guards."

Morgan shook her head. "I haven't heard. There must be a reason. But I expect when the sun goes down, she'll contact us. You changed the subject. How are you feeling?"

"I'm okay. What did you find?"

Morgan handed Rowan one of the folders she had taken from Zacharias's desk and sank down in a chair opposite him. "You should read this. As you can see, the title page reads, *Sodom and Gomorrah*."

"Catchy title."

She smiled. "I thought so as well. We must give humans credit for their provocative way with words. Inside the folder is a list of cities across the globe, and on the line beside each city are rating charts and a box indicating the date for extermination unless signs of redemption are found."

Rowan whistled through his teeth. "Bloody freaking hell. Wizards dedicated their lives to protecting humans. But there is a twisted reality to it. They formed a truce with humans and it's looking as though they were betrayed. With Wizards out of the way, the Talons could do whatever they wanted without the Wizard guardrails stopping them. Do they give a reason for their genocide? Humans also like to create a reason for why they wage war."

"Their excuse is in the title, *Sodom and Gomorrah*. They mention the ancient cities numerous times and the reason that God destroyed them was because the people were evil, concerned only with their own pleasure, and no longer believed in a higher power."

Rowan sat up straighter. "The Talons have long believed they should have the right to root out wrongdoers. It's one of their consistent mantras. Over the centuries, there have been many names they petitioned to be killed, in the name of cleansing the world of evil. Wizards and reasonable humans required proof and the rule of law. It sounds to me as though the Talons want to circumvent that longstanding edict."

Morgan closed the file. "It's worse than that. The Talons may have moved from punishing individuals they feel are immoral or unworthy to dealing with entire cities, states and countries. If I'm reading these charts correctly, they want to destroy places they deem unworthy by using a planned series of natural disasters, blaming each catastrophe on climate change or global warming."

"It's all making sense. That's why they brought in Vlad and the Grey Council. They need the Wizards to manipulate the weather and make it look like a natural disaster. Vlad thinks he's playing Constantine, but it's the other way around. When the Talons have what they want, they will use the Oculist drug to murder anyone who stands in their way." Rowan rested his elbows on his knees and held his head in both hands. "Genius. Is there a timeline?"

"The first phase begins this summer." She left her chair and knelt beside him, placing the back of her hand on his forehead. "You're ice cold."

"I feel like shit. Of course, learning the Talons mean to bring about Armageddon doesn't help. Hard to face the fact that Vlad has turned psycho. He was never a good guy, but this is another level. I'm hoping he doesn't know the true end game. But it would be like him to think that if he does what the Talons want, they won't turn against him. We'll have to find a way to bring this to the Grey Council without Vlad finding out." Rowan clenched his jaw. "I think it's this damn bullet in my shoulder. It's giving me chills. It feels like I've been swimming with polar bears."

Morgan examined Rowan's wound. "I don't understand it. I removed the bullet and cleaned and washed the wound."

Rowan squeezed his eyes shut. His expression shadowed in pain. "You should leave. I think the bullet contained poison, or else I'm still suffering from the side effects of exposure to Oculist power in Stryker's house." He grimaced, holding his stomach. "Either way, you're not safe. Promise me you will kill me before I can harm you."

She brushed hair off his forehead. His skin was like ice. "Rowan. You must know by now that I won't leave you."

"Morgan…" He doubled over in pain and fell to the floor, unconscious.

Silence sliced through the air like shards of glass.

Rowan had said, "…kill me before I can harm you." His words changed everything. He thought not of himself, but of her. He had given up, but she would not, could not.

She was glad Rowan had lost consciousness. He wouldn't have agreed to her suggestion of where she planned to go for help. She knew asking the Grey Council was out of the question. Their solution would be swift. They'd order Rowan killed. The only option was Cassandra and the Trolls' compound. They might turn her down for the same reason the Grey Council would, but she had to try.

She reached for her cell phone, ordered a taxi, and prayed it wasn't already too late. She also sent a message to Wiz. She couldn't do this alone.

****

The ride in the taxi to the Trolls' compound had been uneventful. Now, the difficult part began. "Stop here," she said to the taxi driver and handed him cash that exceeded the fare. Wiz bounded from the cab and headed for a stand of trees and bushes as the driver helped her with Rowan.

"Are you sure this is where you want to go? We're out in the middle of nowhere. All I see are trees and an old rusted-out truck. Your man needs a hospital."

The man was middle-aged, balding, with a wife he loved and three children he adored. Morgan had read all of that in the taxi driver's thoughts on the drive from Sorsha's house on Capitol Hill to the Trolls' hidden compound. He was the kind of man who wouldn't leave a stranded woman and an injured man out in the middle of nowhere. He would have to have a nudge.

She rested her hand on his arm, gently sending soothing words into his thoughts. She told him everything would be okay. She suggested that he'd seen an ambulance pull up and medics help Rowan into the vehicle. For good measure, she placed in his thoughts that he'd overheard one of the medics say that Rowan would be okay.

The driver stepped back and nodded to the woman. "You have a good day. I'm glad your man will be okay."

As the taxi drove off, trees parted and the entrance to the compound opened of its own accord. She fervently hoped that when she'd told the driver Rowan would recover, it hadn't been wishful thinking.

The Trolls were known for healing. Their skills exceeded even those of female Wizards. The magical community praised their goodwill to help others. There was only one group they refused to give their aid—male Wizards. She was taking a big risk coming here. She was unsure of the reception Rowan would have.

Cassandra's voice entered Morgan's thoughts with tight urgency. *"As always, your presence here is a great honor, but why did you bring a Fire Wizard to us? He will do us harm."*

Morgan was prepared for Cassandra's reaction. That she was speaking in her mind did not bode well. *"I am in grave need of your healing touch."*

"What of yours?"

"Rowan was poisoned and is beyond my skill."

Cassandra appeared in the entrance of the compound, flanked by two guards, her thoughts hidden.

Morgan waited for Cassandra's answer. Cassandra was well within her right to refuse to help him. Rowan lay on the ground, his face turned away from them, his breathing shallow. Male Wizards and Trolls had a long-standing agreement to stay out of each other's way. The centuries-old feud traced back to one incident that had never been resolved.

"Cassandra, please trust me. He will not harm you."

"We trust you, milady, but male Wizards are another matter. Trusting them is not easy to do after a lifetime of broken promises. Trusting them costs us lives. Compassion was bred from them. Duty to the Talons and the Grey Council is all they know. You must seek another healer. No one here will risk touching him."

Wiz loped from around the trees, barked and moved closer to Rowan, licking his face. The dog sat back on his haunches and held Cassandra's gaze.

The green aura surrounding Cassandra deepened to emerald. She glided toward the dog and stroked the animal's fur. *"There you are, my pet. I had wondered where you had gone. Really? The Fire Wizard saved your life? Extraordinary. Yes, of course, that changes everything. No, no, calm yourself. Forgive us, milady. We will do what we can for your Fire Wizard."*

A group of male Trolls emerged from the shadows and carried Rowan toward the compound as Morgan followed close behind. *"I am grateful, but why did you change your mind so quickly?"*

"This Fire Wizard risked exposure to save an animal's life. As I'm sure you are aware, Wiz is no ordinary shapeshifter. If he vouches for Rowan, that is enough for us."

Chapter Thirty-Three

A veil of muted golden light draped over Rowan as green and white images glowed beyond his reach. He floated close to the surface of awareness as though partially submerged in a tub of warm water. Even the gunshot wound on his shoulder had retreated to a dull throb. If he was dead, maybe this was the fate of soulless Wizards. So far, not so bad, unless you counted the sulfur smell and the fact his body felt like someone had used it for target practice.

The other reality was that he existed in the in-between time that had gripped his brother before he shapeshifted into his dragon form. Pain, not from Rowan's wounds but the one throbbing from the empty place in his heart, flamed over him. Could Stryker still recognize him? Rowan knew so little about what Stryker had become. He knew only that his brother had the ability to shapeshift into a dragon form and had the power of invisibility. Those with these powers were called Dragon Wizards but had not been seen since the war between Dragons and Wizards.

Would Rowan evolve into a Dragon Wizard as well and seek vengeance on the magical community?

Better if he was dead.

He focused on the possibility Morgan had discovered a way to heal him, and he tried to remember the last events before he lost consciousness at Sorsha's house.

He remembered finding out who was processing the Oculist stones and poisoning Wizards. The files in Zacharias's office supported the man's plan to start an old-fashioned Middle Ages style genocide, in which those the Talons deemed unworthy would be eradicated.

The files also revealed that Zacharias's deceased wife was a Water Wizard, and they'd had a college-aged daughter, but there was no mention of whether she had inherited any powers. Perhaps Zacharias felt he had had to comply with Vlad and the Talons to protect his daughter. She might not have powers, but half-breeds were considered an abomination by both the Talons and the hard-core members of the Grey Council.

The mystery of who was behind the male Wizard deaths was solved. The next was finding who had murdered Morgan's sister Wizards on the island. That one could prove even more difficult—and a moot point if what he suspected was actually happening. He had to face the fact that the most logical reason he was still alive was his connection to dragons. If true, that meant he would likely share the same fate as his brother. Stryker had also lingered in a dreamlike sleep before he'd turned. Was that what was happening to him?

Was this the in-between time before you lost your soul but not your body?

"He's awake." Voices, soft and feminine, drifted in the air around him.

But he wasn't ready! He wondered if that was always the complaint when a person knew they were dying.

He started to rise.

Strong hands pushed him back down into liquid

warmth.

"Do not move." The voice belonged to Morgan. He ruled out being dead. If this were the afterlife, Morgan wouldn't be with him in the same dark abyss. She'd be in the light. The other option hung over him like a smothering shroud. "Am I...a..." His voice felt raw. He worked through the pain. "Have I turned?" Her image wavered in the golden haze, preventing him from seeing her clearly. Something blocked his vision. He blinked and felt a light fabric over his eyes.

Panic rose within him. "Why are my eyes covered? What's wrong?"

"We shall find out soon." Her words didn't fill him with warm fuzziness.

"What's wrong?" he repeated.

Morgan pulled his hands away from his face and began removing the bandages from his eyes. "Cassandra wants you to be still while she examines you. Can you do that for me?"

She was talking to him like a small child. Maybe that was a good sign. He didn't sense she feared him. Of course, she hadn't feared his brother, either. Rowan wished he hadn't remembered that little detail. As the last bandage was removed, light streamed into the small quarters and he squinted against the sunshine, waiting for his eyes to adjust, and noticed two things right away. The first was that he was sitting in a metal tub of mud, and the second was that he was inside a gypsy-style wagon.

"Holy shit."

The walls curved in an arch above him. Murals of life in a medieval farming village swept over the bright yellow walls. An open cupboard displaying pottery and cooking utensils was attached on the wall to his right, while a bed covered with blankets in patchworked prints of purples, reds and greens was tucked against the wall to his left. Completing the feeling of an otherworldly experience was the woman standing before him.

An attractive, petite woman, no more than four feet tall, dressed in a gypsy costume and surrounded by a green aura, moved closer to him. She looked familiar. Where had he seen her? Oh, yes. Vlad's island…and she was a Troll.

He gripped the sides of the tub and turned toward Morgan. "You brought me to a Troll healer? They don't heal my kind, they kill us."

A voice entered his thoughts, pushing past the barriers as though they were made of tissue paper. "*Ease your concern. My name is Cassandra, and you are with us now, and safe. We mean you no harm.*"

"Get the hell out of my head."

The woman pressed her lips together. *"Does he always swear so much?"*

Morgan merely nodded and smiled.

Her reaction annoyed him, but he kept his comments to himself. The female Troll had healed him, and he was behaving ungratefully.

The petite woman smiled, giving him a slight nod. She'd read his thoughts again. When she'd finished her examination, she slid Morgan a glance and nodded. Although they didn't say a word, their expressions were animated, and without doubt they were communicating telepathically.

He felt like an outsider. As he sat up straighter, thick mud sloshed over the sides of the tub and the smell of warm rotten eggs made his stomach churn. "Damn." He clenched his jaw down to bite off a string of additional swear words that would have eased his frustration but would have been disrespectful since he realized the Troll who had saved his life disapproved.

"What's the verdict?" he said. "Will I live? Turn into a dragon? Scurry away like a rabbit?" He'd made the last comments to see if they were listening.

Cassandra turned to leave and, as she did, she glanced over her shoulder. Her thoughts wove into his. *"You have not turned, Fire Wizard, although you must avoid further exposure to the Oculist poison in the future. Twice you have cheated its dark purpose. You will not escape a third time."*

"Thank you." The overused phrase seemed inadequate for what Cassandra had done and what she'd risked. There was no love lost between Trolls and male Wizards. "I'll not forget your kindness."

"You'd better not."

When the door shut behind Cassandra, Morgan moved toward him, bringing the crisp fragrance of salt seas and tropical breezes with her. Rowan drank in her fresh scent and felt more at ease. He was beginning to believe her emotions and her scent were linked.

Morgan smoothed the hair from his forehead. "Cassandra advises you stay here until tomorrow."

"She doesn't like me."

"You are correct."

"Yet I'm alive because of a Troll?"

She tilted her head, smiling. "You saved Donningale."

"I'm pretty sure I don't know who you're talking about."

"You know him by the name Wiz. Cassandra was very grateful. Evidently, you're not as much of a monster as you'd like everyone to believe."

"Saving the mutt was a momentary lapse."

"That is what I told them."

Rowan fingered the bandage over his shoulder. The wound was still tender. "I'm guessing the bullet casings were filled with Oculist powder and that's how my eyes were infected." When she nodded, Rowan reached for her hand, sloshing mud over the side of the tub again. The mud bubbled. "What is that smell?"

She hadn't pulled away. He liked the way her mouth turned up in a smile that touched her eyes, making them glitter like starlight. "It is the medicine Cassandra used to heal you."

What's in it?"

"Believe me, you do not want to know."

He gently squeezed her hand. "I'm glad you didn't give up on me."

"Would you have given up on me if you had to choose between me and duty?"

He knew the response he was trained to give. The one that spoke of loyalty to only the Talons and the Grey Council. Everyone else was expendable, and that included female Wizards as well as male Wizards. Male Wizards were trained to protect their females, but only if it didn't conflict with the wishes of the leadership.

He drew her closer until she was pressed against the side of the tub. She was waiting for his answer. She had saved his life and deserved the truth. "I don't know, Morgan." He expected her to slap him, verbally take him to task, or drown him.

"Your doubt is a first step on a long road." Morgan reached for a folded towel and held it against her chest. "Your uncertainty would not please the Grey Council."

"You got that right. They'd be pissed. Probably have me killed on principle." He gripped the side of the tub and shoved to a standing position, grimacing when pain shot through his body. "That hurt."

"Cassandra said you might have a little pain for a day or two. Is it very bad?"

"Pain of the body I can understand," he said reaching for the towel to wrap around his waist. "It's all the other stuff I can't seem to get right."

As he secured the towel, his muscles flexed and rippled over Rowan's bare chest and shoulders. Morgan felt her face heat as sensual memories flooded over her. "It pleases me you are being honest. It is a start," she managed, refolding a blanket. She was mesmerized by the way his eyes warmed like a banked fire as his gaze touched hers.

"Any chance I can get a shower?"

"Probably not." Her breath caught in her throat. He had moved closer to her and her skin flamed under his scrutiny as the tight quarters of the wagon closed in around her. "The reason you're in the wagon is that although Cassandra agreed to heal you, she won't allow you in the house. I'll have someone bring fresh water and a clean bathtub."

"You're leaving? What if I have a relapse?"

"I will not be long, and Renegade is outside standing guard. Let him know if the pain increases, or if you think you are losing your eyesight again, and he will send for help."

"Why do I have a guard?"

She lifted an eyebrow.

He heaved a sigh. "Got it. Trolls don't trust Wizards, and I'm on probation. I can live with that. Still not crazy about the whole bath experience, though. I'm more of a shower kind of guy—unless you join me," he said with a boyish grin.

She backed toward the door of the wagon until the handle dug into her back. She wanted to stay but knew his presence here was precarious. If she indulged her desires, Cassandra might interpret it to mean that she had been enchanted by the Fire Wizard and was not thinking clearly.

"I could spray you down with a hose."

He cocked an eyebrow. "Promise?"

"I was kidding."

"Too late. I'm going to hold you to it."

Her heart beat so rapidly she thought for sure he must hear its thunder. If she didn't leave in the next few seconds, she knew she never would. She forced herself to turn the door handle. "For now, you will have to be content with the tub."

Chapter Thirty-Four

Morgan left the gypsy wagon, pausing along the path leading to the mansion to catch her breath. She placed cool hands against her warm face. Being so close to Rowan made it hard to breathe. She reminded herself that although he bent the rules when he saved Wiz, and outright broke them by not disclosing her whereabouts, she would be a fool to trust him completely. He admitted he was wavering, and that gave her hope, but she worried about how long that would hold. What would convince him that he had placed his trust in the wrong people?

All she had to do was keep a strong wall around her heart for a little while longer. She shook her head slowly. Who was she trying to fool? The barrier around her heart had begun to crumble the moment she saw him the first night of Bealtaine.

Regaining her composure, she hurried to the mansion. From the water side, shielded by a thick stand of trees, the mansion was a massive four-story building. Beveled glass windows ran the length of the house, with designs of birds and flowers embedded in the brick and on the thick shake roof. The air was infused with a rich cacophony of sights, sounds and intoxicating smells. Gypsy wagons lined one side of the lawn leading to the shore, while bazaar booths lined the other.

Cassandra waited for Morgan at the back entrance. "The young Wizardlings are gathering in the solarium and await your instructions." She paused as her mouth formed a hard line. "How is the Fire Wizard coping with his new surroundings?"

"He wants a shower. Thank you again. Rowan would have died or turned, without your help." A young man and woman, dressed in traditional gypsy costumes and holding hands, rushed past Morgan toward one of the outdoor bazaars, reminding her of the upcoming celebrations. Morgan frowned. "Cassandra, do you think it is wise to have the Freedom Celebration, under the circumstances?"

"If we did not, it would draw attention. This is the anniversary of our independence from the Talons and the Grey Council. To cancel the celebrations would draw undue speculation, and I worry the news might make it back to the magical community." She drew Morgan toward the solarium. "The spirit of the celebration is acceptance. With your assurance that the Fire Wizard is here in peace, and Wiz's account of how he saved his life, my people have agreed to allow the Fire Wizard to attend our celebration."

"His name is Rowan."

Cassandra shrugged. "I know full well his name. Have you noticed that when you attach a name to something it becomes real? You may deny that you have given him your trust, but your heart and the look in your eyes betray you. I cannot so easily forgive centuries of his kind's persecution. A few good deeds will not always lead to redemption. He must leave after the celebrations."

Morgan could not fault Cassandra's logic or her right to expel Rowan from the Trolls' compound. What bothered her more was Cassandra's reference to trust.

Since the moment she first met Rowan all those years ago, she had kept her heart at a distance, wrapping it in a barrier built on the belief he could not be trusted with its care. He had betrayed that trust, and once lost, it was hard to rebuild.

In the last few days, she had begun to believe trust could be rebuilt after all. Rowan had delivered on his promise to discover who and what was killing the male Wizards. She knew he would succeed with his vow to find who'd murdered her sisters.

Cassandra was wrong. Words combined with deeds were a powerful indication of the fate of the soul. Rowan was changing. He had expressed doubts regarding the Talons and the Grey Council. She glanced back through the leaded glass window toward the wagon and prayed that, when war came, he would make the right choice.

****

The Trolls' Freedom Celebration Festival had begun in the compound's solarium. Glass doors opened to frame the expansive grounds that dipped gently down to Lake Washington and welcomed a warm breeze. Lavender-and-rose-scented air crackled with energy and magic. Morgan chanted under her breath, gaining strength from the ancient words while trying to distance herself from her troubling conversation with Cassandra.

Morgan nodded to each Wizardling in turn, encouraging them to repeat the words that would create a powerful spell she hoped would help her defeat Vlad. He had murdered Caitlin and possibly countless other female Wizards. He would have a reason for the killings. Men like Vlad always did. They believed they were the hero of their story. But his reign of terror must end.

Each Wizardling took turns applying body makeup

to arms, shoulders and face. They used brushes dipped in glittering paint made from white and rose gold, applying Celtic spirals, images of dragonflies, unicorns and wildflowers. Pearl-white lights sparkled over the room as the magical words took life, recounting the tales of strong women warriors and powerful sorceresses. The young Wizardlings' skin glistened as though sprinkled with gold dust.

Her spirits soared. Together they created an elaborate spell that swirled around Morgan, increasing her power. She hoped it would be enough.

****

The young Wizardlings had done well. Only time would tell if Morgan had the courage and magical strength to capture Vlad and turn him over to the Grey Council for a reckoning. Her next step was exposing the Talons' plan to destroy Wizards.

She inhaled the air along the banks of the Trolls' compound, smoothing her hands over the long skirt Cassandra had given her to wear for the occasion. Cassandra had insisted she wear a costume more appropriate to the festivities. At first Morgan had resisted. But the ankle-length blue skirt and white short-sleeve blouse made her feel more like herself than the confining long pants and sweaters she'd worn over the past few days.

The compound was infused with a rich cacophony of sights, sounds and intoxicating smells transporting her to another time and place. A gentle time of laughter, long walks and endless nights. The Talons and the Grey Council could learn a thing or two about life and living from these people. Everything about this place welcomed new possibilities.

Morgan hesitated outside the wagon where she'd left Rowan a few hours ago. She wondered if he really understood the mistrust male Wizards provoked in the magical community. Rowan and his fellow Wizards thought they were respected for how they enforced the dictates and laws of the Talons and the Grey Council. The emotion was closer to fear and resentment. Cassandra promised her community would keep their distance and, for Morgan's sake, treat Rowan with respect. The rest would be up to him.

Morgan's hand poised to knock, but Rowan opened the door before she had the chance. Framed in the arched door, filling up the space, he seemed taller somehow, more handsome, more open. Cassandra had seen to it that his clothes were clean and pressed and, despite Rowan's claim he preferred showers, it looked like the bath had relaxed him. The worry and deep frown lines around his forehead and eyes had eased, so he looked younger.

His appearance stole her breath and her words of greeting.

He, on the other hand, seemed poised for conversation as he joined her outside. "Thank all the ancient gods and goddess you are here. Renegade and I ran out of things to say about two hours ago and decided to play cards." His grin was infectious and made her smile as he stepped aside to let Renegade pass, and then exited the gypsy wagon. "We were discussing all we knew about women. A short conversation."

"Agreed," Renegade added with a wink. "Rowan, wish me luck."

Morgan studied Rowan's expression as Renegade jogged down the path toward the mansion. There was something different about Rowan she could not quite place. The friendship building between Renegade and Rowan was just as surprising and every bit as welcome. "Where is Renegade going?"

"To woo Cassandra. You look beautiful. New clothes?"

Morgan was taken by surprise again. His compliment lacked the smoothness of a practiced Casanova, which both pleased her and made his words more potent. Her face warmed under his steady gaze.

"Thank you, kind sir, but I must say how surprised I am by the compliment, as well as your transformation. You seem—happy."

"It's this place, I think, or maybe this is what happens when a man cheats death. I can't explain it either. I also never play cards. It's been an odd day."

A comfortable silence misted over her as she stood bathed in his gaze. She had spent what seemed a lifetime debating whether to deny or accept their connection, believing it a mere product of magic and glamour. Today felt like they were starting over. She wove her arm through his, leading him toward the center of the crowd gathered around an outdoor stage.

"I'm curious. You opened the door before I knocked. Were you expecting me?"

"Renegade said you were coming. They read minds no matter what type of barriers you erect to keep them out. I found out the hard way. Probably why Trolls are so good at playing cards. Where are we going?"

"You shall see."

Chapter Thirty-Five

Morgan found a vacant space beneath the umbrella of a maple tree and spread a blanket on the ground with a clear view of the stage. Other couples were doing the same as everyone vied for the best place to view the festival's performances.

The day was pleasantly warm, and the sun shone over the water like sparklers on the Fourth of July. The lively notes of dueling flutes added a lightness to the air as the set props, platforms and a backdrop of live trees made to resemble a dense forest were arranged on the stage.

"Morgan, if you're asking me to watch a play, you must know, plays are not my thing. I'm more the adrenaline-rush car-chase-movie kind of guy."

"You also told me you preferred showers to baths. I'm hoping what you are about to see will change your mind. Come sit beside me. This one is very special. In ancient times, Trolls did not keep a written history. They were a nomadic race and felt their records could easily be stolen or lost. Instead, they handed down their history in the form of plays. This one recreates the cause of the rift between Wizards and Trolls. It is always preformed at the annual Freedom Celebration." Something in Rowan's expression gave away his unease. She put her hand on his arm. "Do not give me that look. Just watch and learn."

She knew bringing him here was a risk. It was a good sign that he and Renegade had spent so much time together without trying to kill each other. She hoped bringing Rowan to the celebrations would also prove positive. Many might not like that he was here, but it was a risk worth taking if what he learned today helped him shift into more tolerance and awareness.

Cymbals clashed, bringing a hush over the crowd. When it was quiet, a young man and woman burst onto the stage through a wall of paper flowers. The man was dressed in tan breeches, a white linen shirt and a green vest, mirroring the gypsy style of the clothing worn by the crowd. In contrast, the woman wore a formfitting ankle-length black gown, decorated with crescent moons and silver stars. The gown resembled those worn by female mage Wizards during the Middle Ages. The woman cradled an infant baby doll wrapped in a blanket. The couple, their expressions shadowed by fear, wove around the trees on the stage, pausing only long enough to glance over their shoulders.

Morgan rose to her knees to make sure she could see more clearly. She knew the tale of these star-crossed lovers by heart, but each time she witnessed the story, her understanding of the power of love grew. Originally the play was not scheduled until tomorrow night. Morgan had asked Cassandra to have it performed today, before Rowan left, hoping he would reexamine more of his preconceived notions concerning the magical community and his place in it.

Another cymbal crashed over the crowd and silenced the last remnants of conversation.

A third actor appeared on the stage. The newest character was bare-chested and wore dark trousers.

Black tattoos of flames and Celtic swirls decorated his shoulders and right arm, marking him as a Fire Wizard. He wielded a sword in one hand and a dagger in the other. The tattooed warrior shouted for the couple to halt and for the Troll to lay down his weapons. Then came the demand for the woman and child to return with him.

The woman turned slowly toward the Fire Wizard. Her chin raised, she pulled the child closer and entwined her fingers in her lover's hand. Her wordless response was a powerful rebuke.

The Fire Wizard roared out his frustration and anger and lunged forward.

In a lightning-quick move, the male Troll drew his blade, pulled the woman behind him, and blocked the attack. The Troll was protecting the woman he loved, no matter the odds, no matter the cost. Morgan stole a glance in Rowan's direction. Like all those in the crowd, he was straining to see the drama unfolding on stage, pulled into the primal struggle as old as time.

The actors' swords clashed. Their weapons might be made from wood, but the intensity of the fight and the determination in their expressions vibrated through the hushed onlookers as though they were witness to a real battle.

The Fire Wizard drove the Troll backward toward the end of the stage made to resemble a cliff.

A collective gasp escaped from the crowd.

The death blow was only moments away.

The Fire Wizard's sword swung in a wide arc over his head, its song slicing through the air in a deadly melody. When the sword made its descent, the woman jumped in front of her lover and into its path.

An expression of horror gripped the Fire Wizard on

stage as he realized too late what he had done.

Clutching streamers of red ribbon in one hand and her child in the other, the woman collapsed to the ground, her breathing labored.

Enraged and fueled by the need to save his family, the Troll lunged toward the Fire Wizard. Their combined war cries tore through the crowd and their battle increased in tempo and intensity as both raced toward their destiny. Neither gave ground. Both believed they were on the side of right. Blood red ribbons streamed from their weapons, marking the wounds each sustained.

The injured woman, using the last precious reserves of her strength, raised her arm, transferring her remaining strength to her lover. He shouted a protest for her to take it back, not to give her life for his, but it was too late. The power had been transferred. In a burst of speed, gained from his one true love and born from the depths of his despair and loss, the Troll struck the fatal blow to the Fire Wizard's heart.

As the Troll stood over the dead Wizard, wavering on his feet, the weight of the wounds to both his heart and his body taking its toll, the victory was bittersweet. He stumbled toward the woman and child, letting the sword drop from his hand and clatter to the ground.

As he knelt beside her, she reached up to place a trembling hand on his face. Her words echoed his. *"I will always love you."*

They bent toward each other and kissed with the tenderness of a final goodbye. Their words lingered like echoes as they died in each other's arms.

Silence, whisper-soft and reverent, suspended over the crowd. Time suspended in the air, the fragments of the lovers' last words on everyone's lips.

Rowan cleared his throat. His voice was low as he cleared his throat again. "What about the baby?"

Tears pooled in her eyes and blurred her vision. That Rowan worried about the baby warmed her heart. The man surprised her at every turn. She brushed a tear away as she nodded toward the stage. "There is more," she whispered.

His reaction was more than she could have ever hoped for. His first instinct was not to the perceived injustice of a female Wizard choosing a Troll for her mate, but the safety of their child. Her heart filled with a new kind of warmth she'd never thought possible.

A small version of a gypsy wagon was making its way slowly across the stage. An old woman, bent with age and dressed in layers of bright clothes, gold bangles jingling from her wrists, walked beside it. She paused for only a moment next to the fallen Wizard and gave him a silent blessing. Turning to the lovers, she covered them with a single cloth of silk embroidered with images that captured the spirit of a spring rainbow. With the crowd holding their breath in watchful anticipation, the old woman gathered the infant in her arms and disappeared inside the wagon.

Silence hung once more over the crowd before they stood and erupted into applause. One by one, both young and old stood to give honor to the performance. All smiled through their tears, clapping and yelling out their praise.

Rowan was on his feet. "What happened to the child? Is the story true?"

"What does your heart tell you?"

"But it isn't possible. A Troll could never defeat a Fire Wizard, even with a female Wizard's help. Nor would a female Wizard mate with a Troll, let alone have a baby by him. And if the impossible occurred, the Grey Council would never allow the child to live. This story suggests the possibility a Troll with Wizard blood survived."

She slipped her hand in his, knowing his swirling question reflected only a small measure of what must be going on in his mind. "And if the tale was true?"

"It has to be some sort of myth." He whispered the words as though trying to convince himself. His gaze lingered on the stage. "But if it were true and the child lived, those descended from the babe are more connected to us than we've been taught."

Morgan placed a feather-soft kiss on his cheek, loving the way his heart was opening. "Never underestimate the power of love. This is but one play dedicated to Troll and, yes, Wizard history. On the final day of the festival, there is a play that recounts how the Trolls rebelled against the Wizards and became a free people."

Strolling minstrels, their ballads of loves lost and won, began to steal through the crowd. Morgan nodded toward the bazaar. Booths decorated in brilliant colors displayed all manner of tempting goods, from clothes, jewelry, and pottery to toys for the children. Exotic smells from the food booths whispered of faraway lands and childhood memories.

The sensuality created at the celebrations revealed the textures of emotions created at the Wizards' week-long festival of Bealtaine, with one major difference—the laughter, freedom of expression, and lightness in everyone's step was genuine. Spells were not needed to assure pleasure and acceptance.

Morgan liked the way her hand fit inside Rowan's. She stole a glance, wanting to know what he was thinking. She could attempt to read his mind and might succeed. This was not the time. He would share his thoughts when he was ready. She could only guess at the conflicts he faced.

A lull at one of the food booths encouraged her to guide him in its direction. The vendor, his face as round and shiny as a brand-new plate, beckoned her with a chocolate ice cream cone, dipped in multicolored sprinkles. "For you, milady, and..." His jolly smile cracked as his eyes widened to perfect moon-shaped orbs, their focus on Rowan. "The...the..." he stammered, each time his voice rising an octave higher.

She was such a fool. Seduced by the music and the goodwill of Cassandra's people, she had forgotten, or rather, had chosen to forget, the underlying currents of the Trolls' distrust of Wizards. Cassandra's people might distrust all male Wizards, but Fire Wizards, as evidenced in the play, were hated and feared above all.

She turned to leave, an apology on her lips for disturbing the vendor. Rowan slipped his hand out of hers and approached the Troll.

"I don't blame you for being startled. This experience is a little strange for me too. My name's Rowan. And yes, I'm a Fire Wizard. For the first time in my life, I feel I should apologize for what and who I am."

The vendor's hand trembled as he handed a cone to Morgan and one to Rowan, his eyes never blinking as a cluster of squealing girls descended on the booth.

Rowan reached into the pocket of his jeans. "How much do I owe you?"

The vender's head shook from side to side in jerky

movement. "I read your thoughts. They are genuine and true and kind. No charge, Fire Wizard." The ice cream vendor turned toward the group of young female Wizardlings.

Morgan placed her hand on his arm and moved Rowan a short distance away as she silently ate her ice cream cone. The exchange between Rowan and the vendor had surprised her, but one good encounter did not ensure another. "When you finish your cone, we should leave."

The cluster of young female Wizards, their cones clutched in their hands, moved in concert away from the vendor and in the direction of Rowan and Morgan. One of them bumped into Rowan, smearing ice cream on his pant leg.

Morgan recognized the child at once. It was the young Wizardling Anne. In wide-eyed surprise, Anne looked at her empty cone, her mouth trembling over losing her ice cream. But when her gaze locked on Rowan's, fear was reflected in her eyes.

Rowan's mouth quirked in a smile. "Don't worry, little one. I'll get you another."

Deidre came rushing over and tugged Anne's arm, her gaze locking on Rowan. "Anne, you are a silly, clumsy goose," she said in a forced whisper. "You bumped into a Fire Wizard. Say you're sorry."

But Anne didn't budge. Her gaze was fixed on Rowan's.

Rowan seemed oblivious as he paid the vendor for an ice cream cone and then handed her the new one. Anne took a lick of her cone. "Thank you. Deidre said you're... Are you a Fire Wizard?"

"Yes, I am."

Anne took another lick, wiping the excess on her sleeve. "You don't seem so scary to me."

"I'm trying hard to change." Rowan laughed, the sound so open and genuine it startled Morgan and a gathering crowd.

Chapter Thirty-Six

The golden morning traveled into the late afternoon on the wings of the festival's merriment, changing color and texture with each hour that passed. Morgan sat on the pier, dangling her feet in the crystal-clear water. A backdrop of laughter wafted toward her from the crowd as her gaze drifted again and again to Rowan. His one act of kindness toward Anne had changed the way the Trolls treated him. All their histories described Fire Wizards as intolerant and unforgiving toward anything or anyone outside their kind. Rowan's single display of patience toward a small child when she'd accidentally bumped into him, spilling her ice cream cone over his pant leg, shifted their perspective.

He had changed.

Or was this the man he always had been? His enormous capacity for compassion and selflessness must have been kept hidden, buried, caged, waiting for the right moment of release.

The role he was assigned at birth to play was designed and shaped by the Talons and the Grey Council and left no room for self-awareness or compassion. In his case, that role was made worse by the circumstances of his low birth. And now, his brother had turned into a Dragon Wizard and might be lost to him. Rowan hadn't spoken of Stryker, and Morgan vowed she would wait until he was ready.

Female Wizards, even in their short life, embraced their individuality and their ability to care deeply for all living things. She feared Rowan, in not mentioning his brother, was trying to bury his feelings. The Talons and the Grey Council tried to curb emotions of any sort, and in part succeeded. Was the real reason the Wizards' leadership first discouraged—and more recently forbade—male and female Wizards to form life partnerships was their fear each would help nurture the other's better selves? If true, then that would answer many unanswered questions.

Rowan joined her and knelt beside her, resting his hand on her shoulder in a companionable way. "You're deep in thought, milady."

Even the texture of his voice was different. Was it this place? There were moments, like now, that the Trolls' compound reminded her of the fabled Scottish story, where a village had been frozen forever in gentler times and awakened for weddings and celebrations once every hundred years. A part of her wished for the enchantment of such a place.

She covered her hand over his, welcoming his warmth. "This is the first time you have called me 'milady.' Are you aware of its meaning?"

He settled next to her, his gaze traveling toward the cityscape of downtown Seattle. Skyscrapers shared the skyline with the city's iconic Space Needle. Vibrant blue waters framed the shore while ferryboats and sailing vessels traversed the Sound at a leisurely pace.

"Renegade told me the title "milady" means one thing in the human's world and quite another one in ours. And when attached to a female Wizard it signifies that she is not only the leader of the female Wizards but the head of the magical community. A heady responsibility. No wonder the Talons and the Grey Council tried to weaken the influence of female Wizards."

She had spent the last few hours focusing on how Rowan had changed. Now she realized she had as well. When he drew attention to what her title stood for, she realized she no longer felt weighed down by the mantle of responsibility she wore. "I'm not alone in this struggle. Many stand with me."

"Spoken like a born leader who understands the value of giving credit to those who are fighting at your side." He tore his gaze from the city to look at her through his dark glasses. "I'm starting to feel unworthy just to be in your presence." A muscle throbbed at his temple. "Why me?"

"You asked me the same question on the island. Do you remember?" She kissed his cheek, struck by how right just being near him felt. "My answer is the same. How could I not?"

He kissed the tips of her fingers, his voice so low she had to lean in closer. "You are a gift I don't deserve."

She snuggled in his embrace as he put his arm around her shoulders. Words held power, and there was one that hovered between them, a word that would bind them together more powerfully than their brands ever could. It had gone unspoken, and Morgan struggled to keep her silence. She could not be the first to say, "I love you." Before those words were spoken, she must find the strength to tell him of their son.

Love was an emotion female Wizards welcomed and embraced. It would be an easy thing for her to tell Rowan she loved him, had loved him from the first moment she first saw him all those long years ago, and would love him with her last breath. She knew he cared for her, perhaps more than he realized. The burning question was how deep his feelings ran.

Would he choose her above his duty to the Talons and the Grey Council?

Rain, as soft and warm as a spring day floated from the sky. It was a phenomenon of Mother Nature that she could give both sun and rain at the same time, as though reminding the Earth's inhabitants of her sense of humor.

Rowan pulled Morgan to her feet. "Not crazy about rain. Fire and water don't mix. Let's go inside."

His words, casually spoken, were like an arrow. She felt their weight but tossed them away. She wouldn't read more into them. She couldn't.

She wove her arms around him, tilting her head back to see him more clearly. "It is not raining that hard. This is what the Irish call 'a soft day.' You cannot really believe the old fable that a Fire Wizard's core extinguishes if submerged. The rain feels wonderful."

"I don't fear my core's pilot light going out, if that is what you mean. Fire Wizards just don't like water."

"I'm a Water Wizard. Are you afraid I'll summon a tidal wave and drown you?"

He smiled. "Thanks. I wasn't thinking about that until you brought it up."

A crack of thunder followed by a silver streak of lightning heralded a downpour. Sheets of rain bounced off the lake, causing small whitecaps and bringing with it a cold breeze. Rowan pulled the collar of his jacket around his neck. "On the bright side, I won't need a shower."

As much as she enjoyed the rain, his expression was so pitiful she relented, reaching for his hand.

He shrugged away, shoving his hands in his pockets and hunching his shoulders. "Oh, no, you don't. I've changed my mind. You're right. This is a great day. I'm having the time of my life. Never felt better. Don't know why I didn't ever stand out in the pouring rain before." He held his arm out, turning it over. "That's interesting." Steam rose from his outstretched arm and shoulders and fogged his glasses. "Do you think I'm melting? It's going to be hard to track down and punish those responsible for killing the female Wizards if I'm a puddle."

Smothering a laugh, she grabbed his hand. "You are impossible. We are going to the wagon."

"Thank the gods," he said, kissing the back of her hand. "My suggestion is that as soon as we're inside, we shed these wet clothes." He winked. "At last, a perfect reason for getting soaked to the skin."

Chapter Thirty-Seven

Back in cloud-draped Seattle, the sun was losing its hold on the day as rain the shade of tears flowed from the sky. Obscured in the waning light, Stryker, in his dragon form, glided over to the small balcony outside the rooftop apartment where he had first shapeshifted from human Wizard to Dragon.

Hovering over the balcony, he shapeshifted from Dragon to human and dropped soundlessly onto the balcony. Since he was a full-grown Red Dragon, it would not have been able to hold his weight without the shift. Inside, the apartment looked warm and inviting, with shelves of books and containers of daisies, fresh-faced pansies and deep purple violets. It reminded him of a mountain stream in summer, all greens and blues, with its shore dusted with wildflowers. A stark contrast to the snarl of traffic and pedestrians below.

Humans shouldered past each other, avoiding contact and afraid to get too close. For the last few days he'd tried to make sense of this world and its people. They were a mystery to him as he watched and learned. At times he tried to access the life he had had as a human. The memories were difficult to hold onto for very long, possibly compromised by his near-death experience. It was as though he had slept for a thousand years and woken to a time he did not understand. When he tried to locate any of his kind, he found no trace of them in the

Puget Sound area. But the need to reunite with those like him burned in his soul. Had they retreated to the North or South poles, or had the Wizards succeeded in exterminating them?

The Water and Fire Wizards who had been in the apartment were gone. Only the woman they had called AJ remained. He heard her humming in the kitchen. His hearing was scary good, and he chalked it up as another perk of being a dragon shapeshifter.

He had been kidnapped and brought to the apartment. That was the only explanation that made sense. But why would Wizards kidnap him if their goal was to wipe out his species? Was he the last of his kind and they meant to keep him as a pet? Or had Dragons regained strength and numbers, and the Wizards meant to discover their location through him?

Stryker clenched his jaw. He needed answers, and perhaps this human could provide them. But first he would have to gain access to the apartment. The sliding glass door to the balcony was locked, as though they had been fearful he might return. The woman still remaining inside had seen him become invisible and then, once outside the apartment, shapeshift into a Dragon. She was afraid. Understandable. Humans had been told to fear Dragons. But his only alternative was to use the front entrance of the apartment building.

The fire escape was within reach, so getting down in his human form was not the issue. His appearance was. Because of his dark skin and his height of nearly six foot seven, he drew a crowd, and with it the risk that his enemies might be alerted.

And he was naked. His clothes had ripped off when he shifted into dragon form.

Suddenly, the door to the apartment slammed opened and three men barged in as though they owned the place.

Startled, AJ screamed but darted toward a small tote-shaped purse that lay on the sofa. She snatched it and fumbled at the clasp, her hand trembling as she pulled out a small revolver and pointed it toward the three men. "Zacharias!" Her breathing was labored, but she swallowed, gripping the gun with both hands to try and steady it. "How did you find me?"

The man she addressed as Zacharias reminded Stryker of a rodent with a sharp-edged nose and pinched beady dark eyes. He jiggled a set of keys. "That is the wrong question. You should ask who betrayed you and told us where to find you. You ruined me. You and those vamps burned my warehouse to the ground." He motioned to his men. "Look sharp, guys, AJ has a cute gun. If she's a good shot, the gun's sting will bite, but it won't kill."

The two men Zacharias had spoken to looked like ex-military. They circled to either side of AJ, making her jerk her gun first to her left and then to her right and then back toward Zacharias.

Zacharias locked the apartment door while his heavyset comrades moved slowly toward AJ.

Stryker admired her courage. Three against one was terrible odds for a human, even one armed with a gun. She would be lucky if she got off one shot, and dead before she pulled the trigger a second time.

Stryker's anger rose. Legends had it all wrong. They spoke of Dragons killing humans for sport, when it was the other way around. Dragons were dedicated to protecting humans. They only attacked when provoked or believed their families were in danger.

He tried to open the sliding glass door, then ground his teeth, remembering it was locked and likely warded with a spell. But if he could get AJ to open it from the inside, he could help her. He debated leaving and going down the fire escape to the entrance, but the look on the men surrounding AJ told him there wasn't time.

He pounded on the glass with his fists, but those inside were focused on AJ and either did not hear or thought it was traffic and city noise. Or the spell the Wizards cast was so strong that no one could hear or see what was going on outside.

He cursed, pounded again, and received the same result. He spied a five-foot tree in a ceramic planter and threw it at the glass door. The planter shattered, but the door held. If he shifted into his Dragon form, he could rip the glass door out of its frame, leaving nothing but a gaping hole in the wall. But he had already reached the limit of the number of times he could shift today.

He had no choice but to use the fire escape. Inside the apartment, Zacharias nodded to his comrades, and they both lunged for AJ at the same time. She pulled the trigger, wounding one of the men in the arm, while the other snatched the gun from her hand.

Zacharias held up his hand. "Stop. I want her alive. I have an idea." He grabbed AJ and pushed her against the sliding glass door. "You either tell me what I want to know, or I'll let my friends dangle you over the edge of this building. I promise you, it's not a good way to die. You stole something from me, and I want those documents returned, and the identity of those who helped you. Tell me and I might let you live."

"Zacharias." She spoke his name with loathing, as

though it meant rotting flesh, then lifted her chin. "Did you also tell your other assistants you wouldn't kill them if they gave you what you wanted? You pumped my friend's sister and her sister's boyfriend full of drugs and dumped them in a landfill."

He tightened his grip around her neck. "Answer me, or I'll throw you from this building." He reached around and unlocked the sliding glass door.

Stryker was partway down the fire escape when he heard the lock on the sliding glass door disengage and the door slide open. Calling on the shadows to cloak him in darkness, he moved back toward the balcony.

"Boss," the taller of the two men said from the inside of the apartment, "do you think killing her is a good idea? You just said we need her alive."

Zacharias grinned. "Did you hear my thick-headed friend? He says I'm not supposed to kill you. I disagree. And you want to know the best part? I've been told that same thing before, but I always manage to convince my superiors that it was the only solution. No one tells me what I can and cannot do. Get a rope," Zacharias said to the tall man. "We'll see how long we can dangle her over the edge before she tells us everything we want to know."

Smoke and shadows rolled across the balcony like a thick fog as Stryker materialized. "I disagree with your plan." His voice was as black as the shadows that swirled around his feet. "I do not approve of the taking of innocent lives, or those who do, which means you have two choices. Option one—Release the woman and I will grant you an easy death. Option two—Resist and you and your comrades die hard. Pick option two. Please."

****

On the balcony, the smoke and shadows that curled around Stryker's legs thinned before floating on the wind in the direction of rooftop gardens, the waterfront and a giant Ferris wheel. Stryker banked his fury and hid a smile. The startled expressions of the humans told him that his dramatic entrance, although not planned, held certain advantages. They would be hesitant to attack him, which gave him the advantage. But first he needed to get everyone back inside. Things could get messy, and he did not want witnesses to what might happen next.

"I suggest we continue our discussion inside." Stryker moved to AJ's side, leaning toward her. "Do not be afraid. I mean you no harm." Her pale face and terrified expression told him she was not convinced.

Once inside, he closed the sliding glass door. "Now, gentlemen, which option do you want? Option one, or option two?"

Stryker's words seemed to awaken Zacharias and his men from their stunned silence.

Zacharias reached for his gun and pointed it at Stryker. "Neat trick, surprising us like that. Startled us, I'm not embarrassed to admit. Of course, your size is partly to blame. What are you, six-five?"

"Close enough."

Zacharias nodded. "Well, you're still flesh and blood, and unharmed, and this is none of your business. But will someone please get the guy some clothes?"

With a slight blush, AJ handed him a sofa throw. *Note to self. Humans get nervous around naked people.* He nodded his thanks to AJ and tied the blanket around his waist. "I am not leaving. I thought I made myself clear."

"Why are we wasting our time with this guy?" asked

the taller of the two men with Zacharias. "I agree he's not your usual homeless guy. He's built like a brick building. But what else could he be? My guess is he was sleeping on the streets, climbed the fire escape to try and break into one of these apartments, then saw Zacharias and AJ. We need to kill him and get on with why we're here."

"I've no intention of letting the homeless man live," Zacharias said, tightening his grip on AJ's arm. A bruise was forming on her face where Zacharias must have hit her, and yet she no longer looked afraid. The Dragon fire he had banked simmered as he focused on her bruised skin. *There deserves to be a special place in Hell reserved for those who prey on and harm the innocent.*

She turned to focus on Stryker, her expressive eyes reflecting trust.

He gave her a slight nod, hoping she would understand that all would be well.

"Final warning. Let this woman go."

"Isn't this lovely?" Zacharias sneered. "Homeless guy and my ex-office assistant have bonded. Men, I've changed my mind. Kill him."

The two men stalked Stryker, one on his left, and the other on his right, just as they had flanked AJ earlier. He almost felt sorry for them. Almost. He caught the first man to reach him around the throat and broke his neck. As the man slumped to the ground, the second drew his gun, lowered his stance, and squeezed off a round.

As though in slow motion, Stryker saw the bullet leave the chamber and speed toward him. He turned away from the bullet's path, spinning around behind the man and yanking the gun out of his grasp. He crushed the metal with his bare hand and tossed it across the room like a broken toy.

"I don't like guns. Too impersonal."

"What are you?" The man lunged for Stryker and took a swing. Stryker moved to the side and the intended blow connected only with air. As he warmed up for another attempt, Stryker slammed his fist into the man's face. The force knocked him to the ground, where he lay, his eyes open, his head tilted at an odd angle.

Zacharias stepped back, taking AJ with him. "You must be a Wizard. A human can't move that fast." Zacharias's eyes widened as he pressed a gun against Alexandra's head. "Stay back or I'll kill her."

"Not a Wizard."

"Don't kill him," AJ said to Stryker. "Your brother thinks he might know who is murdering Wizards."

"Wizards are my enemy. Why should I care?"

She hesitated, locking her gaze with his. "Okay. What am I missing? This is new for me. I just learned there is a magical community in Seattle, but aren't you a Wizard? They tried to kill you with their poison. Don't you remember?"

He did not remember. Or perhaps the human part of him wanted to forget. "I am a Dragon Wizard, and it is complicated and this is not my fight."

"Well, I know about complicated," she said, taking a calming breath. "There is a poem by Martin Niemöller. It reads: First they came for the Communists, and I did not speak out because I was not a Communist. Then they came for the Socialists, and I did not speak out because I was not a Socialist. Then they came for the Trade Unionists, and I did not speak out because I was not a Trade Unionist. Then they came for the Jews and I did not speak out because I was not a Jew. Then they came for me and there was no one left to speak out for me."

Gods take it! His mother had often quoted these lines. If someone was killing Wizards, his kind might be next. Stryker paused, gauging his opponent. An easy kill. But the words AJ spoke had hit a chord. What would have happened if Dragons had had allies to help them in their fight for survival? He turned toward Zacharias. "AJ wants you alive for some reason, but she did not say in one piece. I'm in the mood to break a few bones."

"You're crazy."

"Pretty sure I am not."

With a tight grip on AJ, Zacharias edged over to the sliding glass door. "Seems we have a standoff."

AJ brought her heel down on Zacharias's toe. He yelped, easing his grip. Stryker moved in, pulling AJ out of the way as he disarmed Zacharias with one hand and then pushed him against the balcony's railing with the other.

"A standoff?" AJ said, rubbing her neck. "That only happens when both sides are equal."

"Let me guess," Zacharias said with a sneer. "You're going to hold me by my ankles and threaten to drop me if I don't talk. But a fast death is better than what they'll do to me if I spill the beans."

"He has a point," AJ said, making a phone call. "We'll turn him over to Detective Lyons. Just an FYI, he is my father, and I can't wait to tell him all about what you had planned for me."

"Lyons is your dad?" Zacharias's voice dropped. "He'll skin me alive or have someone in the magical community do it for him. I'm dead either way."

AJ nodded. "That sounds like a good bet, except my dad believes in the law. If you agree to turning state's evidence, he'll put you into protective custody and witness protection. The phone's ringing."

"I don't know anything," Zacharias said turning to Stryker. "Make her stop."

"Detective Lyons? Dad, this is AJ. Yes, I'm okay. We have someone in…"

Zacharias yanked the phone out of her grasp and threw it out the window. "I told you. I don't know anything."

"My phone has GPS, genius. You have less than five minutes before my father and his men arrive."

Zacharias looked like a deflated balloon. "The Talons were going to disclose to the Grey Council that my daughter's mother was a Water Wizard. The Grey Council is paranoid about diluting the blood lines. The report would be as good as a death sentence for her. What was I supposed to do? She's all I have."

"Where's her mother now?" Stryker said.

"Dead, or at least that is what I was told. She disappeared three years after Katherine was born."

AJ's eyebrows drew together. "You told everyone at work that your daughter's mother overdosed."

"A story. I wanted Katherine to hate her. I thought it would end the questions. It only made her more curious."

Dragon Stryker tried to access the childhood memories of his human side. They were still as hard to grasp as wisps of smoke, but he knew Zacharias's daughter would doubt the story her father spun. Even human children could remember events and voices experienced at a young age. But Zacharias's daughter was half Wizard, which meant her memories likely went even farther back than when she was two or three years old. No wonder she had questions. The child's memories didn't match the stories Zacharias was trying to sell. When AJ turned toward Stryker, she seemed to have the same thoughts.

"We're off topic," AJ said. "Who was your contact?"

Zacharias stood straighter, as though welcoming the shift away from his daughter. "The Earth Wizard Vlad, and occasionally the president of the Talons would drop by unannounced. I got the impression someone else was pulling their strings. They always seemed nervous."

"Any idea who?" AJ asked.

Police sirens blared from a few blocks away. Zacharias twitched as though hit and glanced over his shoulder. "You're sure your father will protect me?"

"That depends. A lot of what you told us is what my father already suspected. You need to give him something new."

Zacharias pointed a shaking finger toward Stryker. "I thought it was obvious. The giant is your proof the Talons' theory is real. Look at him. He's a shapeshifter. A Dragon. I recognized the signs, but I wasn't sure until I saw him fight. The Talons never wanted to kill Wizards, or at least not all the Wizards. Some they killed because they got too close to the truth. The goal all along was to find a way to transform Wizards into the most feared fighting machines created. Dragon Wizards. But to do that they needed Wizards with a strong connection to Dragons."

Police cars surrounded the building and blocked the area, trying to control the growing crowds as pedestrians shoved for a better view of what might have caused the emergency.

"You have to get me out of here," Zacharias said in rising panic. "Something's wrong. How did they get here so fast?"

"The police are good at what they do," AJ said. "Stop changing the subject. What else do you know?"

His voice shaking, he glanced between the crowd below and the entrance to the apartment. "I might have an idea who is really behind this. I can't be sure. I need more time."

In the next instant the door burst opened with such force it broke free of its hinges, flew halfway across the room and crashed to the ground. The hallway was dark, with only the glint of metal.

AJ raised her hands. "Don't shoot," she shouted. "We're unarmed. I'm Detective Lyons' daughter, AJ Zollinger." Over her shoulder, she said, "Don't worry. I'll make sure my father knows you're going to help us."

Men wearing masks, helmets, and tactical uniforms, moved in, their guns raised.

"Trap!" Stryker shouted as he shielded AJ with his body.

Weapons fired in a blur of gunfire and choking smoke. Bullets struck Zacharias with such force he lifted off the ground.

Stryker gathered AJ in his arms and dove through the balcony's railing, unsure if he would shapeshift into a Dragon or plummet to the ground.

****

Spotlights searched the night sky, crisscrossing over the clouds in a frantic dance. The rain, however, had taken a momentary break, as though assessing its options. If the slate-grey, fast-moving clouds were an indication, the break wouldn't last long. In his human form, Stryker, with AJ held at his side, had landed on the rooftop garden sanctuary of a luxury hotel that overlooked Puget Sound and a giant Ferris wheel. He had not been able to shapeshift into a Dragon. Evidently, he was still getting the hang of it. Instead, using a combination of his superhuman core and dumb luck, he had ridden the air currents and landed on the rooftop. The hotel had created a parklike setting, complete with trees, a winding river-rock path, fountains, and—fortunately for him—a tourist shop with "I love Seattle" clothing.

AJ was convinced that the men who had shot and killed Zacharias and then turned their guns on them were not connected with her father or the Seattle police force. It was obvious they hadn't come to rescue AJ but to kill Zacharias and any witnesses.

Stryker did not know if her assessment regarding her father was true. What he did know was that there could be only one reason to search the skies. Someone knew what—or more importantly, who—they were looking for. They were searching for a Dragon.

"You can fly?" Teeth chattering, she rubbed her arms, with the classic deer-in-the-headlights expression. "That's cool."

He shrugged. "More gliding and jumping than flying, this time," Stryker said with a grin. He should have known she would have questions.

She rubbed her arms again. "You're right. It was seriously scary. When I was younger, my father used to tell me bedtime stories of fantastical creatures. I thought he had a wonderful imagination. Now, I realize all the stories were true. So, you said you were a Dragon Wizard. What is that…exactly?"

"That's a long conversation and you're cold. Hold

that question while I find us a way inside the building. We are too exposed. Zacharias was right when he mentioned something wasn't right when those men dressed like policemen arrived so soon after you'd called and left a message with your father. And then there's the question of why someone ordered a search of the skies. You only do that if you think the person you're hunting can fly. The building we're on now is most probably locked, thanks to the crowd and the police, but I think I have enough power to glide us down to the street level. I'm still figuring out how to recharge," he said with a sheepish grin.

Hugging her arms against her waist, AJ moved nearer a walled structure in the center of the rooftop. Her head jerked toward a door. "Or we could use the stairs."

He made a slight bow. "Your wish is my command."

Once on the street level, Stryker led AJ in the direction of the Ferris wheel. He needed answers and had planned to meet one of the contacts he had made over the last few days at that location if anything went wrong. Being shot at and hunted certainly qualified.

A spotlight swept over downtown Seattle, illuminating the city in an artificial glow. He had an eerie feeling that whoever was after him and AJ was getting closer. He could not allow that to happen.

With AJ beside him, Stryker headed toward the perimeter of the Ferris wheel. The wheel kept turning even though the area was closed due to the storm. Lights shone from its spokes like the lights from the northern lights of an Aurora Borealis. A strong feeling of homesickness gripped him like a vise, and he doubled over.

Alexandra rested her hand on his arm. "Are you all

right? You look like you might throw up."

He closed his eyes and gulped in salt-kissed air. "I am fine."

"Oh, really? My father once told me the definition of the word 'fine' when I used it to describe my day at college. He said the word meant 'freaked out, insecure, neurotic and emotional.' Which one of those words describes what's going on with you?"

"Take your pick. I am a Dragon."

She hesitated, while a cacophony of emotions played over her expression, from shock to fear, and finally settled on annoyance. She narrowed her gaze. "No one's perfect. I'm a Sagittarius. What is your point?"

"How about this: I am still trying to figure it out."

"Better. Exactly who are we waiting for?"

He shoved his hands into his pockets. "You're smart for a human. The contact I'm meeting should be here soon. Are you still cold? You look cold." He started to take off his sweatshirt with its image of the Space Needle, but she reached for his arm and pulled him onto the bench seat.

She laughed, shaking her head. "As much as I enjoy seeing you without a shirt, you need to keep your clothes on. Clothes are a big thing in the human world."

"Good to know." He concentrated on the Ferris wheel. It was surprising how comfortable he felt around her. Maybe it was the whole thing of facing death together and surviving that had built a sense of ease. Whatever it was, he did not want to risk examining it too closely.

The lights of the Ferris wheel blurred through the misty rain as the wheel turned. A melody played, but he did not recognize the tune. There was a merry-go-round, and rows of booths set up for food or games where the prizes were giant stuffed animals. Everything about the park evoked a simpler time, a time of childhood wonder, where most problems were manageable. But it was an illusion, an oasis, a place where time was only suspended. Sooner or later, you had to reenter the adult world.

"How well do you know your father?" Stryker said.

****

AJ pressed her lips together and glared at him, a trait Stryker had found amusing when Zaharias was the target. Not so much when he was the recipient. Too late he realized that suggesting she did not know her father as well as she thought she did was the wrong thing to say.

"Are you suggesting that the men who killed Zacharias—and tried to kill us—were sent by my father?" Without waiting for his answer, she stood, hesitated for a moment, and then stormed off in the rain.

He pushed to his feet. "I am sorry. That was a stupid thing for me to say."

She turned and glared at him as though believing her stare would turn him to stone. "Apology *not* accepted."

"I saved your life."

Her glare deepened.

"I am an idiot."

"Yes, you are. The question you should have asked was whether someone might have been listening in on my father's calls. Unfortunately, if that is the case, everyone is a suspect." She cocked her head to the side. "You know, I like you better this way. A week ago, when you were assigned as my babysitter, you never smiled and wouldn't have admitted that you were wrong."

As she turned and headed toward the Ferris wheel, the words she had spoken registered. He jogged to catch up with her. "What do you mean? We never met until the day I shifted."

AJ turned toward him, searching his expression. "You really don't remember, do you? My father and your brother, Rowan, thought I needed protection. I objected, of course, but as usual they ignored me. Anyway, while you and I were investigating the Eye Doctor murders, you were poisoned and almost died. Rowan and Morgan saved your life. I don't remember too much, as I was affected by the poison as well. When you awoke, you turned invisible, shifted into a dragon, and disappeared. The next time I saw you was on the balcony when you saved my life. I thought you remembered."

His memory was as fuzzy as Seattle through the rain. He had no recollection of the Eye Doctor murder cases. He remembered seeing Rowan and Morgan when he awoke, and registering that Rowan was his brother. He hated that he had forgotten the missing pieces of his human life.

The breeze off Puget Sound increased, swirling the rain around them as they stood facing each other. Stryker waited. They were linked, if only by circumstance. Was she in his life to help him understand the connections between his two worlds? There was no such thing as coincidence. The next step was for AJ to embrace the same conclusion.

He heard people running over a gravel path and pulled AJ behind him. "Stay close. They're coming."

Chapter Thirty-Eight

As the rain over the Trolls' compound intensified, festival goers secured tents and their wagons against the sudden storm. Isolated from the others, the gypsy wagon Cassandra had assigned to Rowan was tucked into a grove of trees a short distance from the mansion. This morning it had blended into its surroundings as though the Trolls didn't want anyone to know the identity of its occupant. In a few short hours, however, there had been a transformation. Rowan's wagon was outlined with twinkling rainbow lights. White, red and purple flowers hung from the eves in colorful baskets.

Morgan climbed into the wagon, calling over her shoulder for Rowan to hurry, excited to see inside.

"What do you think it means?" Rowan said, fingering one of the lights.

"It's the Trolls' way of saying they may have misjudged you and they welcome you to their home."

The inside of the wagon exceeded her expectations. The same small lights that decorated the outside were strung over the curved ceiling like stars on a summer's clear night. A carpet of rose petals blanketed the floor and fresh bunches of lavender adorned the open cupboard. The brass tub had been removed and in its place was a table brimming with food.

There was a variety of imported cheeses, from French Roquefort, English Stilton, and Italian

Gorgonzola to Spanish Cabrales. Chunks of one hundred percent dark chocolate from Ghana and Peru, as well as French and Belgian chocolates, were displayed beside bowls of fresh fruit and platters of bright green, red and gold sliced vegetables on polished silver trays.

Rowan popped a strawberry into his mouth. "Impressive. But what I'd really like is a rare steak and grilled onions. What do you think are my chances?"

"Zero." Morgan laughed as she reached for a chunk of dark chocolate and settled on the bed. "Trolls don't eat beef, chicken, pork or lamb." She curled her legs beneath her. "I wish we had a hot plate. We could warm the chocolate and dip in the fruit."

"You forget who I am, milady." He broke dark chocolate bars into a bowl and cradled it in the palm of his hand, melting it. "Usually, I do this to warm a can of chili for my dinner. I'm a lousy cook."

Morgan dunked a slice of orange into the chocolate, the juice running down her fingers as she bit into the succulent fruit. "You are full of surprises, Fire Wizard. You should try some."

He shrugged. "I'll take your word. Fruit and chocolate mixed together is not my thing."

"How can you not like chocolate?"

"I didn't say I didn't like chocolate. What I said was that I don't like it with fruit. You have chocolate on your lower lip."

Her tongue skimmed the corner of her mouth. "Is it gone?"

He shook his head, then leaned over and kissed the corner of her mouth. The brief contact sent warm shivers running over her. Her eyes locked with his and the smoldering passion reflected in his gaze stole her breath away.

His voice filled with the heat reflected in his eyes. "I was right. Chocolate tastes the best on bare skin, or maybe it's you. Whenever I'm around you I'm reminded of tropical islands and exotic seas. Why do you think that is?"

Morgan wiped the remaining juice off her hand with an embroidered napkin, knowing the moment she had both yearned for and dreaded had come. She must tell him. She must tell him all of it. Years ago, fearful and not trusting their love, she'd cast a forgetful spell. That he still remembered images of the magical island of Hy-Basil where they'd thought they could escape the pressures of the Talons and the Grey Council gave her hope. Did his memories suggest that his love for her had conquered the spells she wove around him?

"Morgan."

Startled, she looked up. "I'm sorry. Did you say something?"

"Yes, but I'm not sure how to start. I have a feeling we've met before the Fertility Festival on Vlad's island."

She laced her fingers together to keep them from trembling. Was it possible? No, she corrected. She must not hope. All she'd been taught argued convincingly that it was impossible for male Wizards to have any memory of the female they'd joined with. Yet, he remembered the recent Fertility Festival.

He turned her to face him. "I know it breaks the rules, but I want to know. Have we met before?"

She cleared her throat and nodded. "It was the first Bealtaine I was eligible to attend and took place on Taransay, an island in the Outer Hebrides of Scotland."

"I know of it. It's uninhabited and hardly a tropical

paradise."

She lifted her gaze.

"Sorry. Continue."

She kept her hands locked together until the knuckles shone white in the flickering overhead lights. "My choosing you was an accident, and you were my first. You arrived late and so were not assigned. When you appeared, it sent everyone into a panic. I was so new to the whole process I did not understand the reasons for concern until later. Several years before, during a Bealtaine in Northern Ireland, you fought a male Wizard during the festival, and nearly killed him. The Talons and the Grey Council investigated the incident and judged it self-defense."

Rowan stared out the open window. The rain had eased to a quiet drizzle. "That was a dark time for me. Days before that festival, Stryker had stumbled upon what he thought was a Dragon's lair near the Giant's Causeway. Instead of believing him, I told him we were no longer children and that Dragons had died out eons ago. We fought, and he took off. I was worried for him but never found him. I was angry and frustrated with how I'd handled the situation with my brother and should never have gone to the festival at all. When I arrived there, I spotted an Earth Wizard forcing himself on one of the female Wizards. I pulled him from her and, in my present state of mind, probably would have set him on fire rather than turning him in to the authorities, if other Wizards hadn't intervened. The Talons and the Grey Council took the Earth Wizard's side. He claimed the woman had come on to him and he was fighting her off. The Earth Wizard and I were banned from future Bealtaine festivals until they figured I'd learned my lesson."

Morgan laid her hand on his arm. "The Earth Wizards are forever retelling that story, with Fire Wizards the ones who are volatile and unpredictable, when it is they whom we should fear."

"That part doesn't bother me. But I clearly didn't learn my lesson. My reaction to Stryker the day he shifted haunts me. I thought the worst and should have tried to help him. I've made inquiries as to where he might have gone after he disappeared from the apartment, but he's like a ghost. If anyone knows where he is, they're not saying." He reached over and took her hands in his. "We're off topic. "So, my imagining we knew each other before was not a dream?"

She sighed, the corners of her mouth edging up in a smile. "In a way, our time together was a dream. Like I mentioned, we met at the Bealtaine Festival on Taransay. Our connection was so strong that all the glamours and spells dissolved like mist in a summer breeze. We saw each other as our true selves. After the festival, we fled to the enchanted island of Hy-Basil, off the western coast of Ireland. We planned to defy the Talons and the Grey Council and live out our lives together."

"I have a feeling I mucked it up."

Morgan laughed, reveling in his humor as well as the relief to share this secret. "Both of us were to blame."

He lifted an eyebrow. "I doubt that."

She cupped the side of his face with her hand. "You're always taking the blame. Not this time, my love. We were both young. Too young to understand how to navigate the ways of our world and its restraints and power. When I became pregnant with our child…"

"Wait. We have a child?"

She pressed her fingers to his mouth. "I learned of it the day you told me you were returning to duty. I was angry that you had chosen the Talons and the Grey Council over me, so I didn't tell you. His name is Caden, which means 'spirit of battle.' I hoped the name would protect him."

He paced the cramped quarters of the wagon, shaking his head. "Caden," he whispered. "A strong name. I remember how I was in those days. Too full of myself, by half." He turned to face her. "Is the child here?"

She blinked to control the tears. His reaction was unexpected. "You don't seem angry. You seem…"

"Honored that I am a father," he finished with a grin.

"There is more. Caden was taken from me when he was a child, and I do not know where he is or if he is alive or…"

Rowan silenced her words with a kiss. "Your pain must have been unbearable. He must be almost a grown man by now. How old would he be?"

"He turned sixteen a few months ago," she said evenly.

Rowan reached for her, kissing her as though he would never let her go. She leaned into his arms, feeling the flood of his devotion and love wrap around her like a protective cloak. When he pulled only a breath away, she was out of breath. He traced the outline of her mouth with his thumb.

"I thought I was losing my mind. I couldn't understand how I could love someone so completely in such a short time. You consumed my days and nights. Now, I know. Legends say that Wizards descended from Dragons love—truly love—only once. And now you tell me we have a son. We will find him. I promise."

Her eyes blurred as she traced the contours of his lips with the tips of her fingers. "I am so very glad I told you."

He winked. "Time for a celebration." He reached for the bowl of melted chocolate. "It's a shame to put this to waste."

She laughed softly. "If you are thinking what I think you are thinking…"

"I'm thinking of slathering your body in chocolate."

"Rowan, you can't be serious."

His expression turned mischievous. "Okay. If you insist, we could slather *my* body with chocolate." His grin spread as he ripped off his shirt. "That works for me too."

"I say we do both." She dipped her fingers in the bowl of warm chocolate, painting a swirl over his chest as warm currents of desire washed away her fears. She hesitated, licking chocolate from her fingers. "But perhaps you are still recovering from the poison. You should rest."

His hot breath bathed her in heat. He brushed his fingers over the mounds of her breasts. "Temptress. I am fully awake, as you well know. I have a feeling we're going to need a lot more chocolate for what I have in mind."

She wanted him. Passion stronger than the night they'd shared on the island engulfed her in a longing for his touch.

"Morgan." Her name was spoken like a caress as he kissed the hollow of her neck. Sparks of desire danced over her skin as he found the sensitive spot behind her ear. His breath fanned the sparks into flames.

She pulled back, gasping for breath, answering the question in his eyes as her hands fumbled to remove her blouse and skirt, until she wore only a silk camisole and panties. "Lie down, my lord, and let me please you."

Morgan dipped her fingers in the warm chocolate again and traced the outline of a Celtic tattoo over his heart, then bent to trace its outline with her tongue.

He moaned, entwining her fingers in his. His expression filled with building passion. "No spells. No enchantments."

Her heart raced with the implications of his request. "Without spells and enchantments, we are sealed more strongly, more completely, than even the brands we gave one another."

"I know."

His declaration banished the last restraints she'd held around her heart. Tonight, without spells and glamour, she would know what it felt like to be held by the man she loved.

She set the bowl of chocolate aside and moved toward him. Her breasts strained against the silk of her camisole as her body brushed against the taut muscles of his bare chest. She tasted the heady combination of dark chocolate and man, teasing, tasting and savoring.

His eyes reflected the raging fever simmering beneath the surface. He wove his hands through her hair, cupping the nape of her neck and bringing her lips to his. "My turn."

"But I'm not finished."

"We have all night," was his whispered promise.

Shedding his jeans, he pulled the chemise over her head, bending to kiss her breasts. His hand slid her panties over her hips and down her legs, his touch searing a path along her skin. With the chocolate he outlined a Celtic symbol over her breast. She knew it by heart. The symbol of two intertwining circles held many meanings, but in their world, it meant *Beloved.*

His mouth captured hers, inflamed her as he deepened the kiss, setting her senses on fire, pouring hot waves of molten desire over her skin. His body molded against hers in pulsating flames as he entered her, the heat so intense she knew she must be on fire.

Rowan caressed her skin and inflamed her body with his touch. Away from all the chaos that threatened to drown her into a dark abyss, Rowan was her world and her light. He banished all from her mind except thoughts of the depths of her love for the Fire Wizard who held her heart in the palm of his hands.

****

Morgan awoke nestled in Rowan's arms. She stretched and gazed out the window of the wagon, feeling well loved. The stars dusted the night sky as though an ancient goddess had scattered diamond dust. Dawn was still hours away, though it meant their time on the Trolls' compound would end, and with that ending came a return to the reality of the world she knew, where those she loved were in danger. If just for a few hours longer, she wanted to pretend this time she spent with Rowan would last forever.

But everything ended. She'd learned that the hard way when their son was taken from her.

Rowan stretched and glanced over at her, winking. "I'm awake and starving."

She laughed, knowing he wasn't talking about food. "You are insatiable."

He rose to a sitting position on the bed and kissed

her bare shoulder. "I thought our lovemaking a few hours ago would have answered that question."

She sat and drew her legs to her chest, resting her head on her knees. "It did and most thoroughly. As delightful as making love again sounds, I am also hungry for food."

He flipped off the covers to reach for his jeans and tug them on. "Thoroughly, you say. I like that word. How about I make us sandwiches? Anything more is beyond my culinary talents." He moved over to the cooler where they had stored the cheese. "While I decide what type of sandwich to build, I have a few questions regarding the night you and the young Wizardlings left Vlad's island."

She slid out of bed and reached for a rose silk robe. A few days ago, she would have avoided his question, not trusting that he would not then use her words against her. A lifetime had transpired in a few days, it seemed. She was no longer fearful.

"Even before the festival began, there was unrest among the female Wizards on multiple levels. Our children were being taken from us at younger and younger ages, the Talons were petitioning the Grey Council to take over the teaching of the young Wizards, and there were rumblings that the deaths of female Wizards were not from natural causes."

Rowan paused in slicing a brick of white cheddar, his expression frozen in shock. "You can't be serious. Any one of those accusations would be cause for an investigation. I'm assuming these matters were reported to the Grey Council."

She tied her robe and moved over to Rowan, shaking her head. "That has an interesting outcome as well. Before I answer, have you ever wondered why female

Wizards die so young, while male Wizards can easily live well over one hundred years?"

He set the knife down. "We were told female Wizards have weak hearts."

She picked up a slice of cheese and popped it into her mouth, waiting until she'd swallowed it before continuing. "Yes, certainly 'weak hearts' was the perfect explanation, was it not? The explanation eliminates the need for male Wizards to investigate the murders. Their conscience is clear. Except that Caitlin, the last Leader of the Female Wizards, realized that explanation was a lie. She claimed that Earth Wizards were using their powers to stop female Wizards' hearts, and that this practice had been going on for centuries."

Rowan whistled low under his breath. "That's the reason she was killed, and the reason you all had to flee?"

"There is something else you need to know. The female Wizard you saved from that Earth Wizard died shortly after the festival. Then Vlad's brother, Gordon, the Earth Wizard you confronted, was found dead six months later, and his death was declared a suicide."

"Holy shit, Gordon was Vlad's brother? I had been accused of tracking Gordon down and killing him out of spite. It wasn't true, of course. I heard that not everyone believed my alibi that I was on the other side of the world when his body was found. No wonder Vlad hates me. He blames me for his brother's death." Rowan glanced over to the glasses he used when he was in the human world to disguise the unusual shade of his eyes. "I've been a blind fool, seeing only what I want to see. Someone is tying up loose ends from that event. Why am I still alive?"

Morgan shook her head. "I don't know. Caitlin tried

to warn me about an undercurrent of corruption in the Talons and the Grey Council, but I wouldn't listen. When Caitlin and other female Wizards were murdered during Bealtaine, I could no longer deny what was happening."

"Any chance Vlad is not responsible?"

"There is always that possibility. But it's more likely that he is not acting alone. If only we had thought to confront him the night Caitlin died, we would have had our proof. At the time, we were more concerned for the safety of our Wizardlings. But there is a way we can find out if Vlad was responsible."

Rowan looked up. "What do you mean?"

"If a female Wizard is powerful enough, when she is murdered, her unique tattoo, the one that represents both her name as well as her water sign, is transferred to her killer."

Chapter Thirty-Nine

The white-gold ribbons of dawn wove through the Trolls' compound, waking its inhabitants from their dream worlds as the silver-haired Air Wizard dropped from the sky. Hunter's bow was slung over his shoulder, and a quiver of arrows strapped to his back. He walked among them like an icy breeze, his presence acknowledged, but he knew he wasn't welcomed. A few nodded to him; the rest let him pass unchallenged. Unlike Fire and Earth Wizards, his kind was tolerated. But he knew if they found out he'd unwittingly betrayed their trust, even that small concession would be stripped away.

When he'd told Vlad that Rowan was on the Trolls' compound, it was without the knowledge Morgan might be with him. An unfortunate miscalculation on his part and one he intended to rectify.

Reading the message Vlad had written was the first step, accomplished with a trick of light and air his kind possessed and kept secret. He felt no remorse or guilt in deciphering the message from Vlad. In fact, it proved once and for all that the Grand Vizier could no longer be trusted. Hunter had no problem carrying out the orders of the Talons and the Grey Council to eliminate those they felt had violated the laws of either the magical community or the humans, but there were exceptions— he had never killed a full female Wizard or her children.

Now, he sensed there was a rebellion brewing and

he wanted to gather more information before taking sides.

Hunter had two arrows ready, one to deliver the message to Rowan and the other to kill him if he tried to follow Vlad's orders. Unlike Earth and Fire Wizards, an Air Wizard's only lifelong loyalty was to Water and, by extension, the women and sea goddesses who held that element's power.

Air caresses water, gives it strength and calms its waves with a touch. Water in turn adds healing moisture to the air and increases the power of the storms Air Wizards create. Few, other than female Wizards, knew of this unbroken connection and bond that swept back to the beginning of creation.

He deeply regretted his attack on Vlad's yacht when the female Wizards had fled the island. When Vlad had given him the order to find them and turn their ship around, the Grand Vizier had claimed they were being kidnapped. Fool that he was, he had believed Vlad, without consulting Caitlin. It was only later that he learned Caitlin was already dead then.

The skirmish he waged on the yacht proved Vlad's claim as false. Only female Wizards were onboard, and it was clear they were prepared to die rather than return. They had fought bravely, and Morgan had proved a strong and capable leader. He would not make the same mistake by trusting Vlad's words a second time.

From his vantage point, Hunter watched as Rowan woke, propped on his elbow and gazed down at the sleeping Morgan. The blanket had slipped from her shoulders and Rowan pulled it over her skin gently. The unusual display of tenderness in a Fire Wizard, although common during Bealtaine, was to Hunter's experience unknown outside the confines of the Fertility Festival. Rowan was known for his ability to stay detached. If Rowan had become involved with Morgan, Vlad's message would indeed be a test, the kind perhaps no one could have predicted.

"Well, Fire Wizard, let's see where your true allegiance lies." Hunter notched the first arrow with Vlad's message attached, leveling the tip on a point just above Rowan's head.

The silver shaft flew from Hunter's bow in a blur of gray light, glided through the wagon's open window and embedded in the wall.

Rowan was quick to respond. He retrieved the message, read it, then snapped his attention toward Morgan.

Hunter pulled the second arrow out of his quiver. This one was tipped with a fatal dose of Oculist poison. A gift from Vlad. When he questioned the Grand Vizier on where he'd obtained the illegal substance, Vlad had assured him the Talons and the Grey Council sanctioned its use as necessary under unusual circumstances. Of late, Hunter was beginning to question Vlad's motives. When Vlad ordered Hunter to kill a female Wizard, that ended debate. Killing a female Wizard was a line Hunter would never cross.

He notched the arrow against the string of his bow with Rowan's heart in his sights and waited. If the Fire Wizard made a move to kill Morgan, it would be his last.

Rowan seemed to re-read the note a second time. Then in what looked like a fit of anger, he crumpled it in the palm of his hand. The note burst into flames and turned to ash. Hunter pulled the string tighter. Destroying the note proved nothing.

The Fire Wizard shoved off the bed and yanked on his clothes. A scowl deepened over his expression as he put on his glasses. When he reached the door, he paused long enough to glance toward Morgan again before leaving the wagon.

Hunter eased the tension on his bow, feeling a shift in the air. Vlad's message was clear. Rowan was to kill Morgan the instant he read the order. Why had Rowan waited? Defying a direct order was an offense punishable by death. There would be no reprieve or second chances. In fact, it was likely Vlad would give Hunter the kill order.

"Lower your bow or I'll be having a barbeque over your charred remains."

Hunter froze and did as the Fire Wizard instructed. The Fire Wizard had found him as he weighed his options. Diplomacy won over certain death. "I didn't hear you coming."

"I'm a Fire Wizard, and I get super-motivated when someone shoots at me."

"I was aiming for the wall. If I'd wanted to shoot you, you'd be dead."

"Comforting thought. Why didn't you shoot me when I failed to carry out Vlad's orders?"

"Why didn't you send flames to end me when you realized my location?"

"Curious."

Hunter nodded. "I as well. Vlad is drawing outside the lines of his job description. Thought I would too. Especially since he doesn't seem to have the female Wizards' best interests at heart."

"Ya think? Tell me something I don't know. I'm assuming you read the message. He ordered me to kill

Morgan. Why is she a threat to him?"

"A mystery I very much want to know."

Rowan paused. "Morgan believes Vlad was behind the recent deaths of female Wizards. Do you think that's the reason he wants her dead?"

Hunter replaced the arrow in its quill and slung his bow over his shoulder, using the time to quiet the currents of his growing anger toward Vlad. At first opportunity he would alert his brother Air Wizards. They would not be pleased. Killing a female Wizard was forbidden. "That is an interesting piece of information. Like you said, curious. What's our next move?"

Rowan crossed his arms over his chest. "Your change in allegiance is rather sudden. I'm grateful, because we need all the help we can get if there is war, but you need to give me a reason I'll believe."

"Air Wizards are loyal to female Wizards, first and always. So know this, Fire Wizard—If I, or any of my brother Air Wizards, suspect you mean to harm them in any way, we'll tear you apart."

"Awesome! I feel the same. What do you think would happen if we confronted Vlad with our suspicions and encouraged him to confess and repent?"

"He'll kill you."

"Correction. He'll *try* to kill me."

"It's not going to be easy," Hunter said.

Rowan held out his hand toward Hunter. "Welcome to the opposition. Like my brother, Stryker, likes to say, that's what makes a battle so much fun."

Chapter Forty

The warmth of the morning sun streamed through the panes of leaded glass in the mansion's great room on the Trolls' compound, as its light bathed those gathered within in pale gold. Morgan stood by the window and adjusted the wool shawl over her shoulders, chilled despite its thickness. She had awakened this morning to a cold bed, only to discover Rowan, with the help of the Air Wizard, Hunter, was gathering an army. But it was the message from Cassandra alerting her to the arrival of Connor O'Hara, the representative of the magical community on the Grey Council, that had her filled her with dread. How had Connor learned she was here?

She pulled the wool shawl closer around her as she nodded toward one of Cassandra's guards. "Please inform Connor O'Hara that we will see him now."

Cassandra and the old woman, Danu, sat beside the fire, each dwelling in their own private thoughts. Danu was bent over her knitting, the needles clicking in a controlled rhythm as her weathered fingers created intricate patterns with the yarn. Cassandra was quiet and subdued, her expression a mask, lacking emotion of any kind.

Even now, from Morgan's vantage point in the mansion's great room, she could see a small band of men gathering around Rowan. He stood on the stage, the location of the play they had watched yesterday with so much joy and promise. It seemed like a lifetime ago. So much had happened between them. She had felt they'd reached a new level of understanding. And then the dawn of a new day threatened to change everything.

Footsteps echoed over the polished wood floors, then stilled as Connor entered the room. He stood patiently, his face grim. Whatever comfort she might have gained from Cassandra and Danu was negated by the fact that their thoughts were hidden from her. Were they as concerned as she was about what Connor was here to say?

She straightened, hoping to arm herself against what was to come. It did not bode well that Vlad knew she was here. The moment the Trolls had learned of Connor's arrival, they'd hidden the female Wizards and Wizardlings, hoping it was not already too late. Bad news was reflected in Connor's unusual eyes. Like many Half-Bloods and Shapeshifters, he guarded his lineage. Like a true chameleon, a possible indication of Elven blood, his eyes reflected certain colors found in nature. Outside, his eyes might reflect the shades of blues or greens, while inside they would take on the hues of the wood paneling, parquet floors or furniture. Right now, they looked as dark as aged mahogany.

"Milady," Connor said with a slight bow, the tone of his voice as deep as the color of his eyes. "I will come straight to the point. The Grey Council and the Talons have voted to offer Zephra the position on the Council that Caitlan once held. Their wish is that you, and the other female Wizards, will consider this a step toward mending relationships and they invite you to attend Zephra's installation ceremony."

Morgan moved away from the window with the

pretense of removing her shawl and draping it over a chair near the fire. If Danu or Cassandra had heard Connor's announcement, there was no indication. The old woman kept her gaze on her knitting, while Cassandra's concentrated on watching the flames in the fireplace as they rolled in golden curls over the logs.

Morgan did not trust the Council, and the moment she had the thought, Cassandra raised her eyes and gave a slight nod of agreement. It was a trap. She kept her voice devoid of emotion. "A great honor, and one we will consider with care. I have to say, however, this is very sudden."

Connor's eyes darkened to polished ebony as he clasped his hands behind him. "Yes, milady. Very sudden."

The chill of his gaze matched the cold she had felt all morning and sent shivers of dread over her arms. She wondered how candid he would be with her. He was the magical community's representative on the Council, and many said he disapproved of many of their decisions. But it was unclear which side he was on if a war was declared.

"To what can we attribute the Talons' and the Grey Council's sudden decision to elevate Zephra to the vacancy? They must know that it will take the full membership of female Wizards to approve the nomination." She hesitated. "Ah. Of course. The council believes this will force us to return to the island to approve her nomination."

Connor shifted his feet, noticeably uncomfortable. As a shapeshifting werewolf, he was uncomfortable indoors at any time. But she sensed his unease now had more to do with his offer to her than with his confinement inside.

He cleared his throat. "My thoughts as well, milady. Although the Council does not acknowledge it publicly, it is my belief they felt pressure from the magical community. When the female Wizards and young Wizardlings left the island during Bealtaine, it took them by surprise."

"We left because female Wizards and our young Wizardlings were in danger. That has not changed. It did not seem to bother the Council that three female Wizards died the first night of the festival."

"Not exactly true. Vlad's hold on the Grey Council is tenuous, at best, despite the president's support. The Talons would abandon Vlad if they felt their power slipping away."

The rhythmic click-click of Danu's needles stilled as she bent to pick up a ball of yarn that had fallen to the floor. Cassandra and Danu melded their thoughts together, directing their silent message to Morgan's mind. *"With chaos comes defeat. I foresee an opening."*

Morgan returned a message of her own. *"Theirs? Or ours?"*

"Connor, if what you say is true, how do they view the killing of the Fire Wizards? The murders are unsolved."

He shifted his feet again, this time hesitating as though weighing his words. "Their deaths are viewed as nothing more than a turf war and unrelated to your disappearance."

He was lying, she could feel it in the air, and the shift in Cassandra and Danu's gaze in his direction told her they felt the same. Was he protecting the Talons and the Grey Council, or himself and his position on the

Council?

She cocked her head to the side. "We discovered a warehouse filled with Oculist stones, harvested illegally and brought here for the purpose of poisoning male Wizards. I reject your theory. This is not a small turf war, as you claim. This is much larger."

Connor's eyes widened; the color drained from his face as he slowly shook his head. "It can't be. Oculist stones were destroyed centuries ago."

Outside, a score of Air Wizards glided from the sky and landed near where Rowan was speaking. The sight filled her with hope. The Air Wizards had always been loyal to female Wizards in the past, but she never took anything for granted. Vlad wielded a lot of power, and it wouldn't be the first time a Wizard changed allegiance.

But even with the addition of the Air Wizards, she knew it wouldn't be enough to defeat the scores of warriors the Talons and the Grey Council had at their disposal. Female Wizards needed the magical community. She would have to trust that once Connor learned the truth, he would persuade the magical community to join them.

Morgan motioned for Connor to join her by the table set with tea and biscuits. "Would you care for tea? It is time we shared what we have learned."

Connor slid his gaze toward Cassandra and Danu. "Will the two ladies be joining us?"

"I think not."

He nodded as he sat down at the table across from Morgan and accepted a cup of tea. "I understand. They fear me. I get that a lot. Tell them I'll not shift into my wolf form and harm them."

Morgan smiled as she sipped her tea. "They do not

fear you. Either one of them is more than capable of ending you if you so much as look like you are going to attack. They simply do not trust you."

"But you do?"

"It depends on your reaction to the truth."

Connor looked at his tea. "I wish I had…"

Casandra appeared beside him with a bottle of brandy, pouring a generous amount into his tea, then resumed her place by the fire.

"She read my mind."

"Among other things. Shall we begin? As I mentioned, we discovered a warehouse where they are turning Oculist stones into poison that kills Wizards. Their delivery system is genius. They crush the stones into a powder and add it to a drug they call Magic Carpet Ride. The drug is then sold on the streets. It gives humans a powerful high, but it is deadly to Wizards. A human by the name of Zacharias was in charge, but he was killed, and as far as we know, no one has stepped in to take his place. We suspect Vlad is at the heart of what is going on, but what we don't know is the extent of the Talons' involvement, or if others on the Grey Council are involved. What do you think the Grey Council and the Talons would say if you told them?"

"Hard to tell. It depends on how high this goes. There is a deep rift in ideology between the Talons and the Grey Council. Vlad and the president of the Talons will grasp at anything that will stop the flow of unrest and help them retain power. All on the board are aware of the magical community's growing objection to the policies to subjugate female Wizards. Secretly, many view how they are treated as a form of slavery. Because of this, the Talons and the Grey Council are pushing the theory that female Wizards did not leave of their own free will but were kidnapped by our enemies." Connor hesitated.

"Go on."

"As a way of testing this theory, Vlad offered the solution of giving Zephra a position on the board, with the theory that if you and the female Wizards were free to return, you would attend Zephra's confirmation. If you did not return, Vlad made the case they should assume you were being held prisoner, a fate, might I add, they are hoping for. Kidnapping female Wizards would give them the excuse to wage war and dispel the rumor that their policies drove you all away."

Cassandra and Danu pushed into Morgan's thoughts. Their emotions were strong and their concerns real. Morgan said, "It is a trap, with Vlad winning whichever way I choose."

Connor poured more brandy into his tea and downed it in one gulp. "Exactly. What is more, I believe that if you return, Vlad will not allow you to live. You are too powerful an influence over the female Wizards and the magical community. If you refuse, he will send an army here under the guise of bringing you in safely, and in the chaos, you will be killed and every living thing on the compound will be destroyed."

"A not-so-veiled threat, Connor O'Hara. If I return, I will be killed. If I refuse, not only will Vlad kill me, but he will murder everyone on this compound."

Cassandra appeared beside Morgan. The light green aura that accompanied her had turned a fiery emerald green. "*Connor. Our compound is safe,*" she said into Connor's thoughts as well as Morgan's. "*We are protected on the compound by powerful spells and wards. Only those we wish to allow can enter. We are safe here.*"

Connor rubbed his forehead as though trying to drive out Cassandra's words. "That's freaky. She can read my thoughts." With Cassandra's shrug and Morgan just nodding as though it was perfectly normal, Connor continued. "I need another drink. Where was I? Oh, yes. Under normal circumstances, I would agree that your compound is secure. Except they discovered that Morgan was here, and if they suspect she is on the Trolls' compound, it is safe to assume they believe the female Wizards and Wizardlings are here as well. You should consider that there is a spy feeding Vlad information. It worries me that Vlad is too confident. He must have allies we are unaware of. He is single-minded in his quest for power. No place is safe."

Morgan glanced out the window at the gathering crowd. More Air Wizards had joined Rowan. Was one of them a traitor? Or was it someone on the compound?

What she did know was that even with the reinforcements it wouldn't be enough to defeat Vlad if he attacked. She knew he commanded an army a hundred times the number of the reinforcements gathered on the Trolls' compound. If Vlad's forces attacked, it would be a blood bath. She couldn't allow that to happen.

But she faced a dilemma. Connor suggested there was a spy on the compound. She had to assume that whatever decision she made would reach Vlad's ears. She wasn't even sure she could trust Connor.

She rose, lacing her hands together at her waist. "Inform Vlad that I thank him for his generous offer and will give him my answer in three days."

"Milady…" Connor began.

She held up her hand, interrupting his response. "I understand your concerns, but I'm relying on you to tell not only Vlad but the Talons, the Grey Council and the magical community of my good-faith consideration. My hope is that Vlad, feeling the pressure from those I've mentioned, will at least wait for my decision before he prepares to invade the Trolls' compound. The Trolls are innocents in this battle among the Wizards. My hope is to allow them time to evacuate their children. I give you my word that the female Wizards and Wizardlings will remain here."

Connor stood and gave a bow. "You are a great lady, thinking of others rather than yourself. I promise to relay your message. I hope you well."

She straightened and offered a thin smile as she watched him leave, waiting until the double doors closed behind him.

Cassandra joined Morgan, following Morgan's gaze. "*We must continue to cloak our words. Connor is a werewolf, possessing extraordinary hearing. I thank you for your concern for our children, but I sense you have an additional plan in mind.*"

"*You know me well.*" Morgan glanced out a window. Rowan was dividing the men and women into training groups, some to fight in hand-to-hand combat, others with the sword, while Air Wizards trained those interested on how to use a bow and arrow. She turned back toward Cassandra. "*We will not wait for Vlad to attack. We will go to him.*"

Chapter Forty-One

The grounds of the Trolls' compound were a stark contrast to yesterday's celebrations. The booths had either been taken down or were boarded up tight. Cassandra might talk about how safe the Trolls' compound was, but no one was taking any chances. Rowan started to punch in the number to Detective Lyons' precinct, but paused. The cell phone wasn't his.

He felt like he'd been dropped out of an airplane without a parachute. Why hadn't he noticed before? The phone was his brother's. The one Renegade had given him the night he'd found Stryker unconscious. Rowan had forgotten he still had it.

Rowan shoved his brother's cell into his jacket and reached for his own to dial Lyons' office. After the third ring, the answering machine picked up. Lyons' greeting was short and clipped. After the beep, Rowan started to leave a voicemail, but the phone was picked up.

A woman's voice came through the line. "Detective Lyons is not available. Is there a message?"

Rowan didn't like the sound of the woman's voice. It sounded like it was soaked in thick maple syrup with a generous scoop of sugar-laced whipped cream, as though being nice was an effort. Something was wrong.

Lyons never let anyone answer his phone. He had real control issues when it came to stuff like that. It was probably one of the reasons Rowan and he got along so well. Rowan firmly believed control freaks were misunderstood. They should start a club.

Rowan rubbed the back of his neck, trying to shake his unease. He wasn't going to leave his message—that it was time to evacuate Seattle before all hell broke loose—to anyone but Lyons. "No message. I'll call back later."

There was a long pause and whispered conversation. When the woman got back on the line, her voice had lost its sugar coating. "You don't know?"

His suspicions grew warts. "Know what?"

"Detective Lyons had a heart attack. His daughter was able to get to him in time. They're keeping him at Mountain Hospital for observation. Do you want the number?'

"Thanks. I'll get it myself." Rowan dialed information, then changed his mind. The best place for Lyons and his daughter was right where they were. If he contacted AJ, she'd want to help, when she should stay with her father. And if Lyons awoke, he'd want to join Rowan on the front line. No, Lyons and his daughter were exactly where they needed to be.

He put his cell phone away. "Heart attack, my ass." Lyons didn't have any family history of heart disease, was a vegan before that was a thing, worked out like a man half his age, and didn't smoke or drink. Lyons joked the only thing that would kill him was boredom if he ever retired.

Sure, random heart attacks happened all the time, but Rowan wasn't buying it. He and Lyons were working on a real freak show of a case. If Rowan was a betting man, he'd wager Lyons had gotten too close. This had Vlad's fingerprints all over it. The good news was that the Earth Wizard hadn't been able to give Lyons a full-on killer heart attack like the ones he'd given the female Wizards. If he lived through the nightmare to come, he'd try to learn how Lyons had survived.

"Rowan," Renegade said jogging over to him, "milady is gone, and so is Hunter."

Rowan's core heated. "What do you mean, she's gone? The plan was to wait until tomorrow night."

Renegade shrugged. "Hey, don't set me on fire over it. She changed her mind. Hunter took her to the island. According to Cassandra, they discovered through one of the Air Wizards watching Vlad's island that they weren't going to wait for Morgan to give her decision. They were gearing up to attack the Trolls' compound tonight at midnight."

"I'm surrounded by idiots." Stryker's cell phone rang. Rowan pulled it out.

"Isn't that your brother's phone?"

Rowan nodded as he answered. "Stryker? What the hell? Are you all right? Where have you been? You're not an easy man to find. Are you still a…"

"Dragon," Stryker finished. "You and I will have time to chat when this mess is over. You haven't done such a good job of taking care of your friends, big brother. They almost got Lyons. Would have, if I hadn't intervened. Morgan will be next if you don't make the deal."

"I'm listening."

"Unless the apprentice Wizards and females return at the closing ceremonies of Bealtaine tonight, Morgan will die."

"Vlad will kill her regardless. But how do you know all this?"

"Turns out people are afraid of a dragon threatening to drop them from the air, and you're right. Morgan's dead either way. I'll meet you on the island."

"Why the change?"

"Memory returned. Let's go to war."

Chapter Forty-Two

The aroma of tea, steaming with fragrant spiced leaves, greeted Morgan as she was led to the enclosed garden patio for her meeting with Vlad on his island. A twelve-foot-high man-made waterfall emptied into a pool filled with water lilies and gold-and-white-speckled koi.

Vlad motioned toward a group of high-backed wicker chairs with a view of the ocean. Wordlessly he offered her a cup of the tea. She sipped the warm brew, relaxing despite her suspicions. The comforting and familiar smell seemed at odds with her meeting Vlad. She'd tried earlier to probe his mind and failed. He must have learned a powerful warding spell.

"You surprise me, Grand Vizier. I had not expected a warm reception, or your knowledge that I enjoy chai."

He leaned against the back of the chair, which creaked in response to his weight. He steepled his fingers, and as he did, the cuff of his sleeve slid down his wrist and revealed Caitline's tattoo. Three interlocking spirals connected in the center. The Triskelion represented the physical world, the spiritual world and the afterlife.

Morgan's cup rattled against the saucer. That tattoo confirmed that he had murdered her. She took one breath and then another, trying to calm her racing heart.

Unaware of what she had learned, he continued. "I

truly did not know how I would feel when I saw you again. Awe. Respect. Hatred. Perhaps a combination of all three. It no longer matters. You must realize by now that your plan will fail."

Morgan steadied her cup so it wouldn't teeter off the saucer to the tile floor. "My plan is to support the nomination of Zephra to the open position on the Grey Council."

Vlad drummed his fingers on the arm of the chair. "The plan I speak of is the one to strip me of power and elect a new Grand Vizier. I know about the forces you have hidden, waiting for your command, and the women who have come here with more than a conquest of the heart in mind. You will fail," he repeated. "This island is my own private kingdom. Order your forces to surrender and I will spare those who swear allegiance to me. The alternative is for my army to hunt them down like rabid dogs."

"Your thirst for power has blinded you, Grand Vizier, and fooled you into believing you are surrounded by those who would betray you. The only power we seek is to live as we choose. We wish to love openly without spells and enchantments that hide our true selves and to keep our children with us to train and nurture. We want to live without fear that we will be murdered before our time."

His smile was a thin line across his face. "You ask that we change centuries of tradition. Unacceptable. I know the female Wizards and the young Wizardlings are on the Trolls' compound. I do not wish to take them by force. It sends a confusing message. But I will if they resist."

She saw the red haze of hatred in his mind and

flinched. "Even if the female Wizards come peacefully, you still plan to kill them." She gasped. "And you have already attacked the Trolls' compound!"

His grip tightened on the arms of his wicker chair, splintering the cane as he edged closer. "The moment you and your sister Wizards left the island, I knew what I must do. They rejected the old ways and must be dealt with accordingly." He leaned forward. "But how dare you read my thoughts, witch?"

Morgan winced at the term "witch," knowing he meant it as a term of disrespect, harking back to an era when Wizards thought themselves superior to witches. "I do not need to be a seer to know your thoughts."

"Regardless, I have a remedy for such as you." He extended his arm toward her, turning his hand slowly as though he held her beating heart within his grasp.

The cup and saucer slid from her hands and crashed to the floor, shattering into tiny pieces. The pain in her chest was intense. It was as though her heart was being crushed. Was this how he'd killed the other female Wizards the first night of the festival? Had it caught them so unaware that they had not realized they were being murdered? Morgan drew her hands into tight fists. If she could summon the water in the pool, a wave might knock into his concentration, perhaps break it entirely. She murmured the words of the spell, but only ripples formed on the surface.

He lowered his arm. His hands dwarfed the teapot, making it look like a child's play set as he poured her another cup. Vlad's' mouth twitched in a sneer. "Would you like more tea, milady?"

The crushing pain around her heart eased. But the feeling of fear remained. She stared at the tea. She remembered being offered it the first night of Bealtaine, but she'd been too distracted to eat or drink.

"Poison?"

"More of a way to neutralize your powers by putting Oculist in your tea. A side effect I discovered quite by accident. A small amount can render a Wizard's power nonexistent, while a larger amount can kill. When our kind was made up of mere dark and light witches, and when 'Wizard' was a title bestowed only on males, four god-like creatures, each representing one of the elements of Fire, Earth, Air and Water, challenged the best of our male warriors to see if they were ready to take on the awesome power of the planet. The warrior fighting as the water god's representative was injured. His woman stepped in and finished the fight before we could replace him with another male. It should never have been allowed. She stole the fourth power from us—the power over water."

"Without us, no one, male or female, would have received the powers we now possess," Morgan stated. "Mananea was defending her lover. Our histories tell us that the real reason the god creatures gifted the element's power to us was because of our compassion for one another."

"Your truths, not mine."

A guard burst into the garden. "Grand Vizier. We have a situation!"

Chapter Forty-Three

The Trolls' compound was under attack.

Rowan had never faced an enemy quite like the Ravs. They possessed all the strengths of Nature with none of her weaknesses. In human form, the Ravs were tall, slender, with sinewy cords of muscles. Their wings transformed into long razor-sharp blades, and their strength and agility were unequaled in either the magical or the human world. The creatures sensed each attack, moments before it came, as hatred poured from their coal-black eyes. They may have allied with Vlad, but only because it served some unknown purpose of their own. Once they were unleashed and tasting victory, Rowan doubted if even Vlad could control them.

When it was discovered that Morgan had headed to Vlad's island, members of the magical community and Air Wizards had followed her there. He had no way of knowing if they had succeeded in rescuing her, and blast it all, he had his hands full fighting Ravs.

The Ravs Rowan had fought and killed lay at his feet while others moved to take their place. Their screech-like laughter seemed to taunt him as they danced around him, striking at will. Rowan's clothes were in tatters and his body lacerated by the Ravs' attacks. His body was covered with both his blood and theirs. He'd been surprised theirs was red. He'd thought their blood would be as black as their souls.

Rowan and Renegade's men had secured the perimeter of the mansion, but they were losing ground. The last line of defense was the female Wizards who guarded the Wizardlings in the underground tunnels. The reinforcements had not come in the numbers needed to fight the Ravs' army. He doubted there were enough in the whole of the magical community who could defeat such an overwhelming force.

Renegade's men had suffered heavy casualties. The Ravs were taking their time now, confident of a victory, wanting to savor this moment.

Thousands of birds crowded the sky overhead, turning day into night and blocking out the sun—and thus blocking Rowan's source of renewal for his core's energy, as well. His reserves were dwindling. Conserving as much of his power as possible, he used his knife and bare hands, but such weapons were no match for the Ravs.

How had he let it come to this? He would be dead and Morgan at Vlad's mercy. He'd played this all wrong by refusing to accept the level of treachery permeating the Grey Council and the Talons until it was too late. But while there was breath left in him, he would not give up. Rowan cleared his thoughts of everything but primal defense, lunging toward the two Ravs who circled him with death reflecting in their eyes.

With one hand he grabbed a Rav around his neck and plunged his knife into the creature's heart, pulling his blade free as the Rav's comrade tackled him to the ground. The Rav opened his mouth, cackling in a language known only to them.

Teeth, filed into sharp points, glistened like liquid silver as the black-rimmed mouth formed words whose meaning was clear—the Rav and his kind were bent on genocide of the Wizard race. The Rav threw back his head to gain momentum to sink his teeth into Rowan's neck.

An explosion of flames blasted the sky and Rowan seized on the distraction, slitting the Rav's throat and pushing him away. On the ground, all paused for a split second, mesmerized by the shadow so dark it swallowed up the cursed heavens as it moved with deadly calm overhead. Its wingspan dwarfed the birds around it. The moment was upon them. Vlad had summoned a force to finish what the Ravs had started.

In the next instant flames once more ignited the sky. Instead of the target being Rowan's men on the ground, though, the trajectory of the flames was aimed at the dense population of flying Ravs. The smell of sulfur, ash and burnt feathers smothered the air. Light filtered through the sky as hundreds of birds dropped from the sky in sheets of black rain.

The shock released everyone from their trance. A human-form Rav slashed Rowan's arm with his talon-like hands, then glanced toward the clouds as another blast ignited the sky. Hundreds of sparks of black light flashed randomly as more birds caught fire. Overhead, shrill cries of the dying birds drowned out the clash of weapons and the screams of battle.

"Did you do that?" Renegade shouted over the din.

"Frack, no. I barely have enough fire power left to light a cigarette." Rowan blocked an attack, killing the Rav. "Whatever it is, it's on our side."

Renegade and the Fire Wizards took the advantage provided by their unknown ally and fought back with renewed hope and strength.

Giant wings flapped overhead, turning to make another pass as the ravens merged into a dark formation. Their survival instinct to group together for protection was their doom, making it easier for the massive beast in the sky to kill more at once.

A few dozen of the human-form Ravs, seeking escape, changed back into birds and lifted off the ground. Many were caught in the path of the fire breather before they reached the clouds. Only a few escaped.

The creature that had saved Rowan and his forces glided down to the shore. Its wingspan was the width of a football field, its scales as red as fire.

"What is that thing?" Hunter said.

"Dragon," Rowan breathed, afraid to hope. "It might be my brother."

Renegade pointed his bloodied sword out in front of him. "You're right, Rowan. It's a Dragon, all right."

Rowan put his hand over the hilt of Renegade's blade and lowered it. "If I were you, I don't think I'd point a weapon at him. Remember what he did to the Ravs."

Renegade's eyes widened as he sheathed his sword. "Good point, but I thought Dragons were all dead."

Rowan sheathed his own weapon in his boot. "Not dead. Not all."

Memories slammed into him in crystal clarity. It was as though the appearance of the Dragon had awakened his memories. Memories of the Dragon nest he and Stryker had found as boys. Memories of how they'd camouflaged the opening so no one would stumble into it and destroy the eggs before they hatched. Memories of his brother's reaction and the momentary change of color in his eyes when he accidentally touched one of the eggs.

The Dragon dipped his head, pushing his thoughts into Rowan's mind. *"Hello, brother. I was headed to meet you at the island when I sensed you needed my help."*

Rowan moved toward the beast, his hand outstretched. "Stryker?"

"Aye."

Renegade pulled Rowan back. "What are you doing? You can't touch that thing."

Rowan whirled on Renegade. "That 'thing' is my brother! And just in case you've forgotten already, he saved our bloody lives!"

Renegade lowered his voice, his expression shadowed by concern. "I haven't forgotten. Maybe... maybe Dragons are not the monsters we all believed. It wouldn't be the first time history was twisted into a lie to fit someone's purpose. But you know the legends as well as I, maybe better. You can't take the chance at least some of what they say about Dragons is true. Not now. My elders as well as yours warn that touching a dragon will at the least alter the person's perception of the world, driving him insane, and at the worst, change them into a Halfling, forever caught between two worlds."

Rowan glanced toward the Dragon. Its size dwarfed the compound, where Renegade's men still clung to their weapons, their expressions wary as they gave the beast a wide berth. Rowan didn't share their fears. Stryker was his brother.

Rowan clamped his hand on Renegade's shoulder. "I want you and any man able to fight to meet me down by the dock."

"You're planning on going to Vlad's island. I'll say this much for Wizards—You all have more courage than good sense. That Dragon may have scared the Ravs away from the compound, but it's my guess they're still lurking in the sky and willing to do a kamikaze into the propellers to bring down any planes foolish enough to go to Vlad's stronghold."

Rowan shrugged. "I have a plan."

Renegade shook his head as he motioned for his men. "So did Morgan, and she played right into Vlad's hands."

Rowan turned toward the Dragon, who seemed to be waiting for something. One thing the beast shared with his brother, besides crazy courage, was that they both had a lot of patience. "Stryker. Thanks for saving my life."

"*It needed saving.*" The Dragon paused, his head turning toward Renegade's men, who were loading into two float planes.

"If you can clear the sky of Ravs so I can land, I'll take care of the rest."

The Dragon nodded and spread his wings.

Before Stryker lifted off, Rowan continued, "Stryker, thanks again for saving my life."

The Dragon nodded his massive head again. "*We're brothers first. You've always had my back, and now it's my turn to return the favor.*"

Chapter Forty-Four

Vlad cinched the plastic ties on Morgan's wrists and pushed her into a chair by a window overlooking the sea in his private room on the island. Outside, the ocean was the color of blood and the sky bruised and battered as the war raged between the magical community, aided by the Air and Water Wizards, and Vlad's army.

Vlad gave a final tug on the ties. "In case the Oculist poison neutralizing your powers wears off, I want you constrained when the president of the Talons arrives."

She glanced in the direction of the water for a moment before turning toward Vlad. "You and Constantine are trapped here."

"A temporary situation. My army will win the battle."

Constantine lumbered into Vlad's private room without knocking, on his arm a fresh-faced female Troll, dressed in a gown of pink lace. He was flanked by four dour-faced security guards. He moved directly over to Vlad's desk and set down the bottle of Macallan Scotch he'd brought. "I'm assuming you have proper glasses?"

Vlad reached for two Glencairn glasses and set them down beside the scotch. "Macallan is one of the most expensive in your collection. What's the occasion?"

"First, a toast." Constantine poured the scotch and handed Vlad a glass. "To winning wars. I'm assured that the attack is under control."

"I'm not sure I share your confidence, but I'll drink your expensive whiskey." Vlad clinked his glass to Constantine and drained its contents.

Constantine set his glass aside and shook his head. "I thought a drink before we discuss this war of yours would help. We have tough matters to discuss. The truth is that you've made a bungle of things." His tired expression froze when he turned his gaze toward Morgan.

She gave him a slight nod as she focused on mind-speaking to the female Troll who stood by Constantine's side. *"Regardless of how the war ends, I will do my best to rescue you from Constantine."*

The female Troll blinked twice. *"That won't be necessary."*

"By any chance have you seen my sister Wizards? They stayed behind while we made our escape."

"They are..."

"Holy crap on a cracker," Constantine said, interrupting the female Troll's mind-speak. "I had hoped my informant was wrong. I had to see for myself." He motioned for one of the four security guards, who nodded and left the room. Constantine's eyebrows knitted together. "You succeeded in tricking Morgan, the leader of the female Wizards, onto the island, and are holding her prisoner. What were you thinking? No wonder the whole of the magical community is trying to turn the island to rubble."

"I'm doing this for all of us."

"You forget who you're talking to. You're doing this for revenge."

Vlad glowered, grinding his teeth together. "Still consorting with female Trolls, I see. At least this one doesn't have that annoying green tinge to her skin. She looks almost human. But what are you doing here? I thought you would have left by now." The last thing Vlad needed was Constantine meddling in his business. He ordered one of Constantine's security guards to watch Morgan as he stomped over to Constantine.

Constantine wove a protective arm around the Troll's waist and cast a defiant glance in Vlad's direction. "I'm leaving this doomed island before it sinks into the Pacific. And I'm not the only one leaving."

"What are you talking about?"

"The Grey Council and the Talons have decided it is not in their best interest to stay here. Nor will they continue to support you. They share my human view of not backing a losing horse. I'd advise you to leave as well, but I really don't give a damn if you live or die. Let the rebels have this place. There is more at stake than who controls an archaic Fertility Festival during Bealtaine."

"You fool! This is not about who controls Bealtaine, and you know it."

"Well, that may be so, but that's how the Grey Council and the Talons see this debacle, and they blame you. The last straw was when you allowed Zacharias's warehouse, with a year's supply of our product, to go up in flames. It will take months to recover."

The female Troll touched Constantine's arm and motioned with her eyes in Morgan's direction by the window.

Constantine patted the Troll's hand. "Yes, my lovely, now is the perfect time for you to speak with Morgan." He glanced at the time on his cell phone. "I must leave soon. Your war didn't leave us many options to escape the island. Female Wizards control the seas, and Air Wizards control the skies. Until a short while ago, I anticipated a dangerous journey off the island, whichever way I chose. I'll give you a piece of advice for old times' sake. The Talons and the Grey Council are about results, not promises. For example, if you could deliver the head of one of their leaders, they might reconsider."

Vlad shivered as though someone had walked over his grave. "You used the word 'reconsider.' What aren't you telling me?"

Constantine examined the fingernails on his right hand, then heaved a sigh. "Why, that there has been a contract issued for you dead or alive. Quite a tidy sum. Now, I've said what I came to say. Consider yourself warned. I'd like to say that I will see you soon, but...well, I probably won't." He turned to go.

Vlad blocked his path. "I can offer the leadership Morgan's head." Vlad motioned toward the window—and then his heart nearly stopped beating. "She's gone! And so is that Troll of yours! What did you do?" He reached for Constantine, but two of the security guards intervened, restraining Vlad.

Constantine chuckled. "When I suspected you'd succeeded in tricking Morgan, I made a deal with the Air Wizards. I deliver Morgan, and they allow my plane to leave the island. They were reluctant, until I offered to sweeten the deal." Constantine motioned to his security guards. "Tie him up."

Vlad backed toward the picture of Deborah on his desk. "I'll kill you," he ground out between his teeth. Constantine must have known Vlad wouldn't leave quietly. What was he up to?

The security guards moved slowly toward him as one of them drew out a coiled rope that had been hooked at his belt.

"Fool. I will stop your hearts with a thought."

"I doubt that, seriously, old friend." Constantine smiled slowly, as he returned the screw cap to the Scotch bottle. "I could have given you a fatal dose of Oculist poison, but the Air Wizards want you alive."

Behind his back, Vlad slid the photo of Deborah aside and felt for the latch of the hidden door. "I'm surprised you haven't learned this lesson. Those who betray are often betrayed themselves. Or, as a woman I once loved said, 'What goes around comes around.' "

Constantine frowned and flicked his hand toward his security guards. "What are you waiting for? Tie him up."

Vlad lifted the latch, and a door slid open in the floor. Before Constantine and the security guards could react, Vlad jumped.

****

Along the shoreline, a safe distance from Vlad's mansion and from the fighting, Morgan bent over and threw up. "What was in that drink you gave me to neutralize the poison?"

The female Troll laughed. "A little of this and a lot of that. It was originally created to help when a person drank too much, but it also helps to empty the contents of a stomach in case of poison."

"Well, it worked. Thank you. I think. I feel like I've been hit head-on by a tsunami. I should probably know your name."

"I'm Willow, and I have information for where they have imprisoned your sister Wizards who remained on the island. They are being kept in an underground bunker."

Morgan squeezed Willow's hand gently. "I love that you read my mind and I thank you for the information. The Trolls will be overjoyed to welcome you home."

"I cannot stay. Constantine expects my return, and my work is not over. Blowing up Zacharias's warehouse is not the end. I overheard Constantine tell Vlad that although a large amount of Oculist stones were destroyed in the explosion, they plan to continue. Which means they must have other warehouses. We must find their supplier. Tell my mother, Cassandra, that I am thankful for this opportunity to help our people."

"You're Cassandra's daughter?" Morgan smiled, recognizing the resemblance around the eyes and in the way Willow tilted her head. "That is so wonderful, and I have so many questions."

"In time," Willow said, kissing Morgan as she bid her farewell. "In time."

She then hurried along the shore toward the airstrip and Constantine's plane in a blur of speed. She must have Fae blood to move that fast, Morgan decided. Willow, like so many in the magical community, was not a pure-blood but mixed. Morgan considered the revelation a good thing, and that would hopefully lead to better understanding.

Morgan lifted her head toward the downpour that had begun as they talked. She raised her arms and welcomed its embrace. The rain caressed her, strengthened her, and whispered against her skin, each drop a kiss. *Too long*, they said. *You've been gone too long*.

A bolt of lightning, silver with flecks of gold, creased the sky. Rain reflected its light. Sheets of spun silver unfolded from the sky like yards of polished chainmail. As though in slow motion, Morgan returned her gaze to the men fighting on the far side of the coastline. Her powers were restored. It was time to join the battle and locate the female Wizards who had stayed behind on the island.

Chapter Forty-Five

The island was on fire and the landing strip a mass of bombed-out craters. One plane had taken off, too far away for Rowan to note its markings. By the look and size, he speculated it might belong to a member of the Talons or the Grey Council. That the Air Wizards allowed it passage could mean several things, anything from their considering the occupants of the plane allies of the female Wizards to a purpose known only to themselves.

A puzzle without all the pieces, and one he would have to reconstruct. People were taking sides, and it was imperative to learn the friendlies from the enemies.

Rowan checked the instrument panel on his plane and dipped the wing, heading along the shore toward Vlad's stronghold. Rowan remembered a small area where the Talons and the Grey Council used to land their private planes. Vlad always had a contingency plan for everything. Keeping a plane ready and the landing strip clear for a quick escape would be the Grand Vizier's top priority, but it wouldn't remain that way for long. From the smoke and burst of fireballs, it was clear the battle was moving toward Vlad's landing strip.

Renegade followed Rowan in the other twin-engine plane, keeping below the radar. They'd brought along as many warriors as the two planes would hold, hoping Hunter's forces could hold off until they arrived. And out of the corner of his eye he spied Stryker, in his Dragon form, flying high above them. Their secret weapon.

Flames and bolts of lightning illuminated the dark sky as hurricane-force winds raced across the island. The rain was unexpected, but welcome. Fire, Air, and Water Wizards, along with the magical community, were locked in a life-and-death struggle against the forces controlled by those loyal to Vlad. The storm could tip the scales.

A week ago, the grounds on the site of Bealtaine had resembled something out of a fairy tale. Now they looked like the inside of an active volcano. The tents were in flames, the statues and fountains reduced to rubble and the gardens to ash.

Rowan landed his plane on the private strip behind the castle and cut the engine. Trolls and Fire Wizards from his plane filed out in silence and took cover behind two burned-out vehicles. When Renegade landed, he and his men found cover behind a collapsed helicopter.

Two of Vlad's mercenaries began firing weapons and flames in their direction. From the tattoo markings on their arms and necks, they were Fire Wizards. They wore Vlad's crest embroidered on their tunics, marking them as Rowan's enemies.

Rowan gathered his core heat into a white-hot flame in each hand and hurled it toward the mercenaries. The fireballs hit their target and the Wizards caught fire and turned to ash.

Rowan motioned for the others to follow him into the heart of the island.

He nodded toward Renegade, who, with his men, at a dead run, scooped up weapons left behind by fallen warriors. Meanwhile, Hunter, with a contingency of Air

Wizards behind him, raced for the perimeter of the battlefield to cut off the escape of any of Vlad's men.

Sending fireballs against Earth Wizards was useless. It was like trying to set a diamond on fire. Only the weapons forged and dedicated during the festival of Bealtaine had the ability to kill an Earth Wizard.

With Renegade and his men going to help Hunter, Rowan sped into the thick of the battle. He spun around to gather speed and momentum and cut off an Earth Wizard's head, then finished off another two. Feeling the heat of moving arrows, he ducked as poisoned arrows sped in his direction. They missed their target but embedded in the necks and chests of two mercenaries near Rowan. Screaming their defiance, they cursed Rowan with their dying breaths as they spiraled to the ground.

Rowan's breath caught. He recognized them both. They were amongst the Wizards who had participated at Bealtaine. He'd known both as good men. Somehow Vlad had turned them against their own kind. Rowan feared the open wound Vlad created would never heal.

Renegade signaled Rowan that he was taking his men to an area over by the entrance to Vlad's headquarters. The plan was as old as time. If you cut off the head of the leader, his followers would surrender.

Rowan prayed the strategy worked. The battle was in chaos. Unless an opponent wore an armband or crest, it was impossible to identify who was friend and who was foe. Rowan found Hunter and pulled him into a burned-out alcove littered with dead bodies. "Have your Air Wizards located Morgan?" He needed to find her. If something had happened to her, he'd personally level the island.

Hunter motioned toward what was left of the Grand Vizier's headquarters. "Morgan was ordered to meet with Vlad this morning. That's where Renegade and his men are headed. We got word that members of the Grey Council and the Talons tried to leave the island. We stopped a few, but Constantine escaped."

Rowan ducked as an arrow whizzed past his head. "Was Morgan with them?"

"Not sure. The battle has taken its toll. We've lost good men in the fight. I'm not sure how much longer we can hang on."

"No worries. No one else leaves the island without our permission."

"How can you be so sure?"

Rowan nodded toward the sky and the shadow of a Dragon circling overhead. "My brother. Our secret weapon. Now, will you be able to take control of the island while I search for Morgan?"

Hunter nodded. "With Stryker patrolling the skies, I'll divert all the Air Wizards to the ground. Until now, we've been outnumbered. With your brother and the Trolls, the odds are in our favor. From the little I've seen first-hand, the Trolls fight like they have something to prove."

"They do." Rowan clenched his hand around the hilt of his blade and reached for another one that lay beside a fallen Wizard. He was going to need two swords for what he planned.

Chapter Forty-Six

Morgan, with Willow's help, had escaped Vlad, and her first order of business was to find her sister Wizards. She found them huddling together. The walls and floor of the cinder-block room were blinding white. Every chair, table and bed were made of chrome, and the eating utensils, plates, pitchers, and cups were all from polished silver. The sheer glare, and the cramped space, was enough to drive even the most stable mind insane.

That is what happened when, over a half century ago, humans captured Orca whales by the thousands and sold them to aquariums. The whales were forced to live out their lives in blinding white tanks, barely large enough to accommodate their size. Many died of starvation, others went insane, and the few who survived looked like hollowed-out shells.

Three sets of haunted eyes lifted toward her. The female Wizards leaned on each other to stand. Her heart ached as she rushed into their embrace. Of the seven healthy, vibrant women Morgan had left behind a week ago, only Zephra, Bridget, and Aisling remained, and they were close to death.

Zephra was the first to find her voice. "We told Vlad you'd come."

Bridget's glance snapped with hatred. "I think that's what made him so angry. He couldn't smother our hopes. He couldn't force us to betray the location of you or our

Wizardlings. But I was weak," Bridget said on a sob. "I never revealed your location or that of the Wizardlings, but I gave him a spell that would counteract Water's hold over Earth."

Aisling drew Bridget to her. "You had seen your sister Wizards die at Vlad's command, and he threatened your life. You did the only thing you could to survive. Spells that are made can be unmade." Aisling drew her shoulders back and faced Morgan. "We were under constant threat of death. Vlad murdered Briana. She died instantly. Her heart just stopped. It happened so fast it caught us all by surprise. I believe that was the point. Vlad wanted to send a message that he could kill any one of us whenever he liked."

"When it happened, Patrice rushed toward him with a knife," Bridget added, her anger so evident Morgan could taste it in the air.

"Vlad killed Patrice second," Zephra said, as her eyes blurred. "Right in front of us. When Eva started having pains in her chest, we knew she was next to die and tried to counter it with Water magic. It helped for a few days, but his power was too strong. Eva and Aileen died a short time later, and then he summoned me."

Bridget reached for Zephra and draped her arm over her shoulder. "But you survived, dear heart. He didn't break you."

"Vlad said each one of us would die until we told him your location. Our sister Wizards dying of heart attacks confirmed Caitlin's suspicions. He, and other Earth Wizards like him, are behind the reason we die so young."

Aisling reached out to touch Morgan's arm. "But Vlad doesn't know the true source of our loyalty or the depth of our strength."

Morgan nodded. "Very true, my sister Wizards, yet soon he will find out. I sense Renegade nearby. He will help you leave the island. I have some unfinished business to attend. But first, tell me about the spell you gave Vlad and if you know how I can find him."

****

With the battle raging all around them, Morgan located Vlad in his office.

His orderly domain looked as though it had experienced hurricane-force winds, not surprising, with the Air Wizards searching for him. One thing she shared with Air and Fire Wizards, and with the allies in the magical community who had pledged their allegiance, was the certainty that Vlad must be made accountable for the destruction, mistrust and deaths he'd caused. A message must be sent. But, selfishly, she wanted to learn if he knew the location of her son first.

Vlad picked up a framed picture of a woman Morgan knew was his wife, Deborah. He brushed off the broken glass with a tenderness she would never have suspected.

Vlad removed the picture from the frame and tossed the frame to the ground. "At the end, you start thinking of the beginning, do you not? Did you find them?" His voice seemed far away.

It took her a moment to realize he was talking about the female Wizards. "They are out of your reach."

"Nothing is out of reach. It was a lesson I learned the hard way. He folded the picture of his wife and put it in his jacket pocket, then turned. "Life is full of choices. One day you wake up and realize you crossed the line, but you can't remember when it happened. After that moment, life becomes simpler. And lonelier. I expect you are here to try and kill me."

She held onto her temper. How dare he try to mirror the human emotion of regret! It sounded as though he was asking her for forgiveness. She believed in forgiveness and second chances. It had been a long journey to realize that she was capable of both. He was the cause of so much pain, and yet, seeing him like this, saving a picture of his late wife, told Morgan that there was more to the man.

Morgan had come here to demand Vlad tell her the location of her son. Then she'd planned to kill Vlad. But that would have been too simple and, yes, would be treating Vlad like he had treated others.

"I have no intention of killing you, but you will stand trial for your crimes. I do have a question. You murdered female Wizards. How many more died before you realized you'd crossed the line? Ten? One hundred?"

"One. My wife. Not by my hand, but I knew it would happen and I did nothing. I believed I'd find another woman like Deborah. It is the age-old cliché. I chose ambition over love. She told me we were to have a child."

The reality of what he said hit her, and she pressed her hand over her heart. She had been starting to feel that Vlad perhaps had good in him, but that notion died with his revelation. Her heart ached. "You had both your wife and child murdered to clear a path for your ambitions? You are a monster," she whispered.

"I do not dispute your assessment of me. Yes, my wife is dead. I do not know what became of our daughter." Vlad touched the pocket of his jacket where he'd placed the picture of Deborah. "You are struggling to say the words, and I will say them for you. I cannot forgive myself and I do not expect forgiveness. Therefore, I will not allow you to take me in for judgment. But this conversation leads me to believe you have come for another reason, otherwise you would have tried to capture me before now. Ask your question."

She swiped at the tears gathering in her eyes. She had not known Deborah, nor that he had considered her his wife, which meant they had married in secret. For a Water Wizard to trust an Earth Wizard was extraordinary. But Morgan was also living proof of the power of love. She loved a Fire Wizard. Evidently, there had been something good in Vlad at one time, but he'd killed it the day his wife died. Yet she hoped that some spark of that man still existed.

"I once had a child, but he was taken from me. His name is Caden. I've searched but cannot find him. I was told there is a secret location where children were taken to be trained in your army. Do you know where it might be?"

His smile looked forced. "That is the reason you have not tried to kill me. Human or Wizard, we all have our excuses for why we compromise. You came here to kill me, but your love for your child is more important than seeking justice for my crimes. But once I tell you what I know, you will have no further use for me."

Thunder shook the building and tiny cracks spread like spider webs over the walls. A chandelier crashed to the ground only feet from where she stood.

Vlad moved toward the window, peering toward the sky. An explosion of light torched the night sky crimson, as a shadow soared overhead. He snapped back to Morgan. "You have a Dragon as an ally?"

"Rowan's brother," Morgan said evenly.

Vlad swore under his breath. "The Talons did it. They theorized that the Oculist powder would awaken a Wizard with Dragon ancestry, and they didn't care how many they murdered to prove their theory. I told them it was dangerous, like the ill-conceived notion humans had a while back when they believed they could domesticate a full wolf. It's not that it can't be done. It's that the odds are not favorable. It's nearly impossible to take the wild out of a wolf, and in this case, to tame a Dragon." Vlad grabbed Morgan's hand. "But this changes everything. The shapeshifting Dragon is Rowan's brother, and I'm guessing that means it won't want anything to happen to the woman Rowan loves. You will be my insurance policy for vacating this doomed island. You are coming with me."

Chapter Forty-Seven

Rowan slammed through the door leading into Vlad's headquarters. The absence of guards took him by surprise. For the money Vlad paid his mercenaries, Rowan had expected more loyalty. The doors leading to an outdoor patio were blown off their hinges. Glass crunched underfoot as Rowan entered Vlad's inner sanctum.

Days ago, the place was orderly. Now, there was a gaping hole near the desk, furniture and equipment were overturned, and shredded files were littered over polished wood floors like someone had blown up a confetti factory.

He overheard a woman curse somewhere outside.

Morgan!

Vlad was chasing Morgan toward the shore. To someone without the understanding of Water magic, and how it worked, it might appear that she needed to be in the water to access its power. A woman's body was fifty to sixty percent water, with the brain containing seventy-five percent. No need for Morgan to be closer to water. She had another goal in mind. She was stalling for time.

Rowan fired up his core as Stryker, in Dragon form, emerged from the clouds and dipped a wing. Rowan recognized the gesture. His brother could easily breathe fire and torch Vlad in an instant, but Stryker understood this was Morgan and Rowan's fight. Still, Stryker was letting him know he had his back in case things went sideways.

Rowan tipped his head to Stryker and raced toward Vlad. The Grand Vizier whirled around, fists raised.

But Rowan was faster. He slammed his fist into Vlad's face.

Blood splattered over Vlad's nose as he drove his fist against Rowan's jaw.

The force knocked the weapons out of Rowan's hands as he was propelled into the water. Vlad meant to extinguish Rowan's fire.

Haunting notes of a childhood melody drifted into his thoughts, the rhyme created during the Black Death…

Starve the fire and burn the wind.
Steal the earth and boil the seas.
Ashes, ashes, they all fall down.

Waves rose around Rowan, pounding against him, cooling his core and draining what little reserves he had left. Finding Vlad had proved easier than he'd thought. Morgan might have been stalling for time when she raced toward the shoreline, but Vlad hadn't stopped her. He wanted her by the water.

A trap.

Vlad was counting on Rowan coming to Morgan's rescue.

Submerged in the water, steam enveloped Rowan like a shroud as he fought to the surface despite the pounding surf.

Vlad stood near the shore, holding the woman Rowan loved more than life itself in his vise-like grip, both of them in the waist-high, roiling water. Vlad looked like a mountain rising from the depths of a black sea.

The tide drove toward the shore, stretching out toward the Earth Wizard. Water churned around Vlad in a tidal whirlpool, foaming in its intensity, a sign Morgan was summoning her element's power.

Vlad's arm crushed Morgan's shoulders against his chest as she struggled to free herself. "Turn back, Fire Wizard," Vlad thundered. "The power of Water drains your strength. You will not survive long."

"The same can be said of you, Grand Vizier. Water extinguishes Fire, but it also dissolves Earth."

"I have safeguarded against any erosion with a spell. A gift from the female Wizards when they thought I meant to spare their lives. Why would I? It is a travesty Water Wizards hold such power over us. Our greatest sin was that we elevated them to a level equal to our own."

"We did not grant them anything." Each word Rowan spoke felt like it could be his last as thick waves pulled at him, impeding his progress toward Vlad. "They earned the right to control the element of Water in the same way as our ancestors earned the right to control Air, Fire and Earth."

"Your judgment is clouded by your attraction to this female," Vlad said over the roar of the surf. "Soon our mistake will be made right again. Haven't you ever wondered what it would be like to be free of their control? The time is ripe to rein in their control over Water and…us."

Morgan locked eyes with Rowan. "*Hold,*" she said in his thoughts. "*Vlad believes he has a spell that will conquer Water's power over Earth. It makes him reckless, and that will work to our advantage. I am aware of the spell, and my sister Wizards have reversed its fatal effects. But I need you to stay in the water a while longer. Have faith. My brand will protect you. Can you hold?"* she repeated.

"I can," he said, even though that much effort caused him pain. *"But what is your plan? It looks as though he has weakened you, as well."*

"Looks are deceiving, my love, and meant to cause him to become overconfident. Even now, the Water around him grows stronger, dissolving his core with such care that he is not aware of what is happening to him. Like a frog dropped in cold water on the stove, Vlad will not know the danger he is in until it is too late."

"What is this?" Vlad shouted. "Are the two of you plotting against me in your thoughts?"

Morgan averted her gaze from Rowan's to steal a glance toward the Dragon that circled overhead. "Only that we love each other, Grand Vizier. I wonder, though, do you worry what Stryker will do if you kill his brother? Dragons are not known for their forgiveness."

"But they *are* known for the love of gold, and I have piles of it to offer him. Silence, witch. Time for talk has ended." He crushed her against him.

"Remember. Looks are deceiving." She cast Rowan another glance then went limp in Vlad's arms, and as she did, the intensity of the ocean increased.

Vlad pushed Morgan from him and into the awaiting surf, where seafoam circled around her gently. He ground his teeth and held his hand over Morgan's body. "I wish we had burned all the water witches when we had the chance in the Middle Ages. That some survived haunts us still. No matter. We will right that wrong, and it starts with you."

Rowan pushed deeper into the boiling water, each

step a struggle. He hoped the last words Morgan had said in his thoughts were true. But Vlad was a strong Earth Wizard, the best of the best, which was the reason his rise to power hadn't been a surprise. Could Morgan overcome Vlad's efforts to stop her heart?

The water starved his power, just as the children's rhyme predicted, but why hadn't it affected Vlad? Morgan said her sister Wizards had reversed the spell, but it sure didn't look that way to him. "Stop! You're killing her."

"That's the general idea."

"Let her go. It's me you want."

"At first, that was true. But you have aligned yourself with the wrong side. Distrust has grown between the Talons and the Grey Council. The time for negotiation and peace has ended. They did the magical community a service when they rediscovered Oculist stone. But now their usefulness is over. The Grey Council will take over and Dragons will be our new weapon against all who oppose us."

"You are mad if you think you can control a Dragon."

"I told you. They like gold. It will be a business proposition, one that will benefit us both."

"You and I have always held two different world views," Rowan said, buying time, knowing that Morgan was working on a plan to neutralize Vlad. "I want to bring people together. You want to tear them apart. Your belief is that a broken and fearful world is easier to control. Morgan has earned the right to be called Female Wizard and as such is not a commodity to be bought, sold or bartered."

Rowan worked to keep his balance in the churning

water. "Have you ever wondered what the Atlantis scientist who gave his name to the stones was really searching for when his lab exploded, triggering a chain reaction that destroyed his home world?"

Vlad ground out his words. "You speak of myths, meant to discredit a great man. He did not destroy his world; he was murdered because he wanted to make Wizards invincible."

"Now you are rewriting history."

"Not rewriting, Clarifying. What if I were to tell you," Vlad continued, but his voice sounded weaker and it looked as though the waves were eroding his legs, making him shorter. He grunted, clearing his throat. "Oculist was a Wizard, an Earth Wizard, to be exact, and a direct ancestor of my clan. He didn't just want to make male Wizards invincible. He wanted us to reign supreme over humans and over the magical community. There were many who were afraid to see that happen, even in the magical community."

"History tells us that Oculist was insane."

"Not insane. Inspired. His goal was to create a potion that would unleash Dragon power." Vlad paused as though trying to catch his breath.

Rowan hadn't imagined Vlad's diminished stature. He was definitely shrinking. Rowan edged closer as Vlad continued.

"And he was close," Vlad said, his voice raspy and shallow. "Oculist recorded that many of our male Wizards who'd taken Oculist reported their powers increased. Unfortunately, none of them shapeshifted into Dragons. Instead, they died horrible deaths. Oculist was trying to find a solution when his experiments were cut short."

"You mean when he was blown up and turned into bite-size shark chum," Rowan interrupted.

Vlad glared at him. "True, the explosion of his lab and his death were unfortunate and cut short his experiments, but you fail to see the big picture. With the help of Constantine and the Talons, we discovered Oculist's journals and have been perfecting his work. Your brother's existence proves that Oculist was right."

A short distance away, three women emerged from the water. They joined hands and focused on Vlad.

In that instant, Morgan broke free of Vlad and dove into the sea, swimming toward her sister Wizards, Zephra, Aisling and Bridget.

Vlad's strength was not what it had been on land. As Rowan had guessed, the water had eroded his power just as it had tried to extinguish Rowan's flame. But Rowan had one thing Vlad lacked—Morgan's brand battling to keep his fire alive. He could feel its power creating a protective barrier around his core.

Rowan sent a ring of fire out of his hands. It floated on the surface of the water, its flames dancing and spreading to engulf Vlad in its deadly embrace. Waves curled around Morgan and her sisters. Their arms were outstretched. Their chants flowed like currents as they repeated over and over a line from the nightmare poem—

Steal the earth and boil the seas.
Steal the earth and boil the seas.
Steal the earth and boil the seas.

Vlad cried out. Water poured from his mouth. He held out his hand and turned a tortured glance in Rowan's direction. "Help me!"

Rowan reached out, knowing at that moment that he wanted Vlad punished for his crimes but not dead. It was too late. Vlad's flesh dissolved like grains of sand as he sank into the ocean's watery grave.

Chapter Forty-Eight

Six months later, Orca whales broke the surface of a white-capped blue sea along the coast of a transformed island in the Canadian San Juans. The spring days of the Wizard Fertility Festival of Bealtaine was a distant memory, while snow and ribbons of a crimson-and-gold dawn welcomed a Winter Solstice wedding.

A light dusting of snow frosted the trees and glistened like sugar in the morning light. Cottages, resembling those in the valleys of the Black Forest in Germany with their multicolored doors and window boxes, replaced the gray tents and Vlad's stolen castle.

Bells tolled on the village clock as a pair of white horses drew the bride toward the church.

From Rowan's vantage point on the hill overlooking the journey of the carriage, he slipped his arm around Morgan. "There is still time to make this a double wedding, my love."

Morgan circled her rounded belly with her hand and leaned into Rowan. "This is Cassandra and Renegade's day, dear heart. Besides, I know you will want your brother at our wedding, and he is still searching for the source of the Oculist stone."

Rowan kissed the top of Morgan's head, knowing his love's thoughts. "And our son, Caden. It would be good to have him at our wedding, as well. I know it has been difficult these last few months. So many leads, so many dead ends."

She rose on tiptoes and kissed his cheek and grinned. "We will find him, and the twins will help."

He pulled back gently. "Twins. We are having twins?"

"A boy and a girl, and already they have reached out to me telepathically. They believe they can help us find their brother."

"You can talk to our children? Why didn't I know that?"

She smiled. "It's just one of the many secrets we female Water Wizards share. Come. It is time to join the wedding party."

A word about the author...

Pam Binder is an award-winning Amazon, *New York Times*, and *USA Today* bestselling author. Pam loves Irish and Scottish myths, legends and happily ever afters.

Pam, who is president of the Pacific Northwest Writers Association, and a conference speaker, writes historical fiction, contemporary romance, regency, time travel, young adult and romantasy novels.

http://pambinder.com

~*~

Other books by Pam Binder
and published by The Wild Rose Press, Inc.

Grace Logan and the Goblin Bones
Match Made in the Highlands
Falling in Love with Emma
A Bride for a Day
Thief of Hearts
Christmas Knight
Christmas Deadline
The Inscription
The Quest
Wylder Times
Gingerbread Knight
The Immortal
Christmas Proposal
Raven Spirit
Christmas Secrets